Praise for Suzan Still:

"Suzan Still's *Fiesta of Smoke* is an extraordinary book, encompassing a vast time frame yet bringing the possibility of a contemporary Mexican revolution to vivid life through its beautifully tuned, disparate voices. With a tonality that at times echoes the quiet grace of Gabriel Garcia Marquez's *Love in the Time of Cholera*, matched by passages that have the psychotic edginess of *Breaking Bad*, *Fiesta of Smoke* is a book that will both compel and seduce you to read it to its haunting conclusion."
—Alexander Stuart, author of *The War Zone* and *Life On Mars*

"As with the brush of a muralist, Suzan Still has captured fifty years of the history of Mexico in vivid color. This passionate, nonlinear novel explores the lives of three very different people involved in decades of political upheaval, and sounds the depth of injustices done for centuries there. Gripping in its detail, and daring in its reach, *Fiesta of Smoke* is a moving portrayal of the disparate cultures and complexity of a turbulent, beautiful country."
—M. E. Hirsh, author of *Kabul* and *Dreaming Back*

"*Commune of Women* is a riveting read. The characters are diverse and their stories will find a place in your heart. From Betty's fascination with fake flowers to Pearl's horrifying and tragic life, there is something uplifting in how they found the strength to carry on. A nightmare situation and how the women came out stronger than when it began, along with compassion and the will to survive, *Commune of Women* is a captivating read that I highly recommend!"
—Minding Spot

WELL IN TIME

WELL IN TIME

Suzan Still

This is a work of fiction. Names, characters, places and incidents are either products of the author's imagination or are used fictitiously. Any resemblance to actual events, locales, organizations, or persons living or dead, is entirely coincidental and beyond the intent of either the author or the publisher.

The Story Plant
Studio Digital CT, LLC
P.O. Box 4331
Stamford, CT 06907

Cover design by Barbara Aronica-Buck
Author photo by Mic Harper and Kath Christensen

Print ISBN: 978-1-61188-184-4
E-book ISBN: 978-1-61188-185-1

Visit our website at www.TheStoryPlant.com

First Story Plant Printing: January 2015

Printed in the United States of America

For

Dr. Charles Ladley

who was awarded the Bronze Star
for safely leading his patrol from behind enemy lines,
and who did other things he took oaths never to reveal—
and didn't, despite my cajoling.
Dear friend, loyal, smart, funny, impish, vengeful, and wise

and

Tom Rogers

who gave me a lifetime reading list when I was twelve
on which I still labor,
who nourished countless lives as teacher, curator of Filoli, and
Chinese Grandpa;
whose brilliance, sophistication, aesthetic refinement, passion, and curiosity
were remarkable for their kindness and modesty

Fare onward, friends. We shall meet again.

Like the human body, the cosmos is in part built up anew, every night, every day; by a process of unending regeneration it remains alive. But the manner of its growth is by abrupt occurrences, crises, surprising events, and even mortifying accidents. Everything is forever going wrong; and yet, that is precisely the circumstance by which the miraculous development comes to pass. The great entirety jolts from crisis to crisis; that is the precarious, hair-raising manner of self-transport by which it moves.
—Heinrich Zimmer

The descent into the darkness of the earth, which stands at the center of every initiation, is enacted in modern man, collectively and individually, as an encounter with the underworld; an encounter that fulfills the human psyche.
—Erich Neumann

The cave you fear to enter holds the treasure you seek.
—Joseph Campbell

It is a difficult problem in life to decide whether we should try to develop the germ of goodness in evil men by loving acceptance, or whether we should destroy it unmercifully along with the evil.
—Marie-Louise von Franz

[illegible] the contours of [illegible] more [illegible] every day [illegible] processes [illegible] and [illegible] [illegible] alive. But the manner of its growth is [illegible] occurrences, [illegible] surprising events, and [illegible] accidents. Everything is [illegible] going [illegible] is precise [illegible] the circumstances [illegible] when the [illegible] development comes to [illegible]. The great [illegible] crisis is [illegible] the [illegible] [illegible] with [illegible]
—Heinrich Zimmer

[illegible] into the [illegible] of [illegible] of the [illegible] every [illegible] [illegible] and [illegible] encounter that [illegible]
—Erich Neumann

The cave you fear to enter holds the treasure you seek.
—Joseph Campbell

[illegible] problem in life [illegible] to decide [illegible] [illegible] we [illegible] [illegible] whether we should [illegible] [illegible]
—Marie-Louise von Franz

Prologue

§

Huichol Sierra, Jalisco, Mexico

THE VOICES OF THE WINDS WERE COMMANDING. Otherwise, the valley stood in the somnolence of late afternoon: jagged black rocks emitted solar heat as if just cooled from magma; cactus and low scrub hunkered sparse and pallid against pale, granular soil; the surrounding hills were riven by indigo rivers of shadow cascading down corrugations in each steep, impassable gully.

On the valley floor, the man counted not one, not two, but *thirteen* columns of whirling wind, each taller than three trees, broad as a small herd of deer, and each emitting its own voice. Some screamed, others muttered. Some pounded or pinged, whined or moaned. But the one on which the man focused was the most fearsome of all. It was silent to all but the ears of an adept who could hear its whisper.

Its whisper was alluring.

The man rose from a squat and squared his shoulders. Reaching into his string medicine bag, he fingered the herbs that would sustain him, placed the dried slivers in his mouth, and began to run. There had never been so many whirlwinds. Maybe there never would be so many again. He must understand this extraordinary event.

As he approached, the column of air and dust began to spring slowly along the ground ahead of him. At each liftoff, pebbles and sticks were sucked into its mouth, in the same way that the gods pulled human souls into the abyss of time, whirling them through lifetimes and dimensions, through tempering experiences more numerous than stones or stalks of wild grass.

The column was a black coil, each turning as distinct as yarn on his wife's spindle, and as alive as a den of snakes. He ran faster but the wind eluded him, even as its spirit exhorted him to follow.

This would not be easy or over quickly. He steeled himself to run for days, wiping pain and fatigue from his mind, focusing only on the wind's voice and the secrets that, eventually, it would impart.

Chapter 1

§

Rancho Cielo, Chihuahua, Mexico, 2014

§

Calypso Searcy

TREE BRANCHES BEYOND THE BEDROOM WINDOW WERE SNARLED BLACK CALLIGRAPHY, WRITTEN ON A NIGHT SKY MARLED WITH CLOUDS AND STARS. Calypso wondered what message was encrypted there, as she slipped with her equally indecipherable thoughts into the envelope of blankets.

She lay fingering the enameled golden locket that hung about her neck on a thick chain of gold. She dreaded the dreams that would come should sleep and the locket have their way with her. Looking out at the night, she forced herself to stay awake, knowing it was futile.

It was always like this when she slept without Javier by her side. Despite the thick, sheltering adobe walls of the house and the reassurance of guards on the outer perimeter, she was edgy and alert. She knew it wasn't her own safety that stirred her. It was his.

§

Paris, France, 2014

§

Hill

Hill sat with his laptop before him on the café table, staring at Calypso's latest e-mail. His café au lait was expending its last thread of steam into crisp morning air, but he ignored it. His croissant, too, lay untouched on its white dish. Morning traffic charged down the boulevard with increasing ferocity, but he was oblivious to the noise and movement. Instead, he was focusing with acute awareness on the pit of his stomach, where something old and familiar was moving—a sense of foreboding, of something out of joint.

A newsman was just another critter, really, he reflected. No different than an elk in rut, sniffing a female ten miles distant, or a salmon, smelling one molecule of its home creek while bucking Pacific swells. If there were trouble anywhere in the world, he was the one to sense it. If he were a dog, right now his hackles would be rising.

He stared at Calypso's terse message, so lacking in her usual jollity or quiet wisdom. *Javier is away,* he read for the *nth* time. *I am concerned.* Now, what the hell was he supposed to make of *that?* What does *away* mean? Fallen off the cliff, last seen making a four thousand-foot free fall toward the Urique River? Kidnapped by white slavers? Gone to China to open trade negotiations? Off campaigning for *Presidente de México?*

And how worried is *concerned?* Mildly agitated? Pacing the property of Rancho Cielo, day and night? Frantic? Desperate? Insane with foreboding?

He was bored. Since his last trip to North Africa, he'd been idling. Or maybe several decades of starving refugees, ravening, semimad tribal gun lords, dust, dirt, squalor, and corruption were finally taking their toll. If he saw one more skeletal child with a distended belly he might be tempted to quit investigative journalism altogether. All of which was weighing in on an interpretation of Calypso's e-mail.

What if, as his guts nudged, this was a cry for help? If he responded as if it were, she would shoot back a note denying it. What if he just ignored it and let things develop on their own? *Delete.* He knew himself better than that.

He reached for the croissant without looking, tore off a savage hunk with his teeth and ruminated over it, staring down Boulevard St. Michel, but seeing instead the courtyard of Rancho Cielo, with its fountain of red sandstone, banks of roses and adobe walls scrawled with bougainvillea. How could such a tranquil place invite so much trouble? If it wasn't drug lords abducting the mistress of the house or threatening to raid the place, it was starving Indians staggering through, or family dramas ending in body parts nailed to the front gate.

These aberrant qualities, from his vantage point in Paris and with the prospect of a quiet evening reading before the fire in his apartment on *Place des Vosges*, were sufficiently untoward as to seem from another dimension. That, and the complete lack, in Chihuahua, of amenities which to him had come to seem to be necessities—police who actually upheld the law, for instance, or crème fraiche, or Dover sole—litigated against an active response.

On the other hand, there was the boredom, and the prospect of something contrary, ill-timed, inexpedient, adverse, annoying, and dangerous into which to root like a reportorial sow. Rancho Cielo was a living thesaurus of disaster words. If life was easy in Paris, the *petit pois* ripening and the Opéra about to stage *Carmen*, then by the theory of inverse proportions under which Rancho Cielo operated, murder, mayhem, and primeval forces rummaging archaic karmic burdens would surely be the order of the day in Chihuahua. There would be granitic grit in the tortillas, some form of clan or tribal warfare in progress, and blood on the rocks.

And then there was the ultimate draw. Calypso. Years did not dim it, her union with Javier did not dissuade it, distance did not erase it—the indisputable fact that Calypso Searcy was, now and forever, the love of Hill's life. Like it or not.

He discovered himself in the act of holding half a croissant in front of his gaping mouth, where it had apparently been poised for several minutes. An American tourist at the adjoining table was elbowing her companion and tittering, delighted by his state of waxy flexibility. He slammed the lid of his laptop and roiled his pocketful of coins, gathering up a fistful that he dropped on the table without counting, assured by its very bulk that it would be sufficient.

Rising with what he hoped was supreme dignity, he buttoned his top coat, gathered up his computer, and nodding sourly to his neighbor, departed the café. It was really no contest. Even Paris, Navel of the Universe, with all its charms, couldn't hold a candle to a good ol' shoot-'em-up, dusty, treacherous, thoroughly rash sojourn in lawless Chihuahua. Even Bizet was upstaged by it. Egregious it might well be, but wasn't that the stuff that news—and apparently his friendship with Calypso—was made of?

He dug his cell phone from his pocket and speed dialed Charles de Gaulle Airport. With luck, he could make the next plane out to El Paso. He was two blocks from the café when he realized he was still clutching the mangled croissant in his left hand.

§

Rancho Cielo

Calypso was pruning roses in the courtyard when there was a honk outside the walls. Before she could hustle around to the front, one of the guards had opened the thick wooden double gates and a dusty blue VW Super Beetle was nosing through them. She pushed a lock of hair from her eyes with the back of a gloved hand, shoved her clippers into their holster and went to investigate.

A large, familiar figure was in the process of disentangling itself from the car, which seemed comically small in comparison. "Walter!" She ran to him, and he enclosed her in a crushing bear hug. "What in the world?" She reared her head back to take in his face. "What are you *doing* here?"

"I think I took a wrong turn on my way to Marseille." He held her at arm's length and studied her face. "I've been worried about you. So I thought I'd come and see for myself what's going on."

"What makes you think something's going on?"

"Ha! You are ever dubious of my psychic powers."

Calypso laughed and pulled from his embrace.

"Oh, Walter! I've missed you. Come. Get your things and I'll get you settled in the guest room."

§

Huichol Sierra, Jalisco, Mexico, 2014

§

Javier Carteña

Afternoon shadows cast long, blue runnels across sandy yellow soil, and the greatest heat of the day was just beginning to abate. A small group of Huichol women, in flounced skirts and embroidered blouses, was tending a cook fire in a pounded clearing surrounded by shabby brush huts, while their half-naked children played a shrieking, laughter-filled game of chase.

Javier sat in the scant shade of a scrawny tree and simply waited, as he had been told to wait. Alejandro, the Huichol shaman, had been specific. Although Javier was half indigenous himself, in this place he was considered an outsider. The quest would go on without him. He must await the outcome here on the rancho.

The women spoke in tones too low for him to hear, even if he could understand their language well, but he was fairly sure they were venting their doubts about the big Mexican under the tree, who was half again as tall and broad as the biggest man in their clan. And definitely not indigenous, judging by his blue jeans, scuffed cowboy boots and faded chambray shirt. And too handsome for his own good. The women *tsk*ed and shook their heads.

Old Catarina, her already short frame bent with arthritis so that her skirt swept the ground in front and was hoisted almost to her knees in back, came scuttling across to him holding an unglazed earthen bowl. She thrust it at him without a word and turned away, her old face seamed with worry and distrust. As he ate the shreds of roasted goat meat, the children swirled close to him, casting wary looks, then spiraled away, jabbering like a flock of startled birds.

His thoughts turned to home, to Calypso, and the daily round of Rancho Cielo, feeling their absence as a profound heaviness around his heart. He knew the Huichol ways. He wouldn't be heading home any time soon. The quest could take days and the ritual debriefing days more. Alejandro was a young shaman, but he had shown himself, in the past, to be a man of power and a seer. He was worth the wait. His insights might make sense of the alarm that had been growing in Javier's gut.

He knew that Calypso was having dreams by the way she lay fingering the locket in the morning, her face drawn and pensive. Her usual eagerness to share the vivid and often premonitory visions, however, was absent. Whatever she had learned from the night's eminence, she had kept it to herself.

He stretched out his long, denim-sheathed legs, his boot heels making a ripping sound as they scraped forward in the dirt. He glanced at his truck, sitting tipped on the uneven hillside. He'd need to find a flatter place before nightfall. Last night, sleeping in the bed of the truck, his sleeping bag kept sliding downhill until he lay crumpled against the metal side. Finally, when the stars had shifted above him for many hours, he stopped fighting gravity and slept, snuggled against the inner fender covering the wheel well, as if it were the curvature of Calypso's body.

He liked sleeping under the stars, letting his mind sink into the vastness of space and time, liberating him from pressing concerns of the present. It put his worries in their place, diminishing them to their actual proportion. Even the prospect of death took its proper measure. And since it was death that concerned him now—his, Calypso's, his workers', their families'—he craved the consolation of the stars and their aloofness from all things human.

He thought again of his home in Copper Canyon far to the north and sighed. He knew that his waiting should be active, not passive, that his attention to the question at hand was required as part of the web of power being woven out in the desert by the whirling winds. He pulled his legs under him, straightened his spine, centered his mind, and quieted his breathing. Whatever the outcome, he would have to be part of its making. The westering sun began to burn the back of his neck but he sat still, his eyes half-closed, staring at nothing and everything as his ghostly blue shadow stretched longer and longer before him, also waiting.

§

An old man came out of the god-house and approached him. Javier knew him—Jeronimo González, Alejandro's uncle and one of the clan's singers, who tended the god-house and took part in all the rituals. He was a small, bow-legged man dressed in white cotton pants and tunic, both embroidered in red with Huichol symbols.

"Ha, hombre!" he greeted Javier. "Come over to Grandfather Fire and I will brush you. Then you can go pray in the god-house."

Javier knew a great honor was being accorded him, so he stood. "Thank you, amigo. I would like that."

He and Jeronimo approached the fire and the women retreated. All fire was sacred to the Huichol, Javier knew. It was a source of visions during peyote rituals, and no Huichol felt either safe or at home, day or night, until a fire was lit. Once beside the fire Jeronimo produced a brush and began a ritual cleansing of Javier's body.

"What kind of feathers are those in your brush, Jeronimo?" he asked, to be companionable.

Jeronimo did not stop brushing. "These are not feathers," he said in his soft, cracked voice. "This is a wolf's tail." Javier was shocked. Several of his recent dreams had featured wolves, the shy, seldom-seen gray, white, and russet ghosts that sometimes haunted the plateau around the ranch. "*Camóquime*, father of the wolves, came to me in a dream," the old man said, "and told me to do this brushing for you."

"I had a dream about a wolf, too." The old man stopped brushing and stepped back, looking Javier deep in the eyes. "I was sleeping near a spring and a wolf came and whispered in my ear."

"What did he say?"

Javier grinned. "I have no idea."

Jeronimo shook his head. "Too bad. A wolf only comes with important information. Wolf is related to Father Sun, and his light will help Alejandro on his quest. It was careless of you not to remember."

"I'm sorry." Javier was genuinely chagrined.

"Chaos comes when the taboos are violated and there are transgressions," the old man said. "We must be very careful to do everything in the right way, as the ancestors did. The mining is disrupting everything. All the spirits are unhappy—the wolves, the beaded lizards, *xraiye* the rattlesnake, the black cloud snake, *tohue* the jaguar, the puma, even Grandfather Fire. You are right to come seeking vision." The old man resumed his slow, careful brushing.

Javier had worked for years with the Mexican government, trying to secure Huichol lands against the depredations of mining conglomerates. Lately, however, with the passage of NAFTA and investments by the World Bank and big multinational corporations, Huichol lands were being nibbled along the edges, with vaster intrusions always threatening. With the Huichol, he always walked a fine edge between the spiritual world they inhabited, and the hard facts of political advocacy.

Jeronimo stepped back to inspect him and then nodded his head toward the entrance to the god-house, where the stones of power were housed. Javier tried to collect himself, to focus, before ducking to enter the low doorway. For this small bit of time, he vowed, he would let the machinations of the greater world rest, and dedicate himself to that other world that, in Mexico, always lay behind so thin a veil. The ancestors and the spirits were agitated, of this he was certain. What to do about it was a secret still hoarded in the Great Mystery.

§

Three days passed. Jeronimo sang to evoke *Ea'ca Téihuari*, the Wind Person, sprinkled water from a sacred spring, and did other rituals to induce the spirits to help Alejandro on his quest and to reveal the information Javier sought. The two men ingested sacred *hicouri*, the peyote that is sacramental to the Huichol. Under its influence, Javier was brought once again into close understanding that all aspects of creation are sentient, powerful, and alive with meaning and importance, and that reciprocity between the human and spirit worlds forms the basis of sustainability for all life.

"Look deep into *Tatewari*," Jeronimo said, gesturing toward Grandfather Fire. "Ask him to remind you what the wolf told you in your dream."

The brilliance at the heart of the fire was kindled in Javier's own heart, and he knew himself to be a luminous being with love at his core. Deep in the red embers, he saw his dream replayed, and heard the wolf's voice in the crackling flames. "Wolf walks with the woman," it said, "as guard and guide."

Neither he nor Jeronimo could interpret this, but Jeronimo insisted it was an assurance of spiritual aid in some situation still to be. "There are many dimensions," the old man explained. "They circle and spiral back upon themselves, creating the pattern of the universe which is always dying, and being reborn. Nothing is a straight line. Therefore, somewhere the future is already known, and the spirits are preparing it for us and preparing our protection and guidance so that we learn and grow in safety."

"Does this mean that some danger will come to Calypso?"

The old singer shrugged. "*¿Quien sabe?* Who knows? Mystery is the deepest reality of all."

§

Sleep evaded Javier in the freezing Sierra night, as he curled around the inner fender of his truck, thinking of Calypso and their last night together at Rancho Cielo. At her vanity, brushing her hair, she had set down her brush and come to him, an undulant flow of white gown and black hair in the lamplight.

Sitting beside him, she reached a hand to his face, and held his eyes with a penetrating look.

"You are the rarest of men, my love, the most generous-spirited man in the world. It's why I can't keep my hands off you!" She slipped her cold hands across his bare chest and thrust them into the warmth of his armpits, her knowing smile saying that the reaction was predictable.

"My God, Caleepso!" He laughed and grabbed her wrists. "You trying to kill me? You need some warming up!" He rolled back on the bed, pulling her on top of him, and gathered her hands together to begin nibbling on her fingertips. "I'll start on the periphery and work inward."

Calypso laughed and struggled to free herself, then submitted. "I'm your captive. Do with me what you will," she said, with a sigh that was more delighted than resigned.

Javier held her cold fingers to his lips and kissed the tips. So many years they had been together. So many struggles and cares. Still, contact with this woman's body never failed to move him. Something electric, yet deeply grounded, flowed between them at the smallest contact, as if all joy resided in their conjoined flesh.

On sudden impulse, he drew her body closer and held her tightly. "Caleepso, Caleepso..." he breathed.

She sensed something unusual in his touch. "What is it, Javier?"

He shook his head, his chin resting on the top of her head with a somber weight. Words could not express the painful sense of longing that coursed through him. "It's as if I have to leave you for a long time," he said at last. "As if...I don't know." He held her even more tightly to him.

"You sound so sad, my love."

"I just could not bear to lose you, Caleepso."

She struggled from his grasp and turned so she could see his face. "Lose me? What are you saying?"

"It's just a feeling I have. I can't explain it."

"Sometimes people say, *Like someone is walking on my grave*. Is it like that? Creepy?"

He gazed into her eyes with a look bordering on despair. "I don't know, Caleepso. I just don't want to lose you." And he had pulled her into his chest again and held her fiercely.

The emotion was so urgent that it blasted him out of reverie. Above him, the frosty stars burned and glittered. If they were gods, he thought, pulling the sleeping bag closer around his neck, they were far too remote. How could they know or care what befell men on earth? A cold wind rattled through the surrounding brush, and he listened to it until he fell asleep.

§

At last, Alejandro returned. He had run for three days, fueled by *hicouri*, following the whirlwind as it blasted and sucked and twirled its way through the desert.

"*Ea'ca Téihuari* is angry," he avowed by the fire, his thin face glowing like oiled wood within the wild snarls of his hair.

His body looked sunken, depleted, and one foot was swollen from a cactus thorn inside its battered sandal. "The wind spirits are gathering. The mining is disturbing them. But worse still are the *narcotraficantes*. They are bringing violence to our peaceful land."

Javier sat gazing into the fire, listening solemnly. It was not news that the drug cartels were disrupting things. All of Mexican culture was suffering. Thousands of people had already lost their lives in drug-related violence. Every day there were new reports of the growing power and menace of the drug mafias. Their power even threatened to overwhelm the central government of the country.

Jeronimo, too, listened carefully, nodding his head. "What would the spirits have us do?" he asked at last.

Alejandro began a detailed explanation of the rituals that were to be performed, in rapid Huichol. Javier, whose Huichol was rudimentary, sat staring into the coals, lost in thought, so that he was jolted when Alejandro suddenly turned his attention on him and said, "The Wind Person has a message for you."

"What is it, please?"

"The message is this: there is no time to lose. Danger is everywhere. Protect your home and your loved ones. The times are dark."

Javier stared at him in alarm. "What does that mean?"

"It means," said Alejandro grimly, "that you'd better get your ass out of here. Get into your truck, *now*, and go home. The spirits do not speak in vain."

§

Rancho Cielo

Hill unpacked his small suitcase into the hulking Colonial-era *armario* in the guest room, smiling to himself. It felt so familiar to be here. Memories of his last visit, now more than two years in the past, rose to reassure him that he was welcome.

He thought of the final night of his last stay, when they had sat in the courtyard on the very edge of the canyon, chatting into the night. There were no city lights, no traffic noise. The abyss of the canyon was a cauldron of ink, the sky a poppy field of stars. The world was reduced to firelight, shifting shadows, soft voices. Contained in a cocoon of reminiscence, they scarcely stirred.

"Picasso said that everything you can imagine is real," Hill had offered into the conversational pot already simmering among them. "If that's true, then I need to tell you that this night—being together with you both—has happened before. I remember it. Is that real or imagination? Or is there a difference?"

Javier stirred up the embers in the fire pit and dropped another log into the flames. "Here? What were we? Indigenous? *Conquistadores?*"

"I don't know. Maybe not here. Maybe somewhere else."

"Maybe you're remembering Chiapas. Sitting in the ruin around the cook fire," Calypso offered.

"No. I don't think it's that. But I've sat with you both, just this way, in just this energy."

"Energy? Are you becoming a New Ager, Walter?" Calypso's voice wafted out of shadow like a moth, delicate and pale. Teasing.

A bird muttered as the night wind lifted the branches of the alamos. Firelight washed adobe walls with rose. "Say something, Walter," Calypso spoke into the silence. "I didn't mean to offend you."

"There's nothing more to say." His tone was stubborn.

"Now Walter..." she began sweetly.

"Caleepso"—Javier cut in—"you talk about energy all the time. A group of people. The mood of the weather. Your sense of a new horse. So why question Hill about it?"

Calypso leaned toward the fire, her beautiful face framed in her shadowy mane, like the white moon emerging from cloud. "Because Walter is so rational, and I always think he judges me for saying those things. Do you, Walter?"

Toward the front of the house, a guard coughed, then was silent. Hill leaned back in his chaise lounge, and stared at the starry sky tented over them, taking his time to answer. It was this woman's genius to bring the hidden parts of him to light. If she were to know this about him, he wanted it succinct and accurate, just like the facts he collected for his newspaper articles. He didn't want to have to explain himself later, in some muddled search for understanding.

"I believe," he began at last, "that we live over and over again. We die. We are reborn. And we meet certain people in those lives, doing the same thing. Reincarnating. Working through karma, if you will. Struggling, lifetime after lifetime, to learn lessons that are important to their souls." He clamped his lips, determined to leave it there.

"Hill, you surprise me." Javier turned to him, although their eyes, lost in shadow, were as unknowable as the abyss before them. "You're talking like one of our local shamans."

"I met a Buddhist monk in Cambodia, couple of years ago. We talked for two days straight. By the time he was done with me, I was beyond a reformed-Presbyterian-slash-closet-Catholic. I was cosmic."

"So I wonder where we were, the last time we gathered around a fire like this?" Calypso's voice was dreamy, slathered with the cream of imagination. "Maybe we were players, camped in some forest between castles, planning our next production for a count or a king."

"With you as the heroine and me as the Fool."

"Or maybe we were shepherds on some hillside in Sumeria," Javier volunteered, "naming the constellations."

Hill pointed languidly toward the Big Dipper. "Yes, I remember calling that one *Aunt Agatha*, because it's small on top and big on the bottom."

Calypso pointed southward, to where Gemini's twins, hand in hand, were just stepping over a horizon of black *barrancas*. "And I named those two *Javier-and-Calypso-With-Walter-Trailing-Along-Below-the-Horizon-In-Some-Foreign-Land-All-the-Time.*"

"It probably sounded more poetic in Sumerian."

"That makes me think, Hill," Javier said, his face turned terra-cotta in the firelight, "aren't you getting tired of traveling all the time? Isn't it about time for you to retire? You're welcome here, you know. We'll build a house for you. There's a good flat place, just back from the cliffs, about a quarter mile from here."

"What? And leave Paris?" Hill struck his chest in mock grief.

"You're never there anyway, Walter. You're always off in some God-forsaken land where cholera is killing more people than the resident dictator. Javier and I worry about you."

"I think about retiring, sometimes. But I always imagine myself in the apartment. Strolling down Place des Vosges, mornings, to my favorite café for coffee. Maybe getting season tickets to the opera. Taking the Train à Grande Vitesse to the south and getting a tan on some part of me besides my face and forearms."

"Oh, that's a good one! I can just see you lounging topless on the beach at Saint-Tropez. You and your laptop. And your cell phone on speed dial for the closest airport, in some little pocket of your trunks. You wouldn't make it past the first minor skirmish! You'd be out of there like you were shot from a cannon." Calypso laughed and swatted Hill on the knee. "Be real, Walter."

"I don't want to talk about it now." Hill's tone was petulant.

"Did you know," Calypso volunteered, apropos of nothing, "that the word constellation comes from the word *stella*, and means *star togetherness*? It makes me think, when I look at the night sky, that they and we are linked somehow. We form a togetherness."

"Yes, the only thing vaster than our own interior spaces is that vastness out there." Hill's voice was unusually soft and thoughtful.

"We touch this world with our bodies," Javier volunteered, equally serious, "but that one out there—we can only reach it in our minds, when we let them dream."

"Or when we worship," Calypso added. "Even in prehistory the stars were seen as divine figures. Gods, prognosticating the future, not just of mere mortals like us but of entire cultures and civilizations."

"Caleepso, how do you know these things? You never stop amazing me." Javier reached to stroke her cheek.

"I'll tell you something else she knows."

"What?" Calypso and Javier asked in the same instant.

"The story of that locket." He pointed his chin toward Calypso's chest.

"I thought Father Roberto told you that story while we were in Chiapas."

"Only part of it. Just the very first part, when he was a boy. But you know the rest—I know he told you."

"Well, I can't tell it to you tonight. It's too long."

"Ha! See how you are? I'm never going to get to hear that story, am I? I have to leave in the morning. I'll go to my grave wondering about this thing that dangles around your neck.

How it came to be. Or what its powers are. I ask you: What are friends for? Shouldn't you be obligated by the very bonds of friendship to tell me the story, whether you want to or not?"

Calypso had laughed. "Okay, you! Now you've done it. But it means you'll have to come again. We can't possibly do the story justice tonight."

He had promised then, he mused as he hung his trousers on hangers and thrust them into the maw of the armoire. Promised to come back soon and hear the tale in its full richness. That was over two years ago, and what had he accomplished in the meantime?

War, war, and more war had been the bill of fare, until his enthusiasm for his profession had begun to wane and his heart to feel empty, where once it was charged with the energy of investigation and reporting. It felt right to be again in Calypso's presence, in her indefinable aura of magic. He had to admit to himself that in some very real sense, he had not come in response to Calypso's call at all, but in search of renewal.

§

Hill and Calypso settled into wooden armchairs on the patio, facing the spectacle of the canyon, as it collected the amethyst light of evening and the cliffs deepened to rose.

"Last time I sat here, Javier was here," Hill said, hoping to nudge the story of his absence from Calypso.

She took her time, sipped her Corona, gazed into the canyon, chose her words carefully. "Javier is growing restless," she said at last. "I'm not sure why. Something is troubling him but he won't talk about it. I think it's the cartels.

"A few months ago, there was an attack in Creel, just a few miles from here. They arrived in a caravan of black SUVs. Men just poured out of them, all armed to the teeth with automatic weapons. They shot up the house of the local doctor who's been trying to combat the drug problem among the local kids. Fortunately, he wasn't home at the time. But the message was clear and he left town."

"And Javier thinks Rancho Cielo might be next?'

She shook her head. "I don't know but I suspect so, yes."

"So why is he away? Isn't he worried about your safety?"

"I think that's why he's gone. He went to spend time with a friend of his, a Huichol shaman, down in Jalisco. I'm thinking of it as a spiritual pilgrimage."

"Or a fact-finding mission?"

"That too. His friend does a ritual that helps him tell the future."

Hill hitched forward in his chair so that he could face Calypso fully. "What about you and the locket? Wouldn't it give you a warning, like it did that night in Chiapas when the *guardia blanca* came?"

"Well, that's the thing. I've been having dreams. Disturbing ones. And I haven't been telling them to Javier because I don't want to worry him."

"A Mexican standoff?"

Calypso's smile was tight. "Yes. I guess it is. Neither of us is being as forthright as we should be."

"And what are your dreams telling you?"

He was alarmed when tears sprang instantly to her eyes and her jaw tightened, as if otherwise she might commence to wail. "They're showing me ruin, Walter. Complete ruin."

ʃ

"Let's talk about something else," Hill suggested. "How about finally telling me the story of the locket?"

"You already know the first part. You start." Her voice was still pinched with tears. "If you'll tell what you know, then tomorrow night—*early*—I'll tell my part. Read it, actually. I've just finished a manuscript of Berto's story. But it's long. It'll take more than one night. So if you're called away before it's done because the Continental Divide was just subdivided by Yellowstone's super-volcano or because Atlantis has just arisen from the sea, don't blame me." She managed a ghost of her old smile.

As dusk faded into night, the canyon brooded before them, as unfathomable as the recesses of space. Bats flittered over the abyss, a blacker blackness. Silence fell between them and each was aware of a ponderous shift of energy, as their conversation thickened and coalesced into remembrance and, with it, story.

§

"I can remember that night like it was yesterday," Hill began. "I was feeling like such an oaf. I blundered into your camp uninvited and began, as swiftly as possible, revealing myself to be a gigantic gringo ass. I was mad as hell. At you and Javier. At life. But especially at myself, for having put myself in that position.

"So I went out into the *selva* to cool off, and that was where I met Father Roberto. The minute I met him, I felt things shift. I knew it was all going to be okay.

"He was listening to Maria Callas singing, on his little tape deck. And that got him talking about the capital "F" Feminine. I didn't have a clue what he was talking about, so he decided to explain by telling me his story. And I guess that's why I really need to hear the end of it, because he hooked me. And then, of course, he was called away and I've been wondering ever since.

"So this is what I remember..." Hill sat forward to take a swig from his bottle of Corona and then settled back and folded his arms behind his head, staring pensively into the starlit sky. "I can remember every word, as if I were hearing Berto speak them now..."

§

Chiapas, 1992

"First, my friend, you must understand that the world as you know it—the world of commerce and war and international intrigue—is just a veneer, here in Mexico," Father Roberto began. "This country rests on a timelessness that would be incomprehensible in Washington, DC or in Moscow. Once you leave the main streets of Mexico City, you are thrust back into time before time. First, you encounter the overlay of the Conquest and the heavy burden it has laid on the souls of the indigenous people. Then, if you travel deeper into the country and into the psyches of the people, you will find the mysticism that is the fundament of the Mexican soul.

"I grew up in an upper class family that was quite Europeanized, but the servants—the washerwomen, cooks, gardeners, and maids—introduced me to their worldview, which existed side-by-side with my parents' Catholicism like two layers of an onion. It was a knowledge that I kept to myself, the way most children hide their awareness of sex or their cache of dirty words, because I had no reason to believe that my mother or father would approve.

"It wasn't until my fifth year, when a terrible thing happened, that I learned how wrong I had been..."

§

The Story of Father Roberto Villanova y Mansart

By five, Roberto Villanova y Mansart was aware of the discrepancies between the official religion of his family's home and the subterranean but titillating beliefs of its staff. Priests in stiff black suits came to dinner and disappeared afterwards into the study, where his father wrote them checks on vellum-colored paper with a fountain pen dispensing indigo ink. Nuns came calling on his mother on certain afternoons and left with pockets jingling. Roberto understood that this was not begging, but was a favor done by the clergy, allowing his family to stand in good stead with God.

Meanwhile, in the kitchen with the cook, Esmeralda, or outside with Pepe, the gardener, or in the pantry where old Chimalma sat polishing the silver, another worldview, another dimension of reality even, was developing in his brain like film dipped in chemical solution. In that alternate world, healers could alleviate illness by sucking on one's forehead; adepts of magic could turn themselves into insects and animals which then were able to spy on enemies, unaware; and most shocking of all, tantamount to heresy, the Virgin Mary was really the Great Woman, Tonantsin, in disguise.

At night when his nurse Alma put him to bed, she spoke strange words over him, her face contorted in earnest discourse regarding his welfare with gods whose names he did not know and who, once described, gave him nightmares. When he got a fever, she bound stinky herbs under his nightshirt and made gestures in the air, as if she were writing there. Roberto knew that wasn't the case, however, because Alma could neither read nor write, and this made her airborne calligraphy all the more intriguing and troubling.

Every day a priest arrived to say mass in their private chapel and on Sundays, the entire family—Grandmére, Tía Isobella, Maman, Papa, and any extra aunts or cousins who might be visiting—would troop down the street in somber finery and around the corner to the church, which was tall and layered and intricate as a wedding cake. Inside, the entire wall behind the altar was a *reredos*, a writhing mass of gold-encrusted carving that Maman said had come all the way from Spain in a sailing ship, after the Conquest. It depicted angels and saints supported by billows of cloud and, above them all, riding on the outstretched wings of a dove, the risen Christ.

This Christ was much more approachable than the life-sized one on the crucifix by the altar, who grimaced and glared in a way that made Roberto sink down in his pew and bury his face in his mother's coat. And it only added to his confusion that the servants, who had brought up the rear of their train, now sat in the back of the church looking serenely pious and not at all ashamed of their covert and nefarious ways.

Although, it had just come to his attention that Maman had some peculiar habits of her own, which might be considered outside the pale of strict Catholicism, and these interested him greatly. For one thing, she often seemed to know things before they happened and this was a concern for Roberto, because he wasn't sure how much she might see about him and his doings with the staff. Furthermore, she always wore a gold locket under her clothing, against her chest and even—his wide brown eye to the crack of the door told him—in the bath.

So Roberto began a campaign to elicit from his mother specific information regarding her actual beliefs and practices. This siege, which quickly reached relentless proportions, centered upon the golden locket and its significance to her. Day and night Roberto questioned his mother until, in the space of about a week, he wore down her resistance completely.

"The truth is, Roberto," she began, her eyes flashing with tantalizing mischief, "that you are justified in your curiosity. The locket is a treasure far more valuable than the gold from which it is made. It has a long and amazing history, this necklace. Can you believe that it is not just hundreds but thousands of years old? And that it did not originate in this country or even on this continent?

"No, Berto, my darling, it comes from a distant land, and was made by craftsmen of an ancient civilization that is long dead. And the story of its coming to me, and of the powers it possesses is the most astonishing story you will ever hear."

Roberto felt the skin of his arms prickle at his mother's words, for they were spoken almost in a whisper, as if she were imparting to him the greatest secret in the world. "If you tried for a lifetime, Berto, you could not imagine a stranger and more complicated tale. This locket originated in Egypt, Berto, and by its own magic arts found its way first to Europe, and then here to Mexico. And who can say where it will go next? And do you know what? The power that resides in this locket speaks to me in my dreams, *hijo*. Yes, it tells me things—what will happen and to whom, where lost things can be found, whom to trust and whom to avoid..."

S

Rancho Cielo

To Calypso's disappointment, Hill's voice trailed off into the midnight air. "That's it," he said finally. "I've searched my memory and that's all I can remember. Berto got called away and I never heard the rest. I hope you can fill in the blanks."

"Tomorrow night, I promise. That's it for me tonight. It must be almost midnight." Calypso rose, bent to give him a quick kiss, and went up the path toward the house. Instantly, it brought Hill back to the night two years before when late into the night he had shared these same chairs with both Calypso and Javier. Finally, Calypso had departed, as she had just now, calling, "Don't stay up all night talking, you two," leaving him alone with Javier in the starry darkness.

Javier had drained his beer and risen. "I'm done, too." He banked the fire with a shovel, poured the dregs of the beer onto it and blew out the lanterns. The fullness of night swept instantly over them, rich with insect sounds, wind in trees, and the fragrance of pine. Hill pushed wearily to his feet and the two men stood transfixed for a moment, staring at a sky suddenly looming huge with stars, like a vast meadow filled with wildflowers.

"Amazing," Javier said softly.

"Yes," Hill responded, "There's no end to the amazement, like a well that goes down into the depths and never touches bottom. The well of life."

"Or a well in time."

They had turned toward the house and, picking their way with care, left the living night for the quiet of their beds.

§

Hill lay now beneath an antique woolen blanket patterned with indigenous symbols, not gazing out at the night sky, but at a large painting that hung across from him on the plastered adobe wall. By the light of the bedside lamp its colors were muted, its shadows deepened. He knew it must be one of Calypso's works and so he studied it minutely, hoping to learn something new about this woman who was his life's fascination.

She had painted the cliffs of Copper Canyon as seen from their courtyard, as they plunged nearly a mile to Rio Urique. In the painted world, it was perennial dusk, luminous with cobalt and ultramarine pigments. Reflected light glowed from rose-colored cliffs, with the far barrancas in pale blue shading almost to black as they disappeared into the abyss of the canyon.

It was an image beguiling in its mystery and deep peace. The more Hill studied it, the more he admired the ability and the vision that had brought it forth.

Slipping from bed, he approached the painting and examined the brushstrokes closely. If he'd had a jeweler's loupe, he would have used it. The oil paints were laid down so smoothly that he could scarcely discern the brushstrokes. The entire surface had the closely integrated appearance he had seen in some Renaissance paintings.

He frowned, perplexed. When had Calypso achieved this level of expertise? He had seen her earlier paintings—loosely-brushed, Impressionistic affairs that were lighthearted and sketchy. This painting was of another caliber altogether. It went far beyond technical mastery into a dimension of psychological understanding and inner knowing that commanded respect, if not astonishment. Possibly even reverence. He crawled back into bed feeling shaken.

More than the threads of silver in Calypso's long, dark hair, this painting spoke to him of the passage of time and of his long separation from his friends. Something had happened in the interim. Something of moment. A deepening. The kind he needed himself after so many years on the road.

Hill sighed heavily and turned on his side to extinguish the lamp then lay, still staring at the painting. Even by the light of the just-rising sliver of moon, the painting held mysterious power, as if the vertiginous energy of the canyon were pulling him in, sucking him into a vortex of time and energy against which he was resistless, in a trajectory toward the complete unknown.

§

Morning sun slanted across the *saltillos* of the kitchen floor, casting leaf shadows from the vine surrounding the window.

Hill lumbered in just as Calypso was taking the enameled coffee pot from the stove.

"Good timing, Walter. Did you rest well?" She plunked a mug in front of him as he settled at the rough kitchen table and poured coffee, black, steaming and fragrant.

"Like a rock. And what about you?" Hill used the question to do an intensive study of her face—and found it just as beguiling, just as beautiful, as it had been on their first meeting in Paris, over two decades before. The green eyes held a deepening, a mix of sorrow, understanding, and something else he couldn't define, but that made his chilled flesh tingle, as if it had been stroked by sun.

"Yes, I did. And I feel happier than I could ever have imagined."

"It must be because I'm here."

Calypso beamed silently and kissed the top of his head.

"Happy, even in spite of the drug cartels?"

"Even given that. Javier's trained and armed our ranch hands, you know. They're a small army. No one will mess with us."

"But you still have guards on the walls."

"Yes. We're always cautious. The power of the cartels shifts. Sometimes we're under threat. Then the head of that cartel will be murdered and someone new will take his place who's no problem to us. Or another cartel will come to power, one that doesn't threaten us at all. I've always told you, Walter, Chihuahua is a crazy place, like living in the Wild West. The rules of the twenty-first century just don't apply here."

As she spoke, she was pulling a tray of scones from the oven and depositing them with a spatula on a brightly decorated terra cotta platter. She brought them to the table and placed them before Hill with a flourish. "Apricot scones for your delectation. I don't want you to feel deprived, this far from Paris. There's freshly churned butter in that little crock. And homemade rose hip jelly in that one."

"Drug runners be damned! This place is paradise!" Hill reached with eager fingers for his first scone.

"It is paradise, in its way. I feel more at peace here than ever."

"I believe that," Hill rejoined, as he savored the creamy butter, the delicate, flowery jelly, and the light texture of the sweet pastry. "And I base that belief on my observation of your painting in my room. It seems to come from a place that the Calypso I first knew could not have reached."

Calypso beamed at the compliment. "I'm so glad you like it! I'll tell you its secret: I'm making my own paints from pigments I find here. This place is a mineralogical treasure trove, Walter. Javier and I are always scouring the cliffs, looking for new colors. When I paint with the local pigments, my paintings seem to come alive."

Hill helped himself to another scone, slathering it heavily with butter and jelly while formulating his response. "I see that the colors are true to the landscape, and now I understand why. But it's more than that, Calypso. There's an intelligence...a knowledge...a wisdom...I don't know how to say what I see in that painting. It's as if you've achieved another level within yourself to do what you did."

Calypso busied herself at the stove, her head down, her face closed. She cracked eggs onto a skillet and turned the bacon, without responding. Finally, when they were both seated at the table with plates of breakfast before them, she answered.

"Walter, it's this locket. Ever since Chiapas, when I first started to wear it, it's been altering my perception of reality. I get dreams, insights, visions. Messages whispered into my mind. Sometimes, I know what's going to happen before it happens. Sometimes, I see into a person who's being devious or see value in someone who's an outcast.

"And I see things out of the corner of my eye. Ghosts? Spirits? Angels? I have no idea. But I always feel as if I'm in company. As if I'm watched over."

"That sounds creepy."

"No. It's comforting. They're definitely a benevolent presence. And I'm quite sure that my paintings have developed the way they have because of their guidance. I don't think about it. It's not conscious, really. But there's a kind of reverie that comes over me when I paint. When I'm in that state, magic happens on the canvas."

"It's affecting your writing too. Your last book was very deep, Calypso. It really touched me."

"Were you in Paris?"

"No, in Cairo. Reporting on the debacle that the Arab Spring has become. I'd be out on the street all day, interviewing. Some of the interviews were tragic. Heartbreaking. Then I'd go to my hotel at night and find solace in your writing."

Calypso lowered her eyes, abashed. "I'm so glad, Walter," she murmured.

"So you're still going to read me the story of the locket tonight, right?"

"Well, I can start reading it. It's a long story, you know. If you really want to hear it all, it may take a couple of nights. Maybe more. It took Berto a week to tell it to me."

"I have nothing but time."

Calypso smiled and nodded. "Unless, of course, something more urgent calls you."

"Nope. Let riot and mayhem prevail. Let hell freeze over. Someone else can scoop it. I'm here for the duration. This is the story whose time has come."

Calypso gave him a long look, its depth almost alarming. "Yes," she finally said, "I think you're right. This time, you intend to hear it all." She rose, picked up their plates and headed toward the sink, saying over her shoulder, "You should go out and find Juan in the barn. He can saddle you a horse and show you the way. Pedro and his crew are moving the cattle to new pasture today. I think you'd be interested in the cattle drive."

Dismissed, Hill went outside, determined to involve himself in Calypso's world for the day. But in his heart, he was focused on that moment when the sun would be westering, dinner would be finished, and the locket would open like a portal, spilling its history over him, like light coming through a long-sealed doorway.

ʃ

Chapter 2

THE AFTERNOON TURNED COOL AND CLOUDY AND BY NIGHTFALL, IT BEGAN TO RAIN. After dinner, Calypso and Hill sat in front of a pinewood fire, lounging deep into their chairs and stretching their feet toward the flames. Silence simmering with anticipation filled the shadowed room.

Calypso sat with her long skirt petaled about her, her pale face like the pistil of a dark flower. Hill gazed at her, waiting, determined not to intrude on the deep innerness of her thoughts. At last, she began to speak.

"This rain is the first break in a long drought," she said, glancing at him. "We've been waiting for a month longer than usual for the monsoons to begin. Everything in nature is rejoicing tonight." She raised her mug and took a slow sip of tea, then set it by her elbow on an end table piled with books.

"It seems appropriate when Mother Nature is releasing her waters to let memory flow, too. I've been working a long time writing Berto's story. It's strange and complex. If I hadn't experienced the power of the locket myself, I'd think it was one of those tales embroidered by successive generations until it was more fable than fact.

"By writing it, I've come to understand how quickly life passes. How one generation succeeds another. How lives flame up and then die down to embers and vanish, far too quickly. But objects live on. They have lives of their own, possibly even intentions of their own. Who can say what that bowl knows, for example?"

She gestured toward a cobalt and white porcelain bowl holding apples, on the coffee table before them. "It's Chinese, from the Ming Dynasty. Did it pass along the Silk Road in a camel caravan, I wonder? Was it held in the hands of a noble or a thief? How did it get those little chips, and where? In a hut in the Gobi Desert? In a villa in Italy? And how did it end up in the thrift shop in Berkeley where I bought it? And now, it's here in Chihuahua. It's seen far more of life than we have, Walter, in its five- or six-hundred years. And it will continue, after we're gone. Yet its life is a mystery to us."

She leaned forward and ran a fingertip along the pitted edge of the vessel. "And I wonder the same kinds of things about the locket. Except that I know a few of the details about it that I'll never know about this bowl."

She stopped and glanced at Hill, a mysterious smile playing over her lips. "And so, Walter, at your insistence, the tale begins..." She wiggled her eyebrows teasingly, then bent to pick up a manuscript box from the floor and withdrew a handful of pages.

§

Guadalajara, Mexico, 1963

§

The Story of Father Roberto Villanova y Mansart Continues

In an exclusive suburb of Guadalajara, behind a high stone wall and curly iron gates, beyond a garden anointed by a five-tiered fountain of pinkish-gray stone, stands to this day the villa of the Villanova y Mansart family. It is such an interesting architectural blend of the older Spanish Colonial style with the more recent French Colonial, that students from the local college are often brought there on field trips to pay particular attention to it. Of special noteworthiness and delicate refinement are the long French doors set into deeply carved, heavily ornamented *chiaroscuro* of stone, leading onto balconies of the most finely wrought and cast iron.

It was on one of these balconies, with a frolicking spring wind picking up the corners of the lace draperies and flipping them out toward the parrot-green buds of the trees, that Roberto, then aged five, and his mother stood.

"Berto, my sweetest darling," his mother crooned in French, her accent slightly tinged with Spanish that was like salsa picante to her speech, "this is the most beautiful spring I shall ever see. *Malheureusement*, it is also likely to be the last."

Roberto looked up at her quickly, his dark eyes wide and serious. She was so beautiful, with her auburn hair sparkling gold in the sun. He gazed at her eyes but could not catch them. Her glance slipped off, following the hopping of a bird.

"*¿Que dices, Maman?*" he asked, mixing languages, as he was apt to do. "What are you saying?"

"I am sick, Roberto," she said, switching to Spanish. "The doctor has just found it out. It seems I have a cancer in my brain. A horrid thing, like a big, red balloon slowly being blown up inside my skull."

Roberto began to cry. The fear he felt at that moment was terrible. He sensed in her announcement all the loss in the world—a rending so awful that words could never say it. And he also felt guilty for having pestered her in recent days about the locket.

"Roberto, my love, I know you must cry. I have prayed to God for a way to comfort you at this moment. I have always believed that my prayers are answered, but this time I have gone without response. In God's wisdom and mercy, He sometimes leaves us comfortless. Perhaps, He knows that out of our misery will come our greatest growth into Spirit."

Roberto listened as deeply as his child's heart was able. Between her utterances, the silence was so complete that he was aware of the faint sibilance of water trickling in the fountain and of the distant, muted clinking of lunch preparations in the kitchen, on the floor below. He leaned into these silences, awaiting words that would bring sense to this moment.

"I want desperately to leave you with something that will nurture and love and support you for a lifetime, the way I would if I were able. There will always be your father, of course, but you know how he is so busy with his business. There is only one thing, my darling, that I can offer you. It may not mean anything to you now, or for a long, long time. Yet, I know that eventually it will wrap its arms around you like a true mother.

"So now, I am going to give you something. A token. You must try to understand that it is not the thing itself which has this power. It is a receiver only, like a radio. It holds something so much greater than itself..." She looked into his troubled and uncomprehending face, so handsome, so fragile, and her voice caught in her throat.

With her slender musician's fingers, she undid the top buttons of her white linen blouse and pulled up from the depths of her bosom a long gold chain. On its heavy, curiously wrought length, she held up the locket which had so recently been his fascination. It swung in the spring sunshine like the pendulum of fate.

"This, my darling, as I have told you, is a very wonderful thing. It is a religious medal from Egypt...oh, I know you've no idea where that is...but it's very old. Twenty centuries before the birth of our Lord. That means almost four thousand years, Roberto, which is a long, long time."

She bent down so he could hold the locket in his hand. "It's enamel on gold. A beautiful picture of the Blessed Mother of God, you see? And she is holding Her Son on Her lap. That is how I want you to see me—always, even when I am gone, holding you, helping you in every way possible. Even when you are a very, very old man. I will be there for you, I promise, if the will of God allows it."

"Why is the Virgin black, Maman? Her face and hands are so dark!"

"Why, because she is like our very own *Virgen de Guadalupe*, son—one of the dark ones who brings the mystery of the cosmos, imprinted on her very flesh. In Egypt, she was called Isis. And before that, other names."

She slipped the chain around the chignon at the nape of her neck. Carefully, she placed the locket in Roberto's hand, saying, "You must never wear this yourself. That is very important.

Only a woman may wear it. I have written all about it in a letter that you will find in the box where this locket will live.

"But more important, Roberto my little love, the Mother Herself will always be there for you. She is One who never sleeps, never forgets, never lapses. Her love is eternal and invincible." His mother spoke with such radiance, such sonorous musicality, that she might have been standing beside the piano downstairs, singing while Tía Isobella played.

"It's very beautiful, Maman. How did you get it?"

"It was given to me years ago when I was a student in Paris. There was a very refined and aristocratic man who was the very last of his family, that had lived in France so long that no one knew when they started there. But through various misfortunes, all his family died, leaving him alone, the last of his lineage.

"He told me that the women of his family, his mother and grandmother and ever-so-many-great-grandmothers had worn this locket, and that it had magical qualities so profound that only the wearer could understand them."

Roberto turned the locket in his hands, examining it minutely. "How did his family get it, Maman?"

"It came into his family during the Crusades. He told me it had the blessings of the Holy Mother Herself upon it. Who can say? But I have worn it every day of my life since then, and in spite of my present condition, I can tell you that it is a miraculous thing. I feel confident that its magic will protect you in the coming time, when I cannot."

"What magic, Maman? What miracles? Tell me one." Roberto looked feverishly into her eyes, knowing somehow beyond a doubt that if she could tell him a story convincing enough, he could make the leap of faith that would bind him to the magic of this locket.

"*¡Precioso!*" she crooned, stroking his warm, sunlit hair. "What heavy things I am laying on you, so young!" She turned toward the open French doors. "Come. Let's go inside. I need to lie down for a little while. You can lie beside me and I will tell you a story." Her long, thin arm was lightly furred with sun-shot gold, as she reached to push aside the lace curtain.

She nudged Roberto ahead of her into the bedroom, and he was so blinded from the outside brilliance that he felt pushed into the lake of Death. He turned and grabbed her skirt, crying out in terror and burying his face in her legs.

Lifting and carrying him with infinite gentleness to her bed, his mother sat with him against her breast, then reclined against the pile of creamy pillows and pulled a pale pink cashmere blanket, light as thistle down, over them. She settled him with his head nestled onto her shoulder. The crisp linen of her blouse smelled of starch and a faint trace of *l'Heure Bleue*.

Slowly, his sobbing subsided and turned to hiccuping. The comfort of his head cradled on his mother's breast and the subtle rocking of her torso to some internal rhythm, as if her whole body were singing inside, relaxed him. He closed his eyes in ecstatic comfort, listening as her beautiful voice began to speak, telling him a tale of magic.

§

Loire Valley, France, 1953

§

Maria-Elena Villanova y Mansart's Story

The countryside lying before her was bleak. Frost-burnt foliage of dull umber bordered a winding road with gravel the color of dirty white chalk. Evergreen trees, forming a tunnel overhead and bowed down by pillows of frozen snow, were so dark a green as to seem black in their somber wetness. The chauffeur eased the ancient car through shallow ruts with greatest caution.

Maria-Elena reflected on the story her host for the weekend had told her about this car, as they dined at l'Etoile two weeks earlier. How during the World War II he had driven it into the family chapel, the doorway and windows of which were then sealed up with stone. Then, trees and shrubs were dug up and brought into the courtyard of the chateau and were planted before the newly rocked-up portals.

By the time the Nazis commandeered the place as their strategic headquarters, the chapel appeared as nothing more than part of the old fortifications. Thus, the car had waited, immured in the chapel along with the altar's rare twelfth-century limestone polychrome Christ, whose outstretched arms sheltered the entire property in unseen benediction throughout the War.

"After the War, Christ and the Duesenberg were resurrected on the same day," he recounted, with civilized glee. She remembered how they had laughed together, gazing out the window into the waters of the Seine, *sémé* with a million shards of light shattered on water black as oil.

Maria-Elena was in Paris to study voice. As befitted the family of the great Eduoard Mansart, who had come from France to Mexico in 1763 to found the family's fortunes in mining, sisal, and ranching, it was traditional for the young men of the family to take their educations in London. There they could learn sound business practices and so ultimately run the family enterprises, which had grown to include oil and the railroad. The Mansart women, however, were traditionally educated in the arts in France.

Le Comte de MontMaran was an old friend of her grandmother's from her college days, studying at the Art Institute. It was into his keeping that each successive wave of Mansart women had been proffered, both as a responsibility and a gift of refreshing *jeunesse*.

Since Maria-Elena's arrival in France, her grandmother, Maria-Amalia, had been on a nonagenarian spree of vicarious living. Her letters were filled with directives to go to specific places, view certain works of art, hear particular singers, all of whom were long since retired or dead, and to dine only in special restaurants, many of which no longer existed or the reputations of which had suffered in the intervening seventy years.

Her granddaughter's letters of protestation, begging to be allowed to discover France in her own fashion, only elicited more grandiose schemes and travel plans from Maria-Amalia. Maria-Elena hoped, during the coming weekend with the Count, to lay this burden at his courtly feet and to beg his intercession on her behalf.

The tunnel of trees ended abruptly, and the ancient and perfectly appointed black car purred into a meadow still bent under winter frost and patchy snow. The grassy expanse rolled gently upward to the point where, crowning a small hill, the chateau was now clearly visible.

The Count's family had lived in France, as far as historians and family trees were able to ascertain, at least since the year 732. Men from the MontMaran family had participated with Charles Martel in turning the Moor from the gates of Tours. Later came the Crusades, the First and successive waves.

This inbred warrior mentality was reflected in the chateau, which bore architecturally the ancient imprint of a fortification, only slightly gussied up in the last two hundred years by more effete and less violent generations of MontMarans.

Comte Henri bore all this with dignity and self-effacing humor. "One can scarcely imagine what to do with a thirteenth-century halberd," he had sighed fretfully over dinner, "and I have *twelve* of them! The armory alone is a lifetime's study—and there's still the library and the religious artifacts and the paintings to consider. Little did my military ancestors know that all they were winning for future generations was the right to live as curators and conservators!"

Maria-Elena stroked her hand over the satiny leather of the car seat, cast a wry eye over the window shades, aged to the color of vellum, and the teardrop-shaped silver vase filled with hothouse orchids, on its bracket on the door. Clearly, for all his protestations, the Count had done more than spend a life cataloging and dusting artifacts.

Grand-mère Maria-Amalia had recounted stories quite to the contrary, in fact, of the Count's student days, filled with a kind of Bohemian debauch involving artist's models, Left Bank garrets, poets and painters, and nights swilling in music halls. Grand-mère had told all this, of course, as if it were hearsay and not a thing in which she herself might have been involved. Maria-Elena wondered if this might be why her grandmother was so insistent on filling every moment of her own European years with dry and pointless excursions.

§

The car creaked across a narrow drawbridge spanning a very deep and dry moat, through the dark tunnel of thick outer fortifications and into the castle courtyard, crunching to a halt on immaculate, creamy gravel. The chauffeur, a young and bland-looking fellow in a neat, dark uniform, came quickly back to open the door for her.

Maria-Elena disembarked and stood bedazzled for a moment, orienting herself in this strange setting. In the center of the courtyard, surrounded by a wheel of geometrically laid-out herbs, was an elaborate wrought iron wellhead surmounting an old stone well.

Beyond and encircling were the sheer stone cliffs of the chateau itself. It was part invincible fortification and part aesthetic fantasy. She had expected a fairytale castle with round, conical-roofed towers but discovered instead an austere rectangle of immense weight and proportion, teased by latter-day Baroque whimsy and elegance.

Her wondering gaze was drawn to a door beneath the square north tower where, to her surprise and embarrassment, she now spied the Count. "Oh! Monsieur le Comte! Please forgive my rudeness!" She blushed deeply. How many times in her life had she been admonished never—*never!*—to stare!

The Count came forward to take her elbow and guide her into his home. "Think nothing of it. As I recall, Amalia, too, stopped to ogle when she first arrived. I've grown up here, so it seems not in the least remarkable to me. I'm sure if I were ever to visit Mexico, I, too, should stare. They say there are parrots in the trees, quite wild—is that true?"

With utter grace, he ushered her into the loveliest of rooms. She could not help exclaiming over its wonderful proportions, its walls of boiserie painted soft gray-green and its bank of tall double doors that looked onto what, in spring, would be a flower garden, now a tangle of frost-bent stalks.

"So beautiful!" Maria-Elena murmured.

"Ah, yes. This part was one of the most recently added, you see. It was designed by Louis Le Vau, modeled on his work at Vaux le Vicomte, which was, as I'm sure you know, the model for Versailles. Rooms of this sort—the long windows, the *boiserie*, the high ceilings with heavy crown molding—have become rather the standard and cliché of French interiors, I suppose."

He handed her into a brocade *fauteuil*. "And they do have a pleasing balance of height to width to length that seems to soothe the soul. Based on the Golden Mean or some such thing, I'm told. I don't know—I never studied it. Too busy with the halberds, you know," he said with a wink.

This companionable downplaying of the grandeur of his home relaxed Maria-Elena, and as they chatted before a fire that burned cheerfully beneath the marble mantle, she allowed her eyes to sweep the room again and again, taking in the Aubusson carpet, rich furniture in various antique styles, and family portraits of terribly important- and staunch-looking men and soberly elegant women. Late afternoon winter light laid a flood-tide of gold across parquet floors, the fruitwood fire popped serenely, and beeswax and lavender oil, rubbed for generations into the frames of the furniture, exhaled a sweet and faintly feral scent in the warmth.

Beside the Count's chair, its long slender head lying on its equally elegantly attenuated feet, lay a dog whose gray muzzle bespoke its advanced age. The Count saw her eye fall upon the creature.

"This is Saladin, *ma chèrie*." The Count let his own long, slender hand drift down to the dog's head. "He, like myself, is the last of a long, long line of his family. His grandparents-past-memory were two of six salukis, three breeding pairs brought back from Arabia by one of my ancestors returning from the Crusades.

"One of my ancestors. From one of the Crusades. There were so many over the centuries, and a member of the Mont-Maran family or two seems to have attended each of them. We were ever punctilious about important social occasions, I fear," he said with a small, apologetic smile.

Soon, the Count rang the bell for his housekeeper to take Maria-Elena to her upstairs room. "Madeleine will show you the way. There was a time, believe me, when I would not have relinquished the sacred honor of seeing a beautiful young woman to her room," he said with a glimmer in his eyes. "But now, my knees can't take the stairs, let alone kneel to draw a lady her bath!"

Maria-Elena blushed again, recognizing this not as idle gallantry but a challenge which, twenty years earlier, he would surely have undertaken. It occurred to her to wonder how many generations of Mansart women might have been deflowered in this castle by the gallant and charming Count. This, too, made her blush and she exited the room behind the housekeeper, with her head down in embarrassment.

"Well, you may wonder!" le Comte called gaily after her, deducing her thoughts. "Supper at eight sharp. Don't be late! Take a good rest and we'll talk all night."

ʕ

When she came downstairs, promptly at eight, the Count was waiting for her in the drawing room. "My lovely Maria-Elena!" he exclaimed, coming to her side and taking her elbow. "The dining room seems so...*excessive* for just two people, so I've had Madeleine set us a small table here by the fire."

He shepherded her to the fireplace and pulled out a delicately carved chair for her. She slipped in at a table simply but elegantly set with white linen cloth, monogrammed napkins, and crystal wine glasses. Two tapers burned in gilt bronze candlesticks in the center.

Shortly, Madeleine came silently in, bearing the first course. "Leek and sorrel soup," said the Count, removing the lid to the tureen with a flourish. He ladled the creamy green liquid into her bowl, as her eyes caressed the exquisite painting of birds and flowers in rich polychrome and gold on the old Sèvres tureen.

"We're getting along nicely, aren't we," the Count suddenly remarked.

Maria-Elena was embarrassed and had no idea how to answer, so she fell back on the gracious habits instilled in her by the elder Mansart women. "But Monsieur le Comte, how could one not have a lovely time with one so gracious as yourself?"

Henri de MontMaran threw back his head and laughed, a sound still hearty despite his ninety-plus years. "*Oh, non-non-non-non-non, ma chèrie*, do not be alarmed. It's just that you sounded exactly like your grandmother, when she spoke those very words over seventy years ago! I knew then that the Mansart women were gently reared and not easily dismayed, and I see nothing has changed!"

The meal proceeded in a light-hearted vein. At its conclusion, Maria-Elena, feeling by now relaxed and a little giddy from the wine, was again guided by the Count into a smaller room walled with books. Here, too, a bright fire awaited them and the Count seated her near it.

Saladin, the ancient saluki, came in just as the Count was about to close the door. Head down, his long toenails clicking on the glowing parquet, the dog came to the fire and with a groan, lowered himself to the rug beside his master's chair.

"Now, ma chèrie"—the Count began, settling himself with only slightly less stiffness—"we have passed our first evening quite pleasantly, and I should let you trundle off to bed. But you must know that the true vice of the very old is talk and also that we cannot sleep well at night. These two factors make a lethal combination for one's poor, captive guest, I fear." He smiled sweetly at her and then leaned forward, capturing and holding her eyes with a mesmerizing stare.

Maria-Elena was suddenly aware of him in a very unexpected and uncomfortable way. A mysterious power exuded from him that had been masked completely by his former charm. His eyes glimmered in the caverns of their sockets and his voice was commanding.

"Rather than sending you off to sweet dreams, I must hold you prisoner here awhile. We have a great deal to discuss, you and I."

Maria-Elena gazed at him in fascination, studying the long, thin nose, its bridge bent aristocratically, the high cheekbones and fine, round brow that made him, even in great age, a handsome and imposing man. To what could he be referring, she wondered? Was he somehow aware of her difficulties with Grand-Mère? Had he read between the lines of her few comments about the situation?

A cold wind rattled the panes of the long windows. A draft laid itself across her lap in an icy blanket and made the fire leap and dance. She was suddenly aware that it was winter—true winter such as was never experienced in Mexico—and that she was in a faraway land, in the home of a man she knew and trusted only from tradition. She felt the small hairs along her arm prickle and rise, perhaps not from the chill air.

Madeleine entered silently through the high paneled door, bearing a silver tray with demitasses of black coffee, a decanter of Cointreau, and two tiny, gold-rimmed glasses. She set it on a small tea table beside the Count and went wordlessly to pull the drapes.

Maria-Elena was aware of ambient sounds as if they were words spoken with deepest sincerity—the thin trickle of liqueur into crystal, the rough slide of wooden curtain rings across the iron rod, the soft flapping of velvet as Madeleine flounced drapes together to seal out the draft, the snapping of sparks, the soft, irregular breathing of Saladin, and the muted click as Madeleine departed. And behind it all, the thin, high wail of wind, blowing up for a storm.

"I'm afraid I don't know to what you are referring, Monsieur le Comte," she said at last, in a small voice. "What matter in particular must we discuss?"

His elbows on the arms of his chair, he held his small glass in both hands, observing her through it as a child might look through a crystal prism, delighting in distortion. He remained silent for quite a long time, during which Maria-Elena was acutely aware that they sat in a small cave of firelight, while the rest of the room was curtained in deep shadow. An eerie sensation again covered her with a chill.

"You did not know, of course," he began suddenly, "that you are sleeping tonight in my wife's room? No, to be sure, you would have no way of knowing that. But I want you to know that you are the first of the Mansart women to be accorded that honor." He continued to stare at her in a way that made her distinctly uncomfortable.

"And you would know little of my wife, of course. Her brief transit through my life fell between your grandmother's sojourn here and your Aunt Isobella's, which came a decade or so later. Dearly, as I have loved the Mansart women, I have not spoken of my wife to any one of them—or to anyone else for that matter—these many years. One does not complain of the strokes of ill-fate. But now I feel the necessity to speak of this matter." He hunched his shoulders as if he, too, felt a chill, and settled deeper into his chair.

"Did you know that I had, as well, a son? Perhaps your grandmother has told you? And that he was killed in the War? One of those brave and foolhardy young Resistance fighters, betrayed by his own countryman—a baker, I believe—into the hands of the Gestapo. Shot at dawn at la Conciergerie, I'm told." He looked down to his lap, his lips twisted in an agonized grimace.

"You are wondering why I am telling you these things, I know," he continued, his voice hoarse with emotion. "Is he senile, you are wondering? Is he besotted with the curse of the aged, to endlessly dredge up the past? But no..." his voice fell almost to a whisper, "there is still reason to my story, chère Maria-Elena, so please hear me out, because I am about to lay a tremendous burden on you. And at the same time, to gift you with the rarest of gifts."

He pushed himself from his chair, threw a log on the fire, and went to fuss with the draperies at windows now rattling incessantly in the rising wind. Assured that no gap in the rich blue velvet was allowing a draft, the Count returned to his chair and filled their glasses again.

"It would be usual, you see, for me to tell these things to my own child..." His voice broke and he waited, head down, to regain his composure. "But as we have seen, I have none."

He sipped his Cointreau. "Or perhaps to some relative. But all mine are dead. Except for a small lot of them that took off for America during the Revolution, fearing for their heads. They landed in Indianapolis—a place one can scarcely imagine, let alone inhabit. They sent home once, I think it was in the eighteen-fifties, for vines of wine grapes. They had a wastrel son who intended to begin a vineyard in California, where he had gone to the Gold Rush.

"My grandfather sent them, of course, all wrapped and crated. They went around Cape Horn in a sailing ship and actually reached San Francisco alive. For all I know, they may be growing there yet."

He paused to poke at the fire with an ornately wrought poker. "After that, we lost track of them. Oh, we've received various announcements of marriages, births, commencements, and deaths over the decades. Announcements, I might add, which are no longer handwritten but purchased from stationery companies, with lines to be filled in with pertinent information. I fear this branch of the family, therefore, has succumbed to the American way, as it is called, and cannot be entrusted with what we are about to reveal."

Maria-Elena listened, bemused. How interesting to speak of the generations of one's family in the multiple *we*, as if each generation were party to and answerable for the decisions and deeds of all preceding and succeeding generations. She wondered if she unconsciously yielded such total identification to her own family.

The Count continued to lay out his argument: "*Non!* I distinctly feel that this information is for someone who comes of generations of careful breeding and rearing. Rarefied genetic stock. Call me a snob. Tell me I am unbearably ultraconservative. This has nothing to do with politics nor the rights of the poor."

He leaned forward from the shadows of his wing chair and peered at her. "I understand from your *Grand-mère* that you are psychic? Is that true?" His eyes glowed within their pools of shadow as he stared at her.

"Oh, *oui, monsieur!*" she stammered. "It is true. Since childhood, I have had dreams. In them, a beautiful lady comes to me and tells me things. The information is always, it proves, correct. I can't take credit for knowing what I know. It is she who tells me. But I suppose you would call me mildly psychic as a consequence."

The Count nodded his head slightly in approval, so that Maria-Elena hastened to add, "But I must tell you that these dreams are extremely rare. And as I become older, they are increasingly so."

The Count regarded her now with a fixity that was almost trancelike. The atmosphere between them, within the little circle of firelight, was charged with potent expectation and a mysterious immanence. Saladin groaned at his master's feet and shifted restlessly.

"As you may know," the Count began again, "my family is extremely ancient. We have been present for every major turn of French history at least since Charlemagne's grandfather was walking this Gallic soil. What you do not know, because no one outside the family has ever been allowed to know, is that we have a family secret even more ancient than our lineage. And because there is now no one left in this family to receive this secret, I am passing it along to the Mansart clan with my blessings," he said with a momentary surge of his former charm. "So bear with me, while I tell you a story that will amaze you…Do you need coffee?"

"Coffee? Oh, heavens, *non!* How could I possibly drowse through *this?*" Her heart felt swollen with anticipation and curiosity. Only vaguely in the back of her mind, where unpleasantries so often are deposited, did she wonder if this gift the Count was about to bestow were something she might actually want and not, at some future date, regret possessing.

5

The Story of Le Comte Henri Charlemagne de MontMaran

"As you may know," the Count began, sinking so deeply into his chair that Maria-Elena could no longer see his face and so perceived his voice to be issuing from a shadowy void within its wings, "there was once a region in the south of France referred to as the Languedoc, because the tongue—*langue*—of its people pronounced the word 'yes'—*oui*—as *oc*. The area was ruled over by the Count of Provence, and the speech of one of his vassals, upon his arrival in Paris, would be almost unintelligible in that more northerly city.

"I am telling you this because it is difficult for us in this modern age of relative stability to imagine the divisiveness of the thirteenth century, which is where my tale begins. It seems that every petty chieftain who could raise a scruffy army could set himself up as a count or a duke.

"Consequently, the waging of war was endless. City fought against city and duchy against duchy. If they were lucky enough to have a strong leader who could unite a few of these warring areas, then there would be war of nation against nation.

"It was a terrible time. The clergy alone, and a few of the nobility, could read and write. The vast majority of the populace existed in the starkest ignorance and superstition and were really little elevated above the beasts they tended.

"It was against this flood tide of desperate ignorance and violence that a strange phenomenon arose in the Languedoc region. A group of people deliberately separated themselves from the Catholic church. These heretics, as people deemed them, called themselves the Cathari, which simply means 'Pure Ones'.

"Disgusted by the many degeneracies of the church, these people sought after holiness by attempting to dispense entirely with the material side of life. In the extremes of their belief, many refused to marry, giving rise to terrible rumors of debauch among them, which I believe modern scholars have largely refuted. They were, as well, vegetarians, refusing to eat flesh, eggs, or cheese."

Maria-Elena, already engrossed in the tale, gazed into the fire, quietly sipping her Cointreau. Like the rising wind outside, the Count's deep voice, lubricated by eloquence, seemed an element of eternity.

"Now, you would think that such people would be so completely harmless and inoffensive that no one would bother them and that they would be able to live long and peacefully, communing with God. But like most true innocents, they failed to consider the power of politics in the larger world over their very small and local existence.

"Now, the First Crusade occurred in 1094 or thereabouts. It had been very successful in uniting the squabbling clans of Europe and in directing their warlike energies against a common enemy in the Holy Land. So after Urban the Second, succeeding Popes used the same ploy when their political fortunes seemed shaky or when it suited other of their purposes.

"Pope Innocent the Third—and if ever a man were misnamed it was he—was the head of the church at the time of which I speak. And he had not one, but three Crusades at his command at the opening of the thirteenth century. These were directed, however, not against the Infidel in the Levant but against the inhabitants of Europe, for the pope now applied the name 'crusade' to all wars in which he was interested.

"One war was waged against unbelievers in Eastern Europe, the Prussians. In the West, there was a Crusade against the Saracens in Spain. But of the three, the Crusade against the Cathari, called the Albigensian Crusade, was the most terrible and unjust.

"The spirit of the times was such that the church, and the church alone, could decree one's beliefs. The Cathari, who despised marriage and sex because it perpetuated life on earth, were viewed, therefore, as a cult of madmen. They committed the ultimate heresy, as well, in believing that an individual might commune directly with God, without the intermediary of a priesthood.

"Now nothing could be more an anathema to a bureaucrat—and the church is the most pernicious sort of bureaucracy—than the notion that someone is trying to do away with his job. The purpose of any bureaucracy is, after all, self-perpetuation and maintenance of the status quo. To Pope Innocent, this Albigensian madness seemed so dangerous that he decided it must be suppressed by force. He therefore ordered a Crusade against Raymond, Comte de Toulouse, who had the temerity to attempt to protect those among his subjects who insisted on rejecting the yoke of Rome.

"The Count's realm was, at that time, the fairest and richest district in Europe, and so the prospect of plundering it soon raised an army of great size. A coarse and brutal man, Simon de Montfort, became their leader. He was called by the misnomer The General of the Holy Ghost. In the name of God, this man, who for all his brutality was a skillful general, began a reign of terror and persecution that is ghastly to consider.

"In battle after battle, he was victorious. After each of these, all captives were put to death. No one was spared. Women, children, and the elderly were equally murdered along with their defeated soldiers. It was a bloodbath. This was at the command of Pope Innocent, who, when asked how to tell a Catholic from a heretic, replied, 'Slay all; the Lord will know his own!'"

§

The Count's voice broke with emotion, as if the intervening eight hundred years had done nothing to dim the horror he recounted. To break the spell, he said lightly, "I hope I don't make you feel as if you were plunged back into some dreary grade school history class. I simply am setting the stage, because it is during this time that the first coherent history of my family emerges.

"You see, we did not always have our lands here in the Loire valley. This castle is part of a property that was acquired much later. Originally, we came from Languedoc and it was there that the dark stain of fate seeped into the warp and weft of our family.

"We were not then, you see, MontMarans, because *this*, this chateau, sits on Mount Maran. We were then of the town of Muret. My ancestor was called simply Richard de Muret. He was a vassal under the Comte de Toulouse and so was under duty to his liege to raise an army to fight the oncoming Crusade. It was a terrible decision not only for him, I am sure, but for men like him who were both staunch defenders of the True Church but also loyal vassals to the Count. Richard chose to support the cause of the Count and paid, in the end, a high price for his loyalty.

"But there was more to it than that. There was a secret that influenced his decision, I am sure—his wife, Eleanore, came from a Cathari family. Not only that, but despite her decision to marry and bear children, she practiced, in secret, the heretical forms of worship in the family chapel and her husband, while not completely won over, had great sympathy for her pure and simple ways.

"These two had two children, a son named Godfrey and a daughter, Blanche. As the army of the Crusade advanced, burning, looting, and murdering as it came, Richard and Eleanore made a desperate decision. Sensing that their cause was already lost before it was truly undertaken, they arranged to have the children removed from the south to St. Denys, near Paris, where his brother was a member of the bishop's staff.

"The children, both under the age of twelve, were mounted on swift horses and given into the responsible hands of Richard's closest lieutenant. They left Muret in the middle of the night, leaving behind heartsick parents whom they would never see again.

"That was in 1212, and one year later, you see, the Battle of Muret put an end to all organized resistance on the part of the Cathari. The banner of the Cross waved in victory over a devastated land; the armies of the General of the Holy Ghost performed unspeakable atrocities and orgies, surrounded by their booty; and Pope Innocent was informed that false religion and immorality had been extirpated. Isn't it ironic how inextricably mixed are tragedy and comedy?"

§

The Count paused in thoughtful silence. Outside, the night wind was rising sharply as the leading edge of the storm advanced. Despite the warmth of their fire-lit circle, the peaceful crackling of the hearth fire and the slow, lambent flame of the candles, the wind's incessant violence created a background of eerie tension.

The long French doors and windows rattled in their casements. Waves of air rolled against the castle walls, crashing like the sea. As the night wore on into the early hours of the next morning, its bass voice rose to a shrieking wail that was a Greek chorus of woe, underscoring the tale of terror and loss related by the Count.

Maria-Elena had worried at first that with a fine, rich dinner and two glasses of Cointreau behind her, she might fall into a stupor of relaxation and fatigue. But the Count was a fine raconteur. His deep voice was nuanced and compelling, rising and falling contrapuntally with the wind.

She leaned back in her chair and its deep and brocaded wings sheltered her like guardians standing watch. Her imagination was electrified and she could almost see the terrible doings of 1213 enacted amidst the fierce embers on the hearth.

Saladin wheezed in his sleep and turned, groaning, onto his side. A log shifted on the grate and collapsed in a wave of lava-red coals. Shadows reached out of the corners of the room as the fire burned low and the candles guttered in an errant draft.

It was a timeless scene. She felt it might actually be 1213. It would not truly surprise her to hear music of lutes from the hall or laughter of a banqueting crowd. Time had a limen here, she sensed, a flexible portal where the centuries could mix and pass one another, like celebrants at a masked ball.

§

The Count cleared his throat and recommenced his tale: "Because they were members of the nobility, Richard and

Eleanore were given more important deaths than the run-of-the-mill citizen, who was simply put to the sword. Eleanore was burned at the stake in what was left of the town square. And Richard was drawn and quartered before her, as she stood awaiting her fate. These are terrible matters and I don't wish to distress you, but this is how it was at that time of unbelievable barbarism.

"The children, however, arrived safely in St. Denys and were welcomed kindly into their uncle's home, only to fall into a still more curious fate. It is, in fact, one of the strangest occurrences of that strange time, in which those two children were full participants.

"It is hard to imagine now just what it was that motivated the Crusades. Pilgrimage was an important part of Christian worship then, and to go to the sacred shrines of the East and to the Holy Sepulcher itself was, of course, the ultimate such journey.

"Since the First Crusade of 1094, the Holy Land had gradually fallen again into the hands of the Infidel and Christian pilgrims, while still allowed access to the sacred sites, now returned home with reports that the shrines were being desecrated by the Musalman and that by virtue of being under their rule, these sacred places were in jeopardy.

"We of this century, who hold nothing sacred but our bank accounts, are hard put to imagine the furor this caused and the fighting spirit it aroused. Wave after wave of English, French, and German armies embarked on the futile mission of reclaiming holy soil.

"It was an age of faith, not reason. Yet, religion was at a low ebb and while men fought under the banner of the Cross, few knew the true teachings of that emblem. The instruction they received from the church of the time was a system of absurd superstitions, laced with the questionable deeds of the saints and martyrs."

The Count stopped to poke the fire and to add another log. Glancing to make sure Maria-Elena was still conscious, he smiled encouragingly and sank back within the wings of his chair. He cleared his throat briefly and began again to speak.

§

"Consider for example, if I may digress, the Feast of the Fools observed each year in all the cathedral cities of France. On that day, the priests and clerks met and elected from among themselves an archbishop and a bishop. They were arrayed in great pomp and taken by procession through the streets to the cathedral.

"Once inside, these solemn men of the cloth began orgies of the most sacrilegious nature. They wore masks and dressed in the skins of animals or as women or buffoons, and then cavorted about, screaming blasphemies and singing obscene songs. They ate, drank, and played dice, using the altar as their table.

"They vied with one another, exerting their ingenuity to devise desecrations of the place, such as burning their sandals for incense. They sometimes dressed a donkey as the pope. The debauch was not suitably ended until drunkenness, nakedness, and lewdness of all sorts had taken the day. This was the state of the church in those times—and great must have been the credulity of a people who would follow such leaders!

§

"The whole idea of the Crusades and the reconquest of Jerusalem was really a kind of collective myth and a mass delusion. And no event of that time was more deluded than the mass movement into which Godfrey and Blanche de Muret were about to be swept.

"It seems that in that same spring of their flight to safety in 1212, a young shepherd named Stephen from the village of Cloyes, just west of Orleans, heard the call. That is, he claimed to have had a divine vision that he was to lead a great crusade to retake the Holy Land.

"What was unique in this was that Stephen was only twelve years old, and the army he intended to lead was to be made up not of soldiers but of unarmed children, who would not conquer the Infidel by force but convert him through the strength and sweetness of their faith. He claimed as well to have met Jesus, face to face, while idling in the fields with his flocks. Jesus had brought him a letter proclaiming the validity of this mission, which Stephen was to show to the King.

"No one knows for sure where it came from, but the child did have in his possession a well-written letter on fine parchment, to that effect. Since neither he nor anyone else of his acquaintance in the miserable hamlet of Cloyes could either read or write, his claim was taken, locally at least, for truth.

"There are two interesting theories about how he came to be in possession of that letter and of the grandiose ideas to which it pertained. Neither, I might add, have to do with divine intervention!

"One is that emissaries of the pope, seeking to stir up still another crusade to liberate the Levant—that being the prime foreign policy of Rome at the time—duped this simple shepherd into believing he had been divinely visited and provided him with a letter to prove it.

"A second, even less plausible tale held that The Old Man of the Mountain, the mysterious Chief of the Assassins who lived in an impregnable castle in Syria, had sent two released Crusader hostages to France. The price of their liberty was to send an entire army of children to him for his use as slaves and future assassins.

"Both of these explanations seem impossibly far-fetched. The fact remains, however, that this Stephen, a lad with no education and no background or training, became, following this supposed incident, a highly skilled orator.

"He began locally, stirring up the children with his ideas. Then moving into a larger arena, he went to the great cathedral town of Chartres and preached there, challenging the children to go with him and to take, through saintliness, what adults had not been able to gain through force.

"He passed from Chartres to Paris, stopping briefly to preach there, and then moved on to the greatest pilgrimage site of the time, St. Denys. There, as you may know, the martyr Dionysius, one of the seven founders of the Church in Gaul, was buried. In his behalf, since the time of Dagobert, all the kings and many of the royal family have been buried there. Additionally, this is the city where the sacred Oriflamme, the holy standard of the realm, was kept. All these attractions made it a much-visited pilgrimage spot.

"In St. Denys, Stephen proclaimed his holy mission and was heard by pilgrims from many parts of the country, who returned home fired with his zeal. Minor prophets arose among children everywhere, who claimed also to have had visions and instructions regarding the crusade of the children. The news ran through the cities and villages of the country like a flash flood.

"Suddenly, without warning, children were deserting their homes, collecting into bands, and heading off toward St. Denys. All attempts to stop them were futile. Today, I suppose, it would be called mass hysteria. Then, it could be explained only as a holy calling. Children who were detained from joining their fellows often fell ill and the only remedy was to allow them to go.

"By early summer of 1212, thirty-thousand children had gathered under the banner of Stephen of Cloyes in the city of Vendôme. Finally, near the end of July, the army of unarmed Christian soldiers took to the road, moving southward. The amazing thing about this phenomenon was, the vast majority of these souls were under twelve years of age! And among them, as you already may have guessed, were Blanche and Godfrey de Muret.

"I cannot say I am proud that members of my own family were involved in such mass delusion. I have puzzled over it all my life and can find no corresponding urge in myself that might help me to understand it. Perhaps it's a little like those young women in America who tear their blouses open and scream like lunatics when they see that popular singer of theirs, Sinatra. I don't know.

"But, that they were in this train there can be no doubt. The children went striding out, singing songs, southward toward Marseilles. There, they had been informed by Stephen, the Mediterranean Sea would part and they all would walk to Palestine on the dry ocean floor. There was a terrible drought that summer, which was burning the crops and drying up the streams, and this he took as confirmation that God had already undertaken the great work of drying up the Sea so that the task would be complete by the time they arrived.

§

The Count reached for a log and tossed it on the fire, saying, "That this sort of thing could happen is unimaginable to us, in this age, when we have all manner of protective agencies to both monitor and defend children. But it is a fact of history that these thirty thousand children walked the entire three hundred miles to Marseilles in the space of about a month, begging and foraging as they went.

"The shepherd Stephen was now elevated to new estate and rode in a carriage decked in colored flags, surrounded by the minor prophets on horseback. The children of the nobility were mounted, as well, some with retainers to guard them and carry their belongings. But the vast majority, including my two forebears, were afoot.

"It was sometime in August when their army, greatly thinned through discouragement, malnutrition, kidnap, and death, arrived in Marseilles, still singing songs, carrying their crosses high and waving their cross-embroidered banners. And still, according to contemporary accounts, at least twenty thousand strong.

"The city of Marseilles was in amazement and granted the children only one night's stay there, fearing they might riot or cause some other untoward civil disturbance. But this fitted perfectly with Stephen's plans as, he explained, they needed but a night's rest before the sea parted and they began their walk to Jerusalem.

"And so they slept that night at their jumping-off point, in the streets, in monasteries, or in the private homes of friends, depending on their social status, and the money they could afford to spend. Blanche and Godfrey, we are told, spent that night in a church, though which one I do not know. Nor, I imagine, did they. These children had absolutely no understanding of the simplest geography. Many of them, in fact, while en route, would ask as each new town was approached, "Is *this* Jerusalem?"

"In the morning, these innocents assembled on the shore in the patient expectation that the sea was about to open before them. They waited the entire day and when their spirits flagged, they were exhorted to further faith by Stephen and the minor prophets, *Dieu le vaut!* God wills it!

"As night fell and the sea still had not parted, a great disgruntlement befell the assembly. Many of the children, weary as they were from the long and arduous trek, left the company never to return. Many thousands, however, stayed on to return to the shore the next day. And the next. And the next.

§

"It was into this atmosphere of patient faith and growing dissatisfaction that news of a miracle came, and the troops who remained revived. It seems that two good Christian men of Marseilles, wealthy merchants named Hugh Ferreus and William Porcus, had taken pity on these faithful children and announced that they were willing to supply passage for the entire army across the Mediterranean Sea to Palestine!

"In their sympathy for the children and their interest in the defiled Sepulchre, they intended to ask no money of the passengers. This deed was, they said, *causa Dei, absque pretio*, for the cause of God, and without price.

"As you can imagine, the rejoicing among the ranks was great and Stephen and his lieutenant prophets went about in triumph, proclaiming that this was the miracle that was intended all along and that God had indeed opened a way through the sea for them.

"Being the stubborn stock that we are, Blanche and Godfrey were among this remaining throng, still holding out for the miracle. So within days they were put aboard a ship in preparation for embarkation.

"Accounts from the time say that there were about seven hundred souls per ship and that ten ships in all set out for the Holy Land. There was great waving of banners and voices were raised so loudly in singing that they could be heard even after the ships had disappeared over the horizon.

"This is, I suppose, an exaggeration. But there can be no doubt—the two children and their fellows were on their way across the open sea, embarked on an adventure even greater than the one they imagined.

"The first thing that befell them was a terrible storm on the second day out, which drove two of the ships onto the rocks of a small island off the coast of Sardinia. Over a thousand children were spilled into the stormy surf and perished before the horrified eyes of children aboard the vessel, which managed to slip by the obstacle unscathed.

"I know this because it is written in a first-person account by Blanche herself, which is still in my possession. In fact, it lies in my safe at this moment. She wrote this statement when she finally returned to France, and she swore an oath before God as to its veracity when she presented it as testimony to the archbishop in St. Denys in 1215.

"I have here a copy of it in modern French, and I would like to read you a fragment of it, so that you can hear for yourself the earnest voice of this young woman. It will move you greatly, I think, if you remember that at the time she experienced these things, she was only eleven years old. And when she wrote of them, she was but fourteen."

The Count stopped his long narrative for a moment and emerged from the shadows of his chair to rummage for his glasses on the table beside him. Then he picked up a small volume bound in maroon leather and opening to a spot where an embossed leather marker was inserted, commenced to read.

ʃ

Chapter 3

The Story of Blanche de Muret

WE HAD BEEN TWO DAYS AT SEA WHEN A TERRIBLE STORM CAME FROM THE NORTH. The waves became like mountains and the ship began to dip and pitch most perilously. Many, myself included, became ill and the ship soon stank of vomit.

All were frightened beyond consolation. Our tears were mixed with our prayers to the Virgin, but Our Lady seemed deaf to our pleas. Night fell and the storm worsened. Lucky were they who, tossed violently in the hold, struck their heads and lay insensible, for they were the only ones to pass that night unconscious.

As for me, I clung to my brother Godfrey and would not have released him even had the ship overturned and deposited us in the deep sea. I made it my one goal to survive that night with my brother still in my arms and by the Grace of God, I accomplished it.

Morning came, if such a dark day could be so called, and our situation was not improved. Still, the storm raged and now but two of our nine sister ships were visible through the ragged mists and flying spray. What became of the other seven I shall never know. God grant that the souls therein found happier ports than those of the three beating through that morning's storm!

About midday, we sighted land very close off the leeward bow. The storm had only worsened during the morning, and the wind howled so loudly that we could not hear our own prayers as they issued from our lips. Godfrey and I were on deck, as I could no longer bear the stench below and preferred death by drowning to another moment in that infernal region.

I was, therefore, in plain view of our two sister ships and could see that their situation was perilous. The wind was becoming ever more powerful, and despite the desperate scurrying of their crews about the decks and riggings, I could see that they were set on a collision course with the rocky shores of a small island.

With what terrible fascination did I watch the fates of our comrades played out! What toys in the hands of God are we all! If ever the vanity of Man claims for itself Supremacy, let this story be read as testimony to the contrary.

All that happened was inevitable, and yet, it happened without hurry, as if all of Time had slowed to show this terrible scene in all its vividness. Slowly but steadily, the two ships yielded to the thundering winds and gripping tides. At last, with a final hesitation on the very brink of disaster, first one and then the other of the ships reared on the waves, hovered over the rocks as if suspended on strings, and then crashed down.

Their hulls were broken like eggs against the side of a bowl. Like yolks, out flooded the hoarded treasure from within, the fourteen hundred souls who, until that moment, had been our comrades in this great adventure.

I watched, helpless and stupefied with horror, as the hulls again and again were dashed upon the rocks, until they broke up completely and sank. For many minutes, the water was filled with the flailing bodies of my friends. And then, as if these two ships and their passengers had never been, the sea became once more a faceless cauldron of boiling waters and all trace of the wrecks was washed away.

I have but one prayer of thanks to offer regarding this incident—that my little brother Godfrey saw nothing of it. He passed the entire time with his face buried in my lap, or I doubt not that his little brain of only nine years experience also would have broken like an egg, and he should have been from that time forward a lunatic from having witnessed so great a grief.

It was not until nightfall that the storm began at last to abate. So desperately ill, bruised, hungry, and exhausted were we all that we were beyond thought of giving prayers of thanksgiving for our deliverance from that fearful day. We simply lay down where we were, and as we no longer had to hold onto something in order not to be thrown about, went instantly and soundly asleep, I with Godfrey still wrapped firmly in my arms.

It took several days to recover from the storm. The ship's crew was busy all the day, making necessary repairs to the rigging. Below in the hold, the situation continued desperate. Many of the children had terrible injuries from having been dashed about during the storm. I saw one poor girl with the bone of her forearm sticking through her skin. Some remained sick despite the calming of the seas, and a few, God rest their souls, had given up their lives during that terrible cataclysm, whether from fear or injury I know not. These we sewed into simple shrouds. The men of God who accompanied us prayed over them, and they then were committed to the deeps.

Because of these confusions and complications, I do not now remember for how many days we sailed following the storm. It was with surprise then, as much as relief, when I went one day to the deck and spied land ahead. Perhaps I had come to believe that we would journey on that hellish vessel for all eternity!

News of landfall spread among our ranks. Then what great rejoicing there was that we had survived our terrible sea voyage and come at last to our sacred goal, the land of the Holy Sepulcher of Our Lord!

§

How cruelly shortlived was our joy! For no sooner had we docked in this foreign port, which we soon discovered was not in Palestine but in Egypt, than we were herded together like so many sheep and removed from the docks as prisoners!

Many among us were hopeful, assuming the officials had made a mistake that would soon be rectified. But one of the men of God who accompanied us confided to me that he feared something much worse had befallen us, and in short time he was proven correct.

What our captors now revealed to us was so cruel that it seemed it must break our hearts and kill us all, there in the streets of that strange land. For they could no longer contain their boastful secret but rather jeered at us, making a mockery of our faith. For what do you imagine could be more dispiriting than to learn that our good mentors, Porcus and Ferreus, who had so kindly supplied us with ships for our passage to the Holy Land, had actually sold us into slavery!

Their intentions all along had been to divide the fleet, sending some to Constantinople, some to Alexandria, and some to Morocco. The captains, too, had conspired in this. I was stunned with the coldness and callousness of this plan and of the hearts of these so-called Christian men. May God have mercy on their souls.

ʖ

Now our poor band that had suffered so greatly and with such courage had still mightier sufferings to bear. So exhausted were we and so shocked by our fate, that we no longer could weep for ourselves but stood huddled together like miserable sheep awaiting slaughter.

We were not even allowed water to drink much less to bathe in but were hurried straight from the docks through the streets of a stinking city, which I did not learn until later was the ancient port of Alexandria. You might imagine that merely to be on terra firma again would be cause for rejoicing after so terrible a voyage, but this was not so. The enormity of our plight was just beginning to dawn on us, and our hearts were nearly stopped with fear and grief.

So in this sadly degenerate and filthy state, we arrived by winding ways at a square in the heart of the city. All about us were buildings of antique manufacture, such as one sees at home in the south of France where the Romans have been. At one end of the square, a high platform of stone was raised. It, too, was of ancient construction and the priests among us recognized this place all too soon. We had been brought to the ancient slave market, there to be auctioned off like cattle!

Only then did my true terror begin. I had thought that the sea voyage could never be surpassed but I was mistaken. For now I realized the greatest horror of all: that in all likelihood, I would be parted from my brother, never to see him again. This was a cruelty too heavy to bear. I collapsed in the street insensible.

How long I lay thus, I do not know. When I returned unto myself, however, I knew I had been carried to a different place, for now the high auction platform was to my left, not straight ahead. And what did my miserable eyes fall upon the moment they blinked open upon this cruel world again but my brother, my precious Godfrey, standing upon that block, stripped naked as the day he was born, his head hanging down in misery, humiliation and terror!

I shrieked a sound such as Hell Itself must make. I lost complete sense of myself as a highborn lady and became in that instant a clawing animal. I had but one thought and that was to reach his side. But all my efforts were in vain, for while I lay in stupor, manacles had been placed about my ankles and I was chained to a long line of my miserable fellows.

That the mind does not simply break at such a moment is truly a testament to the human spirit, its strength, and will to live. As for me, my spirit did not break but it bent almost to cracking there in the slave market of Alexandria.

I watched in shock too deep for thought as my brother, my precious friend and my holy charge, was carried off into slavery by an Arab in a flowing white gown. A more vigilant person than I would have attempted to remember every detail of that scene, in hopes of later gaining information of his whereabouts. But I, a hopeless girl of tormented spirit, saw only my sweet brother's face, filled with terror and longing. He looked straight at me, reaching out his little arms, as he was picked up and carried away into the crowd.

§

How long I awaited my turn on the auction block I cannot say. It may have been only minutes or it may have been hours. I had become utterly insensible to my own person. Horror had blocked every part of my mind. I only know that I came out of a dull stupor to find myself being led, free at last of manacles, onto the stone porch.

I was one of ten girls who were sold as a lot. The bidding did not last long and I assume we went for a low price. And small wonder! I cannot conceive that a more unpromising lot of young women existed in all of Christendom! We had not bathed since long before embarking from Marseilles. We had been ill, rolled about in our own vomit, battered and blown until every hair was knotted like fine lace, and our fair skin was chapped and besmeared. Perhaps one can forgive the Infidel for treating us like animals, for that certainly is how we must have looked!

§

We again were chained together, this time by our wrists, and herded through the streets of that most foul and unwelcoming city. The stench of rotting garbage and feces in the streets might have overpowered us had we not, by this time, become indifferent to such horrors.

At the bottom of a particularly foul street, we came to the quays. There we were thrust rudely into a small boat, which set sail immediately up river, the wind and tide being right at that evening hour.

I do not remember a single moment of that voyage up the great River Nile to Cairo. We remained collapsed in a heap in the bottom of the boat, too exhausted and too dispirited to move. How we passed the night, whether moored or moving with the wind, I know not. Nor how many days we passed in the journey upriver. I remember nothing of this time but the terrible ache of my heart, as if I had been mortally wounded there, and the picture, repeated many times an hour in my fevered brain, of my brother's face as he was torn away from me forever.

At last, we came to the great city of Cairo and were loaded without ceremony into a two-wheeled cart drawn by two sturdy donkeys. Again, we were paraded through the streets of the city. Even in my disarray, I could not help but notice that this was a very different city from Alexandria.

Here were prosperous shops and the great bustle that comes with a city involved in successful commerce. The people on the streets in their long Musulman garb were clean and handsomely groomed. As we advanced further into the city, I became aware that the buildings were becoming ever grander and more beautiful. Yet I was beyond wondering whence I was being delivered.

At last we were dumped unceremoniously before great gates set in a high wall. Our jailor paid the carter and turned to speak with the gatekeeper. Then we were led along the wall to a small side door and there admitted.

ʂ

Imagine my surprise, for I had expected to be thrust into a dingy cell, there to rot away captive as so many stories of captured Crusaders had told. When the door opened, however, and we were herded through it, I found myself in an earthly Paradise!

Not since the heavenly beauty of my native Languedoc had I seen such lush and fruitful gardens. In very fact, these gardens were more beautiful than the most perfect garden of France. Here were green grass, flowering shrubs and vines, and palm trees casting deep shaggy shade upon promenades tiled in brightest blue and yellow. Fountains splashed invitingly at every turn. Beds of flowers were mathematically laid out to form geometric designs in brilliant colors. Birds, both in cages and free in the trees, made a merry din amidst the lush foliage.

For all that I was tired beyond measure and hungry beyond caring, I could not keep my amazement captive. Despite myself, I smiled with delight.

I speculated that we might have been sold into the household of the great Sultan of Egypt himself, Caliph Malek Kamel. This, I reasoned, would be a great blessing as he was rumored in France, even among his enemies, to be a man of learning. It was even said that he had studied during many years of his youth in the University of Paris, but I do not know if this is so.

We were brought through this paradisiacal garden to a beautiful building of white stone, graced by a long arcade of low, pointed arches. We passed through doors carved with delicate designs, down corridors paved in cut stones in many precious colors. At the end, we were presented to a guard who stood before polished doors and there, having removed our iron cuffs, our jailor left us.

The guard removed a large key from the folds of his garment and this he inserted into a huge antique lock that turned effortlessly and silently. Slowly the big doors swung open to reveal an antechamber of great sumptuousness. Here stood another man as guard. We were passed into his keeping and the doors were shut and locked behind us.

The second guard herded us forward through heavy curtains wrought in curious, barbaric designs, and behind which was revealed a large room filled with low divans and fat cushions, placed directly on a floor covered in layer upon layer of wondrous carpets. Upon these furnishings reclined or sat many women, all of them dark of eye and hair and all wondrously plump. They languished there in various states of undress and I wondered that the approach of the guard caused no stir among them whatsoever.

The nature of this second guard was very curious and it was not for many days that I learned the reason for this. We had been delivered, it became apparent, not into the dank confines of an Infidel prison but into the soft and feminine boudoir of the women of the house. We were in very fact now the denizens of a seraglio!

§

We sadly bedraggled ten were immediately engulfed in a welcoming way by the women of the harem, and the guard disappeared behind the curtains again. We were obviously a wonder to these women, dirty, ill-kempt, and probably stinking as we were. They plucked at our matted hair and pinched our poor bruised arms, chattering the while in a barbaric tongue that sounded like the purest babel.

While there was much laughter at our expense—and well we must have deserved it—still I felt a certain maternal regard from these foreign women, for they were not rough or rude with us. My eyes fell upon a plate of food lying upon a low table beside one of the divans. My look must have been most predatory, for one of the women, following my glance, gave me a look of great understanding and immediately offered the dish to me and my fellows.

I fear we devoured every morsel on that plate and searched the room with our eyes for more. We had not eaten more than a handful of dried dates since coming to that shore, and we were faint with hunger. The women proffered us food and water until it was clear, by their distressed looks and pattings of the belly, that they feared we would be taken ill if we ate more.

Our strength somewhat restored to us, the ladies now ushered us, en masse, through a series of twisting corridors and brought us at last to a bath house. Here, they helped us from our clothing, if such those poor matted and torn tatters could still be called. Each rag was consigned, by agency of fingertips, and with noses wrinkled in disgust, to a large basket which, when the procedure was complete, was borne from the room by a servant, presumably to be burned.

Now began a ritual that, though administered by the hands of the Infidel, remains still in my memory as one of the sweetest moments of my existence. The women cooed and clucked over our poor thin, pale bodies, still innocent of women's hair, as they slowly lowered us into tubs of steaming water and scrubbed us from our topmost head hair to the soles of our feet. Our nails were pared and cut. Our hair washed and combed. Even our teeth were scrubbed with brushes.

When we were clean as the day our mothers birthed us, still another treat awaited us, for they now, once again in a giggling, jolly mob, escorted us into the neighboring room where steam rose in soft white billows through pierced marble grates in the floor. Here we, as a body, reclined upon thick white towels, turning ourselves like meat on a spit until our bodies were pink as the summer roses of Muret.

I was becoming very relaxed and would have drifted soon into slumber, right there on the floor, but that we now must move again into still another room. Here were low tables and the ladies aided us in positioning ourselves on them with our faces down on soft mats. They then began to massage us, two or three women working over each girl. One rubbed my back and neck, while another stroked and kneaded my arms and hands, and still a third rolled and pummeled my legs and feet.

I must have swooned, for the next thing I remember, I was being carried through the corridors on the bosom of a stout servant, with a gaggle of my new friends chattering along behind. I was placed in a small but beautifully appointed room on a low mattress covered in embroidered fabric. One of the ladies bent kindly over me, stroking my forehead maternally, and that is all I remember.

§

Later, two ladies who could speak a limping sort of French told me that I had slept for three full days and that they had feared I would never awaken but might simply slip away from my slumbering body, not to return. These two ladies of the harem who were able to speak with me were called Farah and Fatima, and they had an interesting story to relate regarding their ability to speak our language.

It seems that during the last Crusade, the wife of one of our French sergeants was captured. Rather than put her instantly to death, however, as is the Musalman custom, she was delivered to that household because of her great beauty.

She became a favorite of the master of the house, and so lived out her life in great comfort until she died of a fever but months before my unfortunate arrival. While she was incapable of learning the barbaric tongue of the Musalman ladies, she yet persisted in teaching them our language. I am most grateful to this unknown woman whom they called Irene, for it was through her efforts that I was able to converse and to learn so much.

We spent several weeks languishing in the harem. The sole delight of these ladies seemed to be to fatten us like Toulouse geese. Day and night they plied us with the richest and most delicious foods, until even the thinnest among us began to look sleek.

During these days, I questioned my French-speaking friends closely, endeavoring to learn all that I could of my situation. It was as well a method I used to quell my grieving after my lost Godfrey, for while I thus conversed, my mind could not dwell on his sufferings.

I learned that I was not, as I originally had supposed, in the house of the Caliph of Egypt. It was, in fact, cause for great hilarity when I suggested this notion. My new master was but a high-ranking official in the office of the Caliph's vizier.

Since the wealth surrounding me was unimaginable, I asked them how much greater must be the palace of the Caliph. These ladies seemed quite well informed despite their sheltered life, and I soon learned that they had spies everywhere, so that they had news of all the latest happenings in the instant. Thus, they were well able to describe for me the opulent surroundings of their king.

First, they told me, I must imagine materials of only the finest sort, for his palace was built of precious stones and woods. There are pillars inlaid with colored stones and jewels and in the throne room, pillars carved to resemble trees with golden leaves upon them. The fountains have basins of a red stone veined in rich pink, in gardens and courtyards that are too many and vast to comprehend. The tall rooms are walled in panels of marble pierced in wondrous designs, and the floors are covered in rich and brilliantly colored carpets.

The Caliph himself, they said, sits upon a golden throne, but behind a curtain, to give audience. Never does he speak directly to those who come to do him homage but speaks only through his advisors, who then convey his will to the supplicant.

He is arrayed the while in the finest linen or cotton fabric, all woven and embroidered with designs of such cunning that they are works of years and years of labor by skilled weavers and craftsmen. And about it all, everywhere one moves, there is the sound of splashing fountains, songs from birds in golden cages and the scent of flowers perfuming the air.

It is, withal, a most pleasurable description. I shiver with wonder to think on it still, for I am sure that in all of France not one such compound exists to compare with its richness.

ʛ

One day when we had been perhaps two months in our new captivity, an astonishing thing occurred which was to change my life forever. We were sitting on our cushions as usual. Some of the women were playing at dice. Some were waxing their legs by rolling balls of beeswax over them very rapidly. The wax caught and pulled out their hair; and thus, their skin was smooth as glass. I was sitting, as was our custom, with my new friends and they were regaling me with tales of their city.

Of a sudden, the curtains parted and the eunuch stepped in—for such my friends had now told me he was. He clapped his hands sharply and called out an announcement that I could not understand. My friends, however, rose quickly to their feet, pulling me with them, whispering that we were to be visited by the master, whose name I now knew was Ali Abu'l-Hasan.

I had wondered many times about the nature of this man whom I had never seen. My friends had told me he was young but this I now would plainly see had been sheerest flattery. For soon there entered a man of perhaps fifty, with black hair, gray about the face, and a visage thin and shrewd. His eyes were so deep-set as to be more like caves of shadow, his forehead was high and finely lined, and his nose was thin and cruelly hooked, like the beak of my father's falcon.

The eunuch again gave an order, clapping his hands officiously, and the ladies of the harem turned upon us ten girls, pinching our cheeks to make them pink, brushing our hair back with their hands, and otherwise quickly surveying us. Then we were pushed into a ragged line before Ali Abu'l-Hasan.

There was much twittering from the ladies at our backs, as if a flock of sparrows had landed there, but one swift glance from their master silenced them. Placing his hands behind his back, this man commenced a slow stroll back and forth before us, eyeing each of us as I have seen bidders do with horses, before the auction at the spring fair. He even pulled back the lips of my friend Jeanne to examine her teeth! When his eyes fell upon me, I felt my face go white and I thought I should faint, so cold and pitiless was his stare.

At last, he turned to the eunuch and whispered something to him. As quickly as he had come he departed, the long white skirts of his garment swishing heavily across the marble steps. Immediately, pandemonium broke out among the ladies. They fairly mobbed the eunuch, clearly questioning him about their master's wishes. The eunuch demanded silence with frantic waving of his pudgy hands. When the assembly had settled, he made a brief announcement that, of course, we girls could not understand.

There was among our poor betrayed party one girl named Agnes, who had come from Amiens to join our sad Crusade. She was consigned by nature to be a stout person. Even our extreme hardships on the road to Marseilles and on the ship across the sea had not completely diminished her. Now, with the fine foods that were insisted upon us day and night, she had again blossomed to her full buxomness. She was fair and full, for all that she was but thirteen years old.

Suddenly, all eyes were upon Agnes. Now it was her turn to be mobbed by the ladies. They shrieked and petted her and made such a fuss that the poor girl was quite bewildered.

Farah finally told me the cause of all this commotion. Arab men, it seems, dislike thin women but must have their ladies plump and round. Because of her stout figure, Agnes had just been chosen first among us to spend the night with Ali Abu'l-Hasan!

ʚ

Never have I been more grateful that merciful God created me small and thin! I felt the greatest pity for poor Agnes, although I did not yet understand the enormity of what had befallen her. Agnes, however, being a simple-minded girl, was delighted with her newfound glory. All day as the ladies worked over her, bathing and combing and massaging her with perfumed oils and manicuring her nails, Agnes was beaming like the sun, full well pleased with herself.

As evening approached, the ladies were still working over her. They arrayed her in a caftan of fine vermillion fabric and painted her face by lining her eyes with black kohl and rouging her cheeks and lips. They had braided her wet hair in tiny braids in the morning. Now these were released and her hair fell in a sheet of wavy gold, past her waist. To me she looked like a poor, silly doll. It was clear, however, that the ladies of the harem found her lovely.

As the sun fell below the horizon, a servant brought in a silver tray bearing one single cup of tea. This was administered to Agnes and although she complained mightily of its bitterness, the ladies compelled her to drink it all. It was, Fatima explained to me, a draught to bring lethargy and to release in a woman her sensuality. Having drunk this opiate, Agnes was escorted from our sight by one of the senior women of the harem.

I am relating all this as dispassionately as I am able, these three years hence. You must know, however, that in that moment I was consumed in horror. Often had my dear mother spoken to me of the sanctity of marriage and the honor of a woman who goes to that bed unsullied. From that hour I vowed to eat meagerly, consuming only enough to sustain my life, so that I should never be appealing to this infidel who held sway over my fate.

I vowed, as well, that beginning that very night while others slept, I would explore these confines, seeking any way of escape. I knew that it was well nigh an impossible task that I had set myself, for the compound of women was surrounded by high walls that were themselves contained within still higher walls surrounding the buildings and properties of Ali Abu'l-Hasan. Nevertheless, I preferred death itself to the fate I now knew awaited me within the seraglio.

§

Well after midnight when the sleeping quarters were at last filled only with the deep breathing and snores of sleeping women, I arose from my mattress and slipped into the corridor. I intended to move toward the back of the building, where the kitchens and laundry were situated.

I had only gone several feet, however, when a sharp whisper brought me to a halt, with my heart beating in fear as if to break from my chest. From behind a curtained doorway, in the dim light of the few oil lamps situated in wall niches, I saw the wan face of another of my companions, Marguerite. Slipping a hand from behind the curtain, she beckoned me with silent urgency.

Quickly, I darted into her room and the curtain was drawn behind me. Marguerite clutched my hand in terror and pointed toward the floor. There in the dancing shadows of the oil lamp lay a bundled heap that, on examination, I discovered to be none other than Agnes!

Marguerite told me that a servant had just brought her thence, completely insensible, and dumped her upon her mattress. I bent quickly toward her in concern. Her fine dress was no longer upon her body, but merely wrapped about her like a blanket. Her round face was smeared almost beyond recognition with the remnants of her once glad makeup. Her hair was twined about her in disarray like a net about a large fish.

I set to work to straighten her, pulling straight her legs that were crumpled beneath her and smoothing her arms. I set her head aright upon her pillow. Then I began to pull the caftan from around her and that was when the full horror of her situation was revealed to me!

As I pulled away the dress, I saw red welts and scratches upon her torso. Bending closer in the dim light, I saw to my grief that her poor nipples were mauled, as if gnawed by rats. Worse sights awaited me, for as I removed the gown completely, I saw that this young girl, too young for her first bleeding, was yet flowing with blood from between her legs. I drew back from her in fright. You may be sure, I felt so ill I could scarcely breathe!

Beyond thought, I rushed from the room to the sleeping chamber of my friend Farah. Without even pausing to knock, I threw aside the curtain and dashing to her bed, began to shake her awake without ceremony.

Begging my sleepy friend to accompany me, I dragged her, still half-clothed, down the corridors to the chamber where Agnes lay. Farah had only to glance at the pathetic child on the mattress. She made a clucking sound universal to women when they have seen something that is a great shame and injustice. My own mother used to make such a sound. Telling Marguerite and me to wait with Agnes, she disappeared from the room.

It seemed forever that we waited. Marguerite and I held one another, to give ourselves courage. Agnes lay moaning upon her bed, while the blood flowed endlessly from her, soaking into the mattress in a stain almost as black as ink.

At last Farah returned, drawing behind her the senior lady of the harem, one of the master's first wives, who had taken Agnes away earlier in the evening. The two stood but a moment speaking in low and hurried voices, and then the older lady bent toward Agnes and Farah again departed.

The woman made clucking and sighing noises, as if it were her own daughter who lay before her so cruelly violated. She gently opened the legs of my companion and with the hem of her garment, began to wipe away the blood.

Soon Farah returned bringing towels and a basin of water. The two women first ripped one towel into strips. One of these they gently began to push within the orifice of my poor friend. Gentle as were their ministrations, Agnes began to moan and cry out, as if they were causing her the greatest pain. Terrible as this scene was, I could not tear my eyes away. My only thought was that, but for the sacrifice of Agnes, I myself or another of our company would now be suffering this terrible anguish.

The two women worked long over Agnes, wiping her clean until the basin of water was as red as blood itself. When they had sufficiently cleaned her, they discovered that her second orifice in her bottom was bleeding as well. The two women passed a dark look containing purest outrage.

At this moment, the curtain was drawn aside and a man entered. I had seen him before, for he was the doctor who ministered to Ali Abu'l-Hasan's harem. He bent quickly to the bed and having taken but one look, turned and shooed all but the oldest woman from the room.

Marguerite and I stood shaking in the corridor until Farah emerged from the chamber. She embraced us both most gently, then shepherded us back to my room. There she put us both in bed together, as we were so frightened that we could but cling mindlessly to one another.

Farah sat beside our bed, singing and crooning to us until through sheer exhaustion we slept. When I awakened in the morning, Farah was still there. In answer to the first question that sprang to my lips, she answered sadly that Agnes had departed this earth during the night and that she rested now in the loving care of Allah.

I was unhinged by this report. I shrieked, asking Farah how such a terrible thing could have happened in a house where we had all otherwise felt so welcome. It was then that Farah, treating me as an equal and one far older than I was in fact, told me a dark story.

S

During the last Crusade, she said, Ali Abu'l-Hasan had gone to Jerusalem to fight. While there, he witnessed atrocities visited upon local women by our own invading force. Women were raped, mutilated, and killed. The brutality of this treatment fairly undid him. When he returned from the Holy Land, he was a different man, dark of countenance and dark of thought. His treatment of Agnes obviously reflected his wrath regarding the treatment of Musalman women by the Crusaders.

This line of reasoning I could understand, if not condone. But then, I protested, how could it be that Irene, she who taught Farah the French language, was a favorite of the master? Why did he not brutalize her, as well?

Farah gave me a long look, as if assessing my ability, at so young an age, to understand. There are certain women, she explained delicately, whose temperament and physical form outfit them in such a way as to make them irresistible to men. This dispensation makes them invulnerable to the affairs of the world. Politics, philosophies, religions, and enmities mean nothing when faced with such a woman.

Irene had been one such as this. Despite his hatred of the Crusaders, Ali Abu'l-Hasan could not hate Irene. In fact, her physical attractions and abilities made of her a soothing balm to his fevered psyche. Doubtlessly, because Irene was no longer available to catalyze his emotional intensity, poor Agnes had borne the brunt of it in its raw and virulent form.

From that moment forward I became a different person. Where before I had languished, eating the food provided me and whiling away the hours conversing with Farah and Fatima, I now pulled together all my wits. I still conversed with my new friends but I now asked questions of a more pointed nature. I found out how food was delivered into the compound of women and how and when the laundry was collected and delivered. Slowly, I formulated a plan of escape.

§

About two weeks after the death of Agnes, I put this plan into action. During my nightly forays, I had discovered that the laundry contained huge baskets. These were filled with freshly washed bedclothes of the harem and then transported outside to be spread in the sunshine to dry.

Early one morning, I crept into the laundry where the servants were just starting to be busy at their tasks and crawled into a basket already half-filled with washing. I pulled a wet sheet over me and curled up tightly beneath, still as a mouse.

Soon one of the servants brought another batch of wet laundry and threw it in on top of me. I thought I would suffocate beneath the hot, heavy weight of it. As more and more sheets and towels were added, I was sure that I had chosen my coffin instead of my escape route!

At last the basket must have been full. I felt the load being lifted. I heard the servant grunt, as if from the unexpected weight of it, and I held my breath, for I knew that this could be the moment of my discovery. The burden was shouldered, however, and I felt myself being carried and jostled.

I was blind beneath the smothering load and saw nothing of what surrounded me. My sole hope was that as the laundry was unloaded, I might find an undiscovered moment in which to hide myself away outside. Then, it was my plan to await the cart of the vegetable sellers that daily delivered goods to the harem kitchens and to stow away thereon.

As with so many other plans in life, this one was destined for failure. The basket was dumped out without ceremony and as I lay gasping beneath the steaming load, some part of my body, my foot or elbow, must have lain exposed. Of a sudden there was an outcry and I felt the laundry being pulled from above me with alarming rapidity and force!

I gathered myself to spring into action and when the last sheet was pulled away, I saw two stout old women, who grabbed at me. I leapt to my feet, dodged to the side, and began to run, I knew not where. But the sure knowledge that an attempted escape from the harem was punishable by death and that to stay in the harem was a living death acted like twin spurs to my ambition.

I found myself in a walled yard of sun-baked bricks. Everywhere were bedclothes and towels hanging on lines, stacks of baskets filled with produce, and carcasses of meat swinging from hooks. I darted into this confusion.

For all my speed, however, my quest was hopeless. The old women had raised such a hue and cry that every servant was soon alerted and as I rushed past, would grab at me and then take up the pursuit.

Soon, I found myself running down the center of the yard with a full army of servants at my heels and ahead of me, only the firmly closed gates in the high walls. My situation was hopeless. Only one obstacle remained between the walls and me, and that was the well, which rose before me with its heavy wooden bucket swinging from an iron wellhead.

Preferring death by drowning to being rent into pieces by the mob that pelted after me, I gathered my strength, placed my hands on the stone lip of the well, and vaulted into its yawning black maw!

§

Chapter 4

§

Rancho Cielo

"Oh dear!" Calypso stifled a big yawn and stretched her arms over her head. "That's got to be it for tonight. My voice is going."

Hill, slumped down in his chair and staring into the embers of the dying fire, shot upright. "What? Right when she jumps down the well? You can't quit now!"

"I have to, Walter. Look at the clock. It's after one in the morning."

"If this was Scheherazade's tactic, I'm surprised the king didn't kill her from sheer frustration."

"Now, Walter. Try to curb your narcissism and remember that this isn't just about you. I'm telling you, I won't be able to talk in the morning if I don't quit now." Calypso shuffled the pages into a more orderly lump and dropped them into the manuscript box. "To bed with you now!"

Hill's lower lip curled down petulantly, but he rose and then pulled Calypso to her feet. "You're one hell of a storyteller, you know that?" He bent and kissed her lightly on the lips. "Until tomorrow. You promise, right? That you'll read more tomorrow?"

Calypso smiled and nodded. "I promise."

§

Morning light was just seeping into the kitchen as Calypso lit the stove, put on the kettle and ground coffee beans. Lonely for Javier, she smiled to hear a male voice in the house.

"Walter?" she called. "Can that possibly be you?"

Hill shambled in, tousled and disheveled. "I was so tired last night I forgot to undress." He slumped into his chair by the fireplace, where embers still winked among the ashes.

"That's because 'last night' was really this morning. We didn't get to bed until after one." She threw him a compassionate glance. "And it will be a few minutes before the coffee's ready."

Hill groaned and ruffled his hair with his fingers. "That damn story will be the death of me," he said, and then bent to throw kindling on the coals. "It's good, you know. I mean, you've got all the details right, but you've improved on Berto's telling. My advice is..." Bent double using bellows to fan flames from the sleeping embers, he was interrupted by the shrilling of a siren of ear-splitting intensity. He jerked upright. "What the hell?" he shouted.

Calypso stood in the middle of the kitchen floor as if paralyzed, her face gone suddenly ashen. "Oh, God!" she mouthed over the din.

"What is it?" Hill shouted again.

She turned to him then, like a woman sleepwalking, and shook her head as if denying to herself what she knew to be true. "The siren," she said.

"Well obviously!" Hill jumped from his chair and moved toward her, alarmed. "What the hell is going on, Calypso?" He took her by the wrist, unsure what to do. She looked at him but appeared unable to speak. Hill began to guide her toward the couch but she resisted.

"No!" she cried, pulling back and turning as if to go outside.

Just then, the door burst open and Pedro raced into the kitchen. "Boss Lady!" he shouted, dashing to her. "You've got to get out of here. They're coming!"

"Will someone please tell me what's going on?" Hill bellowed over the incessant wailing of the siren.

Pedro turned to him, still clutching Calypso's arm. "We're about to have visitors. The lookout's started the siren. Everyone from the village'll be coming to take shelter."

Hill grinned, unable to help himself or to register their alarm. "Well, I realize how isolated you are but surely there's a better way to welcome visitors."

Calypso rounded on him. "Not funny, Walter! He means *them*, the cartel. We're under attack!"

Hill was instantly sober. "Oh." He looked to Pedro. "What can I do?"

"You can take Boss Lady outta here."

"*No!*" she shrieked, outraged.

Pedro turned on her, impatient. "We talked with the Boss about this. You know what you gotta do. I can't fight, worrying about you. You're my responsibility 'til he gets back. You have to leave!"

"What does leaving mean?" Hill shouted. The rising and falling shriek of the siren was making him a little crazy.

"Boss Lady knows. She'll show you. She's in your hands."

Calypso was hanging on Pedro's arm with steely fingers. He pried her hands loose, his face grim. "You have to do this for the Boss."

There was pounding on the door and he thrust Calypso from him. "I have to go. This is it, Boss Lady. Do your part." He strode to the door and opened it to find Juan, his next in command, on the doorstep.

"They coming! About a mile away now. Coming fast."

"Is everyone in from the village?"

"They're coming, too. Almost all in."

"Good. You go organize the men. You know your job, Juan. Don't fail me. I'll be there in just a few minutes."

"You got it. Good luck!" Juan turned and raced away, and Pedro closed the door. He turned to look at Calypso. "So" he said, "this is it. You gonna do what we planned?" He held Calypso in a firm and questioning stare.

Hill watched her hanging there, mid-kitchen, as if suspended on a string, wavering indecisively. Pedro stepped toward her and she held up a commanding hand to stop him. Slowly, her face galvanized into a mask of resolve. She took a deep, ragged breath and squared her shoulders.

"All right," she whispered, her voice inaudible above the siren's continued wail. "Here we go"—then, turning toward Hill with regal poise she said—"come, Walter. It's time to leave."

§

Calypso ran to a closet, threw the door open, and reaching inside, withdrew an empty backpack that she threw at Hill. "Go to your room and put only necessities in this. A coat, socks, your passport, money, credit cards, whatever. Think survival. You have two minutes."

Hill stood rooted in indecision. "But—"

"Go!"

Hill went, taking the stairs two at a time. Calypso turned again into the closet and brought out her own pack.

"Is it loaded?" Pedro asked.

"Always." Without turning and with her shoulders braced she asked, "How bad is it?"

"Bad. Ten SUVs. Comin' like bats outta hell."

Calypso slung her pack over her shoulder as she went to the foot of the stairs. "Hill!" she shouted. "Time's up. Let's go!"

Hill came clattering down the stairs, the pack swinging from his elbow. "Now what?"

"Now for a little adventure." She jerked her chin at Pedro. "We're ready. Let's go."

Pedro opened the courtyard door and ran out with Calypso on his heels. Hill followed her, then on impulse, turned back into the house.

"What are you doing?" Calypso shouted, glancing back at him as she ran.

"Forgot something," Hill called, opening his pack as he darted into the kitchen.

"For God's sake, Walter! Come!"

Hill reemerged at a gallop. "I'm here," he shouted. "Lead on!"

The three raced across the courtyard. Behind them, all along the sides of the house, shouts of men and women and the wailing of children arose as the inhabitants of the workers' village pressed inside the sheltering walls. Ahead lay only the abyss of the canyon with its four-thousand-foot-drop to the river. They ran down the stone path until they were brought to a halt by the low stone wall that protected the very lip of the cliff.

Hill looked wildly at Calypso. "Now what? Do we grow wings and fly?"

Calypso, her face closed and taut, only jutted her chin indicating Pedro on the other side of the wall, who already was working a gray nylon climbing rope through an iron ring set into the bedrock of the cliff.

"No," she said, "we're going to rappel." She scooted over the top of the wall as she spoke.

Hill felt his face go white. "To *what?*" he gasped.

"Rappelling uses a rope for controlled descent down a rock face. It's a technique climbers use when a cliff is too steep and dangerous to descend any other way. Put on your backpack, Walter. Good and tight."

As she spoke, Calypso was donning her backpack and then a climbing harness of nylon webbing with attached D-rings and steel adjusting buckles that fit around her thighs and waist. Pedro tossed the anchored rope over the cliff.

"Watch how I do this because you'll be next."

Hill felt his chest tighten. "You've got to be kidding!"

Just as Calypso opened her mouth to answer, a volley of shots echoed from the front of the house. "Shit! Listen, Walter, I'm not kidding. Watch me when I go over. I'll send the harness back up, then Pedro will set you up."

She stood, leaning over the cliff edge on the attached rope with her back to the drop. "You'll make sure the women and children are secured in the house?" she asked Pedro.

"Of course. I know what to do," he snapped. "Now, check yourself. Your harness doubled back?" Calypso checked the harness buckles and nodded. "Carabiner screw gates closed?" Again, Calypso checked the metal figure eight around which the rope was looped and that attached the rope to her harness through a locking carabiner. She nodded. "Okay then, Boss Lady. Over you go!" And with that, Calypso pushed off the edge of the cliff and disappeared.

"Holy shit!" Hill threw himself over the wall and, taking a wide-legged stance, bent to peer over the edge. There, only about ten feet below him, was Calypso, hanging by the gray thread over thousands of feet of pure space, her feet braced against the cliff.

She looked up at him and grinned. "It's not rocket science, Walter, but it works," she called up to him. "Watch this." She pushed off from the rock face and descended another five feet. "Just hold the rope like this. Keep your right hand down by your hip like I have it, and don't let your left get close to the figure eight. Keep it above there as you descend. It'll do the rest. I'll be down there to catch you when you arrive."

She gave another shove with her legs and bounded into the air, landing ten feet lower on the rock face. Craning her neck and squinting against the sun, she called up to him, "There's a bulge here. You won't see me once I've gone over it. There's a ledge just below it. See you there!" Then she pushed off the rock and sailed out of sight.

Hill backed away from the edge, his breath coming in short gasps. "No way am I going down there," he said to Pedro, then ducked as another volley of shots sent lead ricocheting across the courtyard. "Shit!"

Pedro was busy hauling up the climbing harness. "She's down," he said. "Your turn."

"I told you, I'm not going." Gunfire almost drowned out his voice.

"Look, asshole, I made the Boss a promise to get Calypso to safety and that's what I'm gonna do," Pedro snarled. "But the Boss isn't here, so I'm in command, you dig? That means it's up to you to take care of Calypso."

"I am *not* going over this cliff."

Pedro gave him a disgusted look. "We can do this two ways," he said. "Either you go over conscious or unconscious. Your choice." His face was hard and uncompromising.

"I said *no.*"

Quick as a ferret, Pedro was in Hill's face. "If you're gonna waste more of my time, I'm just gonna do it my way." The fist he doubled looked hard as a sledgehammer. The two men stood glaring at one another.

"Show me how to get into the harness," Hill sighed finally. He was convinced that death awaited him either way: Pedro would punch him unconscious and toss him over the cliff, or the rope would break while he was fully conscious and he would have almost a mile of free fall during which to consider his sins and make amends. "It's as good a day as any to die."

§

"Just walk backwards." Pedro was clearly trying to sound reassuring but Hill wasn't buying it. "You won't fall. The figure eight'll slow the descent. It acts as a friction multiplier."

"I was always bad at multiplication." Hill's toes hung on the last margin of the cliff.

"Just sit back. Get your butt down lower. Good. Now, just step off."

Hill stepped backward, his hands gripping the rope with insane strength. What madness, to suspend his life over an abyss by this slender thread! Sweat trickled down the bridge of his nose but he was too paralyzed to wipe it off.

"Kick off the cliff!" Pedro's dark, vulpine face appeared over the edge of the cliff a few feet above him. "Kick off and let the rope carry you down." Hill remained frozen. "Or maybe you'd like me to just cut the rope and get it over with. I haven't got all day." Behind him, sounds of all-out war had erupted. Pedro drew a .357 from his belt and aimed it at Hill. "Get the fuck down this cliff or I'll give you a shortcut."

Hill kicked off the cliff, flew into space, and slammed his feet back into the rock again. Pedro and his .357 were now a good ten feet above him. He kicked again and the rope sizzled through his fingers as he descended again. He tried not to think of his rear end sitting on nothing but air, almost a mile above the Urique River. He concentrated instead on kicking the cliff as he swung against it and on learning to control the tension on the rope with his right hand.

His feet found momentary purchase on the bulge of rock over which Calypso had disappeared. Then momentum and desperation took over, and he bounded off the curved face and found himself swinging through air. Red canyon walls flashed through his peripheral vision. A glimpse of the aqua thread of the Urique below him made his stomach turn. Then, powered by weight and gravity, he swung with tremendous speed toward the cliff again, careened off it with his left shoulder, and catapulted again into space.

He was turning a pirouette in midair when he heard a familiar voice calling, "All right, Walter. Enough of the Peter Pan act!" He spun on his tether just in time to see Calypso standing on a narrow ledge, a sheer drop below her, and then he slammed into her full force.

Calypso's arms came around him like steel pincers as she dragged him to the cliff and held him against backward momentum. Hill's knees gave out and he slithered down her body until he lay collapsed on the cool stone—panting, while Calypso's fingers dug at him, unbuckling the harness. Vertigo reduced him to complete submission as she removed it.

"How did you do that?" Hill finally was able to gasp. "I could have pulled you off the ledge."

"I'm roped in. See?" Calypso showed him a short tether that passed through an iron ring set in the rock face and then to another harness buckled over her torso.

"Where did that come from?"

"We keep it here for just this kind of thing. It's our escape route, Walter. We've had it in place ever since I was kidnapped by El Penacho's henchmen." She began reeling in the rappel rope. "That's it," she said, as the end of the rope came sailing down. She coiled it under the iron ring. "No going back, now—but no one can follow us either."

"Great," Hill said, with feigned enthusiasm. "Is there, perchance, also a way forward?" He leaned on his elbow and glanced outward briefly at the yawning red canyon and its airy interior and then reeled back, overcome with vertigo.

"There is." Calypso took Hill by the elbow. "Just turn toward the cliff and crawl, Walter. Don't look at the canyon or the vertigo will get you." Hill turned onto his side and scrambled to his knees, while Calypso extricated herself from the harness and snapped it to its metal ring with a spare carabiner.

"It's like I'm iron and the canyon is a magnet pulling at me," he rasped.

"I know. I've experienced it myself. Just crawl."

Hill crept along the ledge, with Calypso walking beside him to guard the drop-off. About twenty feet ahead of them where the ledge widened was a leaning flake of stone, big as a garage door. As Hill crawled under its shelter, the powerful pull of vertigo lessened. Then his mouth gaped in amazement. Hidden behind the stone was the opening to a cave.

§

Hill pulled himself into sitting position, his back to the cliff, and his view of the canyon shuttered by the leaning slab. He found he was panting and over the steam engine puff of his own breath, heard volley after volley of gunfire echoing through the canyon from above. He realized it had been a constant backdrop to his efforts ever since stepping off the edge of the cliff. Somehow, he had interpreted it, in his rattled state, as the hammering and exploding of his own nervous system.

"Gunfire," he said inanely.

"Yes."

Something in Calypso's tone made him look up. Her face was contorted with grief and Hill was instantly ashamed. He struggled to his feet.

"This must be hard for you. Let's go inside." He took her by the arm and pulled her toward the entrance to the cave but she resisted, as if she could not bear to leave this last, disastrous contact with home.

"What will come of this, Walter?" Her voice teetered along the ragged edge of breaking. "What if Javier comes home in the middle of this? I can't lose him, Walter! I couldn't bear it!" Her eyes met his, wild with anxious tears.

Hill swept her to his chest and held her tightly. "Calypso," he breathed into her hair, "Javier will survive this. You've got to believe it." He felt her body go rigid and knew she was fighting to control the fear that was overpowering her. Then, with a wrenching sob, she broke. Leaning into Hill's chest, clinging to him like a drowning woman, she wept.

ʖ

Rancho Cielo

ʖ

Javier drove straight through for sixteen hours. It took three hours just to extricate his truck from the lattice of barely visible tracks that lead from the Huichol village out of the hills toward the highway. Once on the paved road, he sped through the mango groves of Jalisco where the tall, shaggy trees were laden with ripening fruit. He drove too fast over the Devil's Spine, a perilously narrow twist of road winding vertiginously atop dizzying cliffs. In crossing the mountains, the road crossed the Tropic of Cancer as well, before descending to the deserts and scrubby hills of Durango.

As he traveled, he knew he was passing through the very growing fields of the cartels, where marijuana and opium poppies occupied every growable space in the near-vertical mountains. The little village where he stopped for gas was hostile with paranoia and secrecy.

Once back in Chihuahua, he wheeled his truck up the Boca del Lobo, the Throat of the Wolf, far too fast, his tires squealing on the steep, looping turns. Once on the high plateau with still almost a hundred miles to reach the ranch, he floored the truck, streaking down the narrow highway heedless of wandering cattle, and slowly lumbering trucks.

Caught in a vortex of worry and dread, it was as if Wind Person were speeding him along. All he could think of was Calypso's safety. He went over the preparations he and Pedro had made for the defense of Rancho Cielo, looking for any chink in their armor. He reviewed the promise Calypso had made to vacate if trouble should erupt and followed in his mind the route they had set up if she should have to flee.

They had thought things through so carefully, but he had always assumed he would be present if things went bad. What if everything had gone wrong while he was away? The thought maddened him and he drove on into the dawning day like a dark wind howling across the Sierra.

§

Just as the sun rose, Javier passed through the neighboring town of San Juanito with its ambient smell of pine sap and diesel from its sawmills. Outside the vividly turquoise and white church, women in black were already congregating for early mass beneath its square bell tower. The interior of the little corner restaurant where he and Calypso often enjoyed empanadas, a specialty of the house, was invisible behind steamy front windows, indicating breakfast was ready to serve.

Outside of town, he turned at last onto the dirt road leading to Rancho Cielo. His hands felt bonded to the steering wheel and the gas tank was nearly empty. Pushing the truck mercilessly over the washboards in the road, he roared toward the ranch with mixed relief and foreboding.

At last he entered Rancho Cielo property, jolting across the first of several cattle guards of railroad rails welded over concrete pits. Cranking the wheel to the left, he took the road to the house, snaking up the long drive as if devils pursued him.

Ahead, he could see the high defensive walls of the courtyard where, instead of a solitary guard, men were swarming, further raising his sense of alarm. As he slowed for the final, circular drive centered with a tall, three-tiered fountain, the big double gates swung open. He skidded around the right hand arc and swung the nose of his truck through the opening, barely missing the gatepost as the tail end whipped through. He heard shouts as the gates clashed shut behind him.

Slamming on the brakes, he threw himself from the cab. The entire courtyard was frenzied with movement. Men were running, carrying weapons, while the women and children from the workers' village were being herded through the kitchen door of the main house. He ran toward the house, thinking only of Calypso.

"What's going on?" he shouted to the first man he came to, a ranch worker named José. Before the man could answer, shots were fired somewhere outside the courtyard and an answering volley came from atop the walls.

"The mafia, señor," José yelled.

"Where's Caleepso?"

José shook his head. "*No sé, señor.*"

Javier pushed past him. The interior of the house was a chaotic mass of swarming women and children. He couldn't make his way through the crowd and shouted, "Where is Caleepso?"

A woman sitting near the door with her two small children nestled against her responded, "Señor Pedro took her away, señor."

Javier spun through the door and raced along the side of the house toward the cliffs, just in time to see Pedro running up the walkway toward the house.

"Where's Caleepso?" Javier shouted.

"She just went over the cliff." Pedro ran up to him, winded. Another burst of gunfire drowned out the rest, and Javier grabbed his arm and dragged him down next to the foundation of the house. "She's okay," Pedro gasped. "And Hill."

"*Hill?*"

"He came yesterday."

Javier slumped against the foundation stones in relief and reached to give Pedro's shoulder a pat. "Good work, Pedro. Now, what's going on?"

"It's the mafia, Boss. The guard saw them coming. He sounded the alarm. We got everyone in I think. When'd you get here?"

"Five minutes ago. They must have come up from the canyon because I didn't see them on the road from town."

"Yeah. We saw them when they were still deep in the canyon or we wouldn't have had time to get everyone in."

Their eyes met as the volleys of shot increased. "Let's get up on the walls and give these bastards hell," Javier said.

"You got it, Boss."

They crouched, ducking their heads, and ran.

§

From the walls, they could look down into the road where several black SUVs with darkly tinted windows were clustered, just out of rifle range. Men must have poured out of them, because it looked as if at least forty were milling around the vehicles, throwing occasional shots in the direction of the walls. In between, they were passing plastic bags from which each man pulled a handful of something and then sniffed deeply. The remainder they flung from them and clouds of white powder floated in the damp morning air.

"They're coked-up to the max," Perdo hissed. "*Chingada cabrones.* They're gonna think they're Supermen."

"*¡Hideputa!* That *perico's* worth enough to run the government of Mexico," exclaimed one of the ranch's cowboys. He spoke with his eye squinted for his first opportunity at a good shot, his rifle muzzle resting on a crenellation of the wall.

"Shit, man!" Pedro responded. "Cocaine *does* run the government of Mexico!" A shout of laughter went up from the men and that plus Javier's presence did much to steady and unify them.

The men on the ground must have heard them laughing, because they suddenly looked up at the walls, pointing. Bags of cocaine were shoved into pockets or thrown back through open SUV windows. Suddenly, every hand was wrapped around an assault rifle and one man, obviously the leader, was signaling them to spread out and surround the walls.

"Here they come, men," Javier said softly. "Wait until they're in range and then hit them hard." He crossed himself and the men followed suit.

At that moment, Calypso did not exist except in that sacrosanct place where she always lived in him. He felt his muscles tighten, his heart rate quicken and his fingers dig into the stock of his weapon like steel hooks. Everything he held dear lay behind him—Calypso, the workers and their families, his home, and his ranch. Before him was only death. He took aim. There would be death coming from his direction too.

§

The men on the wall fired first. The response was a blanket of automatic fire from the ground that kept Javier's men ducking, crouched on the catwalk. Fortunately, Javier had anticipated this during the building of his fortifications and had included gun ports at that level. His men thrust their muzzles through these and sent out a solid wall of lead that dropped several of the invaders in their tracks and sent the others scurrying back out of range, dragging several wounded and dead with them.

They took shelter behind their vehicles where Javier watched them holding an excited powwow, arms gesticulating. Javier used the interim to check his men. "Everyone okay?" he called. Shouts went up along the wall, assuring him that his men were still at their posts.

All the preparations he had made over the years were paying off. His men were all well trained in handling armament. Three had been sent to Ciudad Chihuahua to study to be medics and were well-supplied and ready in case of injuries. Some of the younger teenagers were trained as runners who would bring ammunition up from the armory at the base of the wall and keep ammo clips loaded, supplying their fathers and uncles. He knew that in the house, the women would already be preparing pots of beans to keep their army fed.

The thugs of the cartel were displaying no such organization. Shouting had erupted from among the parked SUVs. Bodies were being loaded in the backs of the vehicles. A fist-fight broke out and several men joined in, while others tried to break them up. Then, as abruptly as they had arrived, everyone piled into their vehicles and drove away in the direction of town.

To do so, they had to pass in front of the walls and Javier's men peppered the cars with shot as they passed. One veered off the road, its driver wounded. There was a hesitation and then the SUV lumbered back onto the roadway and sped away in the wake of the others.

§

Javier's troops were jubilant. A shout went up, and there was a spate of high-fiving and laughter. Javier held up his hand for silence. The men were instantly quiet.

"I congratulate you!" he said. "Each of you performed just as we trained to do and with real courage. I hope you're all very proud." The men grinned and jostled one another with their elbows. "The enemy has left and we are victorious—but..." he hesitated for emphasis, "they will be back. And next time, they'll be angry and they'll be prepared. That means we have to be even more prepared. We have to work very hard and very fast. Are you with me?"

A shout went up. "We're with you, Boss," Pedro called. "What do you want from us?"

"We have to implement Phase Two. That means getting your families out of the house and up into the crags on the west end of the ranch. Juan, you and Felipe get them organized and get them out, right now. Make sure they have food and blankets from the storehouse.

"Pedro, you're our demolitions expert. You know what to do.

"It's time to bring the big guns up. Who's going to do that?" Several hands shot up.

"All right. Let's get to it. Boys, you make sure to get the ammo up here and all the extra clips loaded." The teenagers, eyes wide with their first combat, nodded and skittered down the stairs to the armory.

Javier beckoned Pedro to him. "This is going to get really ugly," he whispered. "Make sure we can do as much preliminary damage as possible."

"I'm on it, Boss." Pedro turned away, stopped and turned back, holding out his hand. "Just in case," he said.

Javier knocked his hand aside and the two men embraced.

§

The Cave

"This cave runs for miles," Calypso said, wiping the back of her hand across her eyes, mopping tears. Only twenty feet inside the cave, the light already was growing dim. She dug in her pack for LED headlamps, handed Hill his and shone hers ahead, illuminating a rounded tunnel with smooth, curving walls of red stone.

"It's kind of like being inside a big intestine," Hill said. "As long as there's no peristalsis, I'm good with it."

Calypso smiled through her tears. "It does get pretty narrow in places."

"Not something a man with the chest of an American bison can't navigate I hope?"

"Well...if only Pedro were here to pull, while I push..."

"He'd carve the extra parts off me more likely. Do you know he threatened to shoot me if I didn't rappel?"

Calypso shook her head. "But he wouldn't have."

"You'll never convince me of that." The shaft was wide enough for them to walk side by side. "How do you know where we're going?"

"We've practiced this many times." She stopped to face him. "I need you to know, Walter, that I'm not running away from danger. Javier made me promise that if we were ever under attack, I'd do this. And he made Pedro take a vow to get me to safety. Javier knows that the first instinct both Pedro and I have is to back him up. But he says he can't concentrate or fight or even survive if all he's thinking about is my safety."

"Makes perfect sense to me. And I never would have accused you of running away. I'm the one who knows you've got the heart of a lion, remember?"

Calypso nodded, satisfied. "Good. I just couldn't bear it if you thought I was cowardly." She swept the light ahead to where the passage made a sharp inward turn. "The cave narrows beyond that turn. We'll have to go single file. And watch your head. The ceiling lowers, too."

The cave narrowed considerably beyond the turn. Calypso snaked through, crouching, with the grace of a dancer, while Hill huffed and scraped his way along, occasionally barking his head on the low ceiling.

"*OW!* Shit! How much more of this?"

"Lots. But we're almost to a resting place. Are you hurt?"

"Nothing that a bottle of Saint-Emilion, a rare sirloin, and a few sutures couldn't mend."

"You're hungry. Well, hang in there, Walter. We'll be able to eat soon."

"There should be a warning chiseled in the rock over the entrance to this place: ABANDON HOPE, ALL YE WHO ENTER HERE."

Hill kept up his genial grousing, as they wended deeper and deeper into the heart of the bedrock. Both were aware of the cooling temperature, the gently descending slope, and the growing sensation of weight. The massive walls enclosed them; the ceiling seemed to press down ponderously.

It was the opposite of vertigo, Hill reflected as he scuffed along. Instead of the almost irresistible urge to throw himself into the canyon's gulf, he now felt suffocated, as if this solid rock would become his tomb. The only positive thing was that, this deep inside the mountain, the sounds of gunfire could no longer be heard.

§

After more than an hour of ducking, weaving and sliding through tight spaces, they were suddenly aware of the distant sound of falling water.

"What's that?" Hill asked, stopping. "Have we connected with Rancho Cielo's sewer system?"

Calypso glanced over her shoulder at him. "It's a surprise," she said with a mysterious smile. She moved forward then, her vigor renewed by anticipation, with Hill lumbering after her.

The narrow passage began to widen and the close air was relieved by a cool, damp breeze that moved toward them, fanning their sweating foreheads. At last, they broke out of the corridor into a vast rock chamber. The headlamp beam could not encompass it in a single sweep, but Hill could tell by the echoes that the room was high and wide. The sound was of falling water, thundering into a pool.

"Is that what I think it is?" he shouted to Calypso.

"Yes! Look at this!" She flashed her light over a pool of black water, its surface chipped with wavelets, and followed the flow backward toward its source. The narrow beam revealed an area of turbulent, frothy water, and then the glassy ribbon of a waterfall. She directed the light upward so that Hill's eye could follow the water to its source, high on the far wall of the cavern.

"It must be forty feet high!"

"At least." Calypso lowered her light and searched with it along the edge of the pool. "There's a flat spot over here where we can rest. We've got water bottles cached. We can fill up for the rest of the way. This is the only water for miles."

She led the way along the verge of the pool and then turned left behind a sloping wall of stone. Hill followed her into a sheltered nook where she was already lighting a suspended camp lantern. By its light, he saw a hanging mesh bag of empty neoprene water bottles hooked over a thumb of stone and a couple of metal hampers with locking lids sitting against the stone wall.

"This is pretty cozy! Did you stash a couch down here, too?" he asked hopefully.

Calypso chuckled. "You'll just have to sit on your own padding I'm afraid." She unlatched a hamper and brought out a small camp stove. "Here, pump this up for me. I'll get some water. We've got dried soup here. You must be starved."

"I could eat." Hill fiddled with the stove and lit it, while Calypso went to dip water from the pool. "Is that water safe to drink?" he asked when she returned.

"Are you kidding? This aquifer is ancient and filtered through layers and layers of bedrock. It may be the purest water on the planet." She poured water into a small aluminum saucepan, added a foil pouch of dried soup mix, and set it on the stove. "I wish we had some bread to go with this, but..." she sighed, leaving unspoken her thoughts of her kitchen and its delicious foods on the plateau above them. "We have another stash of air mattresses and sleeping bags up ahead. But it'll be hours before we get there."

"You and Javier did all this?"

"And Pedro. We've felt for a long time that it might come to this. And we had no intention of fighting to the death. We always wanted a sure escape route. Of course, we always planned that Javier would be here too."

"Instead of me."

"I didn't mean that. I mean our plan was never complete. Did I really expect that Javier would leave his workers undefended? Or his property? Maybe he always knew it would be like this, but I had the idea we'd be doing this together." She stirred the soup, averting her face, but Hill heard the crack in her voice. "His plan all along was probably to send me with Pedro and I just never realized it."

"Do you have any idea where we are?"

"Yes. This cavern is about five hundred feet lower than the plateau where the house sits and over two miles east of it."

"No kidding!"

"The passage slopes much more steeply from here on. There are even a couple of places where we've installed ropes. And we've marked the places where the tunnels split, so that we don't wander forever under here, like the Piper of Keil."

"The who?"

Calypso poured soup into a small aluminum bowl and handed it to Hill along with a camp spoon. "The Piper of Keil. He made a bet that he could play the bagpipes better than any fairy piper. Of course, he lost. His punishment was to wander forever under the ground in the mazes of fairyland, playing as he went. In Scotland, you'll find people who swear they've heard him passing under their feet."

"How do you know these things?" Hill's voice registered his amazement.

"My grandmother was a Scot from Clan Ross. She was born in the Orkney Islands, up in the North Sea. She used to regale me with stories about Scotland."

"So Celtic mysticism runs in your blood."

"Pretty much. I think my grandmother's sense of the occult made it easier for me when Berto gave me the locket. She'd told me about similar precious objects—especially the Holy Grail. It's supposed to be in a vault deep under Rosslyn Chapel in Midlothian, you know."

"That sounds like someplace in Tolkien's Middle Earth."

"No. It's in Scotland. Almost as many stories attach to it as to this locket." She touched the necklace that lay beneath her shirt as she settled beside Hill and leaned against the stone wall. She blew on her soup to cool it.

Hill rummaged in his pack and with an "Aha!" came up with two crumpled scones. "Your bread, madame," he said, handing her one with a flourish.

"My scones! That's what you went back for this morning?"

Hill grinned wickedly. "I can have surprises, too."

They bit into the pastries and savored them in silence. "Apricot," Hill said at last.

"Um-hum." Calypso's voice was small. "I picked these apricots last spring and dried them." Her eyes, filled with sorrow, found Hill's. "There are so many little reasons why I love it here,

Walter. Mainly because Javier loves it so. But these apricots are reason enough, aren't they?"

"They are," he agreed solemnly.

"The hardest part isn't sitting here in the dark, surrounded by tons and tons of stone, is it? It's not knowing what's going on up above. That part is almost more than I can bear."

Hill nodded. There were no words in any language to comfort the desolation in Calypso's voice.

She began to clean up their lunch mess. "Wash these in the pool, will you? We need to move on now. We still have a long way to go." She turned to the open hamper with such solemnity it might have been a sarcophagus. "And we'll need to fill the water bottles. There won't be open water again for a long time."

§

"This cavern must have been an initiatory chamber in ancient times," Calypso said as they shouldered their packs. "Before we leave, I want to show you something." Her headlamp beam played along the edge of the black pool until it lit upon a narrow ledge, just above water level. "Come over this way," she said as she sidled onto the ledge, facing the wall of stone.

Hill, realizing he would never be able to anticipate Calypso's sudden changes of direction, sighed resignedly and followed her onto the rock shelf. It was just wide enough to accommodate his size fifteen shoes as he sidestepped along. "This better be good," he grumbled.

About twenty feet onto the ledge, where the wall of rock curved to encircle the pool, Calypso halted and directed her headlamp beam onto the stone in front of her. "Here it is! Look at this!" She turned toward Hill, who was blinded momentarily, as he tried to steady himself and keep the weight of his pack from pulling him backward into the water.

Hill squinted at the stone wall in front of them. "What? I don't see a thing." In the same instant, he saw them: handprints. Actually, stencils of hands. "Oh! What are they?"

"They're the signature of one of our ancient cousins. They blew pigment through a reed, leaving a negative imprint of their hands. See . . . this hand fits mine perfectly! The fingers are the exact lengths of mine." She held her long, slender hand against the stone for Hill's perusal. "And that one over there fits Javier as if he'd made it himself." She indicated a large imprint with tapering fingers. "You try this one. I bet it will fit you!"

Hill edged closer to Calypso, raised his thick, square hand with fingers spread and carefully aligned it with the hand outlined on the wall. As he did, he felt the hair on the back of his neck rise. The handprint fit him like a glove. He had the uncanny sensation that it *was* his handprint, left there long ago as a reminder to himself. It seemed preposterous, yet the sense of ownership of the print was overpowering.

By his headlamp's beam he examined his hand, looking for overlaps or places where the print was too big for him, and found none. He stared at his hand with its surrounding aura of timeless red pigment and lost all sense of himself as a twenty-first century man, of his place in the world, of time altogether. He stood suspended in the eternal moment, with time's linearity collapsed into the ever-present and ongoing Now. A deep sense of wonder and humility pervaded him.

And then the moment passed. He was aware again of the weight of the pack, the thin spray from the waterfall, of Calypso's large, solemn, observing eyes.

"Well?" she breathed.

Hill didn't answer but began sidling back off the ledge. Calypso followed him silently. When they had regained solid footing, she put her hand on Hill's arm.

"I know," she said. "You don't have to say anything." Then she turned and, hitching her pack up on her hips, started into the void of the tunnel.

§

Rancho Cielo

When it came, it was as bad as Javier expected. A convoy of SUVs and trucks came racing down the road at dawn the next day. The beds of the trucks were filled with men and bristled with guns. Javier watched with field glasses as the convoy turned across the first cattle guard onto Rancho Cielo property. First one, then another, then another laden vehicle pounded forward, tearing across the second cattle guard at the base of the driveway.

Javier muttered under his breath, "Let them come, Pedro. Just enough. Not too many." Six vehicles were inside the perimeter, and the seventh was just crossing the upper cattle guard, when there was a tremendous explosion. The front end of the seventh SUV rose up and the vehicle flipped over backward, bursting into flames as it rose in the air. Parts flew off and bodies hurtled, as it landed upside down on the hood of the truck following. That vehicle, too, burst into flame, and the two SUVs following rammed into it, in a massive collision.

A victorious shout went up from the men on the walls. Javier turned and caught the eyes of his gunners. He raised his arm and brought it down decisively, and three men stood up, with rocket-propelled grenade launchers on their shoulders, took aim, and fired. The three lead SUVs exploded. The men sank down behind the parapet wall again, and Javier signaled three more to stand. Their RPGs took out the next three vehicles in line, leaving bodies and burning metal littering the driveway.

Behind the cattle guard, all was chaos. Men swarmed from the stalled vehicles, shouting, to congeal behind one of the trucks. Javier followed them with his field glasses, but could not make out what they were doing. At last, the crowd began a concerted effort and suddenly, from behind the truck, they rolled out a howitzer and positioned it facing the walls.

Javier's heart sank. He could see they had positioned it about two hundred yards away, just beyond the reach of the RPGs. He knew that, using comparatively small propellant charges, the artillery piece could propel projectiles at relatively high trajectories, with a steep angle of descent. Against such a weapon he, his men, and their fortifications were powerless.

Ordering up his long-range snipers, he commanded, "Kill as many as you can around that howitzer. Keep up a steady barrage. Don't let them get a shot off."

It was too late, however. With a deep *whoosh*, the howitzer launched a shell, just as the snipers got off a volley that dropped several men around the artillery piece. Javier watched the shell arc up into the sky, as if in slow motion. He could hear his snipers firing again and again, but the sound was distant and muffled. With all his being he watched the shell descend, calculating where it would hit. It seemed to hang suspended for a lifetime before it plummeted down, right through the tiled roof of his home.

§

The Cave

Almost immediately the passage grew much more difficult. "Be careful near this siphon," Calypso yelled.

From the waterfall's basin, water poured down a stone chute and cascaded into a whirling pool, with a sucking vortex at the center. The way past was slippery and the roar of the descending water terrifying. Hill shouted something but Calypso couldn't hear it and shook her head, concentrating on crossing the slick stone. When they were sufficiently past the monster, she turned back to him, asking, "What did you say?"

"I said," Hill called over the diminishing din, "it's like a big bathtub drain. I wonder what would happen if I fell in there?"

"You'd probably end up in a chamber like the one we just left—only with no way out!"

Soon they came to another cavern, this time from up near its ceiling. Calypso waited for Hill to catch up.

"Javier thinks we've been following the original water course," she explained. "Where we're standing would have been another waterfall. But for whatever reason, the water got diverted. Maybe the rock wore thin and the water just dropped through as a siphon, into a tunnel below. It probably has an outfall in the river somewhere. Anyway, that's the last we'll see of it. Our challenge from here on is to be like water ourselves."

"What do you mean?" Hill stood on the lip of the drop-off, running his headlamp beam along the vertical wall beneath them. The light was lost in the abyss of the cavern below.

"Water, of necessity, flows on. That's our challenge now too."

"Going over this drop looks more like a big splat than a flow."

"It's not as bad as it looks. This is one of the places where we've set up ropes. Over this way." Calypso led along the lip of the drop off. Back in a shadowed nook, her light caught another iron ring set into the stone, with a rope already attached and coiled on the stone floor. "This won't be nearly as scary as that first rappel. It's only about fifty feet to the floor of the cavern."

"Great!" Hill couldn't muster sufficient confidence to sound sincere.

"Relax, Walter. We're almost halfway there," she said as she busied herself, setting up the rappel.

"And just where, pray tell, is 'there'?"

"Our stopping place for the night." She fiddled with the equipment. "Okay," she said at last. "It's ready. Do you want to go first or last?"

"I don't want to go at all." Hill sounded as petulant as he felt.

"Fine. Then you can stay here, if that's what you choose." Calypso slipped the climbing harness around her and buckled it tightly. "If you change your mind, just let me know, before I pull the rope free." And with that she pushed off, disappearing into the chasm of darkness.

Hill rushed to the edge and followed her looping trajectory to the cavern floor. He watched as she unbuckled the harness. When she turned her face up to him, it was set and grim and she refused to speak. Her hand on the rope said it all.

"Okay. All right. Send the harness up," he sighed resignedly. "And if I ever agree to go adventuring with you again," he muttered under his breath, "just shoot me."

"I heard that." The harness came whipping over the edge. "The acoustics in here are like a cathedral."

"Speaking of cathedrals, I could be in Paris right now"—Hill growled as he buckled the harness—"sitting in a café, admiring Our Lady's flying buttresses and eating something delightful. Actually, a stiff drink of fifteen-year-old scotch also comes to mind."

He backed toward the edge, clinging to the rope, trying to remember where he should hold his hands so as not to have his fingers devoured by the figure eight. "But no! Instead I'm immured inside a mountain of stone, performing trapeze acts in pitch blackness." He sat back and let the rope slide a few inches.

"Just quit your resistance and get it over with, quickly and simply. Like water."

"Okay. Here comes the big flush." And he pushed off into space.

§

Calypso caught his arm and steadied him as his feet hit the cavern floor. "Careful! It's really uneven here." She could sense the quivering of Hill's limbs, more than feel it. "You did well, Walter," she conceded.

"Right! Consider that last act an evocation of my undying love for you." He pulled at the buckles of the harness with trembling fingers.

"It's your pure heart that got you through that, for sure. Because it certainly wasn't your technique."

"I could experience self-pity about now," Hill sniffed, "but I won't. I will be noble and stalwart and steadfast, despite the hellishness."

"Walter, you and I both know that you'll write a report about all this that will probably win you the Pulitzer."

Leaving the rope and harness hanging in place, they shone their lights ahead and chose a path through the rock-strewn chaos of the cavern floor, grousing and sniping companionably as they went.

"The passage is over this way," Calypso said, waving her light across the far wall. Then she turned to Hill and said with deep sincerity, "You had great courage up there, Walter. Don't think I don't know it." She turned and trudged on, before he could master his astonishment and think of a suitably cavalier response.

§

Calypso stopped before a low, black opening in the cavern wall and turned toward Hill, who still was navigating a series of rough, rounded boulders with difficulty.

"It's like climbing around where old Volkswagens go to die," he huffed. As he approached, she held him in a solemn stare that alarmed him. "What?" he asked defensively. "Am I slowing you down?"

"No, Walter. It's just that... I have to tell you about the next part. But first, we need to put fresh batteries in our headlamps."

She knelt and dug into the open top of her pack.

"Here. Put these in and give me your old ones. They must be just about used up." She busied herself with her own light and the cave suddenly went dark. "Oops!" Her laugh came out of utter blackness. "Let's do it sequentially, shall we?" Her light flicked back on and Hill felt himself take a deep breath.

"I think I stopped breathing for a second there." He slid the batteries out of his lamp and she handed fresh batteries back, with a stare that was so intense that Hill became nervous. "What?" he asked again, a little shrilly.

"I have to tell you about the next part."

"You already said that. What do I have to do now? Swing hand over hand across a bottomless chasm filled with sightless albino snakes?"

Calypso took her time answering, choosing her words carefully.

"The next part is...well, honestly, the hardest." She held up her hand to stop the response that was already forming on Hill's lips. "Once we're through it, everything else is a piece of cake. But this next part is..." She let out a little sigh. "Is hard."

"Well, that was enlightening."

"I'm sorry. It's not easy to describe it. It's going to be harder for you because you're bigger. And it's hard enough for me. But!" she held up her hand again, to stop his exasperation. "Javier can make it through, so I know you can, too."

"Through what?" Hill's voice was laden with his growing suspicion.

"The next part is very...very *small*."

Calypso's eyes held a particular kind of pleading that made him distinctly uncomfortable.

"At first, you can crawl. But then, very quickly, you have to...well, I would call it *slither*. The tube gets very...*close*. I like to do it face down, because I can't stand to see the ceiling so close to me. And I do it in the dark, by feel, for the same reason. But Javier likes to go face up, because in the narrowest part he says there are handholds in the ceiling that he uses to pull himself along."

She stopped and stood staring at her feet. "So that's it. Any questions?"

"What about my pack?"

"We take our packs off and drag them behind us on leads. You have to maneuver them with your feet so they don't get caught crosswise in the tunnel."

"This sounds like swell fun! And how long does this passage go on?"

"I'm not sure. It seems like forever but I'm thinking it's probably no more than a couple of hundred yards."

"A couple of hundred yards. I see."

"It's not wonderful, Walter. I've done it many times and I never really get used to it. The first time is the hardest though. So you've got to believe me when I say that it *is* possible to get through. When you think you can't, that's when you're closest to it getting better. Does that make sense?"

"Perfect. And I suppose it's not an option to just sit and wait for a demolition team to come and blast me out of here?"

Her smile was meager and it told Hill everything he needed to know. If even Calypso's courage was daunted, then the party was about to get rough.

Calypso showed him how to tether his pack so that he could drag it behind him. Then, ducking to the low opening, she said, "Let's get this over. We don't have helmets, so watch your head."

She inserted her head into the hole, then withdrew it and sat down, looking up at Hill.

"Two things, Walter. Be like water: flow, don't fight. And remember that there really is enough room for you to get through. It's not your body that will have the most trouble. It will be your mind."

S

Calypso crawled into the tunnel, determined that this time she could do it calmly. No matter that she had done this passage more than a dozen times. It still made her heart race just to think about it.

"Best not to think about what's ahead," she called back to Hill. "Just take it one second at a time. It's easier that way."

Hill squatted and looked into the tunnel as far as he could see by the headlamp. At its furthest arc, he could just make out Calypso's retreating form scuttling along on all fours, her pack trailing behind her, before she disappeared around a turn. He sat back and put his head on his knees. He hadn't had the heart to tell Calypso the truth—he was a claustrophobe.

Already the day's exertions in the dark and close confines of the cave had challenged him. His nerves were shot. He couldn't imagine how he would accomplish what lay before him, but the thought of being left alone in the center of the mountain was even worse. With a ragged sigh, he inserted his head into the opening and began to crawl.

He made it round the first turn with no trouble, even though his pack hung up. He had to kick it loose because the tunnel already was too narrow to reach back for it. Ahead, his lamp showed that the ceiling sloped down to under two feet high. He caught a glimpse of Calypso's retreating rear, as she wriggled out of sight.

Realizing that this was the juncture where he would have to decide on going face up or face down, he decided on face down, despite Javier's preference for the former. Somehow, the thought of looking up at solid stone, right in his face, was more than he could bear.

He lowered himself onto the floor and squirmed forward on his forearms. The floor of the passage was fine sand and not abrasive. Raising his head to look forward, he cracked his skull on the ceiling.

"*Ow!*" His voice was muffled and he heard no response from Calypso. All he could do was crawl ahead, following the rut left by her pack in the sand.

The tunnel ran fairly straight, with occasional high and wide spots where he could draw his knees under him and crawl for a bit. All too soon, however, the ceiling would lower and he would find himself face down again. Resting in one of the wide spots, spread eagle in the sand, he tried to estimate how far he had come. He thought it might be about two hundred feet. A third of the way! Heartened, he dragged himself to his knees and crawled on.

When he estimated that he must be well over halfway, the tunnel began to constrict. He could lift his head a scant six inches and his elbows were hitting the sides. He could feel his heart rate rising and not just from exertion. Remembering

Calypso's promise that in coming to the worst spot he was almost through, he wriggled on.

The passage, however, became smaller still. This must be the place where Javier preferred to be on his back, pulling along with ceiling handholds. Hill tried to turn over but the space was too tight. The ceiling was now too low for him to lift his head.

Suddenly, panic swept over him. He tried to push outward with his arms, but they were pinioned to his sides. He had the sensation that all the air was being sucked from around him and he began to gasp. Cold sweat broke out all over his body. He could not control his mind. Panic galloped through him and every fear of a terrible death that he had ever imagined overtook him and then was superseded by his present predicament. He felt he was dying and it was terrible beyond comprehension.

He lay rigid, fighting for composure. Just kick with your feet, he reasoned with himself. Push forward a few more inches. He tried to do it, but his size fifteens caught on the ceiling. He leaned his feet sideways, and was able to push forward with his toes. He made a few more inches and realized that, unbelievably, the space was becoming smaller still. He thought his heart was about to burst and he lay gasping on the sand.

The weight of the stone above him was immense. The ceiling, a couple of inches above him, seemed to press down with living animosity. He could not control his breath. It sobbed through his lungs like hot wind. He knew that he had to get control of himself or he would pass out. Control, however, eluded him.

Scenes from his life began to flash through his mind. There was the time in Vietnam, when he was just new to the journalistic profession, when he went into the field with a Marine recon unit and they were hit with enemy fire. Flashes of gunfire erupted in his brain and he saw the jungle floor again as he dove toward it, heard the shouts of the men, and smelled, just as vividly as if it were flowing from his own body in present time, the metallic smell of blood.

Just as quickly, he was in Ethiopia with his Land Rover's axle broken in a ditch and the ground temperature soaring past a hundred and twenty degrees. He was swigging the last drop of water from his canteen, when a ragtag group of local militia hove into view, Kalashnikov rifles bristling from the beds of a couple of battered Toyota pickups. He could feel, again, the steely, simian grip of those hands that pulled him into the truck, smell the reek of unwashed flesh, and hear the excited jabber of his captors.

Again, his mind skittered and he was in the cockpit of a bomber as it swooped low over a thatched village in the jungle. Mozambique! The CIA's covert operation against the rebels there. The plane dove, strafed, took fire. Bullets ripped through the floor right next to his boot. The pilot's feet both spouted blood, as he slumped on the stick and the plane slid crazily sideways.

Hill could not stop the progression of wild memories, nor quell the intensity of the visceral sensations they brought. His mind was fevered and he felt as if his skull might break open like a melon, spilling his brains into the sand. He lost all sense of where he was in time and space and felt himself spinning into oblivion.

§

Calypso slithered desperately forward, keeping her head tilted sideways beneath the crushing ceiling. Her elbows barked against the rough stone of the tube. She was in the lowest place, the one that always made her feel, no matter how many times she passed through it, as if her death were imminent. Only the thought of the freedom of movement that awaited her kept her from panic. *Just a few more yards to go*, she told herself. *You can do it! You can do it!*

Turning her head sideways, she slipped her skull under what she knew was the very tightest place of all. She dug her hands into the sand and swiveled her hips, worming her way through the obstructed passage. Just a couple of yards now.

Then a few feet. Finally, her head broke through to open space, then her arms, and she was able to pull herself forward into the next cavern.

Just as she was pulling her legs from the tube, she heard it. The sound was muffled, but that did nothing to stifle the horror of it. It was so anguished, so tormented, that it turned her stomach.

Hill! The sheer abandon of the shriek was telling. He was losing it. Tears leapt to her eyes. "My God!" she gasped. "That poor man!"

She experienced an instant of pure revulsion at the thought of going back into the tube, then she unsnapped her pack from its tether and kicked it to the side. Diving onto the cavern floor, she lunged forward and, denying herself the right of protest, wriggled back into the tube.

§

When Hill came back to himself, his first sensation was of a cool breeze blowing onto his fevered face. He lay with his eyes closed and savored the freshness of the air, the sweetness of the scent of pine. He rolled his head to the side and glanced upward. A rend in the stone ceiling revealed a silvery night sky luminous with stars. Directly above him, the thin sickle of a new moon rode the river of the Milky Way like a slender boat.

"Just push with your feet, Walter," he heard Calypso's voice say calmly. It echoed slightly, like a voice from another dimension. "Be like water. Wiggle your hips like a fish. Paddle with your feet. Keep your head turned to the side so it will slip through. You're almost there. Just let yourself swim through."

Her voice calmed him. He smiled up at the moon as he pushed his feet into the sand. The sensation of floating was marvelous. He wiggled his hips and moved forward. He felt the stone above him brush his cheek, then scrape across his shoulders and back, but he was oblivious, reassured by the sight of Calypso, standing free against the night sky. She bent her kind face toward him and smiled. Her hair wreathed on the night wind and her skirt arced and ruffled about her. "Just swim, Walter," she said again. Gently, he wafted forward like a fish in dark water, drifting in the moonlight.

§

Hill lay on the rough floor of the cavern in fetal posture, his breathing coming in ragged gulps. The strange sensation of floating still bore him on illusory waters.

"It's over, Walter. You made it. It's all over now," Calypso's voice crooned.

Her hand on his shoulder gently rocked him. That was his first realization that he was sobbing. He registered this with distant amazement, while the fact-finding and -keeping part of his brain informed him that he had not cried since he was nine and broke his arm playing touch football. There must be a good deal pent up, given the intervening decades, his rational mind reasoned distantly.

While this internal dialogue proceeded and the sobbing continued unabated, some new and fresh place in his psyche was bathed in a delicious sense of peace and wellbeing. He lay beneath the confusion of voices like a big trout in the calm space beneath turbulent water. He felt absolved of every sin, shriven of all burdens, as innocent and vulnerable as a newborn babe.

Finally, Calypso was able to get him to his feet and, supporting his hobbling, half-delusional stagger, she guided him a short distance into a side room off the main cavern, where she leaned him against the wall while she lit a lantern. Hill promptly slid down into a heap and lay crooning and chuckling to himself, as Calypso went about setting up camp from the stored supplies. She lit a camp stove and put water on to boil, rolled out self-inflating mattresses, and spread sleeping bags on top. She brewed two tin cups of tea and handed one to Hill, who had propped himself against the wall and was now staring blankly at the shadows jiggling and dancing over the stone walls.

"What is this place?" His voice surprised her with its youthful lilt. The question might have been asked by a curious ten-year-old.

"After that horrible tube, Javier and I both felt we needed to provide some comfort for ourselves, so we prepared this room. We liked it because it's about the size of our bedroom at home." She smiled and glanced at the ceiling that stood a good four feet above her head. "Plenty of breathing space."

"And how far are we from getting out of this place?"

"When we get up from sleeping, it will basically be a stroll and then we'll be outside under the sky."

Hill accepted the bowl of soup she handed him and tilted it eagerly to his lips. "I'm starving! How long has it been since we ate?"

"You're the one with the wristwatch."

Hill pulled back his cuff and squinted at his watch, did a double take, and stared at it in amazement. "It's after eight o'clock! But it was almost nine, when we were having breakfast, so that means…But it can't be. Can it? Have we really been in this cave almost twelve hours?"

Calypso smiled at him with mischief sparkling in her eyes.

"Twelve hours you think, huh?" She laughed. "Walter, it takes a full day to get through this cave. We've been spelunking for almost twenty-four hours!"

"You're kidding." His voice was deadpan.

"No, Walter. I'm completely serious. If you feel exhausted, now you know why."

"I had no idea…"

"You lose all track of time in a cave, without natural light." She collected his cup and refilled it with soup. "There's really no way to anticipate whether it will be light or dark when we come out. I'm always surprised." They drank their soup in silence while Hill contemplated this.

When they had drunk all the soup, Calypso rummaged in her pack, came up with two oranges and handed one to Hill.

"Dessert."

"Every adventure I go on with you, I end up losing weight. It beats regular attendance at the gym." Even Hill's thumbs felt tired, as he peeled the orange. "After this, I'm going to need to lie down."

"Me, too." Calypso gathered their cups, scoured them with sand, and rinsed them in a meager stream of bottled water, then stored them again in the metal hamper.

"How'd you get that big thing through the tube?"

Calypso smiled. "We brought it in from this side. You think we're crazy enough to try to wrestle it through there?"

"Crazy is what I think this entire place and your lifestyle in it is," Hill muttered. He rolled onto his knees and crawled to the nearest sleeping bag. "Do you mind?"

"Not at all. I'm right behind you." She switched on her headlamp, blew out the lantern, and came to sit on the bag next to Hill's, busying herself untying her shoes and flexing her feet. "Oh but it feels good to get those off!"

In answer, there was only Hill's soft breathing. Calypso dragged her pack over to serve as a pillow, crawled into her bag, and zipped herself in. When she turned off her light, the blackness that engulfed her was already part of her dreams.

Then softly, through the fog of sleep, she heard Hill's whisper:

"You were wearing a skirt."

"Um?"

"A skirt. Why did you pack a skirt?"

Calypso did, in fact, have a skirt at the bottom of her pack along with her lipstick, but she had not worn either.

"You're dreaming, Walter."

"No." She heard him shift onto his side, facing her. "I'm not dreaming. I saw you, standing in that opening in the rock. The wind was blowing your skirt."

"What opening in the rock?"

"The one right above the tightest part of the tube. If it hadn't been for that—the sight of the stars, the fresh air flooding in, and you standing there talking to me—I think I would have lost my mind. You saved my life. Thank you."

Calypso opened her eyes to the limitless blackness and stared. Memories of her own initiation into alternate consciousness filled her: Santa Rita prison, the steely grip of the guard's hands, the rape, the overwhelming of her natural boundaries, the pinioning of her innate strength. And then the euphoria afterwards: the strength derived from having survived, the sense of expansion, of floating, of becoming one with all that is.

Finally, she sighed and murmured, "You're entirely welcome, Walter. Now, go to sleep."

ና

Rancho Cielo

After the explosions and the firing of the howitzer, the battle raged on. Men advanced on the ground, only to be mown down by Javier's gunners on the wall, who fought tenaciously, reloading and firing with trained rapidity and accuracy. The snipers managed to keep anyone from firing the howitzer again. Another of Pedro's traps erupted from under the roadbed, lifting trucks and SUVs into the air, exploding them.

All the while, Javier's home was burning. The heat of it became intense, then almost unbearable, for the men on the walls but they would not be dislodged. Scorched and exhausted, they kept cramming fresh clips into their rifles and firing, until there was no one left to kill.

A sudden, eerie silence fell. The only sound was the crackling of flames as they consumed the house. By the time the men were free to fight the fire, there was nothing left to save.

ና

Chapter 5

ʖ

The Cave

CALYPSO AWOKE TO PITCH BLACKNESS AND AT FIRST, IN PANIC, COULD NOT REMEMBER WHERE SHE WAS, ALTHOUGH SHE KNEW THAT WHEREVER IT WAS, SHE WAS WITH HILL. He must be having the same sensation, because she could hear him scrabbling for the switch on his headlamp. With a click, sudden illumination revealed the folded and veined wall and ceiling of the cave and remembrance flooded her.

"Good morning, Walter," she muttered, still half asleep.

"Good morning to you! Just stay put. I'll get the tea water going." Hill pushed from the ground and rummaged for a match, then lit the camp lantern and stove. Calypso squeezed her eyes shut and turned on her side, away from the light.

"Still tired?"

"Um-hum."

"Some of this glue that passes for instant oatmeal ought to fix you right up." He ripped open a foil pouch, sounding positively chirrupy.

Calypso sat up, her hair wrapped about her shoulders like a shawl, and observed Hill more closely.

"My, we're a merry little ball of sunshine this morning."

"Never felt better in my life." He began to whistle and the beam of his headlamp zigzagged about the space in time. "*When the red, red robin comes bob, bob, bobbin' along...*" he sang softly, as if his whistle were still accompanying him. "*Dee dum, dee dum, dee dum da dum...cheer up, cheer up the sun is red. Live, love, laugh, and be happy-y-y-y-y...*" The final words were sung in full-throttle bass, his arms spread wide.

Calypso turned on her stomach and pulled her pack over her head.

§

Two hours later, the gloom of the cave began to brighten to twilight as they clambered up a final bouldered incline and saw sky glimmering within the black template of the cave's mouth. By Hill's watch, it was close to six o'clock, but neither could say with assurance if it was six in the morning or six at night.

"It's like being on one of those transpacific flights where you cross the international dateline and you don't know even what day it is, let alone what time," Hill said, pulling himself up the final incline. He stuck his head out of the cave and peered around like a groundhog assessing the weather. "The sun seems to be over there, behind a mountain," he reported, pointing to his left as he clambered out into the light.

"That's west, so it's evening." Calypso stepped from the cave, shrugged off her pack and dropped it on the ground. They were standing at the base of a cliff soaring into an ultramarine sky that, to her cave-weary eyes, sparked electrically in the slanting rays of the sun. Before them was a steep downhill slope of tumbled boulders and low, scruffy brush.

"We've dropped almost a mile in elevation," she said, glancing at Hill, who also seemed bedazzled by the sight of the sky. "That's the Batopilas River just below us. It's probably only a mile away."

"I thought it was the Urique."

"No, we've moved right through the mountain, from one river drainage to another."

"Amazing! Where to now, fearless leader?"

"There's an old mule trail that follows the river. It was built in the seventeenth century to bring supplies to the mines and to bring the bullion out. We'll follow that into Batopilas. We keep a safe house there."

"Is it far?"

Calypso picked up her pack and slung it over her shoulder. "Far enough. We won't come close to getting there before dark."

She began to pick her way down the slope toward the river. Hill started after her and then turned back, leaning his shoulders into the opening of the cave.

"Thank you," he called. He didn't know why he was doing it or to whom he was addressing his gratitude, but somewhere deep within him, he knew it was the right thing to do.

§

The western sky, clasped between twin prongs of cliffs, began to flame with radiant crimson and gold, and deep indigo shadows nested in the swales of the canyon. Calypso led the way down a steep scree slope made more difficult by the falling light.

"We can't make Batopilas tonight," she called back to Hill, who was lowering himself gingerly through a notch between two car-sized boulders. "It's just too treacherous. We don't need a broken leg to add to our woes."

"I agree." Hill's legs were shaking with exhaustion and his entire body ached from the exertion in the cave. "Is there somewhere we could hole up for the night?" They were out of water and his words clicked off a dry tongue.

"There's a spring up ahead." Calypso's voice was pinched with fatigue. "We'll stop there for the night."

A quarter hour of carefully lowering themselves down the treacherous slope brought them to a game trail beaten faintly into the loose gravel.

"We have to head back uphill a little," Calypso said, pointing up the trail. "It's not far." Hill only nodded, then followed as Calypso turned right onto the trail.

A few more minutes of scrabbling uphill and they pulled themselves onto a tiny plateau. An extension of the cliff, like the flounce of a lady's skirt hem, backed the flat space and from within the ruffled rocks came a delicious sound.

Rounding the edge of the outcrop, they came on a scene of astonishing beauty. The base of the rocks formed a shallow grotto, covered floor, walls and ceiling, with moss and hanging ferns. Water eddied down the back wall into a shallow pool that shown in last light like a silver shield. At the back of the pool, beside the falling water, was a figure of the Virgin of Guadalupe carved from the living stone, daubed with ochre and cloaked in shadow.

They dropped their packs and rummaged for their water bottles. Calypso entered the grotto first and knelt on the lip of the pool.

"There are animal tracks here," she said. "Deer and raccoon." She cast her eyes along the bank as she held her bottle submerged in the cool water. "And something else. . ." she frowned and bent to squint at the muddy border. "Sometime bigger. Maybe a large dog or a cougar. It's hard to tell. The prints are all muddled."

She pushed to her feet and backed out of the grotto, inviting Hill into it with a sweep of her hand. Then she raised the bottle to her lips and swallowed the sweet, cold water gratefully, in long pulls until the container was empty, her head thrown back and her eyes on the first stars winking above the iron clamps of the cliffs.

§

"How did you find this place?"

They were lounging around a small brush wood fire. Above them, the moonless night sky was limpid with starlight. A cold wind tugged at their mylar space blankets and made the fire gutter and smoke. Calypso drew her blanket more tightly around her shoulders and stared into the fire, remembering.

"It was the first time we made it all the way through the cave. We'd been trying to find the passage for months. A *Rarámuri* shaman told us it was possible, but we'd only come to blind ends before."

She turned her eyes toward Hill.

"You can imagine how we felt once we'd started into the tube. I was sure we were going to die in there. I only kept going because Javier was ahead of me and I didn't want to get separated from him. And he says he only kept going because I was behind him and he didn't want to make me back up!" She laughed, shaking her head.

"So when we finally staggered out, we were exhausted and ready to die from thirst. It was summer, too, and so hot! I don't know what we would have done if *Suré* hadn't appeared, like a miracle."

"Suré?"

"A Rarámuri man. We just looked up and there he was, standing on a boulder. He led us here."

Calypso could still see him in her mind's eye, with his long, bronze runner's legs, his breechcloth and sky blue cotton shirt with long, gathered sleeves, staring at them as if they were as startling to him as he was to them.

"*Kuira*," Javier had said. *Hello.*

"*Kuira*," the man responded, his voice almost a whisper, as was customary among his shy people.

"*Wawik?*" Javier asked hopefully. *Water?*

The man shook his head. "*Ke.*" *No.*

At the time, they had only been at Rancho Cielo for two years and were still learning the language of the local indigenous. His linguistic cache almost expended, Javier asked, "*Wawik—dónde?*" Apparently bilingual, the man had pointed downhill and beckoned for them to follow. In due course, he led them up the game trail to the spring in the grotto.

"Suré works for us now," Calypso said. "He had to give up his native ways because the cartels wanted him to grow marijuana instead of corn. When he refused, they threatened to kill his family, so he had to leave his little farm." She sighed. "It's so unfair, Walter. You really ought to write an exposé. The Rarámuri are being pushed off their lands, just like the Mayans in Chiapas. It's the story of modern Mexico."

"Not so very modern. Remember, it started with the Conquest, in 1519. It's not exactly hot news." Hill tossed another stick on the fire and chafed his hands together. "I thought Mexico was supposed to be hot and tropical."

"It's autumn, Walter, and you're two thousand feet up in the Sierra. But when we get to Batopilas, you'll see that it's tropical. Up on our plateau there are pine and fir, but down here in the canyon there are date palms and citrus trees."

They sat in silence, listening to the night wind moaning through the cliffs and spires of the canyon and the nearer, more companionable crackle of the fire. "It must be all over by now at the ranch," Calypso ventured at last. Her voice was small and tight with worry. "When we get to Batopilas I'll call. Or maybe there will be news waiting for us. Or maybe even," her voice brightened, "Javier."

Hill sat wrapped in his mylar blanket and stared glumly into the fire. He didn't want to think about what had happened at Rancho Cielo, and he definitely did not want to voice to Calypso the nagging concern that weighed on him as if he were carrying a set of barbells.

"Maybe so," he replied. "Maybe so."

§

The growling of their stomachs woke them long before dawn. The fire had burned down so that not even embers remained, but the cold wind that had gained in ferocity during the night had died with it. Despite the emergency blankets, they were both stiff, sore, and deeply chilled.

"Do you have any food left in your pack, Walter?" Calypso had pushed herself upright and was stacking tiny sticks in the blackened fire pit. "I'm all out."

Hill sat up, dreading the next stage of ascension that would require him to rise to his feet.

"I'm out, too."

Calypso lit the pyramid of sticks and sheltered them from the wind with her body until they flared into flame. She filled an aluminum bowl with water and set it on rocks near the flames.

"I still have some tea. When we've had that, I'll see if I can find the ingredients for an energy drink the Rarámuri make. It fuels them to run day and night, sometimes for two hundred miles or more."

"I feel like that, sometimes, when I've had my second espresso."

"Yes, but do you *do* it?"

"What?"

"Run."

He reached to a boulder, and with a grunt, pulled himself to his feet.

"I'll be grateful if I can still walk."

After tea, Calypso scouted the vegetation around the grotto.

"There's a wild lime tree here and we're in luck. It still has some fruit." She came back to the fire with a handful of small, leathery green limes. "Now for some chia seeds."

She followed the trickle of water that emanated from the grotto and crept darkly down through the rocks toward the river.

"Chia's a member of the mint family," she called back to him. "It grows wild along water courses here in the canyon. The seeds are very nutritious."

Hill's eyes followed as she picked her way through the rocks, bending to harvest seeds into her bowl from dry, wind-beaten seed head spires, and he marveled at her resilience. Despite the hell of the last two days, she looked fresh and beautiful, with her cheeks rouged by wind and her hair in a long braid over her shoulder. Her blue jeans were faded and abraded and she wore them, he reflected, as if she were on the street in Paris, with indefinable chic.

From his vantage point on the edge of the grotto plateau, the backdrop of canyon fell away behind her in shadowy shelves of indigo. She was so at home there, so comfortable in the wildness and chaos of it all, that Hill felt the old tug. He would never be free of it. For him, Calypso was the summation of womankind and rather than make him morose, this realization brightened his mind, like the sun that was just beginning to spill over the high cliffs to the east.

Here he was, in this impossibly feral place with the woman of his dreams, who was, in fact, a waking reality. In the sacred ceremony of life, he had just ingested the wafer, or the sliver of peyote, or the sacred mushroom. With the day's dawning, his being flared like gates of light opening, allowing the holy moment to enter.

Even one instant of this pure and vivid life was worth all the rest, with its bills and sweltering airports, bad food, boring and officious people, and all the other accumulated ills of Western civilization. He would not trade this instant for all the rest of it put together. This, he knew in a flash of insight, was the purity of love and he rejoiced in it.

§

Calypso came to the fire, her face glowing from the climb back to the plateau, and set down the bowl with it's small clutch of mottled gray and tan seeds. Then she went to the cliff face and bent toward the riffles of water-worn rock as if searching for something.

"It's still here!" she said and held up a round, fist-sized stone in triumph. "I've used this every time we've come here," she said over her shoulder, as she washed the rock in the pool.

Settling cross-legged by the fire, she set the aluminum bowl with the harvested chia seeds in her lap, then tore open two small pouches of honey from her pack and dribbled the amber runnels over the seeds. Finally, she threw in the limes, poured a small amount of water over everything, and then commenced macerating and grinding the lot into a paste using the stone as a pestle. When everything was a nasty, greenish-looking pulp to Hill's watching eye, she began to add water until there was a thick, sludgy drink, clear to the brim of the bowl, which she held up to him with a smile.

"Here. Drink this. It'll give you strength."

Hill took the bowl from her and stared into it.

"I've never felt more dubious," he said. "We're a long way from medical assistance."

Calypso sighed in exasperation.

"Here. Give it back to me." Hill complied and Calypso tilted the brew to her lips without hesitation and drank deeply. "If I die in the next few moments," she said acidly, "just bury me here. Don't trouble yourself trying to lug me down the mountain." She smiled at him brightly and when he reached for the bowl, held it just out of his reach. "You're sure?"

"Yes."

"I don't want any medical emergencies." She shifted the bowl further still, as he leaned, reaching for it. "And no gagging, grimacing, or agonizing allowed."

"I promise," Hill said and his stomach gave a vicious growl as if in agreement. "I'll be manly as Socrates with his hemlock."

She relented and handed him the bowl. He sipped the liquid reluctantly and then his face brightened with wonder. He took another tentative sip and raised his face to the warmth of the just-risen sun.

"Well, I'll be damned! It tastes good! Delicious even." He buried his lips in the green liquid and drank deeply.

Calypso sat by the fire, snapping sticks and throwing them into the flames, a small smile playing around her lips. She could feel the tangy brew making its way inside her. Its living warmth, along with her fondness for Hill and his nattering ways, was the heat she needed to fuel another day of exertion.

In her mind's eye, she clambered downhill through the boulder field, all the way to the old mule trail that ran along the riverbank. The river would be rushing over its stones, with a slight morning breeze riffling the surface and water ouzels bobbing on spray-misted rocks midstream. Alders, bare now in the autumn cold, would lift their dark limbs in silhouette against the clear and piercingly blue sky. It would be a scene of serenity and peace and it would belie all that the dreams had told her.

§

It was an image straight out of her dreams but it was real, and it was standing not five feet away, elevated on a flat outcrop of rock. Without a sound, a large animal had materialized and with a gasp, Calypso turned to face it. She heard Hill give a yip of alarm and brought her hand down, in a gesture demanding his silence and immobility.

This, she knew instantly, was the creature that had left its prints in the mud of the grotto. It was not a large dog or a panther, as she had suspected, but a wolf.

"Good morning," she crooned softly. "You're looking very beautiful this morning."

It was true—the wolf was a magnificent animal, tall, lean and sleek. Its charcoal and gray coat, deep, soft, and silvery, russet around the face, sifted gently in the morning breeze. Its yellow eyes stared into hers unwaveringly and Calypso stared back.

The standoff continued for several seconds, during which the wind brought the sound of the river's rushing far below, the chirp of birds in nearby bushes, and the green scent of the grotto. Calypso's mind was frozen. She could think of nothing to do about their situation. The wolf seemed equally undecided.

The small sound of rolling pebbles broke their trance. The animal turned its head toward the noise, and Calypso's eyes darted in its direction, as a man emerged from the foliage near the mouth of the grotto.

"Down, Lobo!" he commanded and the wolf sank dutifully to the stone. Calypso had expected a Rarámuri but the man was Anglo or part-Hispanic and spoke English. He was tall, lean, and gray-haired like the wolf and his stance was tense, as if any quick movement on her part would set him into instant and deadly motion. She had met men like him before, men cut off from the mainstream of society, accustomed to making their own laws, imposing their own judgments. Altogether, she thought fleetingly, she would rather take her chances with the wolf.

"What are you doing here?" he asked, scanning Calypso and Hill behind her with pale blue, expressionless eyes.

"We're hiking in the canyon," Calypso answered. "We spent the night here. We're just preparing to leave."

The man continued to stare, and the wolf's yellow eyes were also unwavering. Calypso felt a crawl of dread move through her. Had they escaped the battle at the ranch only to fall into far worse hands? She squared her shoulders and stared back at him impassively.

The man moved closer. He was wearing faded jungle camouflage pants and a black windbreaker, and something in the way he moved caused his image to blur into the surrounding shadows, rocks and greenery, and then come into focus again, mirage-like. Ex-Recon, her intuition told her. Silently, on crepe-soled boots, he crept closer until he was standing above her, with the wolf at his feet.

"I won't hurt you," he said, never breaking his stare.

Calypso did not believe him. Everything instinctual was aroused. Red lights flashed and alarm bells clanged beneath her immobility. She felt her body tense, her breath coming in short gasps, and her leg muscles tighten. She knew she should run, but instead watched him warily, feeling already overpowered.

The move was too sudden for her to anticipate. In an instant, he had leapt beside her and her arm was in his vice-like grip. Before she could react or even cry out, he whipped his hand from his jacket pocket and flung a fistful of white powder into her face. She heard Hill's yell and felt the collision of his body against hers as he tried to intervene. Then a wave of dizziness hit her brain and she felt herself slip down, away from the man's grip. Her last impression was of the stones coming up to meet her and then everything went black.

§

A confusion of sounds, like voices on a tape being eaten by a boombox. Through one squinted eye, a sliver of piercing light. The voices warped and gurgled through the background, alternately liquid and viscous. She felt deeply ill. The hard surface under her seemed to be spinning and the centrifugal force of it blasted her out of consciousness again, sending her into a blackness slashed with yellow sabers of light.

§

Light and voices again. A splitting headache. Mouth unbearably dry. Heart hammering arrhythmically. She tried to concentrate, to understand. A mixture of English and Spanish. The word *drug*. A surge of oblivion, overwhelming her like a black wave.

§

Finally, the ground under her stopped spinning. Voices no longer eddied and chuckled around her like fast-flowing water. Still the headache, still the dry mouth, but her heart no longer felt as if it were bursting.

She heard her first coherent sentence: "She ought to be coming out of it soon." English. The voice deep and male. Not the voice of her attacker. She lay still, gathering her strength; gathering her wits.

A hand gripped her shoulder and rocked her, not ungently. "You in there?" The same deep voice. Rocking again. "Come on. It's time to wake up." She thought she detected an element of concern. She tried to speak and heard an unintelligible mutter in what might be her own voice. The hand shook her again.

Calypso opened one eye and winced at blindingly bright light. She clamped her eye closed again and whispered, "Water."

There was a pause and then a hand slid under her neck and her head was bent upwards. A glass was pressed against her lips. Water coursed into her mouth and down her throat. She choked, gagged, began to cough. The coughing made her head ache unbearably.

The hand had not moved from her neck. When the coughing subsided, the voice said, "Take another sip. Not so fast this time. Just a sip."

She sipped. Cool water penetrated the parched recesses of her mouth and a trifle of the desperation subsided behind its fluid promise. She sipped again and then rolled her head back as a wave of dizziness hit her.

"Dizzy." Her voice was scratchy and weak.

"It'll be wearing off soon." The hand went away. She lay inert, savoring the wetness of the water, asking nothing more of herself. Then she slept.

§

When she awoke, there were no voices. Through slitted eyes, she took in a room washed in evening light entering one small, high window set in a wall of roughly plastered stone. Her hand wandered out from her side and felt the abrasion of a wool blanket. She blinked, tried to focus.

Above her, a ceiling of pale plaster was washed with rose in the falling light, with triangles of deep indigo shadow hanging like kites in the corners. She raised her head and caught sight of a crude wooden table and chair and a fire burning low on a small hearth, before her head dropped back of its own weight. She closed her eyes. The nausea had passed, and the headache. Her mind felt clear but she was completely without volition.

She heard a heavy wooden door scrape open and then closed. Footsteps. They stopped next to her bed.

"You're awake." The same male voice. Not unkind. Not frightening. She opened her eyes.

A man of medium height stood over her. He was broad-shouldered and powerful looking despite his age. Calypso put him somewhere in his late sixties. His skin was brown like the local indigenous, but he spoke uninflected English. Black hair salted with white framed a slightly pocked face made handsome by strong bones and deep-set, intelligent eyes.

"You were out a long time."

"How long?" she whispered.

"Twelve hours or more."

"Why?"

"The Devil's Breath."

Calypso shook her head.

"Scopolamine. You got too big a hit."

She rolled her head to see him more clearly and was surprised that he was wearing a black cassock.

"Priest?"

He gazed down at her and said with a small smile, "Of a sort."

Calypso frowned and tried to sit up. The man reached down and restrained her with a hand on her shoulder.

"Better stay down awhile." He reached behind him, dragged the wooden chair beside her bed and sat. "What's your name?"

Calypso was suddenly wary. She and Javier and Rancho Cielo were known throughout the canyons. How could she be sure it was safe to reveal her identity? She countered: "What's yours?"

"You can call me Father Keat." He said it with the same small, self-deprecating smile.

Calypso nodded. "You can call me Jane."

The man nodded with a chuckle. "All right, Jane." He cocked his head and regarded her appraisingly. "So how do you feel?"

"Better now. I thought my heart was going to burst."

He nodded. "Tachycardia. And then bradycardia. Your heart rate was down to thirty-three beats per minute. You had me worried."

"What happened?"

"You met up with Los Lobos, man and wolf. They're quite a team."

"Why did he. . .?"

"It's our policy."

"I don't understand."

"You will. Just rest for now."

Calypso had a sudden rush of remembrance and pushed herself up on one elbow.

"What about Hill?"

Father Keat did not answer. Instead, he took a stout Mexican tumbler of handblown glass from the table and held it again to her lips.

"Drink. You're dehydrated." She drank. "I'll come by later." He stood.

"What about Hill?" she asked again. Even to her, her voice sounded like the wail of a child.

"We'll talk about Mr. Hill later." Father Keat rose, threw a log on the fire and exited, closing the door firmly behind him.

§

Calypso awoke to a deep, mellifluous voice speaking English.

"Hey! You're awake."

She blinked her eyes, frowned, and squinted in the low light. The fire burning on the hearth sent soft, undulant waves of light across the man's face, half of which was burnished by firelight and half hidden deep in shadow. One massive hand rested on a black-clad thigh thick as an oak trunk. The hand was black.

"How are you feeling?"

"Better. Hungry. Thirsty."

The black hand moved, reached, brought the white glass to her lips. "Icepick'll be bringing some food, in a few minutes."

"Icepick?"

"You'll get used to the names. Mine's Lone-R. That's capital-L-o-n-e-dash-capital-R." He smiled down at her serenely. He had huge, dark, wide-set eyes, the kind she had seen in photographs of Tibetan *rinpoches,* that bespoke lifetimes of spiritual evolution. His head was shaved and it shone in the firelight like an orb of onyx. She noticed he wore a black priest's robe like Father Keat's.

"*Father* Lone-R?" she asked, with a ghost of her old verve.

"Not yet. I'm still an acolyte."

"You're wearing the same robes as Father Keat."

A chuckle rumbled out of his vast chest.

"Yeah. We watched *The Matrix* and really dug seein' Keanu Reeves kickin' ass in that black coat. So we decided to wear 'em, too."

"Where am I, Lone-R? Who are you people, anyway?" Despite his impressive size and the rock-hard muscles of his forearm as he served her water, Calypso felt safe with this huge man.

"You're in our monk house, here in the bottom of the canyon. A few miles from Batopilas."

"You're *monks?*"

"Yeah. In a manner of speaking. We call ourselves The Ghosts."

Calypso frowned. Was she still under the influence of The Devil's Breath?

"I don't understand."

"You will."

"Am I safe here?"

He chuckled, again.

"You kiddin'? This place is a fortress. You wouldn't be as safe in the Pentagon!"

"A fortified monastery."

"Exactly." He clenched his hands and cracked his knuckles. It sounded like a pistol going off and Calypso jumped. "That's exactly right. We're a fuckin' fortified monastery."

There was a sharp knock at the door and Lone-R went to answer it. He opened it just as the man on the other side—Icepick, Calypso presumed—was turning his back to give the door another clout with his boot heel. He held a tray of steaming food in both hands and above his black cowboy boots he wore the same style of black robe that Lone-R wore.

As he came to her bedside, Calypso observed him. On this man, the small, high collar of the flowing robe looked appropriate. The skirts moved gracefully, as if the man were a dancer. Above the collar, however, his face was ashen and blank, as if he had spent too many hours in a cell meditating. About seventy, wrinkled and with a thatch of steely gray hair, he exuded an icy chill that forbade any contact. Without speaking, he deposited the tray on the table, turned as if pirouetting, and departed, pulling the door closed almost soundlessly.

After Lone-R had helped her rise from the bed and sit at the table, Calypso tried again.

"I guess what I really mean is," she said, holding the fork poised over her food and shooting him a glance, "am I safe here with all of you?"

Lone-R didn't answer directly. He looked at the floor for several seconds, while Calypso dug into the pile of black beans and rice on her plate and found them disappointingly bland.

"I'm going to tell you a Mexican joke," he said at last. "Up in the Sierra, there's a knock at the door of this little cabin. The owner goes to the door and opens it. On his doorstep there's this seven-foot tall Indian, a real *hijo de la chingada*, wearing a double banderilla, a .9 stuck in his belt, and he's carrying an AK-47.

"The Indian says to the guy, 'I'm a householder and I need your help.'

"The guy's pretty tough-lookin' himself, with three days growth of beard and a pistol stuck in the waistband of his pants. He doesn't even answer. He just takes out his gun and shoots the Indian dead.

"The guy's pal gets up from the table, where he's been drinking tequila and taking little hits of coke from the end of his knife, and he comes over and looks down at the dead Indian and says 'That guy was a real *hijo de la chingada. Muy peligroso,* very dangerous. *Tiene el derecho*. You did the right thing to shoot him.'

"The guy looks at his friend and says, 'You fool! I didn't shoot him because he was dangerous; I shot him because he was a householder!'" Lone-R threw back his head and laughed uproariously.

Calypso managed a half-hearted smile. She understood the joke because she was inured to the upside-down, macho humor of northern Mexico that vaunted death. No man of the Sierra would admit to being afraid of a seven-foot Indian *hijo de la chigada*, but his overblown machismo would demand death to tender feelings for a householder in trouble.

"Good one," she whispered.

"So how can I tell if you're safe or not? You're no seven-foot Indian—but you're probably a householder." He watched for her reaction with his fathomless eyes.

Calypso kept her head down and toyed with her food. "What do you want?" she asked finally. "Money?"

Lone-R shrugged. "Not for me to say."

"Whose job is it to say?"

"The brotherhood's. It'll be put before all the Ghosts."

"What will be?"

Lone-R grunted and shrugged. "Your fate."

"And what about my friend? Is he okay?"

Lone-R shrugged again and turned away. "*¿Quien sabe?*" he muttered. "Who knows?"

§

The food must have been laced with drugs. When Calypso came to, she was in a barren room of the same plastered stone, lying on the floor on a bare mattress. A flat screen TV was playing a rerun of *The Sopranos* without the sound. She tried to sit up, was hit with a headache as if a hatchet had been buried in her skull, and flopped back with a groan.

She lay looking around the simple room: the bare, ticking-covered mattress and the television made up the furnishings. There was a hearth, on which a fire had burned down to embers, and a small barred window. In the corner a door stood wide open, revealing a tiny cubicle holding a listing toilet and a basin with exposed pipes underneath.

She sat up, holding her head in her hands to stifle the headache. Her mouth was dry as dust. She staggered to her feet and made her looping, weak-kneed way to the window. Even though she was accustomed to the canyons, where the ground refused all horizontality in favor of universal verticality, the view out the window made her gasp. She was perched high on a cliff that plummeted at least a thousand feet, to be lost in the tops of trees. Immediately below her she could see, by craning her head, that there were two stories of stone building beneath her, blending seamlessly into the living rock below.

She reeled to the door and tried the latch. Locked. She went to the bathroom, used the toilet, washed her hands, dashed water on her face, and drank from the faucet. Then she collapsed back onto the mattress, pulled her knees into fetal posture, and stayed that way for hours.

Sunlight swung a slow arc through the room and then, with a burst of rose light against the eastern wall, died. From where she lay, she watched a few stars emerge, pale and glittering against the lingering electric blue of the sky. There was no sound except her shallow breathing and the shove of wind against the outer walls.

Something in the austerity and loftiness of the room soothed her. Despite Rancho Cielo's vertiginous perch on the edge of the Urique Canyon and the miles of unimproved roads between it and the nearest town, the house was often as busy as a Greyhound bus terminal. Ranch hands, indigenous women and children coming for classes, and local elders holding political meetings with Javier, all passed through, day and night. She and Javier lived busy lives.

She lay listening to the whine of the wind against the window and fell into a deep reverie that took her far from her fear. Something in her situation haunted her with its familiarity, and she thought of her manuscript and the story of the locket. She fingered the necklace through her shirt. Surely, if the Ghosts hadn't stolen it while she was unconscious, it was a good sign.

And then it hit her: Lone-R, huge and black, sitting beside her bed! The strangeness of her predicament and the odd parallel of his presence swept her back nine hundred years, to the part of the locket's story that she had related to Hill, as they navigated the cave.

ʖ

Chapter 6

The Story of Blanche de Muret Continues

It was not my good fortune to fall straight into the water below, but I must tumble in air, barking elbows and knees and head upon the rocks that lined the well. I grazed my scalp and it all but knocked me senseless. It was as if I were within my very worst nightmare of falling. And all the while there was a terrible, high-pitched sound accompanying me that I did not realize until later was my own scream of terror.

The shock of icy water, as I plunged headfirst into it, brought me again to my senses. I went down and down into absolute blackness, fighting with arms and legs to slow my dive, and then to regain the surface. I came puffing and blowing into air again and clung straight away to the rocks of the wall, although they were slimy and smelled most dank.

As I hung there kicking my legs to stay afloat, my eyes slowly adjusted to the gloom. Around me, I could see nothing, so profound was the darkness but looking above, my eye could follow the shaft of the well to where it ended in a dazzling dot of light, far above me.

In very truth, I did not know whether to congratulate myself for having survived this ordeal, or to be bitterly disappointed that my fall had not been my demise. For it seemed my condition was now hopeless beyond redemption and that I were better dead.

Just as I was thinking that my situation could not be worse, it swiftly became so. I looked above me and, around the light at the top of the shaft, I could see dark dots that must surely be the heads of those who were peering within, hoping for sight of me. Then I saw something cross the disk of light and fall, and I realized in terror that they had thrown the bucket into the well!

Hastily, I filled my lungs and dove, and not a moment to spare, for the bucket hit the water above me like an explosion. In the darkness, I felt it drift down to my right, as I fought once more toward the surface.

The bucket was immediately pulled up again, and then those on the surface commenced pelting me with stones. These came rattling down the shaft like thunder and filled me with terror. I dove again and felt a stone graze my shoulder as it plummeted past me through the inky water into oblivion.

I stayed beneath the water until I could no longer and then I surfaced. Still rocks rattled down toward me, but I must have air or die.

As I struggled, gasping and thrashing in the water, I heard a sudden noise that sounded like an exclamation of astonishment, a sound I was sure that I myself had not made. As I blinked water from my eyes and looked frantically about me, I saw a faint glow coming from the far side of the shaft.

To my amazement the light grew brighter, until I could plainly see an opening, like that of the tunnel of a mine, and therein, straining my own credulity, stood a woman, bucket in hand, staring at me in alarm.

I floundered toward her and reached out my hand to her in desperation, and she, in a reflex of common human solicitude, reached back to me. Our hands met and she pulled me toward her. At that moment, a stone came racketing down the shaft and as I was almost saved, struck me on the head with such force that I was instantly senseless.

§

Now begins what is surely the strangest part of this chronicle, for if I had not myself experienced what follows, I doubt not I should believe another such account to be a lie. And yet, these things did happen to me and I am rendering as honest an account of them as I am able. I beg the reader, therefore, to remember my status as a highborn lady and to consider my character, known by all to be unblemished, as he reads what next befell me and to credit me with speaking the truth.

For when I came again to myself, I found I was in a most strange and marvelous setting! What first I saw was the face of her whom I assumed to be my rescuer, bending over me in honest concern. As I came slowly back to myself and was able to look around, I found I was lying in the oddest chamber imaginable.

It appeared I must be still underground. The ceiling and walls of this room were hung with stones in the shape of rough cylinders and cones. Some hung from the roof, pointed at the ends, like daggers suspended there. Others rose from the sandy floor on which I lay, like teeth embedded in a jaw. Still others extended from the floor full to the ceiling, making columns. And withal, these shapes were of the purest white, but in the light of the many oil lamps burning there, glowed with a moving and swirling opalescence like the aurora borealis that once my dear father showed me on a cold winter's night in Muret.

So odd was all this that I immediately surmised that I was dead and had arrived at some wondrous Purgatory or the antechamber to Hell itself. This caused me great confusion, between terror and wonder, at the beauty of a place so ill reputed. And so I lay for many minutes with both my eyes and my wits wandering freely.

About me were other people moving around the room, performing various tasks. There was nothing particularly odd about their faces. They looked much like the people of the world I had just departed. I was drawn, however, to notice their clothing, which was spotlessly white, but rather than falling to their ankles, ended at their knees. This same simple tunic was worn by men and woman alike.

At last, the shock that had held me immobile released me and the pains of all my injuries came throbbing back. I was tormented by a headache and upon exploring my pate with careful fingers, discovered a bump as big as a hen's egg on the top of my skull. I drew my hand away and found it bloody. My elbows, too, and my knees were scraped and bloodied and I was beginning to be cold as well, for I lay still in my wet clothing and without a blanket.

Now, to add to my miseries, came a new shock, for there was a movement on the far side of the room, and through a low door appeared a man more curious than I had ever seen. I knew instantly that I was in the presence of the very Devil Himself.

The man who approached me was a good two meters tall, with huge shoulders and a body powerful as a bull's. His skin was as black as midnight and emblazoned upon his forehead, because it was branded into his flesh, was the sign of the Cross.

I shrank from him in terror. At this, he stopped and came no further nigh me but began to address me in a strange tongue. When he saw that I understood not a word, he spoke again, in a language different from the first. This he did several times until, as clear as the May sky, he asked me in French, "*Êtes-vouz française?*"

I could barely speak from fright but answered in a weak voice, saying "*Oc!*"

He smiled then, a huge smile full of teeth and so jolly that I ceased to fear him, even if he were the Devil. Then he told me that if I would permit him, he would take me to a place where my wounds could be tended and where I could rest comfortably.

To this I readily assented, as I now ached from top to bottom. My pains seemed to be growing steadily rather than diminishing, and I was shuddering from cold.

It was nothing for him to scoop me up in his arms, as I have seen shepherds lift up a little lost lamb. This act was both so tender and so inherently painful that I began to cry, and once the tears had started, I could not stop them to save my soul.

He carried me through the doorway and down many strange corridors glittering with crystals and hanging with the long rocks. Everywhere, light was provided by oil lamps burning in niches along the walls. I lost all track of the countless turnings we made, but at last he brought me to a chamber wherein was a bed and on this, he lay me with infinite tenderness and then withdrew.

Soon he returned, bringing with him a small woman with a round and serious face, withered like a winter apple and her gray hair gathered into a knot at the nape of her neck. This task accomplished, he bowed from the waist to me and departed.

The woman carried with her a basket filled with small jars stoppered in crystal and semiprecious stones, carved in delightful shapes. Also, she had small bits of clean cloth and a pail of warm water that, by its scent, was tinctured with herbs. With these, as soon as she had relieved me of my dress, she began to wash, anoint and bind my many wounds.

We quickly found we could not communicate in a common language and as I was suffering greatly, I lay back quietly, glad that I did not have to speak. Finally, her work accomplished, she covered me with a soft blanket.

Just as she was finishing, a second woman arrived bearing a bowl of soup. As my elbows were now tightly bandaged, I could no longer bend my arms, and so this kind woman held the bowl for me as I drank the warm broth, which had an excellent effect on my chilled bones. These two then withdrew and I soon slept.

ꟸ

When I awoke, I knew not whether it was night or day, for this community under the ground had no sun. I was surprised to find the black man sitting beside my bed, patiently awaiting my awakening.

"Where am I, please, sir?" I asked, for all that had befallen me had left me most confused. "Am I in Hell then?"

At this, he laughed a most uproarious laugh! *"Ma pauvre petite,"* he responded, "you have never been farther from it! By falling down the well, you have entered a heaven such as this world scarcely dreams of. You are greatly blessed by your accident this day!"

Whereupon I told him with great dignity that I had not happened to fall down the well but had escaped thereunto, and how I had preferred death in this manner to the fate which might befall me. He listened gravely to my tale and asked me many questions. For all that he was such a strange looking man, his manner was very courtly and I was sure that his lineage was noble.

Now the second woman reappeared, bearing a tray of steaming food, and my new friend withdrew so that I should eat in privacy. Again, as before, the woman fed me with kindest concern. The food was delicious, being rice nicely seasoned with herbs and mixed with vegetables. There was a cup of warm, fresh goat's milk, as well.

When my meal had been cleared away, the black man returned and resumed his position by my bed. As soon as he was seated, I asked him, "Please, sir, can you tell me what manner of place this is into which I have fallen? For I have nothing in my experience in this world to explain it."

He answered that he would respond to my question, but in a very roundabout manner. Looking wryly at my bandaged limbs, he made a small joke, saying that it seemed I had time to spare and wouldn't be rushing off soon. So he began to regale me with his own story, telling how he had come to this odd place himself.

§

The Story of Caspar, King of Nubia

I am, he began, the king of a country of which you doubtless know little, if at all. Perhaps you know my country as the ancient land of Kush but to me it is called Nubia. It is one hundred days hard march to the south of this city of Cairo, or Al-Qahira, as my people call it.

When I left my country, there were sixty of my subjects with me. Ours is a Christian nation, and I had the intention to visit all the holy places of this world and they were eager to accompany me. So terrible was the journey northward, however, that by the time we reached Jerusalem, which was our first destination, only ten of these good souls remained.

I stayed in Jerusalem for six months, regaining my strength, and then I journeyed on to Constantinople. Again, the traveling was so desperately hard that when I reached that miraculous city, only two of my companions remained. We who survived gazed at that jewel of the Bosphorus in wonder, for we had not believed there could be so rich a city in all the world.

It had high walls and mighty towers that enclosed it all around and rich palaces and lofty churches, of which there were so many that one could not believe it unless he had seen it with his own eyes. By her length and breadth and her richness, she is surely the queen of all cities.

The Emperor, Alexius the Third, received me and my diminished retinue most kindly. He was amazed to see that a black man could yet be a Christian, and to learn that in my country all the citizens are Christians, and that when a child is born and baptized, a cross like mine is branded upon its forehead.

I was to the Emperor as great a marvel as his city was to me. And so he invited me to tarry there, which invitation I gladly accepted, for I had taken a fever in our wanderings through Syria and much needed rest.

The Emperor lodged me in a very rich abbey and made me the guest of it for as long as I wished to stay. What a joy it was to awaken in my chamber, high in a tower room, to the early sun streaming over that fair city of domes and towers, to hear the church bells ringing in the morning in a hundred voices, and to watch the swallows twittering and swooping over it all like spirits of gladness itself! You might imagine that I would be tempted to give up my pilgrimage and to languish there forever—and you would be correct.

Even after my fever had passed and my health was restored, I remained in Constantinople, for it was an infinite delight and every day's exploration brought new discoveries.

One of my chief pleasures was to visit the Hagia Sophia, the great cathedral dedicated to Holy Wisdom, for it was wisdom I sought on my pilgrimage.

It is impossible to describe the vastness of its dome, rising against the sky, effortless as prayer itself. Its interior was as lavish as the exterior was elegant in its austerity. The choir was adorned with silver and the place where the priest stands was upheld by twelve columns of silver. The walls were covered in holy icons of exquisite rarity and beauty. Upon the altar were twelve crosses, two of which were carved like trees and were taller than a man.

There was a wonderful table set with precious stones, with a great gem in the center. On the altar were forty chalices of gold and silver candelabra so numerous I could not count them. And there were many vases of silver, used during the greatest festivals.

There was a Gospel used to celebrate the mysteries that was painted most wondrously with rare pigments and forty censers of pure gold. In cupboards along the walls were other incomparable treasures in such quantities that it would be impossible to count them. All this in the Church of Hagia Sophia alone, and still there was the richness of the Church of Sainte-Marie des Blachernes, in whose complex the holy relics of the Virgin Mary were housed, and hundreds of other churches, as well, to admire and wonder over.

Yet my heart was not content, for when I embarked on my pilgrimage I did so with one prayer in my heart and this was it: that somewhere in my wanderings I might meet and study with a living saint so steeped in the Holy Spirit that he would be able to ignite my slumbering spirit, as well.

For you see, I had in my country a wife and three children, whom I loved beyond all things. In the year before my journey began, each of these beloved ones was carried away into death. Two of my children fell ill with fever and died. My oldest child, a son, fell from a cliff while hunting and was shattered like an egg.

At last, there was only my wife and me and she was with child. Crushed as my heart was, I had hopes that we might begin again to build our family. The grief of our losses, however, caused complications with her pregnancy. She began to deliver early and in so doing lost great quantities of blood. She died, taking our unborn child with her.

So great was my grief that I went quite mad. I raved against the God whom I had worshipped from my childhood and I questioned His mercy and justice. At last, after days when I was too morose to attend to affairs of state or even to feed myself, I reached a decision. I would go on pilgrimage and seek through all the world for one who, through their great saintliness, would answer for me this one terrible and burning question: *Why?*

I left my brother to govern the country in my stead, and with the sixty brave souls I have already mentioned, I set out. So great was my bitterness that I watched my companions drop along the way without surprise. I considered myself accursed, so that everyone around me would sicken and die. My wish was that I, too, might pass into death and so leave my troubles behind me but this fate was not to be mine.

§

The time in Constantinople healed my body and brought back to my fevered mind an interest in things of this world but it did nothing to heal my soul. Still I longed, and with growing ardor, for one whose touch or look would be a balm to me. I sought the impossible, for in my madness, I came to believe that only the Savior Himself could heal me.

So after many months as the guest of Alexius, I took my leave and embarked upon a ship bound for Rome, leaving behind me my two remaining subjects, who were happily adapted to their new city. In Rome, I gained audience with Pope Innocent III and while I found him a stern man and an able administrator, I knew immediately that he had nothing that would soothe my wounded spirit. He gave me his blessing when I departed the Vatican that day, but I left its gates as barren as when I entered.

I did not tarry in the city of Rome, for after Constantinople it was squalid and hostile with political strivings. I once again embarked, this time on a boat bound for your country, France.

After a long sea voyage, I passed through the Straits of Gibraltar and up the Atlantic coast to an obscure port in Normandy, from whence I made my way to the great Abbey of Mont St-Michel. There I was received kindly but the Benedictine fathers had nothing that would feed my growing spiritual hunger. So I soon traveled on to Paris, where I beheld the great Cathédrale de Notre Dame under construction and prayed before the relics of Sainte Geneviève, the patron saint of that fair city.

All the while I traveled, I repeated my prayer again and again: to be led by the Goodness of God to a great saint, with whom in personal conversation I might discuss the sad events of my life, and through whose pure emission of Divine energies I might be instantly and completely healed in my soul. Perhaps you will think this was an heretical desire. For does not the church claim for itself the right to forgive sins and to intercede in our behalf with the Savior? Perhaps you believe that I was asking too much of God or the wrong thing. But as I traveled, I grew in the conviction that, sooner or later, my faith would be rewarded, and I would meet one of those holy ones of whom Jesus said, *Ye are as gods. All that I do, you can do and more.*

Departing Paris, I turned southward, intending to go to Spain to the shrine of Saint James at Compostela. I booked passage on a boat heading down the Rhone River and there, a strange thing happened.

ꕤ

We had stopped one day, somewhere in the heart of your fair country at a little village, to take on grain and to purchase perishables for our evening meal. As I wandered through the streets of this nameless place, an old woman approached me.

Her hair was long and wild and gray. She had no teeth and her clothing was an exotic mixture of gay colors and tattered rags.

She was, it seems, a gypsy, that being an ancient race called Romany, whose origins are so distant in antiquity that no one remembers them. These people, as you may know, are nomadic and make their way through the countryside of all Europe, pillaging chicken flocks, mending pots and telling fortunes. And this is exactly what this old dame offered to do for me.

Having nothing better to while away an afternoon in a small and sleepy village, I agreed. She sat me down on a wall beneath a shady apple tree and took my black hand into her grimed and wrinkled one. Long she gazed upon my palm, making grunts and wheezes as she did so. She had the animated expression of a monkey I used to keep near me at my court, and I was becoming increasingly amused by her expressive brow and was about to burst into laughter, when she fixed me with a stare as burning as coals themselves and began to speak.

"I see," she said, "that you have a strange and terrible destiny. You are one imposed by fate to lose everything, that you may find something of still greater value. The first half of your life has been spent in loss and grief and terrible suffering. You have wandered long and far."

She had now my full attention, as you may well imagine. For here, it seemed, was the first person on my journey who understood part or perhaps all of what I had suffered, and that which I was seeking. No longer amusing myself at her expense, I begged her to continue.

She regarded my palm another long while. Finally, she said with great compassion in her voice, "That which you seek is not here, but you are drawing closer. You must continue southward three days more, to the *Bouches-du-Rhone*. There, in the swamps of the *Camargue*, you will find a clue that will lead you to your goal. I can say no more."

With that, she dropped my hand and turned to depart. I hastened beside her, offering her a large sum of money, for I felt in my heart that she had seen me truly and guided me well. But this old woman, who had spent her life, I was sure, bereft of all material comforts and begging and scratching for the meagerest living, refused my coins.

"No, my son," she said, piercing me again with her burning eyes, "one never accepts payment from those who are involved in their true destiny. Only from *les perdues*—the lost ones." And with that, she turned firmly from me and stumped away down the street.

You may be sure that I passed the next three days on the boat in a fever of anticipation. The long stops at obscure villages seemed now a torment, and we could never break our night's mooring early enough in the morning to satisfy my urgency.

On the third day, we arrived at the river town of Arles, where my boat had achieved her destination. I questioned the captain closely before I disembarked. "Are there swamps near at hand?" I asked him.

"*Mais oc!*" he answered immediately, as if it were the most self-evident thing in the world. Pointing down the river he said, "You may find a boat of some local fisherman and go down river, clear to Les-Saintes-Maries-de-la-Mer. There, you will find swamps, to be sure."

The charms of this famous town of Arles, of ancient and fascinating Roman manufacture, were completely lost on me. Even though I could see the Roman coliseum rising on the hill above the stone quays, I was not tempted to investigate the sights. My one and only objective was to locate a boat going down river to the swamps.

To this end, I went to take my breakfast in an inn nearby the quay, hoping to find there some local folk who could guide me. My luck was good, for as I was relishing my meat, I chanced to overhear a man saying he was leaving momentarily for Les-Saintes-Maries. Immediately, I accosted him and begged passage on his boat, and as I offered him a good price, he was only too happy to oblige.

Before the morning was half passed, I was seated in the prow of a small fishing boat as it made good progress down toward the sea. The river was broad and deep, the color of a turtle's carapace. The wind was coming at our backs and the captain raised a small sail, so that we seemed to fly over the smooth waters.

As we went along, I asked this good man some questions about our destination. In answer, he commenced a tale, which was so strange and wondrous that I will tell it to you now, in its entirety.

§

The Fisherman's Tale

We are a blessed people, began this worthy man, for we have received, in times long past, the holy presence of the very companions of the Christ. This was seven years after the murder of our dear Lord and Savior upon the Cross.

The Romans in Jerusalem would harry and persecute His followers still. Finally, those closest to Him were brought before Pilate, as was Our Lord before them. The great man was tormented by his role in the murder of the Lord, and could not bring himself to pronounce the death sentence upon these good people. So to relieve his conscience, he decreed that they were to be set adrift in an open boat, with no rudder and no sails. This was as good as a death sentence, mind you, but Pilate could flatter himself, you see, with the lie that he was actually saving their lives. But in this, as you will see, the hand of Our Lord was active.

So it came to pass that five people were placed in a boat on the shore of the sea: Mary Salome, who was the aunt of Our Dear Lord; Mary Jacob, the wife of His uncle; Mary Magdalene and her sister, Saint Martha; and Joseph of Arimathea, he who supplied the sepulcher for our Blessed Savior. When they were all loaded aboard, with no provisions even for the sake of appearances, they were cut adrift and the out-going tide caught them and bore them away.

Many there were who stood upon the shore and wept, all followers of Our Lord who grieved to see their saints thus misused, but who were unable to help their cause. Among them was a servant girl named Sarah, whose wailing rose above all others, for she had great love of her mistress, Martha.

Now, they be some who say it different, mind you. The gypsy folk call this Sarah *Sarah-la-Kali*, meaning Sara the Black, and they say she was as black as you yourself, sir. And then they be those—who whisper it, to be sure—who say this Sarah was the daughter of Mary Magdalene, and that the father of this Sarah was Our Lord Himself!"

The fisherman stopped to cross himself conspicuously, before continuing.

Now, as the boat was cut loose and began to move from the shore, this Sarah broke from the others, ran to the quay and without hesitation threw herself into the waves. She floundered her way toward the boat and upon reaching it—more by agency of the waves than by her skill as a swimmer, I'll wager—she begged to be pulled on board.

All the passengers decreed she should turn back, for they knew their voyage was a dark-fated one, doomed beyond doubt to thirst, privation and then capsizing in the first rough sea, their boat being oarless and rudderless as it was.

But the girl was half-drowned already. She swore that she would give up all struggle and sink like a stone, rather than return to shore.

Finally, her will won her what she desired. One of the Marys threw her coat upon the water, and it magically turned into a raft, sir, which buoyed the girl up until she could be pulled aboard by the others.

In normal course of events, a boat without rudder, oars, or sails would be swept out into the open sea, there to capsize, when the winds grew strong over the open waters and the waves were high. You must see, however, that this was no ordinary vessel, for these passengers were not regular persons but those especially beloved of Our Lord. And so it happened that the sea remained calm and a wind was always at their back, pushing them along.

After many a day, God in His Mercy brought these poor outcasts to rest on this very coast, at the very place to which we are journeying now, named after the three Saints Mary, come from the sea. And each as hale and hearty as if naught had been amiss with their voyage.

Mary Salome, Mary Jacob, and this black Sarah, too, founded a church on the very spot where they came ashore, on the site of an ancient pagan temple, they say. Martha went off to slay a dragon in Tarascon. And Mary Magdalene straight away went up into the hills to live all by herself in a cave. They say each day she was raised to the cliff tops to pray by a band of angels. And Joseph went over the sea to Britain, carrying with him the Holy Grail.

It is a curious tale, is it not? And strange it is that, as the church is dedicated to the Marys, it is really Saint Sarah who reigns there. When we come there, you will find a statue of her under the altar, in the crypt. She is dressed in fancy garments brought by the pilgrims, but her face, sir, is completely black, because of which they call her "The Egyptian." It is a face of such beauty that I believe, sir, you will be moved by her, in spite of yourself.

ʖ

The Story of Caspar, King of Nubia Continues

Thus saying, he ended his tale. My pulse pounded, for I felt assured that he had given me the clue of which the gypsy had spoken. I now was determined to proceed directly to the crypt in Les-Saintes-Maries-de-la-Mer.

By now, the main channel of the Rhone had narrowed, with side channels branching off. The fisherman explained that we had reached the estuary, where the great river sank into a maze of marshes and winding waterways, before finally flowing into the sea.

He began to turn his boat skillfully this way and that, maneuvering through the mazy channels, where any but the most experienced person would speedily have become irrevocably lost. He told me that many there were who had come this way to their peril, for the swamps were filled with quicksand bogs into which, once fallen, one would never again emerge.

At last, toward evening, we debouched from a narrow channel so shallow that it had been necessary to pole our way for the final hour. Before us lay a tranquil lagoon, turned coppery in the failing light. To my amazement, it was brilliant pink along its margins from the millions of flamingoes that roosted there, for as the fisherman explained, they annually migrated from Africa to those shores. This sight was so startling and so lovely that it was some time before I raised my eyes and espied our destination, the lights in the distance marking the little village of Les-Saintes-Maries-de-la-Mer.

It was with great relief that I stepped from the fishing boat, and my knees both gave great cracks as if to agree that they, too, were glad to be free of such cramped quarters. So uplifted did I feel, that I invited the fisherman to have supper with me at the local inn of his choice and he gladly accepted.

As we walked from the shore the short distance into town, I became aware of an unusual turmoil in the streets, which were very crowded for so small a village. Music from lutes, along with singing and the click of castanets, arose from the alleyways on all sides. Along the streets, we soon encountered gypsy wagons painted in bright colors and drawn by sway-backed nags. "Whatever is going on in this place?" I exclaimed to my new friend.

"Did I not tell you?" he cried. "I have missed the best part of my tale, then. Why, in May and October, gypsies from all countries converge on this village to throw a great festival in honor of Sarah, who is their patron saint!"

ʃ

It was full in May and the festival obviously was well underway. After supper, I parted with my fisherman friend and made my way to *La Place de l'Eglise*, where stood the solid and beauty-less bulk of the Church of the Marys. It was built of a light-colored stone, very rough and simple, and looked as much a small fortress as a church. It seemed an unlikely place for me to find my promised solace, after so many of the grand monuments of that continent had failed me in that regard.

I had intended to go straight away into the crypt to see this black saint, Sarah, for I thought that perhaps it was fitting, after all, that one who was black like me should prove to be my deliverer. But my intention was thwarted by the throngs of people that mobbed the church.

Around me was the most unusual assortment of folk I had ever seen, even in the bazaars of Constantinople. For these were gypsies, who had come from disparate parts of the world and their costumes reflected this. The women wore petticoats of bright colors, embroidered shawls, and tortoise shell combs stuck into their long, coarse, black hair. The men wore vests, many of them embroidered with bright designs, and hats that shaded their already dark eyes. They were there by the thousands, and every one of them was striving to enter the little Church of the Marys.

Several times I attempted to enter, only to be repulsed and swept away on the tides of the mob. I could but think of Sarah, floundering in the surf, for this experience gave me a fuller appreciation of her determination.

At last I had to admit that I would not be able to enter the church that night, and I went to find lodgings. To my surprise, there was yet a room in one of the inns, this being, I suppose, because the gypsies came equipped with their homes drawn behind them. I fell into bed and was soon fast asleep, despite the cacophony that rose to my window from the street below, of music, shouts, singing, crying children, and neighing horses.

§

Sometime in the early hours of the morning, I awoke with a start, unsure where I might be, as the perpetual traveler often is. When I had reoriented myself, I realized that I had awakened because a profound silence had finally fallen on the streets. I arose and peered from my window to discover that not a soul moved in the moonlight. My hour to meet Saint Sarah had come at last!

I made my way down the steep stairs of the inn, groping like a blind man in the darkness. The night air was almost cold that May night and carried a pungent smell that I could not define but was, perhaps, an amalgam of smoke from gypsy camps and the prevailing smells of the surrounding marshes. I moved down the street like a shadow and felt my blackness to be a protective cloak, given to me by my good mother, the night.

I feared that I would find the church doors closed and bolted, but when I arrived there, this was not the case. The doors were still thrown wide open and within the sanctuary votive lamps were flickering. I entered warily, expecting momentarily to be accosted by some night watchman or vigilant priest. As I moved further into the church, however, I could see plainly that I had the place completely to myself.

Now, I wondered how I might find my way into the crypt, but this question, too, was soon answered. For here was a very unusual construction, with the altar raised above the floor of the rest of the church and, right below it, a low stone arch through which steps led downward into the earth. From the semicircle of the arch, a glow, as of internal fires burning, was coloring the stones a dull red. With wonder as to what I was about to discover, I stooped under the arch and set my foot upon the stairs.

I had been before in the crypts of many churches, during my days investigating Constantinople, and they were invariably dark, cool places, dank, and smelling of mold. What amazement did I feel, then, as with each step into the crypt of Saint Sarah, I felt heat rising to meet me and the light intensifying!

Descending but a few steps, I reached the crypt itself, which was a simple curving vault of stone, so low that at its edges I could not stand upright. Keeping to the center where the ceiling almost grazed my scalp, I advanced, struck with wonder. For there in the right hand corner stood the Saint, robed in a crimson gown of silk, and surrounded by a veritable bonfire of half-burned tapers.

How long I stood, gazing awestruck, I cannot say. I stared into the sweet, solemn face of the Saint, and she stared back. She had a tiny nose, high cheekbones, and a pointed chin. The light of the tapers played across her painted eyes, making them flicker and dance.

The heat of the place was almost unbearable and seemed too much to be accounted for by the flames of the candles. The entire room seemed to pulsate and throb, as if I were within a living heart. The air fairly crackled with an energy I was past attempting to define. For suddenly, I was moved to throw myself on the floor at her feet and worship there, and as I did so, my heart broke open and all the pent-up grief and rage came pouring out in a molten tide.

Never will I know how long I lay there sobbing. But when I came back to myself, a pale daylight was seeping down the stairs from the church above, the candles had all burned out, and my face, embedded with grit from the floor, lay in a puddle of my own tears.

The footsteps of the first pilgrims of the day echoed across the floor above me and I arose hastily, wiping my cheeks on my sleeves. Saint Sarah still stood in her corner, looking stern now and forbidding, without the light of the candles playing across her. Yet the chamber still pulsed with heat and energy, although I knew the dawn above must be a chilly one.

I groped along the wall until I found the little table where the candles were displayed for purchase, dropped some coins into the iron box and took my taper. As I advanced toward the Saint, I realized that there were no flames left from which to light my candle, and I felt my heart would break at the prospect of leaving this place without having lighted a candle there.

Drawn by an invisible magnetism, I stepped to within three feet of Sarah, holding my candle before me. Suddenly with a small sound like a blown out breath, the wick of my candle burst into flame! I nearly dropped it in my astonishment!

The first pilgrim came down the stairs behind me, his feet scratching on the grit. I stood transfixed but a moment longer, staring into the face, so still and inscrutable, of The Egyptian. Then I inserted my taper into its holder, turned and fled the crypt.

§

I made my way through the awakening streets, not thinking of a destination, only attempting to put as much distance as possible between myself and the crypt of *l'Eglise-Les-Saintes-Maries*. At length I found myself on the shore of the sea and, unable to proceed further, I perched on a big rock. There I sat for many hours, mindlessly watching the tepid waves roll up the beach and flow ever back again.

I could not think on what had befallen me in the night, for it was too strange and too affecting. I can tell to you, now, what I could not admit to myself that morning: that in that last instant before I fell to worship at the feet of the Saint, her dark and placid face was transmuted. For in that moment, so delicate that my heart ceased beating for fear of rupturing it, I saw the face of my beloved wife hovering like a vaporous mask over the Saint's, there in the candlelight, and she smiled at me sweetly and with infinite love. This it was that punctured the blister of my grief and released those long-held toxins.

Many times that day by the sea I laid my head upon my knees and wept for all that I had lost. But in these tears was balm. No longer did I rave and rage under the delusion of my birth, for I had been told since childhood that I was king, and all things must obey my will. There by the sea I grieved as a simple man grieves his losses, and in so doing began to heal.

§

I stayed upon the rock until the setting of the sun. As the waters of the Mediterranean lay gilded at my feet, I felt the pangs of hunger and came back into my body at last. So

I arose and made my way back to the town, aware as I walked that for the first time in many, many months, my heart, if not completely at peace, at least did not gnaw with anguish in my breast. Rather, my limbs felt loose and strong and my head clear and open to receive something new.

In this state I arrived on the Place de l'Eglise, seeking a tavern I had noticed the day before, from whence the smells of cooking food were particularly inviting. The pace of the gypsy festivities seemed to have accelerated, a fact which the tavern keeper confirmed. More and more of this odd race were arriving each day, and there was excitement in the renewal of old acquaintances and the forging of new bonds. Several weddings, he said, had occurred that day, and the dancing and singing and feasting would go on until all hours of the night.

After my supper, I roamed the streets, stopping to listen to the music of various groups gathered there and to watch the dancing of their women, which was sensual and haunting. As I stood in the background, leaning against the wall of a building and robed in shadows, I felt invisible in my blackness. For the first time since the death of my family, loneliness stabbed my heart. For so long my rage had armored me, but now I was as one stripped of all defenses, and these poignant celebrations of the gypsies but accentuated my isolation in the world.

As if this feeling were a beacon that called to itself its antidote; however, I was suddenly aware that a man had come quietly to stand by my side. In the shadows and dancing firelight, his face was obscure, but what I could see of it gave me quite a shock. Here was a wild and dangerous-looking character, indeed!

He was a small man, dark as a chestnut, and his right eye was sealed shut by a terrible scar that ran from the angle of his jaw to the center of his forehead. His hair was cut at jaw length and stuck out in all directions, like the mane of a lion, and was of the blackest black. He wore a rumpled shirt under a shabby vest and baggy pants stuffed into boots scuffed and worn almost past serviceability.

I felt sure that he had come close to me only to cut my throat and rob me. I drew back from him in fear, for all that I was half again his height and might have broken him over my knee like limb wood, if such were my desire. Still, he alarmed me, for his one good eye was inscrutable in its blackness, and he had about him a wild and fierce energy. If I were to awaken in the deep watches of the night with such a one bending over me, I would be sure the hour of my judgment had arrived!

He smiled at me in such a way that every blackened tooth in his head was revealed, but it was a smile without mirth. "I frightened you," he said, and it was a statement, not a question.

"You startled me," I replied gruffly, for I did not want to show weakness to this man.

"You are alone here," he said, again as a statement. "I saw you at the tavern. Come with me to my camp and join my family. We are celebrating the wedding of my nephew tonight, and there is a feast laid out."

I immediately refused him, for I suspected that his intention was to lure me out by the lagoon and there assault and rob me.

He cocked his head and smiled again, nodding in a knowing way, and fixed me with his good eye, in the same manner as the parrots that were kept in my court in Nubia. This mannerism had always endeared these wise birds to me, so I was predisposed to hear what next he said to me.

"The solitude of a king is his safety," he said softly, "but the solitude of a common man is loneliness." So saying, he turned from me and began to slip away through the crowd.

ʃ

Suddenly, I was as desperate to go with him as I formerly had been eager to avoid him. My heart, in a quick flaring, told me that this was the clue I sought in the swamps of the Camargue. Hastily, I shouldered my way into the crowd, which was closing behind him like the sea around a fish.

Several times I thought I had lost him, for the light was poor and the press of the crowd was great. Because he was a small man, he slipped easily through the throng, while I must bull my way through clumsily. But each time, I would espy him again, moving like a minnow through water grass, and my rudeness was great as I pushed all in my path aside to follow him.

When at last I came to the path that led down to the encampment by the lagoon, I could see him hurrying ahead, for the moon was gibbous and gave a little light. I relinquished my pride and called out to him, saying, "Wait, my friend! I have changed my mind!"

He did not stop but slowed his step, and I hurried to catch up to him. Without turning to me, he continued on and I followed as we entered the encampment. He knew his way through clusters of wagons and past campfires that looked all the same to me. Music was coming from all sides, children were running and playing hide-and-seek among the carts, and the whole was lit by both blue moonlight and the flickering red light of the fires, lending the scene a wild and unearthly appearance.

Suddenly, he darted to the right between two wagons. I squeezed myself through this space behind him and found myself within a circle of carts whose center was a blazing fire. Around it, men were dancing with their hands on one another's shoulders, while the musicians sat back in the shadows on rough stools. Women were in the process of laying out food on plank tables, as mobs of children ran squalling and shrieking and jumping, round and round.

It was a scene not unlike many in which I had partaken myself, when I had a family. Often I would go out on hunting expeditions with my court, with children, wives, and servants in tow, and we would camp in the hills with just this sort of exuberance.

In the moment that I stopped to take in the scene, my guide had disappeared. So I simply found a place on the ground, leaning against the wheel of one of the wagons, and settled myself to watch.

To my right, old women were tending cooking fires over which, on iron cranes, big pots bubbled with marvelous smells. Beyond them, a knot of young men was gathered and I assumed that the bridegroom must be among them, for they were drinking and there were shouts of hilarity and good natured jostling among them. To my left were the musicians and, beyond them, a bevy of young women turned in to face one another, like mares in a defensive circle. They were giggling, and occasionally one would look over her shoulder toward the young men's group and then turn back with excited whispers.

How it made my heart ache! Many times I had witnessed similar things in my own country. It proves, I suppose, that we truly are all the children of one God, for no matter what our country or our race, so many of our behaviors are the same.

§

People began to collect at the tables now, for the smell of hot food was compelling. I had been invited to the feast, but my guide was nowhere in sight. I felt awkward intruding on this family's party, but one of the old women found me in the shadows, thrust a wooden bowl in my hands without a word and threw out her hand toward the tables, commanding me silently to take my place.

Room was made for me on a bench without surprise or comment. Soon steaming kettles were ladled out into my dish. When everyone was served, there was a clapping of hands and all fell silent, turning to the head of the table where, to my surprise, I now beheld my guide, but much transformed.

He had changed his clothes and now wore a soft white shirt with full sleeves, under a vest embroidered in green and red. Loose black pants were tucked into boots of red leather. For all his wild hair and ugly scar, he looked lordly, and I knew he must be the head of his clan.

He spoke a blessing over the food in a language I did not understand and took to be the Romany of his race. Then the feasting commenced and, along with the eating, there was much laughter and joking and wine was passed, again and again.

When finally all the food was eaten and we all were a little tipsy from the wine, the musicians again took their stools and began to play. Now, my host revealed himself to be a singer, and he began the wailing chant of his people, that some say is an amalgam of the cry of the Muslim muezzin and the mournful song of the Jewish cantor, compounded during the gypsies' wanderings in Spain.

Whatever their origins, the songs were deeply moving, and the crowd began to shout its enthusiastic response to the singer as he sang. Women began to dance, especially the old women, who moved into the circle with their bent shoulders suddenly straightened, and their stiff, padded hips swaying like those of young girls.

Again, I settled myself against a wagon wheel, content to be even an observer of this family festival. But soon I felt a movement to my right, and a woman stood there who quickly took her seat beside me.

"Welcome to our camp," she said quietly. "My name is Allia."

I nodded to her and then half turned away, for I did not know the ways of her people, and if she were being forward, I did not want to cause an incident. She seemed content simply to sit beside me without conversing, and as the evening progressed, clapped her hands to the music, and several times got up to dance. But always, she returned to my side.

While she was dancing, I watched her closely. She was an attractive woman, I saw, but not beautiful. She was neither young nor old and had the long nose and flashing eyes of her race. Of medium height and frame, she was somewhat on the thin side. In all, she seemed completely unexceptional except for two things. One was her expression that was both sad and dignified and seemed to have deep thoughts and feelings dreaming beneath the surface, like schools of fish beneath dark water. The other was that she had chosen, when others had not, to sit by me.

§

Gradually, the pace of the evening began to slow, as mothers gathered their children and took them off to bed, and old women cleared the debris of the feast and then stumped off to their wagons on swollen ankles. The bride and her groom departed to the shouted jokes and well wishes of the crowd, and in the shadows of the wagons, a few of the young men and women met in shy flirtations.

At last, only a single instrument still strummed, sending its haunting melodies and cadences over a camp half sleeping. I rose, and nodding good night to the woman who still sat beside me, I turned to depart.

I had not gone ten paces beyond the circled wagons, however, when a gruff voice stopped me. "You are leaving," it said, and I knew by the declarative tone that it was my guide and host. I turned and bowed low to him, replying that I was, and I thanked him heartily for his generosity and hospitality.

"You are not going to stay with Allia?" This was a question, and the note of surprise, if not alarm, in his voice was new.

I drew closer to him, much disconcerted. "Forgive me, sir," I said, "because I do not know your customs. I had the understanding that the men of the Rom are very protective of their women."

"This is true"—he replied, coming closer still to me—"but Allia is a special case, you know."

"How would I know the smallest thing about Allia?" I asked in dismay. For now I was beginning to perceive that in trying not to give offense, I had given offense. "Out of respect for you, I have ignored the woman, all evening!" I said in frustration.

With this, he threw back his head and laughed. He was more than a little drunk and very much on fire from the passion of the singing and dancing. His face flushed and his shirt untucked on one side, he reached his right hand to my shoulder and pulled me in conspiratorially.

"Allia is a special case," he whispered again, his breath rich with alcohol and garlic. "Allia has the second sight, you know. She has refused marriage since she was a child, when her mother first tried to arrange it. She announced then, when she was five, that she would have no children but would have many men.

"Of course, we all thought she was having a girl's delusions and was playing out her fantasies, heh? But no, in the next breath, she turns to our uncle and says, 'If you do not give back the bracelet, you will die within a week!' And then she flounces off into the night.

"Well, a week later, our uncle dies—and in his bedroll is found a precious bracelet that had been stolen from our mother. From that day onward, we have listened with respect to all that Allia says." He pushed his weight into my shoulder, rocking me gently, as if to awaken some sleeping faculty of reason in me.

"You...you are related to her?" I stammered.

He looked at me wild-eyed in surprise, his eyebrows almost buried in his mane. "Did I not tell you? Ha!" He threw his head back and uttered this cry of self-deprecation at the top of his voice. "Of course I am related to her—is she not my sister?"

The situation had become most peculiar. "Is Allia, then, accustomed to saying with whom she will spend the night?" I asked, to mark time and get my wits about me.

"She does not decide it, sir, she foresees it. It was she who sent me looking for you today. 'Go and find a huge black man with the sign of the Christ on his forehead,' she told me, 'and bring him here to our camp. He is a king, but lonely, and in need of our aid.' So I went and there you were and here we are and now, sir, I am going to bed before I fall down. Allia's wagon is that one there, with the yellow wheels. Good night to you!" And with a stagger to the right, he wheeled about and made off into the shadows.

I looked toward where he had pointed and there was the wagon with the yellow wheels, and on its steps, Allia was sitting. Her petticoats were pulled up to her knees, and her bare legs and feet glowed like old ivory in the moonlight. I approached her cautiously, for I had no attraction to this woman and no intention of being her lover for the night.

When I was within range of her voice, she looked up at me and said softly, "Come," and patted the step beside her. I took a few more steps and stopped again, hesitating. "I won't bite you," she said, with a sly smile.

Two more paces and I stood at the foot of the three little steps that were the entrance to her cart. The door behind her was ajar, and the glow of a candle lantern lit a tableau of hanging copper pots, above a wall covered in religious icons.

She reached out her hand to me. "Come closer," she said, "and I will read your palm again."

"Again?" I said, as if in a trance.

"Yes, as I did that day in the village on the Rhone," she answered, taking my right hand in hers and running her left hand, cool and smooth, over my fevered wrist, to my elbow, and back.

"That is impossible," I said, confused. "That woman was old. Ancient."

"I know. She is my grandmother. But I was the one who sent her to meet you. And I who told her what to say. You are a man of destiny, King of Nubia. Even at a great distance you cannot be ignored, for the Power has news for you."

She turned my hand between her two hands and a warmth stirred in my palm. She ran her fingernails from the tips of my fingers down my palm to the heel of my hand, then back again. I was powerless to withdraw it from her.

She lowered her head, and I felt her tongue softly brush the cup of my hand. She raised her head and, looking me full in the eyes, said, "I taste loneliness here. It tastes like brass." And she commenced stroking my hand with her fingernails, again.

Who knows how long we might have stayed thus? If the decision were mine, we might be there yet, for my brain had turned to porridge.

Gently, she tugged me closer and then, leaning her weight on my shoulder, pushed herself up from the step. She pulled the little door open and put one bare foot inside the wagon. "Come," she said softly. "Come inside and you will not regret it."

I protested meekly, "But I am a pilgrim," meaning I had been chaste.

Allia only laughed softly, saying, "Then, pilgrim, you have reached your mecca!"

§

The night had grown cold. The camp, after so much revelry, had collapsed into exhausted slumber. Even the horses slept, white breath rising from their nostrils as from a den of dragons. I, too, was weary. My head ached for a bed; my body, to be horizontal.

Yet even more, my heart longed for the comfort of a woman's presence, to be pillowed against her bosom, to be held and kissed and murmured to. My quest had been arduous and my will adamantine. Now, in the presence of Allia, it all fell away. There was nothing for me to do but to surrender.

As Allia opened the door to her wagon, a rich and complex scent rolled out toward me as I stood behind her, her petticoats in my face, waiting like a child my turn to mount the three small steps. The smell was compounded of dried herbs, beeswax candles, patchouli, and that sweetest of perfumes, the bodily oils of the woman herself, steeped into clothing, cushions, and implements. This essence was much like sandalwood, a perfume dear to me, as it was a favorite of my departed wife.

The wagon, which was gaily painted on the exterior, with yellow wheels and a red body banded by intricate designs and flowers, was equally lavish and colorful within. The walls were of polished wood and were hung with many small, but very finely painted icons in the Byzantine fashion. A tiny stove occupied one corner. Across the back was a bunk with a thick mattress, layered in rich blankets and colorful shawls and heaped with cushions in fine brocades. Underneath were cupboards, two on a side, their fronts painted with flowers and birds.

To the right, a narrow table attached to the wall, supported by two carved legs at the front, with two stools beneath. On the left wall were hooks holding her possessions—dresses, shawls, baskets with jewelry and shoes. It was altogether a jewel box of a place, rich in reds, yellow ochres and deep blues, and twined with lovely designs.

I took it all in for a moment and breathed deeply the smell of a woman—a scent that I had so long denied myself as to believe I was immune to it. But now I understood I was immune only because I had not exposed myself. Or perhaps because I had not yet met Allia. She was a woman, while not beautiful in the classical sense, whose own feminine essence was so complete that no man, once invited into its aura, would be able to resist.

I closed the door behind me, half stooping, for the room was not high, although I soon realized I could stand erect without hitting my head. She stood with her back to me, allowing me, I imagined, a moment to look around and collect myself. But this I could not do, for the opulence of the perfumed air and sudden warmth after a night of chill, and the closeness of this mysterious woman, overwhelmed me. All my strength and high station left me and I stood, arms slack, mouth agape, like a bumpkin.

Allia moved languidly to the stove, where a kettle of water was steaming. Taking up a copper basin, she poured hot water into it and finally turned toward me, her hair shining in the candlelight like a black wave of the night sea.

"I will bathe you," she said.

She set the basin on the table and came to me, pressing her body close to my chest, and began to undo the buttons of my coat. She pulled the heavy garment from me and hung it on a peg. Then she returned to do the same with my weskit and my shirt. The while, I stood as one transfixed, limp and unprotesting, too exhausted to protest, too hungry to resist.

She continued to strip me, pulling from me my boots, my pants, my under garments, until I stood naked before her. Then, using a soft cloth, with the tenderest care and most sensual strokes she laved my body with water. She washed every inch of me with equal attention, showing no fear or embarrassment when she applied herself to my intimate parts. I was as one bewitched.

When I was clean, she led me to her bed. I trailed behind her, as resistless as wax in the sun. She sat me down, pulled pillows behind me to support me, all the while her eyes averted from me. Finally, when I was propped in my waxy state like a dressmaker's dummy, she turned the full, wild essence of her gaze upon me and began to dance.

Slowly, her hips moved from side to side as she hummed a strange, haunting melody in a minor key. Her shoulders undulated. Her arms were two snakes, mating in water; her hands and fingers like lambent flame. She turned her back to me, so all I saw was the night waterfall of her hair, the slow lifting of her slender hips, and the soft swaying of her long skirts that whispered, as they swished, of the hidden place to which she was leading me.

When she turned back to me, the top buttons of her blouse were undone, and I saw that she wore no bodice beneath. Her breasts shone in lamp light like heaps of coin. Before my riveted gaze, she slowly drew the halves of the blouse aside. Dropping it to the floor, she danced on, softly singing a bewitching melody, in the tongue of her people. One by one, her skirts and petticoats dropped to the floor, until she danced naked, like a goddess upon a frothy sea.

As I watched, my tired body came slowly to life. What had been benumbed, or denied, experienced resurgence. When finally, with a last twirl, she came to me, covering me in her black hair, I was ready. She straddled me and drove her hips into mine, and my mind reeled at the sheer, hot pleasure of her. At her scent. At the rhythm of the dance which she brought so palpably to my body. At the sweetness and fullness of the breasts she offered me, with a panther-like arching of her back.

What more transpired that night is beyond telling. I was as one near drowning upon a night sea, tossed by waves, supported on the broad back of the waters. Lost. Hallucinating. My peril became my ecstasy.

I did not know before that night—even with my beloved wife—the secret meaning of a man and a woman, coupled. After that night, the world was changed. What had been lost in deaths and long wanderings was restored. What was dying was resurrected. My tongue cannot convey the profound gifts given by Allia. But I sit beside you today because of her and I will never forget.

§

Perhaps I have gone on too long or said things that are not appropriate for the ears of one so young. I must tell you, my dear Mademoiselle de Muret, that I am old now, and recounting one's life story is a vice the elderly nourish with relish. And by your own tale of your friend Agnes, I know you have need to understand that the coupling of a man and woman may be a sweet—nay, even a sacred—thing.

All that has gone before is but a preamble to the answer you seek: Where are you and what manner of place is this? Well, my dear, you have been guided by fate to a most unique and secret place. Only one with Divine guidance might have found access to this place, as you have done.

You are, as I am sure you are aware, underground. This cave was in use long before you or I ever were born. For many hundreds, perhaps thousands of years, this cave has sheltered those who preceded us in this life. It has always had a religious function, apparently. In other rooms than this, there are paintings on the walls of extreme antiquity, showing people in the act of worship.

Egypt, as you may know, is a nation whose history is so long as to be lost in the sands of time. Always it has had a tradition of worship of a Mother Goddess, one that you might comprehend if you think of your own country's adoration of the Madonna.

This cave was one of the places where the Goddess was worshipped for longer than human memory can recount. And it remains so today. Only those chosen by the Goddess ever find this place, and so, my child, I consider you a very blessed person indeed, as am I, for my own arrival here would never have taken place had it not been for Allia. Let me tell you how that came about.

S

I stayed with Allia for the several weeks that her people camped at Les-Saintes-Maries-de-la-Mer, and while I was with her, she taught me many things that were a revelation to me. Her people venerate the statue in the crypt, Saint Sarah, she who is also known as The Egyptian, as an earthly representative of their own dark-skinned Romany mother goddess, Sara-Kali.

The very site of Sarah's church was originally a temple to the Egyptian Goddess Isis, in an earlier time, when the town was known as Ratis. The place was much beloved of Egyptian sailors who plied the Mediterranean, because its swamps were reminiscent of their own Nile Delta. So it was natural that their goddess should accompany them and be established there.

As a Christian, I was at first affronted by these notions and said so in no uncertain terms. But over the days, Allia won me over.

"Why," she asked me, "do you find it strange to worship the Goddess? Your own religion is but twelve hundred years old. Yet we agree that God is eternal. Who do you suppose Mother Mary was, before your religion was born? Just because the names are different, do not imagine that the Goddess is different. Her earthly manifestations may change, but She is unchangeable and eternal."

Finally, I came to see that Allia was correct. Whether we call her Isis or Aphrodite, or Mary or the Mother of God, the Divine Feminine is always there, sheltering and teaching and loving humankind. Rather than making me feel apostate, this realization gave me great comfort.

Toward the end of my stay with the gypsies, Allia again read my palm. Long she held my hand, gazing down into it, as if it were a crystal ball through which all time was fleeting.

Finally, with a sigh she laid my hand upon my knee but kept hold of it, as she raised her eyes to mine and began to speak.

"You have a strange and wonderful fate, King of Nubia," she began. "I have read many palms in my life, but never have I seen one both so powerfully star-crossed and so blessed. Many have been your misfortunes and great your suffering. However, because you have borne all this with dignity and forbearance and never have faltered in your quest, your great will and determination have altered your fate.

"Now, your torments are in the past. Now, you go forward to claim your reward. How rare an event is this! So many are called but so few endure until the end.

"Now, our time together is nearly at an end. Tomorrow, you will set forth again on your journey. But this time you will not engage in vain wanderings, for you have a destination written in your fate."

It was then that she told me of this place, of which she is an initiate, and where her presence is familiar. For here in this cave, under the very foundations of the palaces of the Muslim overlords, is the sanctuary and holy community, consistently renewed over thousands of years, of the Great Goddess Isis.

ʂ

Allia held me fiercely, that night, as if passing into my very body her own fire and passion. And I, for my part, clung to her, reluctant even to imagine parting from this woman whose very heat had kindled in me, again, my waning life force. Never will I forget Allia, and I present her each day to Isis as a precious gift of memory and gratitude, praying that her life will be long, prosperous and joyous.

I journeyed to Egypt by boat, beginning the very next day. And here I will live out my life, for I am old now, and also deeply contented, for my heart is healed in the presence of the Great Mother. And now I understand that you, too, belong here, but in a very different way, Blanche de Muret.

You see, over the years Allia has visited here. She comes to worship Isis, of course, but she and I are, in some strange fashion, married in our souls. She is very old now, as am I, and it is a great blessing that she has recently traveled here, probably for the final time. Mademoiselle de Muret, what I am telling you is that you will be blessed with an audience with Allia!

ʖ

Chapter 7

The Story of Blanche de Muret Continues

WORDS CANNOT EXPRESS HOW VASTLY RELIEVED I WAS TO HEAR THE KING'S STORY! For now I knew with certainty that I was not dead and lost forever in the holds of Hell, but was fostered in a human community, however strange. During the king's long recitation, I grew increasingly more relaxed and optimistic. Perhaps, by God's good grace, I should live to see my homeland again, after all!

After the king's departure from my chamber, the old doctor came to me again. Gently, but firmly, she unbound my bandages, bathed my wounds in fragrant herbal water, reanointed them with her salves, and wrapped them again in soft cotton. It was plain, even to my uneducated eyes, that my scrapes, bruises and cuts were healing at an almost miraculous rate. The old woman met my eyes when the last bandage was wrapped and smiled, wordlessly speaking the universal language of pleasure at my progress.

I slept long that day, as if some guard that I had erected, from the day Godfrey and I departed Muret for St. Denys, could finally step down from its post. Above all, my heart rested in the King's promise to locate my dear brother, Godfrey!

The arrival and auctioning off of so many Christian children had created quite a stir all along the Nile, he told me. Therefore, he felt that it would not be too difficult to gain news of Godfrey's whereabouts. This twin assurance, that I was not in Hell and that my brother might soon be liberated from the living damnation of slavery, released me deep into healing slumber.

I know not how long I lay thus, enslaved to exhaustion and pain. For in that sunless world into which I had fallen, day is the same as night. At last, however, the time arrived when my doctor pronounced me healed and the bandages were removed, not to be replaced.

The good king came to see me shortly thereafter. "How are you feeling, dear child?" he asked me kindly.

At last I was able to answer, in full honesty, that I was completely recovered. My energy was high, and I felt ready for any adventure he might propose.

ʕ

Then began yet another strange episode in my already odd account. If my tale stretches the credulity of my readers, they may well imagine how it was with me who experienced these things and without foreknowledge, whatsoever. Truly, I was as one lost in a dream. For on that fateful day, I was delivered by the king into the hands of women who were priestesses of the Mother Goddess. As the women of the harem had done before them, they bathed and clothed me, but this time in preparation for an audience with Allia.

These ablutions were carried out in a deep and secret part of the cave, far from the daily hubbub of the community's mundane life. Back and back I was led, by winding passages dimly lit by lamps and glittering with crystals. In niches along the walls were votive figures of ancient manufacture, and even upon the walls themselves were painted devotees in the act of worship at the feet of the seated goddess.

The women who led me were of all ages and robed in the simple white linen tunics common to their kind. Their faces were calm and serene, as if nothing merely human could bother them, and this, combined with an amulet, which each wore about her neck, alone set these women aside from their brethren as a special caste.

When at last I was bathed, anointed and dressed in a fresh white tunic, I was led by the eldest of these women, with no fanfare but with great reverence, to yet another room, accessed by a passage so narrow that we must go singly and with our heads bent low. In this humble posture, we arrived in an antechamber where a single chair of gorgeous and antique fabrication sat upon a reed mat. Indicating that I should sit, the priestess bowed and departed and I was left alone.

§

I looked about me in wonder, for the room was plastered and then painted, every inch, with scenes of great vivacity. Here were hunters with spears menacing flocks of wild geese, women bending to thresh grain, and masons hewing blocks of stone. Indeed, many of the activities of human community were represented there.

When I had glanced at these scenes, I rose from my chair and examined it, for it was a wondrous thing of ebony, overlaid with sheets of gold, hammered into repoussé figures of the Goddess and her child, and inlaid with coral, carnelian and onyx.

So astonishing was the workmanship and so opulent the materials, that I was utterly charmed, and so did not hear Allia when she entered. How long she had been standing, observing me as I scrutinized the chair, I do not know. At last, with a start, I realized that I was not alone, and turned to find her by the door to the inner chamber, staring at me with detached amusement.

"You find your chair problematic, Blanche de Muret?" Her voice was low and contained a bit of a growl, as if beneath her smooth chestnut skin, a leopard might be lurking. That voice fairly gave me a chill for, although it lacked menace, yet it promised a character half-wild and practiced in uncanny things.

"Oh no, Madame!" I managed to stammer. "Quite the opposite. It is a thing of such beauty that I am scarcely fain to sit upon it."

"Then come hither and leave it undefiled," said she and, without further invitation or urging, she turned and disappeared through the inner door with a swirl of her long white skirt. For Allia was dressed differently than the others, her dress being of very finely woven linen reaching to her ankles. In that one turning movement, I saw the dancer that my dear King Caspar had described, and wondered what it might be like to watch her dance, fully and passionately.

I followed her into the inner room and at the doorway was arrested in astonishment. For here was a large room furnished with divans, chairs, and tables, all assembled in a way similar to that of the anteroom chair. Never in all my life before, not even in the great house of Ali Abu'l-Hasan, or in Farah's or Fatima's descriptions of the great Caliph's palace, have I encountered such furnishings! They were as if wrought by the hands of a mighty magician or by the angels themselves.

ʃ

Allia, meanwhile, had arranged herself upon a divan and waited with languid grace for me to contain my curiosity and wonder. Finally, I collected myself and took a seat on the chair that she indicated, beside her couch.

"I see you are amazed by these furnishings, which pleases me," she began. "It shows that you have an eye for beautiful things and an appreciation for their degree of excellence. What is more, I perceive that you are entranced by their vibrational quality. For be assured, these are objects of very high energy, and anyone who is not similarly attuned would be repelled by them rather than attracted."

Now my attention was full upon Allia, and I was again amazed. For despite my understanding, made plain by the king, that this woman was greatly advanced in age, yet she appeared ageless. Truly, I could not have guessed whether she were thirty or three hundred. Her body was slender and supple as she reclined upon her divan, and her long hair, which hung past her waist, was glossy and black. Yet her eyes, fathomless as the waters of the well from which I had been rescued, exuded the wisdom of ages.

"You must surely be wondering what has befallen you in arriving here. I have wandered the earth, and I can assure you that few other places as curious and as potent as this one exist. You have a strange fate, Blanche de Muret. It is not unlike that of the good king who has ministered to you: you are fated to lose everything and then, after long and terrible adventure, to find something of even greater value."

She stopped speaking then and regarded me with her bottomless onyx eyes and, although I felt myself unmannered not to respond, my tongue was bound speechless in my head. I somehow understood that it was my duty to listen only. Still, my blood ran cold at her assertion that I had lost all. Had she then news of my Godfrey? I awaited her next words with trepidation.

"You have heard, I am sure, from the King of Nubia how I am gifted with second sight to an unusual degree. This is a great gift from the Holy Mother but one, I confess, that is not always easy to bear. What I see is often difficult and sometimes unspeakable. Perhaps this is the price exacted for the placement of such power within human grasp." She stopped to arrange a fold of her skirt, fingering the fabric with a meditative air.

When again her eyes shifted to mine, they were filled with compassion. "You must be brave, Blanche de Muret. I see that, these many months, you have already displayed a courage and intelligence far beyond your years. But now you must be stronger still. For the news that I must give you will weigh down your heart to breaking. When you have heard it, your childhood will be over."

This dire prediction was like a cold blade in my heart. I looked upon Allia with dread and would have hated her, had not her gaze been so entirely filled with loving sympathy. For already, as if by reading her thoughts, I began to suspect that I knew the import of her serious words. And with that knowledge, magically, at the same time, I felt an influx as if of warm milk, an energy that pervaded my torso and limbs with both succor and strength. Fed by it, I knew that I could withstand even the most terrible news.

I squared my shoulders and sat forward on the seat of the chair. "I am ready," I said.

§

No words can convey the grief of those next moments in which Allia reported all that she knew. Then and thus, I learned of my parents' deaths and the manner of them. And when this seemed too horrible to bear, Allia added to it the information hardest of all to hear: my Godfrey was dead! My poor little brother! My heart felt it must burst asunder at the news.

I howled in pain. I fell to the floor and beat my fists against it. I rolled about as if my body were encompassed in flames, screaming, "No! No! No!"

All the while knowing full well that every word Allia had spoken was true.

§

The Monastery of the Ghosts

Calypso lay awake in the darkened room with the story fading as her hunger grew. No one had brought her supper and now, in the depths of the night, her stomach growled like an angry dog. The embers of the fire had long since died into ashes, and there was no more firewood. Without a blanket, she was beginning to grow chilled. She got up and dragged the mattress closer to the fireplace, lay down again, and turned on her side to warm her back by the still-warm ashes.

The flat screen TV had finally gone off sometime in the night while she drowsed. The only light came through the small barred window that looked west, away from whatever hint of dawn the early hour might offer. A sickle moon floated in the black velvet rectangle of the window, shedding silvery light over her austere prison.

For imprisoned, she had to admit to herself, was what she was. She held out hope while talking to Lone-R, but that was before the second drugging, and before awakening in the bare, locked room.

Maybe no one had come because the Ghosts were in session, deciding her fate. And Hill's. His destiny concerned her more than her own. Was he even still alive? And then, there was Javier. She felt blunted and angry. The locket should have warned her; should tell her now what was going on. Just when she needed it most, it had gone silent.

And who was the woman Hill had seen, standing in the nonexistent opening in the tube? It was this vision, and the fresh air he gulped as it poured through a crack in the stone, that relieved his panic and saved his sanity, although Calypso was absolutely certain that no such crack existed.

She rolled to her other side and curled toward the hearth to warm her front. Every avenue of thought led her to blind alleys or mazes that turned her back upon herself. No single question had an answer—and she had dozens of questions. Her intuition told her that she needed to go deeper. Somewhere in all this, solace was lurking, if she could just hunt it out.

There were questions that she wanted to avoid, but they nibbled at the restraints with which she blocked them until she gave in. Had this all happened to her before? Was she reliving the outline of a former life? And if so, why? Had she failed to learn the lessons of the former existence? Or did certain archetypal patterns simply repeat themselves, over and over, like the cycling of the stars? She thought of the night in the courtyard with Javier and Hill, and their joking about being Sumerian shepherds naming the constellations. Maybe there was more truth than poetry in it.

She gazed out the window at the tail of the moon, already sailing serenely westward past the window frame. Then, pulling up her knees, wrapping her arms around them, she wept. Exhaustion followed tears, and as the moon voyaged silently on to set behind the western cliffs, in the blackness between moon- and dawn-light, she slept.

ʕ

Rude thumping on the door awakened her. A long streamer of sunlight, striped with shadows from the bars, flowed from the window. The room was cold and so was she. She tried to get up, but her muscles were too rigid to respond—and besides, she was locked in anyway. She subsided on the mattress and glowered at the door, hating the intruder.

Lone-R's deep voice came muffled through the thick wood. "You up? I got grub. You decent?"

"I am," she shouted back.

A key ground in the massive antique lock, and the door creaked open, revealing Lone-R, jaunty in his black, single-breasted "Matrix" cassock, with a baseball cap on backwards over his bald head. He picked up a tray from the floor of the corridor and brought it to her, kicking the door shut with his heel as he passed.

"Hungry?"

"Hell yes. Starved." She wanted it to sound lighthearted, but it came out as a grumble, so she continued in like vein. "Cold, too."

Lone-R nodded. "Yeah. I got wood for the fire."

He picked up the end of the mattress and dragged it, Calypso and her breakfast away from the hearth, as if it were nothing, then went out to the hall and returned with a leather sling filled with kindling and firewood. He busied himself at the hearth, while Calypso surveyed her breakfast, a repeat of yesterday's beans and rice.

"Is it safe?" she asked, realizing only after the question was out that she had asked him the same thing yesterday.

"What?" Lone-R was stacking the kindling carefully, after having dug through the ashes for the few remaining coals.

"The food. I can't take another drugging. I'm fuzzy-headed."

"Naw. No drugs in there this time. They were just messin' with you."

"Why?"

"Cuz they can, I guess. It's their way. They like to show who's boss."

He got down on the floor with his rump in the air and blew on the coals. Ash rose around his head like a volcanic cloud. Fanned by the hurricane blast of his massive lungs, the fire burst into flame.

"Well, they can consider me duly messed with." She lifted an unglazed cup to her lips and was encouraged to taste coffee and not a bad brew, at that. "What about Hill?"

"What about him?"

"Did he get breakfast this morning, too?"

"Can't say."

"Because you don't know or because they won't let you?"

He sat back on the floor and clasped his hands in front of his knees. "Could be," he said noncommittally.

"So what's next?" She stabbed her fork into the plate of rice and beans, her jaw set. The food was as bland today as it had been yesterday. She chewed it grimly.

"Today they're gonna come for you."

"To do what?"

Lone-R shrugged. "Who knows?" He scrambled to his feet. "Hey! I almost forgot." He went back into the corridor and returned with her backpack. "So you can freshen up," he said, tossing it beside her on the mattress. "Gotta go. See you later."

Before she could think of a way to detain him, he was gone, locking the door behind him.

ʕ

Of course, they had been through her backpack. Her passport and driver's license were shoved into a pocket she always used for batteries. So much for pretending her name was Jane. Everything else was there including her money, a change of underwear, and the skirt and sweater she'd kept stored in the pack as a celebratory outfit when she and Javier had survived their strategic retreat.

Now, she was without him, without Hill, but needing a change of clothes badly. Feeling disloyal, she went to the tiny bathroom and sponged herself clean with the cold water that dribbled from the faucet. Then she donned the skirt and sweater, combed her long hair and put on lipstick. Feeling far better, she sat cross-legged on the mattress again, and finished the tasteless plate of food.

An hour passed. She set the tray by the door, wandered to the window and stood staring at the canyon. A wind was rising, sending small clouds scudding across the sky, and their shadows fleeing along the cliff face like jubilant black sheep. The room was slowly warming, but air seeping around the weathered wooden frame told her that the day outside was cold, despite the sunshine.

Her mind was as scattered as the clouds, and she decided to meditate. Sitting cross-legged on the mattress, she closed her eyes and centered her mind. Soon her body began to rock gently from side to side, as kundalini energy rose undulating up her spine and her mind filled with colored patterns of light. She had a fleeting thought that being locked in an impregnable stone room at the top of an equally impregnable cliff was not so bad. Then, she floated into bliss.

§

When they came for her she was ready—clean, dressed, calm, and centered. Lone-R opened the door, followed by Icepick, and she was led down a maze of corridors and a flight of stairs, with one of them guarding her on each side.

They stopped before high double doors, deeply carved with matching crests. If her high school Latin still served her, the motto on the left read *I teach*, and the one on the right, *I conquer*. Lone-R tapped on the right-hand door with scarred and calloused knuckles. A voice from inside called "Enter!" and the doors opened outward, each propelled by a man in a black cassock.

Lone-R and Icepick escorted Calypso onto a dais surrounded by a turned bannister of old and polished wood. A straight chair sat waiting, but she chose to stand, taking in her surroundings. She resisted the urge to let her eyes dart around the room and instead swept them with the steady calm of a surveillance camera. Hill was not in the room.

To her right, sitting at a high wooden desk, was Father Keat, like a judge before his court. In front of her, ranged in straight wooden chairs five rows deep, sat an assortment of men, all in black cassocks, and all staring at her impassively. A man stood on guard in front of each of the double doors, and Lone-R and Icepick went to replace them.

The room was large, square and warmed by a huge fireplace at the rear. A fire tender stood beside it, his hands folded before him. The wall to her left held a bank of long casement windows letting in the slant of autumnal sun through wavering antique glass and thrumming with wind. Despite the fire and the sunshine, the room was chilly and she was glad she'd worn her sweater.

It did not occur to her that she had adopted Javier's habit of taking in any new place fully, looking for danger, until Father Keat interrupted her scrutiny. "I hope you're satisfied with your surroundings, Miss Searcy?"

"Father Keat," she said, turning toward him with dignity and bowing very slightly and ironically in his direction.

"Please be seated."

"I prefer to stand."

"We prefer that you sit."

She sat. Deep silence filled the room. The fire snapped. Wind rattled the windowpanes, beyond which the canyon walls shone rose and copper in morning light. The rows of men sat silently immovable, hands folded in their laps. Calypso's quick count put their number at around sixty.

"You present us with a rare dilemma, Miss Searcy," Father Keat began. Calypso did not respond. "We do not allow trespassers on our land, and you and your companion have trespassed. We are here today to decide what the penalty should be."

"May I speak?"

"Of course. You are your own sole defense."

"I was not aware that the area of the grotto was private land. My friend and I were tired and thirsty and needed a place to camp for the night. If you release us, I promise that we will never bother you again."

"I'm afraid it isn't that simple."

"I can pay a ransom, if that's what you want."

"No. Money is not the objective, here. Secrecy is. You see, Miss Searcy, you've stumbled on a well-kept secret. You've lived in these canyons for almost twenty years and yet you never knew of our existence."

Something in the man's assurance nettled her. "How do you know how long I've lived here or what I do or do not know?"

"Scopolamine, Miss Searcy. You've been under the influence of a truth drug. The first time you almost OD'd. The second time, you underwent interrogation by our resident expert. There's nothing we don't know about you, except your hat size. And we can find that out, too, if need be."

Calypso frowned, glaring at Father Keat. "I don't remember giving you any information about myself."

"Scopolamine turns you into a zombie, Miss Searcy. You won't remember a thing you do under its influence. But let me recap your life, just so you know that I'm not lying to you."

He glanced at a paper lying on the desk in front of him, picked it up, and read. "You were born in 1950 in Berkeley, California. Your father was a university professor and your mother was a concert pianist. Your parents were killed by a drunk driver on Shattuck Avenue, coming home from one of your mother's concerts. You had just turned eighteen; therefore, required no legal guardian. The estate you inherited from your parents was less than one might have expected. In order to finance your education, you sold your family home and moved into an apartment on Dwight Way. You received your bachelors degree at UC Berkeley, in 1968.

"During your time at the university, you met and fell in love with Javier Carteña, who was recently arrived from Mexico. You taught him English. You were raped in Santa Rita prison by a guard, following a peace march in Oakland. Mr. Carteña helped you during your recovery. Then, he hunted down and murdered your attacker, jumped a freight train for Mexico, and disappeared from your life for the next twenty-five years. Shall I continue?"

During this recitation, Calypso held her clenched hands lying helplessly in her lap. What kind of drug was it that could pry her deepest secrets from her? How could she possibly have revealed to complete strangers that Javier had committed murder? She choked her panic down and raised her head defiantly.

"No. I'm convinced."

"Good. Now the problem is, you see, that we don't call ourselves The Ghosts for nothing. Not unlike Mr. Carteña, each of us has reason to keep certain aspects of his past secret. In fact, the necessity for that is so great that each of us has had to disappear completely from the world, by staging our own deaths. So we are doubly Ghosts, Miss Searcy: we live an invisible existence, and we are all—officially—dead."

§

Calypso shook her head in confusion. "I don't understand. What are you doing here? What is this place, anyway?"

Father Keat took his time to answer. He gazed out the windows, choosing his words. Finally, his eyes met hers.

"On June 25th, 1767, the Order of Men in the Company of Jesus—the Jesuit order—underwent expulsion from Mexico. They were under suspicion by the king and were arrested and shipped out of the country. I'm sure you know this.

"In this canyon, they had done extensive missionary work and were in the process of building a big church near Batopilas, the mission of San Miguel de Satevó, just outside of town. You know, because it was revealed during interrogation, that the church is called the Lost Mission, because there are no records describing its existence. There's a reason for that which you do *not* know, according to your own testimony while under the influence of the drug. So I'll tell you what even historians don't know.

"The Jesuits in this canyon decided to defy the expulsion order. Because of its remoteness, the king's agents didn't arrive to arrest them until after news had already reached Batopilas of the expulsion order. So the fathers had time to hide themselves in that very cave you claim to have traversed two days ago. Local Indians were the only ones who knew about the cave because of its inaccessibility. One of them led the fathers to the cave and kept them supplied with food until the king's men had given up finding them. The local rumor was that the Jesuits had fled northward to Alta California, and that was the official word sent back to Europe to account for their disappearance.

"Now you know that the Jesuits were a hardheaded lot. They'd begun their missionary work and weren't about to give it up. First, they built this place, to house themselves. You can imagine the labor required to raise these three stories of stone on this steep land. For water, they developed a spring that rises behind this building. They cultivated small fields. All this was hidden from the town of Batopilas because of the remoteness of this hanging valley and its distance from the mining operations.

"When they'd established this monk house and their food supply, they were determined to finish the church that they'd started. But they couldn't show themselves in town on danger of arrest. So they hit on the plan of building only at night. People would go to bed with the church in one building phase, and wake up the next morning to find it in a further stage of completion.

"The Europeans in the community found this very unnerving and felt the place was haunted and so avoided it. The local indigenous population, however, with their thin scraping of Christianity, believed it was a miracle and they've been worshipping there ever since.

"So that's why it's called the Lost Mission and why it was never recorded in the official church records. Like us, the Jesuits were ghosts. Eventually, of course, they all died off and this place was left abandoned. Even the Indians avoided it, because the Jesuits would torture any of them that they found nearby. So it just sat empty until we bought it, twenty years ago."

Calypso couldn't help blurting out, "But how did *you* find this place, then?"

Father Keat smiled thinly and said, "I'll let El Lobo tell you that part."

He raised his hand and gestured toward the audience. Calypso caught a quick movement from the corner of her eye, as El Lobo rose from the assembled brothers and made his way to the front of the room. He came to stand in the center, between Calypso's dais and Father Keat's desk, and clasping his hands behind his back and staring straight ahead, began to speak.

"I was a fugitive," he said. "I had done a contract killing for one of the drug mafia and instead of paying me, they decided just to kill me. I got out, but I had to kill one of the big guys to do it. And I was injured. I knew this canyon a little, from when I was a kid—how remote it is. So I came here and lived off wild mangoes and avocados, and just kept way out on the margins of things. Eventually, I found the grotto and then the little trail that the Jesuits had built, climbing into the hanging valley. And then I found this building.

"It wasn't in bad shape, considering that it'd been abandoned for over two hundred years. When I first entered, I found the last Jesuit's skeleton, still lying in his bed. Some of the windows were broken and swallows and owls were nesting inside, but that was about it. There weren't even any mice or rats. The library had a complete account of what they'd been doing since the expulsion, and I'd sit and read their journals at night, by the fire.

"So I set up housekeeping here, until I thought it was safe to make a break for the border. That's where I met Father Keat—in Texas. Eventually, I told him about this place and with..." he looked questioningly at Father Keat who nodded, "with money we made doing...stuff...we bought this land using my name, because I'm a Mexican citizen. Then before I 'died,'" he flipped his fingers in the air to indicate quotation marks, "we set up a corporation for ownership. It's complicated but it's working."

Father Keat answered his questioning look with a nod, and El Lobo made his way back toward his seat. Calypso's eyes followed him. Even indoors, his movements were swift and stealthy, with an animal-like hyperawareness. He truly was a wolf of a man, she thought warily.

"And you wanted this property because...?" she asked Father Keat, as her eyes followed El Lobo to his seat.

"Because I was getting older and I wanted out of what I was doing. And I knew a lot of other guys who did, too. You're among a rare group of men, Miss Searcy. Altogether, we've personally killed over a thousand people. Those are the ones we know about. When you do aerial bombing, like I did, you don't get to count coup."

An entire assembly of assassins! Calypso fought to keep her composure. She felt her chances of survival, like the tube in the cave, gradually but ineluctably diminishing. At the end of this kangaroo court would there be some small hole still left, through which she could just barely wriggle to safety? She glanced at Father Keat's granitic jaw and doubted it.

S

"We are united by a spirit of democracy, Miss Searcy," he continued, oblivious to how absurd that assertion sounded to her. "So the men thought it was only fair if they shared their stories with you, since against your will they've gotten to know yours." His eyes swept the assembled men. "Who wants to go first?"

"I do." The voice came not from the body of men, but from the door. It was Lone-R. Father Keat tilted his head and someone rose from the seated men to take Lone-R's place as guard. Lone-R came to stand where El Lobo had stood and took up the same posture.

"Begin," Father Keat commanded.

"My name is Lone-R. I have another name, an official one, but it was never really mine. The State gave it to me because I didn't have no father. My mother was a prostitute. I was born addicted to crack cocaine and almost died when I was a baby, comin' off it. When I was just a kid, my mom started sellin' me to weirdos for sex. When I got to be nine, I thought *fuck this*, and I ran away. I lived on the street, doin' what I had to, to survive.

"I grew up big, like you see me. On the street, if you're strong everybody gots to take a swing at you, to test theirselves." Lone-R held up his scarred hands, covered in callouses thick as rhinoceros hide. "I learned to fight. Ha yeah! When people started dyin', then people started leavin' me alone. But I kept driftin' west, and I had to prove myself again, in every city I came to.

"Finally, I got to LA and I took up with some guys who were on their way to do a robbery and I said, *What the hell?* and went along. Well, they gave me a .9 and when things started to go wrong, I used it. I killed a cop and that was the first time I went away to the pen. They never could prove it was me, though, so after nine years, I was out again and I was still only twenty-seven.

"When I got out of prison, I was full of anger and hate. I wanted to kill everyone, no exceptions. I paroled in LA and out on the street I was always in fights. One day this guy comes onto me about some shit and I cold cocked him. He was dead before he hit the pavement. Well, you might know, a cop was just drivin' around the corner and seen the whole thing. Bam! I'm back in prison on a second strike.

"I ended up doin' time in San Quentin, twenty-five to life. But I got lucky. The California prison system was overcrowded, and the federal court said they had to let twenty thousand people go. I don't know how it happened, but my number got pulled, and I was out on the street again, after only doin' seven years. So now, I'm thirty-four years old and mean as hell. I knew it was just a matter of time before I got slammed for somethin' else, so I broke parole and ran to Dallas. And that's where I met Father Keat and my life got changed."

Lone-R glanced at Father Keat, who nodded almost imperceptibly. Lone-R turned his eyes to Calypso. "I guess he'll tell you about that." He turned and walked back to the door. The relief guard returned to his chair and everyone looked expectantly at Father Keat. Rather than explain, however, Father Keat called for another testimony.

"I'll talk." A hand went up in the middle of the assembly.

Father Keat nodded saying, "Go ahead."

A short, elderly man threaded his way past the others and came to stand before them. Calypso studied him closely, finding it hard to believe that he, too, was a killer. He had the inoffensive face of a grandpa, a balding head fringed in gray hair, and glasses. His robe looked like a black barrel, giving evidence of a stout body beneath. He cleared his throat and began in a gravelly voice.

"My name's Tito, but everyone calls me The Knife. I grew up in Chicago, South Side, Back of the Yards. My father was a tailor from Armenia. He married my mother when she was fresh off the boat. He was fifty-three and she was sixteen. That's how they did things in those days.

"It was a tough neighborhood. As I kid, I had to fight to survive. I was small, so I bought me a knife.

"One day in front of the barber shop, this kid twice my size starts pushing me around, threatening to pull my gizzard out through my mouth. So I take my knife and I stick him right in the gut. Well, I must of hit an artery, 'cause the guy falls to the ground, bleeding like a broken hydrant, and in a few seconds, he's dead.

"I'm in shock. I'm just a kid. I don't even have the sense to run. I hear a siren coming and I'm just standing there, staring at this guy lying on the sidewalk in a puddle of blood, and I'm still holding the knife.

"All of a sudden, I feel this big hand come down on the back of my neck and somebody drags me into the barber shop. Whoever it is has got a death grip on my neck. He pushes me right through the shop, out the back door, into an alley. I'm thinking, *oh shit, my time is up.*

"The guy's got a car parked back in the alley, and he's got a driver. He says to the driver, *Open the door!* And when he does, the guy throws me into the backseat and says, *Let's get outta here.* The driver pulls out fast and away we go, with the guy holding my head down so nobody sees me through the window.

"Well, long story short, turns out I'd connected with Big Joe Gratz, one of the biggest mobsters in Chicago. He tells me, *You got sand, kid*, and he says he wants to train me to be a hit man. Well, hell. What have I got to lose? So he puts me in with these really tough guys and they teach me all they know. And for over twenty years, I do Big Joe's dirty work, even when he's spending time in the slammer.

"But then, one day..."

"That's enough for now, Knife," Father Keat cut in. "We'll hear the rest later." He looked at the group. "Next?"

One by one, the men came forward, stood with hands clasped over their black cassocks, looked straight ahead, and told the most ghastly stories of mayhem and murder. There were thieves, pimps and assassins, interrogators, drug dealers and gun runners, each one with a nickname evoking his trade. Some of the worst were Latin American soldiers trained in counter-insurgency at the School of the Americas at Fort Benning, Georgia. They told their stories of the torture of innocent *campesinos* with the bland confidence lent a twice-told tale, sometimes with a hint of pride, sometimes with the barest breath of shame.

Calypso's attention was riveted to each. She studied their faces with their stress lines, scars and baggy eyes, their thinning hair, their powerful hands. As the stories went on, she began to feel overwhelmed by the enormity of their cumulative crimes, the weight of which seemed to be filling the room and snuffing the light from the windows. To her surprise, it wasn't disgust that filled her but a ragged sort of compassion for these lives so marred and mangled by violence and crime.

At last, Father Keat announced that they would break for lunch. Calypso was escorted back to her room, where a tray was waiting for her.

"It's nice to see they sometimes alternate rice and beans with beans and rice," she said acidly.

She plopped down on the mattress, pulled her legs into lotus posture, then balanced the tray on her thighs. Maybe, she thought as she chewed the tasteless mess, instead of killing her they might let her bring some inspiration to their kitchen as their cook.

§

After lunch the stories went on. Calypso began to differentiate the lesser from the greater offenders against the human race. Mere murder of rival drug soldiers began to seem petty, compared to wholesale slaughter of innocents by agency of airplane, helicopter and automatic weapons or through sadistic torture. Initially, she felt nauseous, listening to the gruesome details of death and destruction. Later, as the afternoon wore on and each man came forward to tell his tale, she became numb.

Finally, the ordeal was over, with no apparent verdict having been accomplished in her own case. She was led back to her original room, with its low wooden bed, primitive table, and chair. A fire was lit and extra wood brought. A tray of food arrived, featuring the same monotonous rice and beans.

As she chewed morosely, she thought of Hill, wondering where he was salted away in this pile of stone. She could hear his voice, in sardonic mode, saying, "Too bad Pedro's not with us. He could shuck and jive in assassin, and maybe win us our freedom." She smiled, despite herself.

She was so enervated by the day and its revelations that she scarcely ate. The sun had barely sunk behind the cliffs when she lay on the bed, pulled the woolen blanket over her, and fell into exhausted sleep.

§

In the depths of the night, Calypso suddenly found herself standing in a barren stone hallway before a pair of elevator doors. She could hear the mechanism of the lift rumbling, feel the slight tremor of it rising up her legs from the floor. It was cold and she shivered as she waited under a bare bulb that shed sickly yellow light.

The grinding of the elevator ceased and after a pause, the doors parted. Calypso peered into an interior that seemed to hold shadow and nothing more. Then with a slight rustle, as of dry leaves shifting, a figure appeared from the darkness. It was tall, thin, and all in black, and she thought it must be one of her captors. Her eyes swept up the long, inky garment to the face. Then she gasped and froze, too paralyzed with fear even to scream.

The face, hooded in black, was fleshless. There were no eyes, only gaping sockets were eyes should have been. Nevertheless, Calypso had the distinct impression that she was under intense scrutiny. The two black holes were leveled at her like twin barrels of a shotgun.

Mesmerized, Calypso could not tear her eyes away from them. Her mouth went dry; her heart hammered. Her thoughts were gelatinous, unstable, amorphous. She could not move, but remained captive of the vacant but intense stare, as hypnotic and lethal as a cobra's.

Despite the figure's similarity to the Grim Reaper, Calypso began to discern that it was female. What was more, this was no mere mortal, but a divinity: *La Flaca*, "The Skinny Lady," *la Señora de las Sombras*, "Lady of the Shadows," *Santa Muerte*, "Saint Death"—she went by many names among the poor and disenfranchised of Mexico, who venerated her and invoked her against violent death, especially by gunshot.

Death Herself had come to call, and Calypso had the impression that this visit was in response to the day's litany of Ghostly crimes and in defense of their victims. Punchily, she realized that some sort of respect must be paid to so august a visitor.

She tried to speak, but her mouth was frozen in a rictus of terror. Gathering her will, exerting maximal effort, she tried again, and achieved a ragged hiss of air. At last, contorting her face in sheer determination, through clenched teeth and shuddering lips, she managed a rasping whisper.

"Bl-bl-bless you, Mother."

Before her startled eyes, the terrible faceless face began to morph. From within the skull, a hazy mass pushed outward and began, layer upon layer, to solidify, first into muscles criss-crossing, and finally into flesh. In the place of the hideous skull, a ravishingly beautiful face appeared, of an angel, of a goddess. Calypso, unable to fathom its loveliness and delicacy, gazed upon it with wonder and delight.

The figure made the smallest movement with its hand, that moments before had hung down only bones of *la Huesuda,* "the Bony Lady," but now was long fingered and graceful. *Santísima Muerte*, "Most Holy Death," raised Her fingers in a gesture of blessing. Calypso felt hot, stinging energy shower over her like sparks blown from a fire. She stood encompassed in the fiery breath of *la Dama Poderosa,* "the Powerful Lady," entranced.

The doors of the elevator began to close and the car to descend. Calypso's awed gaze followed, as it sank from view. Her last glimpse was of the sweet face, smiling up at her from floor level, as the doors closed completely.

§

The ponderous grinding of the inner mechanism recommenced; the floor shook. Calypso's eyes burst open, her breath coming in wrenching gasps, heart racing so fast it felt like it would explode. A tremendous flash of brilliant white light was followed by an enormous bomb blast of sound. She screamed and ducked, shielding her head with her arms.

It was her first realization that paralysis was gone. She could move. She could speak. She lay trembling, attempting to locate herself in time and space. Another flash of painfully bright light illuminated plastered stone and the looming mantel of her room.

Lightning! Followed by thunder. Calypso took a deep breath, trying to calm herself. Storm. It was only a passing storm. Her entire body shuddered uncontrollably, as her rational mind explained that she had just had a nightmare, brought on by violent weather.

Her deep heart, however, where *la Señora de las Sombras* now communed, insisted that something mighty and terrible had shown itself, offering its naked awfulness, and asking something of her in return: respect, homage, recognition of her own fate.

Having given it, Calypso received a blessing. In the final transformation of the epiphany, Her robes had turned from black to white, a color symbolizing purity and protection from negative energy. The Goddess, showing the beneficent side of Her nature, had smiled upon her.

Calypso began to relax. Knot by knot, her muscles released the terror. She rode the wail of wind and hammer of rain like a boat with reefed sails. Somehow, she would survive—or, if she did not, *Santa Muerte* would offer her kind sanctuary.

ʃ

She could not return to sleep. The twin terrors of encountering the phantom of Death, and the terrible lacuna where knowledge of Javier's and Hill's fates should be, kept her staring at the ceiling, where firelight and lightning alternately lapped and bolted. She fingered the locket beneath her sweater, angry that it had failed her. She was tempted to take it off and stow it in her backpack, but some nagging inconsistency kept her from it.

Could the dream be a gift from the locket? If so, what was its message? Her brain was too seared from the experience to puzzle it out. She returned instead to the story of the locket itself. How Blanche de Muret had undergone imprisonment, just as Calypso was enduring it now, in not unpleasant circumstances that yet held menace of pain and death. She realized that her captor Lone-R, and Caspar, King of Nubia, had become entwined in her mind so that, against better judgment, she trusted the man.

She lay entangled in these maddening allusions like a swimmer trapped in a kelp bed. Long streamers of thought wrapped around her, tugging, impeding progress. She remembered a friend's description of his terror, fighting the grasping kelp while scuba diving off the California coast. He'd said the only way to release himself was to stop fighting. To relax. To glide through the long, waving sea forest without resistance.

Calypso willed herself to stop thinking and rethinking her situation. To simply float with the current of her thoughts, which was wafting her always backward, to the story of the locket. The storm was passing over, moving on. She watched the lightning illuminate the far cliffs, transforming them into a blank white screen where memory could be projected, the story replayed.

§

Chapter 8

Blanche de Muret's Story Continues

ALLIA KEPT ME IN HER PRIVATE APARTMENT FOR A WEEK AND TENDED ME AS LOVINGLY AS A MOTHER. Gradually and gently, she told me the circumstances of Godfrey's enslavement and death. These details, at least, gave my heart some peace.

He had been purchased by a noble family of great spiritual elevation, who had treated him kindly during his brief passage through their household. Sadly, his little heart must have been broken, for he soon contracted a fever and was gone before a month had passed. During that time he was treated as one of their own children would be, with a doctor's attention and delicate victuals, in a clean and sun-filled room. This simple account gave my grieving heart some small solace.

At times, during the week I spent with her, Allia would speak to me of the mysterious community into which I had quite literally fallen and of their history and beliefs. At other times, she simply held me against her bosom while I wept, or exhausted from weeping, collapsed against her strength like a sack of barley grain leaning against a wall.

At those times, I could feel a strange, wild energy exuding from her. At first, this force alarmed me, but I soon realized that in its presence I was revivified and healed, and I came to crave these times of closeness with her. Truly, I began to understand all that King Caspar had told me regarding Allia's curative powers.

When I asked her about this, however, Allia was evasive. She would smooth my brow with a gentle stroke, smile into my eyes, and change the subject. Perhaps she felt it inappropriate to speak of the gifts granted her by God.

During the hours that Allia left me alone to rest, I was kept amused by the community of workers surrounding me. Painted onto the plaster with which the cave walls had been coated, they yet seemed to breathe and jostle by the light of the oil lamps. Their colors were rich and their postures vital and realized with great charm, so that they seemed painted but yesterday. Allia informed me, however, that they were of great antiquity.

"These are works from very long ago," she told me. "The ancient leaders of our people, the pharaohs, knew that their lives would continue on the other side of the passage we call death. So they had their tombs outfitted with all the necessities of everyday life—tools, food, weapons, furniture. Even servants in miniature, going about their daily chores. And these scenes were painted to keep memory of the world of men fresh."

"Are we in a tomb then?" I asked in alarm, for this was a morbid notion and sent me into a panic. Quite suddenly, the great weight of earth pendant above us seemed ineluctably beginning to descend.

"Yes," Allia said. "This was one of the many chambers of the tomb of one of the earliest pharaohs. You needn't look so worried, though. It will not be yours. I can see quite clearly that your end will not come in Egypt but in your home country, and many, many years hence."

"I do not understand, at all, why you and the others are doing this!" I cried with pique. For suddenly the entire adventure seemed too arduous and mysterious. As a sign of its own healing, one might suppose, my mind demanded answers.

"Then, perhaps today is the day for me to explain to you what this community you have fallen into is all about," Allia said with a twinkle, not the least put off by my outburst. "You have recovered from your injuries and your shock sufficiently to grasp what I am about to tell you, I think.

"But you must understand that this is all a great secret. Nothing can be conveyed to you without your absolute promise, sealed in your honor and that of your family, to keep everything I tell you secret for now. Later, when you return to your own country, it will be imposed upon you to tell some of it and this you can do without compromising our safety. We will discuss those matters later. For now, I need your promise to hold what I tell you in profoundest confidence."

Of course, I made a solemn and sacred vow to her, to keep her confidence. In part, I confess, I was motivated by an urgent need to know more about my circumstances. But even more, I was deeply desirous of the safety of these good people who had nurtured me after my escape from the house of Ali Abu'l-Hasan. Nothing could induce me to endanger any one of them, I assured Allia from my heart.

"Very well then," she said, after I had sworn my oath. "I will tell you now about this community and why we are so secretive. Have a bit of this food before we begin. And a little tea." She handed me a cup fashioned with wondrous delicacy. "I want you to be strong and alert, for what I am about to tell you is long and complex. I want my student awake for her history lesson!"

I smiled at her teasing and broke a large piece of bread for myself. For, in truth, more than my appetite for information was stimulated. After weeks of wan energy, I felt myself rebounding, hungering, and restless for action. I chewed my food with exaggeration and returned her humor, saying around a wad of bread and cheese in my cheek, "I vow to you to stuff myself, if you will only begin!"

Allia smiled, arranged her skirt about her legs in an artful way, and commenced.

§

Allia's Story

As you know, Allia began, this community lives underground in a cave. What you do not know is why we choose so odd and difficult an existence or even how we effect this lifestyle. How we get food. How we do not fall ill without exposure to fresh air and sunshine. All this and more I will convey to you today.

To begin, you should know that the religion of Egypt is quite different from your Christian one. I am speaking here of the ancient beliefs of which you probably know very little, if anything at all. In some ways, they are so foreign to your beliefs as to seem heretical. Yet in another way, they may be quite comprehensible to you, since the progenitor god of the Egyptians, like your Christ, is a dying and resurrected god. For, like your Jesus, the god Osiris was unfairly murdered but then brought back to life.

Osiris, it is said, fell in love with his sister, Isis, while they were still in the womb of their mother. So they, who were brother and sister, god and goddess, became husband and wife, king and queen. It was they who taught the early people of Egypt the arts of civilization and raised them from brutish cannibals into a people sustained by agriculture and crowned by music, poetry and evolved religious practices.

Two siblings were born with them: Nepthys, their sister, and Set, their brother, who was the Lord of Evil. Set married Nepthys, for a god could only be wed to a goddess, never a mortal. But his hatred of both Isis and Osiris was great, and he plotted how he might kill Osiris and take over the land of Egypt for himself.

§

With seventy-two conspirators, Set hatched a plan. He had a beautiful box made of cedar from Lebanon and ebony from the land of Punt, for in Egypt there are no woods hard enough for this purpose, but only the soft wood of the palm tree. The box was inlaid with precious stones and gold and was a work of wonder.

Next, Set and his evil friends prepared a great feast, to which they invited Osiris. So the great god-king came, to sit eating and drinking and jesting, surrounded all the while by a viper's den of enemies. After everyone was well fed and loosened by drink, Set's henchmen brought the amazing box into the feasting hall. Every eye was dazzled by it, including that of Osiris.

Now, Set made what seemed to be a host's generous and playful offer: whoever could fit perfectly into the box would have it for his own. Of course, his cronies knew that the box was a perfect fit for Osiris alone, but they played along. One after another, they climbed into the box, to be found too short or too long or too wide or too skinny.

Finally, Osiris took his turn and found that the box fit him perfectly, whereupon he cried in triumph, "The box fits me! It is mine!" At which Set leapt forward with the quick suppleness of a beast and snarled, "The box is yours indeed, my brother—for all eternity!" And with that he slammed the top, and his helpers brought molten lead, with which they sealed the lid tight. And then the whole mob of them carried the box to the banks of the Nile and threw it into the river!

And so the brothers parted: Set, in triumph, to establish his rule over his brother's kingdom, and Osiris, to die in the box, and be carried down the river to the sea. I can see that you are distressed, Blanche, by this story. And a terrible story it is, indeed. But it is not yet finished, and in the end you shall see that, just as with your beloved Savior, Osiris will live again. For the great wisdom of this tale is yet to be revealed.

So far, as you already have witnessed in your short life, we have a story of the triumph of evil over good. But the story never ends there, Blanche. Never. And the necessary containment of death, whether in a sepulcher or in a box, or at the hands of madmen who commit the bodies of their victims to torture, as with your parents, is only a predecessor to the great and triumphant flowering of life.

ꞩ

Now, as you can imagine, when Isis heard what had befallen her love, she was undone with grief and rage. Leaving her court without a single attendant, she ran to the riverbank, hoping for sight of the golden box bobbing on the waters. But she was too late. The current of the river had already carried the box northward toward the sea.

Isis was undaunted. Following the bank of the river, she too traveled northward, asking each and every soul she passed along the way whether they had seen the box upon the waters. Each would answer that, indeed, they had seen this wondrous sight and it had passed them by, moving with the waters toward the sea. The children, especially, who played upon the banks of the river were eager to give an account, and later, to honor their helpfulness, Isis blessed all children that they should always speak words of truth and wisdom.

Many days Isis traveled down river in pursuit of her love. Her hair grew wild, her skin was burned by the sun, her clothing was in rags, but still she persisted. Nothing could deter her from finding Osiris, for nothing in this world, Blanche, is stronger than the bond and power of love.

Finally, Isis came to the sea. She stood upon the beach, her hair all tangled and flying in the wind, and surveyed the vast expanse of water before her. Truly, her heart must have been about to break with hopelessness. But we must remember that Isis was no mortal woman but a goddess, and that means she had powers of which we mere humans know nothing.

Let us call the power she used, there upon the bitter sands of her search, the powers of intuition or insight or revelation. Call it what we will, there was a voice inside her that said hope must not be lost and that turned her to her right, toward the east.

Again for many days, she journeyed along the coast, again collecting accounts from children, fishermen and other simple folk who plied the waves or lived close to the waters, of a passing marvel—a golden box that traveled eastward, as if propelled by the gods themselves. And so she traveled on, sun-blistered and ragged.

§

Now, while Isis traveled thus, footsore and weary, Osiris in his box was making progress like a ship under sail. At last, his coffin—for that is what the glorious box had become—came to the coast of Phoenicia, near the capital city of Byblos, and there the waves cast it ashore, to land in the branches of a tamarisk tree.

This tree, stimulated by the energy of the god within the box, grew prodigiously and soon was of such girth that it encompassed the box completely. So poor Osiris was doubly encapsulated: first in the box, and then within the tree, so that it seemed he would never be found.

This all must sound fantastic to you, but you must remember that these are the doings of magic, the power that the gods use to effect their will and desire. And while there are those among us here in this cave this very day who are adept at such powers of visualization and thought-made-form, no one in the present time can match the magic wrought by those first beings.

Even your own Savior has said, *ye are as gods*, and it is so, dear Blanche, but we are weak and corrupt, compared with those mighty ones from the beginning of things when this story was made. And we must realize that Osiris allowed all this to transpire in order to demonstrate a most important universal principle: containment precedes regeneration. Remember this, child, should you ever find yourself again in captivity, for Osiris suffered, that you might know this.

§

Now, it soon happened that news of this marvel, a tamarisk tree of unusual size and wonderful fragrance, traveled to the city of Byblos, and into the hearing of King Malcander and his queen, Astarte. Together they journeyed to the seashore to see this wonder for themselves. So impressed were they by this marvelous tree that they ordered it cut down on the spot, to be carried back to the palace. There, it was erected as a pillar in the throne room, a thing of beauty and mystery.

Finally, after many months of hard travel, Isis arrived at the shores of Phoenicia. There, the children excitedly told her of a wondrous tree that had suddenly grown by the shore, of so great a wonder that it had been visited by the king and queen.

Hearing the fate of the tamarisk, Isis grew hopeful, for she suspected that only the presence of a god could work such a miracle upon a simple entity of nature.

Some say it was as she rested on the stump of that great tree and some that it was later, when she refreshed herself at a well in the city of Byblos, but at some point soon after her arrival, Isis encountered the young women who were in attendance upon Queen Astarte. Whether they came to the sea to bathe or to the well to draw water is of little importance. Isis, even in her state of dishevelment and bereavement, was a goddess still and the maidens of the court were drawn to her. It is what transpired from this fortuitous meeting that interests us today.

For this is one of the great truths of life, dear child—when you have traveled long and honestly upon a given road, be it a real road of dust, hunger and sweat, or a way involving much artistry and effort or one of great moral restraint and wisdom—the gods and goddesses, in their infinite mercy, will send helpers at the very moment when your own will and energy are depleted and all seems lost. So it was, as you have heard, with our dear Caspar of Nubia when, after long and terrible suffering, he was close to despair. And so it was with you, when you chose death over terrible defilement and fate flung you into our waiting arms. And so it was with Isis, who had traveled with such noble intention upon the hardest of roads, for now the gods decreed that she should have her reward.

§

In her generosity, Isis saw that these maids of the court were yet untutored in the refinements of womanhood that she had so long nurtured among the people of Egypt. Taking pity on these roughly coiffed but kindly girls, she offered to plait their hair and they readily agreed. With delight they then rushed off to show Queen Astarte their newly styled hair, in the process drawing with them the divine scent of Isis that pervaded them like strong perfume.

The queen, enchanted both by the lovely hairdos and the scent that wafted around the girls, soon extracted from them how they had come by these refinements and sent a servant to invite Isis to the palace. Isis was in the guise of an old, bedraggled woman when she arrived, and still her essence was so sweet that the queen invited her, then and there, to become the nursemaid to her two children, young Prince Maneros and his baby brother, Dictys.

Isis accepted this assignment because, upon entering the palace, she knew her quest was at an end. She could sense the closeness of her love and she was determined to locate him. So she cared for the little princes by day and at night searched the palace for Osiris.

Before long, she discovered his essence exuding from the vast tamarisk pillar in the throne room. Confounded by its imprisoning structure, each night she turned herself into a swallow and flew round and round the pillar, crying her love in anguish to her husband and brother.

Isis was of such a sweet and loving nature that the little princes flourished under her sway. The baby Dictys especially was fond of her and she of him. So Isis made a decision such as only a goddess can make: she would confer immortality upon baby Dictys!

So each night, when she had tired of flying about the pillar, calling to Osiris, she did further magic. Taking baby Dictys by the heel while chanting mystical words, she would dip the infant into the flames of the evening fire, in the same way that an armorer would commit a sword to hot coals to temper the metal.

This was her routine for many days and nights, until one night when Queen Astarte discovered Isis in the act of holding her child into the flames! You can imagine, I'm sure, how it must have appeared to the frantic mother, who screamed that the new nursemaid was trying to kill the little prince!

A furor was raised in the palace of King Malcander that night and before the coming of the dawn, all was revealed. Isis showed herself in all her glory and reproached the queen for rupturing the magic that would have gifted her son immortality. For their part, the king and queen cowered before the radiance of the goddess and offered her whatever treasure she might wish in their kingdom. But Isis asked for only one thing, the great tamarisk pillar, which they granted her without hesitation.

§

Immediately Isis caused the tree to be hewn open and discovered the golden box within it. At the sight of it, she threw herself down upon it with wails of such terrible anguish that it is said poor baby Dictys died of fright upon hearing them, thus punishing his mother for subverting the will of a goddess.

In fact, we now see the terrible side of the goddess, for every god and goddess possesses one. The good King Malcander now supplied Isis with a ship to return her and her treasure to Egypt, and sent young Prince Maneros to accompany her. But once they were at sea, Isis caught the boy spying on her as she opened the lid of the box to tend to Osiris. In a rage, with one blow-like glance of her eyes, she knocked him overboard and into the sea.

Soon, their ship was navigating across the mouth of the Phaedrus River, which was in flood. The force of the current was so powerful that it threatened to sweep the ship away from sight of land, out into the open sea. Isis was outraged by this impediment to her homeward journey. She shouted a curse at the river, which immediately dried up and has remained so ever since.

Such is the power of the goddess, my child. We mortals cannot comprehend it nor the morality that propels it. There are some who call the gods unjust and whimsical in their actions. But it is a universal law, which even the gods and goddesses cannot violate, that every curse shall lead to an even greater blessing. And so it was with Isis, whose one objective was to return Osiris, in all his benevolence, to the land of Egypt. And so, as we shall see, it eventually was with Set, whose black magic only conferred great blessings upon all, through his downfall.

§

Some say Isis took Osiris to a cave and some that she hid him in the marshes of the delta. In any case, she stowed him away in a secret place and began working her magic over him. Because he was a god and incorruptible, his body was perfectly preserved and unblemished, even in death. And because she was a goddess, she knew the magic spells to return life to his lifeless body, even as your Savior Jesus is rumored to have done to Lazarus.

At last, Osiris's eyes fluttered open and the first thing he beheld was the beautiful face of his beloved Isis. Immediately, while he was still in a barely conscious state, they desired one another, as couples sometimes do who have just awakened from sleep. After so long a separation, it was a joyous and passionate coupling, and Isis knew from the instant it occurred that she was pregnant with a son.

Afterward Osiris rested while Isis went to find food, leaving her love unattended. Now, it happened that Set and his henchmen were hunting that night, by the light of the moon, for Set was of a beastly disposition and felt most comfortable hidden in the cloak of night, as is often the case with evil ones. Imagine his amazement when, on the night wind, he smelled a whiff of his brother Osiris!

Like a wild predator, Set followed the scent until he arrived at the hiding place prepared by Isis. When he saw his brother alive and resting sweetly, Set flew into a titanic rage. He fell upon Osiris, rending his body into fourteen pieces. These he gave to his henchmen, telling them to distribute them as widely as possible, from one end of Egypt to the other, so that the parts could never again be reassembled. Off into the night loped these evildoers, bearing away the separate parts to be hidden.

When Isis returned, expecting the adored company of her love, she came instead upon an empty, blood-soaked box. How great was her anguish then! No consolation was possible. And here we see how great is the power of love. Exhausted and grieving as she was, she set forth immediately to discover what had happened to Osiris, with the sole intent of bringing him once more to life.

It did not take long for Isis to receive confirmation of the murder.The minions of Set could not stop bragging of their exploit, and Set himself went about shouting his triumph. The news was soon buzzing even among the lowly people of Egypt, how Set had brought his brother low for a second time.

§

This time Isis enlisted the help of her sister Nepthys, who had left Set in disgust and horror because of his evil doing. They also begged aid from Nepthys' son, Anubis, who turned himself into a jackal, so that he might use his delicate nose to sniff out the hidden parts of Osiris.

By day these three traveled on land, guarded by seven deadly scorpions. By night, they moved upon the broad breast of the Nile in the royal barge. So great was the radiance and power of the goddesses that crocodiles in the river and scavenger birds of the air refused to touch the pieces of the god.

Slowly, Isis recovered the parts of the dead Osiris. At each place where she found a part, she caused a temple to be erected, honoring him. That is how there come to be thirteen holy temples dedicated to Osiris in the land of Egypt.

I see you are alert, dear child. The bread and cheese have served you well. For you are wondering now why there are only thirteen temples, when Osiris was rent into fourteen pieces. That is because one of the pieces was lost. The phallus of Osiris was thrown into the Nile and was swallowed by a fish! The loss of the phallus was divinely ordained, you see. It went into the great river that waters all Egypt and in this fashion inseminated the entire land, bringing fertility to humans, animals, and plants alike, and demonstrating, even in death, the dominion of Osiris over his brother Set.

Isis made Osiris a new phallus of cedar wood and gold, and through her magic, fused it to the reassembled body. But the soul of Osiris had been too long in the underworld, and even the magic of Isis could not return him to life on this earthly plane. His spirit had flown and taken up residence in the Hall of Timelessness, there to act as judge upon those traveling between this world and the next.

So Isis went to an island in the Nile called Philae, at the southernmost boundary of Egypt, close to the First Cataract. There she erected a great temple, the holiest of all, for there was where she had found Osiris's heart, and it was there that she buried the body of her beloved, the god who had brought the joys of civilization to Egypt.

By then, Isis was heavy with child. It was time for her to give birth, but she was harried by Set and his hoard of evildoers. She was driven forth from the towns and took refuge in the swamps of the Nile delta, and there, accompanied only by wild dogs, she gave birth to their son Horus, who one day would avenge his father and mother against Set.

You must be wondering why I am telling you this story. Entertaining as it is, it is not apparent what is its connection to the explanation I have promised you regarding this community. But have patience, dear child, for I am about to embark on a story that will make all clear to you.

ʂ

Now, we move forward in time, to the years following the Crucifixion of the one you call the Lord Jesus Christ. These many centuries later, a temple still flourished on Philae in the Nile River. This temple, sacred to the goddess Isis, was built more than three hundred years before the Christian era by the last dynasty of Egypt, the Ptolemys. It was erected on the site of the temple built by Isis—in fact, including the earlier structure in its architecture.

Because it was believed to be the burying place of the god Osiris, it was still a deeply sacred site to the Egyptians. Only priests and priestesses were allowed to live there and so the island was known as The Unapproachable. It was so sequestered that it is said that fish did not visit its shores nor did birds fly over it.

I regret that you will not be able to travel with me to Philae. You would be overcome with awe at its beauty and grandeur. But your path leads elsewhere, my little friend, while mine will lead to Philae one last time. To me, it is the most sacred site in all the world. It is likely that when I go this time, I shall not return. I ask nothing more of the Great Mother than that She allow me to pass from this world while within the sacred compound at Philae.

Since you will not see this marvel in your lifetime, I will describe it to you. Imagine that you are approaching a small, low island by boat on the river. Rising from the green water is a building of such magnificence that I can scarcely convey its beauty to you. A double colonnade extends to greet you at the water's edge. Before the entrance to the sacred courtyard are two huge lions, carved in granite, and behind them two obelisks, each tall as a great tree.

The great gate to the temple is formed by two immense pyramid-shaped pylons, carved with monumental figures of Isis and Osiris, and behind them, across a courtyard, are two more, forming the entrance to the most sacred area. The columns that support the temple roof are massive, completely covered in hieroglyphs carved into the stone and painted in bright colors, and at the top there are capitals in the shape of papyrus bundles and palm fronds.

No, I cannot convey to you the grandeur of this place that is so dear to me. And dear, for a multitude of reasons, not the least of which is that it is the resting place of the body of Osiris. Or that the temple is sacred to Isis. But there is yet another reason and it bears directly upon the history of the community in which you now take shelter.

You may not know that dynastic Egypt of the Pharaohs was conquered, first by the Greeks and then by the Romans. Yet all during that time, for a period of close to a thousand years, Philae remained a sacred site where the ancient Egyptian religion was practiced, even while foreign influence and persecution flourished.

Because it was the last outpost of Egyptian religion, many devoted followers went to Philae on pilgrimage. The temple even attracted Greek and Roman pilgrims, who came to pray for healing and wisdom from the mysterious goddess Isis. Even after the Romans converted to Christianity, three hundred years after the death and resurrection of the one you call Jesus, still the temple and its religious practices survived for another two centuries.

Finally, in the Christian year 550, the Byzantine emperor Justinian officially closed the temple of Isis on Philae. It was the last so-called pagan temple active in the Mediterranean world—although I have visited a Roman temple to Isis that still remains active in England. The chapel that was dedicated to Osiris was rededicated to the Christ, and the temple of Isis was converted to a church honoring the Virgin Mary. All was then maintained by a Coptic Christian community that lived on the island, until even that was closed down by Muslin invaders in the seventh century.

ና

So you see, dear child, that the temple on Philae has had a long and tumultuous past. It was during the time of Emperor Justinian, when the temple was closed to ancient Egyptian practices, that we again pick up the thread of my tale. For this transition from Egyptian to Christian religion on Philae was not a peaceful one.

One day, as the priests were going about their sacred rituals within the temple, a mob broke in! These were Christian zealots who could not tolerate the thought of another religion besides their own. You must understand that they were coarse and uneducated people, while the priests whom they attacked that day were inheritors of thousands of years of knowledge, culture, wisdom and magic.

The Christian mob swept through the Temple of Isis, sacred to Egyptians for a thousand years, defiling the place—breaking statuary, hammering off hieroglyphs, and killing as they went. Perhaps never before on this earth has there been such a wasteful slaughter—one which set human culture back by centuries.

ꟹ

You can imagine the panic that swept through the Egyptian religious community that day. Priests and priestesses were running in all directions, trying to save the precious artifacts and sacred objects. Trying to save themselves!

There was a special urgency because there was among them a family of such importance that all were willing to lay down their lives to protect them: the remaining lineage of the last true Pharaoh of Egypt! This family had escaped following the takeover by the Greek Ptolemys, and they and then their lineage had been sequestered at Philae for eight hundred and fifty years, in an unbroken line of succession!

Thus, on that terrible day when the Christian mob swept in, every heart and mind among the Egyptian priesthood was turned toward the safety of this sacred and irreplaceable family. We have first-person accounts of that day, written in hieroglyphs, and stored in this cave to this day. And there are storytellers among us who have preserved these accounts orally, from one generation to the next, for these last nearly seven hundred years. Therefore, I can assure you that what I am about to tell you is as accurate as any human history can be.

ꟹ

There were, of course, guards around the temple at Philae, and they were the first to raise the alarm that a ragtag mob of people was heading toward the sacred island in a variety of boats, mostly small fishing vessels. Clearly, these were no pilgrims coming to be healed, for they brandished weapons and were shouting as they came.

Immediately the high priest, named Aapep, which means Moon Snake, understood the dire nature of this invasion and ran like the wind to the royal chambers. Without salutation or any ritual respect whatsoever, he shouted that the royal family must take flight instantly. He grabbed the baby from its cradle and taking its mother, the queen, by her arm, dragged her from the room and through a series of twisting corridors, with the remainder of the family racing behind. And at the desperate procession's end was an ancient crone, carried by servants.

At last, with shouting, crashing, and screaming echoing through the hallways behind them, they came to a small chamber into which Aapep guided them. Drawing aside an embroidered curtain, he revealed a low door, which he opened and through which he hastily shoved one after another of the family: the mother and her princelings, their father, the present Pharaoh, and finally, the old crone, whose identity you shall know presently.

When all were secured inside, Aapep slammed the door, and barred it from within. Now, they were in a low chamber that diminished in height toward the far end, leading directly into a tunnel. The only light was from a torch that Aapep had managed to grab from a wall sconce as they raced along. There was, however, a stack of unlit torches lying beside the entrance to the tunnel, put there in case of urgent need. These he lit, one at a time, and handed to each member of the group who was capable of carrying one.

By the flaring light of these, the startled and badly frightened family looked into the tunnel that descended sharply into an abyss of blackness. Aapep gave them no time to fall into trepidation, however. "Majesties," he cried, "there is no time to hesitate. This way lies your salvation!" And so saying, he plunged into the tunnel, with the royal family straggling after him.

That day, dear child, old Egypt died on the surface of this beloved land. The priests and priestesses of the temple all were slaughtered most brutally. The Christian mob looted, burned, and smashed until the temple was desecrated and ran with blood. But under their very feet, running like a secret river in the darkness of the earth, the precious seed of Egypt was preserved, to await another day in the light of beloved Ra, the Sun.

ʖ

For hundreds of years the priesthood had prepared for just such an emergency. Stored in underground labyrinths were food that was continually renewed, clothing, bedding, utensils—all that the family might need to survive for a given time beneath the ground. What they did not expect, of course, was that there would be no return to the sunlight in their lifetimes, or in the lifetime of any of those present that day, but one.

It is that one most extraordinary person about whom I will tell you shortly. But first I will say that the underground area where they were now gathered was manmade, but it connected, by design, with a natural cave the runs along the course of the River Nile for many hundreds of miles.

Sometimes the cave deviates and runs out under the desert. And sometimes it sinks right under the Nile and water drips through its ceiling. In places, long ago, it had collapsed, and the segments had been reconnected by human agency. But for those who knew the way—and it was part of the secret knowledge of the priesthood at a certain level of advancement to know these things—it was possible to move from the southern boundary of Egypt at the First Cataract, all the way northward to the delta where the Nile enters the sea, completely under the ground!

Who knows? Perhaps it was in that very cave that Isis sheltered with the reborn Osiris.

§

Now, for a day the family huddled in the manmade chambers beneath the island of Philae. Through secret windows in the foundation of the temple, they were able to spy the doings above and thus learned the terrible outcome of the day's events. Then, with the religious objects that were supplied there, the pharaoh and his wife performed solemn rituals of atonement and in honor of the dead. When these were at last complete, they gathered their family, the priest Aapep, and their servants about them, and took council.

"It is just a matter of time," said the wise Aapep, "before these invaders find the secret door. Therefore, I recommend taking the most extreme measures possible for your protection." There was silence then, for the parents and the old woman knew to what he referred, and it was a thing of such gravity and finality that their hearts quailed before it.

"Can we not hope, then, for any kind of rescue?" asked the queen, her hands enmeshed in the hair of her oldest child. It was clear to see how she grieved that this boy would be subjected eternally to a sunless realm, and never again run and play in open air as any child should.

In answer, the Pharaoh simply pulled her to him in the tenderest of embraces, for he could see that her heart was about to break. "We must have the courage of our ancestors," he said gently. "Many generations of our family have lived in peace. It is our lot and responsibility to sustain our line through the greatest challenge since the coming of the Ptolemys. We must be brave."

So it came to pass, there in the sunless world, that the little group made a terrible, irreversible decision. For, hidden inside one of the giant pylons of the portal to the sanctuary was a device of ponderous weight and import—a huge slab of stone which, when triggered, would slide downward into the tunnel and form an impenetrable barrier to all pursuit. But of course, it also would cut the royal family off from the temple at Philae forever.

With trepidation and heavy hearts, the little group moved in single file into the tunnel that would take them to this heartbreaking juncture. In due time, they reached a place where the smooth floor of the tunnel gave way to a sudden abyss, bottomless in its blackness. Across this stretched a delicate bridge of rope and wooden slats, the further end of which was just visible in the light of the guttering torches.

§

On the edge of this pit, the family stopped to rest. There the pharaoh performed yet another ritual in which he thanked the gods for the family's many peaceful years at Philae and for their safe escape, and invoked their help on the journey into darkness which they were about to undertake.

He was just uttering the closing prayer when they all were jolted from their meditative silence by a sound that struck terror into their hearts. Muffled by the length of the tunnel, but closer than they cared to know, were the shouts of pursuit! Stopping his prayer in mid-sentence, the pharaoh swept his son into his arms and stepped onto the bridge, saying, "Come, my dears. It is time."

The bridge swayed and swung under their hurrying feet. The servants, in particular, set it swinging as they tussled and half-dragged the poor old woman along its narrow length. When at last they were all assembled on the other side, the pharaoh turned, and with his knife cut the ropes of the bridge, which sagged against the final fibers and then, cut free, swung away into the darkness of the pit.

Aapep, meanwhile, raced to a spot in the far wall where a small stone, carved with the hawk-head of Horus at the end, protruded from the surrounding stones. With a mighty tug, he pulled the stone from its slot. There was a moment of profound silence during which the entire group held their breath. Then, slowly at first and then with increasing force, a stream of sand appeared from the ceiling above the pit. It fell first in a tiny trickle and then a flow, and finally cascaded down into the abyss like one of the rapids of the First Cataract.

All the while a sound, at first a dim rumble in the invisible regions above them, increased to a roar that drowned out both their labored breathing and the cries of their pursuers. It was a terrible grinding, wheezing, rumbling sound of massive masonry moving, as if an earthquake were in that instant demolishing the temple above their heads.

The ground under their feet began to shake and the queen looked wildly around her for her children, screaming, "We have to get back! Get out of the way!"

At just this instant, out of the mouth of the tunnel opposite them came a stream of dark figures, brandishing torches. So fast were they moving that the first among them could not see his peril in time and simply plunged over the edge of the pit, where he and his torch instantly wheeled into darkness. The others managed to stop in time, and they clustered on the edge of the abyss, gesturing wildly with their torches and shouting. For the holy family must have been clearly visible to them across the divide by the light of their own torches.

All the while, the earth was rumbling and stones were shrieking as they grated and tumbled upon one another. The cataract of sand had turned into a solid deluge, as the entire ceiling gave way, and an ocean of sand descended.

At the last moment, one of the pursuers pulled an arrow from a quiver on his back, slammed it into his bow, and pulled back. Just as his arrow was released, flying like death itself toward the royal family, there was a deafening roar. Like the blade of a huge hatchet chopping, a giant slab of stone slid thundering down from the ceiling. With a horrific jolt, it landed, straddling the pit, completely blocking one side of the tunnel from the other!

S

The royal family and their retainers huddled against the wall, weeping with terror. A blast of hot, stale air blew past them, extinguishing their torches like the breath of some infernal god. Plunged into complete blackness, it seemed their minds would break from the utter lostness of their position.

But then, out of black silence came the voice of Aapep, shaking a bit, it is true, but calm, saying, "I have a flint, here on my belt. We will have light in a moment. Take heart." And surely as he had spoken, there was a scratching of flint, a spark was kindled, and in a moment, a torch flared like hope returning after despair.

With the relighting of their torches, the group hovered between gratitude that they were safely defended from their pursuers and dread of the dank kingdom which was now theirs to rule. As they moved once more into the tunnel, their way now being irrevocably chosen for them, they did so both with thanksgiving and trepidation. It was not long, however, before their attention must once again shift to matters of gravest concern.

§

The royal entourage made their way forward for some time and finally broke from the hewn tunnel into the first of a near infinitude of natural caverns. This one was quite spacious and glittered magically by torch light from myriad tiny crystals embedded in the limestone. More important, it had several large side chambers and these were of such special importance that each was fitted with a massive door, secured with a lock.

Since these were no mere wanderers but the royal family of Egypt, the content of these chambers was well known to them and to the high priest Aapep. Here was sealed a treasure of such vast value as to be immeasurable, for they were now in the royal treasury! Here were collected, through many hundreds of years, the unparalleled treasures of their wealthy kingdom, removed to these impregnable rooms at the time of the Ptolemy takeover.

Of course, they had no use for gold or jewels or precious woods or gorgeous jewelry, which could neither be appreciated in the gloomy dark, nor eaten by their hungry band. Fortunately, their years of preparedness were paying off, for in the initial chamber also were stored foodstuffs fit for a king and sufficient for an army. And so they rested and ate, and as they ate, discussed. Slowly and painfully, a plan began to form that gave hope of a way forward.

Aapep, as part of his priestly training, had traversed the entire length of the secret cave and tunnel system, from Philae in the south to a humble fisherman's shack that hid the entrance, in the northern delta. "With the supplies that are stored here, we can travel underground all the way to the north in safety," he said. "It will be a slow process, but if we carry food forward, making several trips each day between this and our next stopping place, we can keep ourselves supplied. Further on, there will be more stores."

"How will we know if it is a day we labor thus, or a week, since there is not Ra to guide us?" asked the queen.

"Aapep speaks wisely," the pharaoh said. "We will do as he suggests and we will rest as we grow weary, no matter what the hour on the surface above."

And so, they settled on the details of their plan, and would have begun immediately but for yet another misfortune in a day black with them. Surely, the stars of heaven were frowning on them that day, for no sooner had they eaten and rested and begun to stir around, eager to begin their labors, than the old woman, who had been valiant and stoic throughout the day's ordeal, began to suffer a critical decline.

ʛ

And now, dear Blanche, I will tell you about this mysterious old woman. For she touches your own future, strange as that may sound. The name of this old woman was Sa Tahuti and she was—and is—the high priestess of the House of Tahuti, who is known on your continent as Thoth, the God of Wisdom. She was at the time of their escape over one hundred years old and her condition was very fragile. Yet, I tell you a wonder, young Blanche: Sa Tahuti is *still alive!*

I see I have greatly confused you and that is as it should be. For what I am telling you now is not only a great secret but one of the great spiritual wonders of Egypt. Through great spiritual elevation, Sa Tahuti has found a way to pass her soul from one body to another without ever having to experience death. And what is more, she has been doing this for several thousand years!

Yes. It is astonishing, I know, and scarcely believable. And yet it is so. And believe it or not, Sa Tahuti is not unique. In my wanderings with my people the Romany, I have met one other in the land of India, a man named Baba Ji, who shares a similar ability and fate; and high in the Himalayan mountains, I have heard whispers of yet another. This ability is a mark of spiritual elevation at a level which is unimaginable, even to those of us who have studied the ancient ways.

Now, when Sa Tahuti transfers from one body to the next, she carries with her all the wisdom and knowledge of ancient Egypt, from the days of Isis and Osiris forward—spiritual science, astronomy, and astrology, mathematics, metallurgy, healing, magic and the history of the Egyptian people, to name only a few of her areas of understanding. She is so prescient that she knows when she is about to die and in her wisdom, already has a body chosen into which she can transfer. For you see, throughout the ages, children have been born specifically so that their bodies may become a vessel for the soul and spirit of Sa Tahuti.

Yet here was their dilemma: the child who had been designated to be Sa Tahuti's next incarnation had been murdered when the Christians stormed the temple! And so disturbing was this to the old woman, who now faced sudden loss of her accumulated wisdom should she die, that the very thought of it brought on the physical crisis most to be feared.

So taxed was her old heart that Sa Tahuti collapsed and could not be revived for some time. The queen and her attendants worked over the old woman, for the queen was no mere figurehead but a practitioner of the deepest arts of Egyptian healing and magic. Just as Isis revived the dead Osiris, so the queen was able to revive Sa Tahuti, who teetered on the threshold of death.

Once her condition was stabilized, Sa Tahuti took counsel with Aapep. Their urgent whispers buzzed away like two angry wasps for a considerable time, and it seemed to those around them that they were arguing, a thing unheard of formerly. Finally, Aapep rose from his position beside the old woman's reclined body and came to the pharaoh with long, grievous face.

"My Lord," Aapep began, tears brimming in a deeply troubled countenance, "Sa Tahuti says she will not last the night in her present body. Furthermore, she is aware that the child whose body she was to inhabit next has been murdered." At this pronouncement, a gasp of horror arose from the royal couple, for they understood the dire consequences of losing this living repository of wisdom.

"We have discussed this matter at length and have come to a decision, one which tortures our very beings to suggest."

The pharaoh was a wise and prescient man himself, and he could sense where this conversation was heading. Instinctively, he reached out to embrace his queen and their infant son, who lay nursing sweetly in her arms. "Speak it," he managed to spit out, as if he were ejecting sand from between his teeth.

"My Lord, Sa Tahuti is the priceless treasure of your realm. I believe you know that she must not be allowed to pass away without renewal."

The pharaoh, his jaw clenched against a rage he knew was directed at no living person but at the gods, could only nod.

"Sa Tahuti and I have conferred. She tells me that your son, the youngest prince, is of feeble constitution." This could not be denied. The baby was colicky, cross-tempered and always uncomfortable in his little body, no matter how tenderly his mother ministered to him.

Aapep looked down at his feet, his mouth twisted with difficult words: "Sa Tahuti, My Lord, believes that the prince will not complete the journey northward. Lack of sunshine, dampness and stale air will be too great a burden for his little soul to bear."

At this, the queen gave a shriek and clutched the child fiercely to her breast. The look she hurled at Aapep was both anguished and enraged.

Stoically, the high priest continued on: "Sa Tahuti believes that it would be possible for her to do something that she has never before accomplished. Because the soul of the baby prince is so loosely tied to his body, she proposes to exchange bodies with him. This would mean that he would expire tonight, with her body, rather than several days hence. Sa Tahuti also believes that, given the strength of her own soul, she can heal the baby's body and thus survive. She wishes you to know that, because of his great sacrifice, the prince will be welcomed by Osiris and the other gods into the Hall of Timelessness and will abide happily there forever."

Aapep finished his terrible message with bowed head. Backing away, he left the pharaoh and queen to confer. It was beyond a doubt the most anguished decision of their lives. Yet, in the end, they proved themselves to be truly royal. They considered the welfare of the kingdom before their own grief and consented to this magical soul transfer.

ʖ

All present gathered around the recumbent body of Sa Tahuti, who held the baby prince against her breast, heart to heart. As the pharaoh and the high priest enacted a solemn ritual, their chanting echoed and re-echoed through the vast reaches of the cavern, as if all generations of priests and pharaohs were present, participating in this moment of profoundest magic.

Then, Sa Tahuti added her voice to theirs, a high, tenuous, reedy wail, like wind over winter marshes. It carried such ominous potency that the women of the group began to weep and Aapep and the pharaoh could scarcely continue. Their voices rose and fell, mixing and swirling with their rebounding echoes, as if an entire contingent of the dead had arisen to aid in the soul transfer. The sound encompassed each person and seemed to enter into their very bones, so that they throbbed as if trapped inside a huge drum.

Then abruptly, Sa Tahuti's voice ceased. Aapep and the pharaoh stopped their chanting. The echoes died away into the depths of darkness surrounding them. The instant hung, breathless and quivering as a pendant drop of rain on the end of a twig...

Suddenly, the little prince let out a yelp and began to wail in exactly the same cadence as Sa Tahuti's chant. At the same moment, Sa Tahuti's body gave a great spasm and with a rattling gasp, lapsed into the utter stillness of death.

The women began to wail and tear their hair. The baby kicked his feet and shrieked, until the queen rushed to pick him up and comfort him. And Aapep knelt to minister to the body of his old friend, Sa Tahuti.

Every soul present testified later that they were unsure if the soul transfer had happened at all. Their group was completely undone by all that had transpired that day, and lacking anything else to do and being absolutely physically and emotionally exhausted, they lay themselves down on their individual bedrolls and slept.

§

I will not tell you more of the journey endured by this little band, dear Blanche. Suffice it to say that they encountered many adventures and hardships on their journey northward. Eventually, they came to this area of the great cave, which we presently inhabit. Here they stopped and set up housekeeping, and here this community has been ever since.

Contact was made with the outside world through certain trusted portals. The land above us was purchased and a great house with walled gardens was built there, using funds from the treasury. This provided a place of secret egress through which each member of the community might, on a regular basis, have access to sunshine and fresh air and all the amenities of the upper world. The attendants you have met here will rotate with those in the house above tomorrow. You will meet an entirely new group, invigorated by their time above. They will come bearing baskets of fresh fruits and vegetables and meat. And so it has been, these many centuries, Blanche my child.

Christian rule in Egypt was eventually replaced by Muslim rule. The great estates of the Muslim lords were built next to ours, including that now belonging to Ali Abu'l-Hasan. But here we have stayed, a community of true Egyptians, still worshipping as we have for thousands of years.

We are like a secret heart beating beneath the breast of the land. The pharaoh still performs his rituals...I see you are surprised. Yes, chère Blanche, a pharaoh still reigns, a direct descendent of the one who fled Philae so long ago. And Sa Tahuti, who became Sau Tahuti when she lived in the male body of the young prince, is once again restored to a feminine body.

Ah! You are surprised again! Yes, Sa Tahuti, the very one, is still with us and is now so old, after so many incarnations, that no one except she can count it. It is because of her that I have told you this long, wandering tale. For soon, you will receive an audience. We must prepare you now to meet Sa Tahuti!

ʖ

Chapter 9

Monastery of the Ghosts

CALYPSO STOOD GAZING FROM THE WINDOW AT THE LIGHT SHOW IN THE CANYON. The chasm lay in utter blackness until an explosion of lightning and thunder illuminated it, turning cliffs into shimmering sheets of silver and the abyss into a vast amplifier.

A similar storm agitated her mind, as it alternated between a gulf of unknowing and the radiance of timeless wisdom. Her thoughts churned with the story of the locket and the strange parallels that were beginning to manifest in her own life.

Just as she and Hill had made the cave crossing from one river canyon to the next, escaping the cartel's attack, so the pharaoh and his entourage had resorted to a cave to save themselves. And both efforts were sustained on supplies already laid in for just such a contingency. And what of Hill's vision while trapped in the tube? Wasn't it a miracle as surely as Sa Tahuti's transformation?

Even more abstractly, wasn't it stone that had saved both groups? In the Egyptian case, the massive stone cutting off the enemy's advance and in her own, the monolithic stone of the cliff over which she and Hill had disappeared as if they had never been. And in each case, a river was the source of life toward which they journeyed.

More importantly, she was separated as grievously from Javier as Isis was from Osiris. Would she have to lose him and find him dead in order to fulfill the pattern? The thought was too terrible. And yet, the myth of Isis showed the Goddess in both her terrible and benevolent forms, just as in tonight's dream. Calypso had come too far in life to expect happy endings.

A blast of lightning and thunder shook the windowpanes, filling the room with a shock of blue-white light. Alarmed, her thoughts skittered and bolted onward.

Did people really reincarnate again and again? It all seemed too huge and too fantastic. And yet, she felt in her bones that all people were really Light made matter, suffering amnesia about their true origins. Were she, Javier, and Hill, and the rest of humanity, all part of an ancient lineage of which beings like the Christ and the Buddha were the shining exemplars, the realized ones because they had overcome the forgetting?

Could she dare to believe that she was conjured from the same divine fire? Was that hubris or simple knowing? And did it exalt or exhaust her to think that she had been around since the beginning of time and would be here after its end? Wasn't that knowledge almost as heavy to bear as the locket?

She had to smile despite herself. Her weary body certainly felt tonight as if it had seen the passage of the ages.

She gripped the window bars and leaned her forehead against the cold metal. The storm was moving off down the canyon like a great battle transiting, with cannons roaring and bombs dropping. The hard white light of lightning was replaced by the glow of the fire, the crashing cannonade with the slow drip of rain on the sill outside.

Calypso pulled the chair close to the fire, threw on another log and bent her head to her hands, her elbows on her knees. It must be nearly dawn, although it would be a dark one, hidden behind clouds. Somewhere in her own life, light must be dawning, too, despite all appearances. Her body was leaden with weariness, but somewhere deep down she had connected to a bottomless aquifer of energy. Come what may, she knew herself to be unshakable.

§

A sharp knock on the door startled her from a doze, her face still supported in her hands. She jerked awake, her eyes darting to the window. It was still black behind the bars and the fire had scarcely burned down on the hearth. Who would be summoning her at this early hour? Before she could call out the question, a key turned in the lock, the heavy wooden door swung inward, and a black-robed figure glided through it.

Calypso reeled back in shock, momentarily caught in the illusion of her dream repeating itself. There was no black cowl, however, and when the figure stepped out of shadows into firelight, she saw that her visitor was Icepick.

Of all the men's stories, his was far from the most gruesome. Yet he was one of the men for whom Calypso had felt the least compassion. It came, she realized, from his apparent lack of compunction. He had told his life's tale as if he were reading from a book written by someone else about a fictitious character.

There was an isolated quality to the man. His face was pitted and desolate as the lunar surface, with a haunted yet somehow vacant expression, as if he had lived too long in an orbit far from human warmth. He was not young but the years had been kind to him. He moved with an uncanny grace that more resembled stealth. Yet he was a gray man—hair, flesh, aura. Instead of giving off energy like other living creatures, he seemed to suck energy in, leaving a void around him where air and vibrancy should be. He was, in a word, creepy.

Calypso rose from her chair and stood behind it, keeping it between them.

"Icepick," she said. "To what do I owe this visit? It's very early."

Icepick did not answer. He flowed soundlessly around the room, keeping Calypso edging around the chair, as she turned to face him. Her eyes never left his face as she thought of his story: how he had first killed at only twelve, while working in his father's little corner market.

A thug had come in, he'd recounted, to collect extortion money. Icepick, knowing that the amount was needed for rent, had crept up behind the man as he wrangled with his father and slipped an ice pick under the back of his skull. It was the first in a very long string of assassinations, all carried out with the original ice pick that he kept hidden in a leather case on his wrist.

Calypso looked for the telltale bulge of the case but Icepick was in constant motion, the skirt of his black cassock swinging about him like a dancer's.

"What is it that you want?" she asked again, trying to keep a rising panic from her voice.

Having circled the room once, Icepick came to a halt in front of the window and stood sideways to it, glancing out into the featureless blackness, but keeping an eye on Calypso. They stood that way for several moments, he in a posture of readiness, she with her hands on the back of the chair, imagining how she might use it as shield and weapon.

"You're causing a big problem for us," he said at last. His voice was soft, almost seductive.

Calypso did not respond. The intimation that Icepick had come to remedy the situation was all too clear. She did not imagine that he was the kind of man who would be swayed by argument.

"We never have women here." His voice was accusing.

"It was never my intention to trouble you with my presence." Her response sounded more nettled than she intended. If this was the situation for which the dream was attempting to prepare her, then how in the world could she manage to bless this repugnant personification of death?

"It's a problem," he repeated.

It suddenly occurred to Calypso that he might never have killed a woman, only men. On impulse she asked, "When you killed the thug who was shaking down your father—what did your mother say?"

He swiveled to face her with snaky suppleness.

"What did you say?"

She could see he was flustered and followed up her small advantage.

"It must have been hard for her. You were her son. She loved you. Yet you'd done this thing that was irrevocable. I'm trying to imagine how she must have felt."

Icepick's face had become even more bloodless. Calypso knew that they were at the crux of his visit. Either he would attack now because of her impudence, or the situation would shift in her favor.

They faced one another across the small room like two animals gauging their attack. Icepick's eyes narrowed and he circled his nose through the air, the instinctual gesture of a hunting animal picking up a scent. Calypso's heartbeat quickened and her muscles tensed in readiness. Her fingers dug into the top rail of the chair back like steel screws being set into the wood.

She watched him with all her instinctual being, waiting for the slight tension that would be the gathering of his muscles for attack. And when she saw it, she threw down her final ace.

"I think she must have blessed you."

There was a misstep in the choreography of his kill. He went rigid and glared at her.

"What did you say?"

"Your mother. I think no matter what she may have said to you, that in her heart she blessed you. For rescuing your father. For saving the rent. For sending a message to the gang that was squeezing your family. I'm a woman. I know these things."

Calypso could see that Icepick was completely flummoxed, as if she had somehow manifested his mother's ghost in the room.

"You were just a poor kid doing what had to be done. It was dog eat dog. Probably no one ever told you so but you were a hero. You saved your family that day. And you've paid a heavy price for it. I know in my heart that your mother was proud of you."

If she had fired a handgun into her opponent, she could not have reduced him further. Icepick shifted his feet, settling out of attack stance, and sagged against the wall as if he had taken a bullet. He lifted eyes heavy with tears that had needed shedding for over sixty years. His voice, although still soft, had lost its seductive menace.

"You think so?"

"I'm absolutely certain of it."

Calypso resisted the urge to go to him. To touch him. He was too much the wounded animal. So she followed up her advantage with another blow to his defenses.

"I need you, too, Icepick. I need you to be heroic for me. I'm in a bad spot and I don't know the rules here. I don't know how to defend myself. Would you defend me?"

She surprised herself with the depth of her plea. It came from a place not of fear but of newly roused compassion for Icepick. In those few instants, she had seen him vulnerable, undefended, as he must have been before and just after his first kill.

In every human, she realized, there is a Before and After persona, one innocent and principled, the other bruised and defensive. Somehow, through the grace of the locket and its dream, she had touched the pulse of the former.

Icepick straightened, and with a flick almost too quick to register, pushed the icepick up his sleeve like a magician. Calypso had not even seen it in his hand. A wave of weakness swept over her and instead of gripping the chair like a weapon, she leaned into it for support. They stood staring at one another, each trying to imagine how to go forward from this unexpected juncture.

§

Suddenly they both flinched in alarm. With a tremendous crash, the door flew violently inward. Lone-R was revealed in the weak light from the hallway, his leg still descending from the mighty kick he had delivered. He rushed into the room, crouched in a fighter's stance, his scarred and leathery knuckles up, his torso weaving.

"You son of a bitch!" he screamed, and he lunged for Icepick, who retreated behind the table.

"Get out! Get out!" he yelled, and Calypso didn't know if he was telling her to run or if he was trying to eject Icepick.

Lone-R caught the edge of the table in one hand, flipped it on edge, and used it as a battering ram to press Icepick against the wall.

Icepick did not fight back. His shoulders and head hit the wall with a sickening thump, and he raised his arms in a gesture of surrender.

"Lone-R!" Calypso shrieked. "No! Stop!"

"This son of a bitch came here to kill you!"

Lone-R slammed the tabletop over and over into Icepick's body, using the full force of his massive body. Calypso was reminded of a bullfight she had attended years before, in which the bull trapped the matador against the bullring wall with one horn and then crushed him repeatedly with its vast chest.

Calypso burst into tears. "Lone-R, please! Please stop!" she sobbed. Icepick's eyes were unfocused and she could see he was nearly unconscious. "Please! You've got to listen to me! Stop for God's sake!"

Something in her tone finally broke through Lone-R's killing rage. He kept the pressure on Icepick, but ceased ramming him. He turned to Calypso with a look of consternation.

"He's gonna kill you, don't you understand?" he asked, shaking his huge head, as if her reaction were too naive to comprehend.

Calypso dashed her tears with the back of her hand.

"We were just negotiating a truce," she panted. "Ask him." She waved her hand at Icepick and then collapsed into the chair, lifting the hem of her long skirt to wipe her eyes.

Lone-R turned again to Icepick and, shoving the tabletop against him with less vigor, snarled, "Well? What about it?"

Icepick tried to answer but couldn't speak. Lone-R backed the pressure off a trifle and Icepick wheezed, "Broken ribs. Can't breathe."

"This a trick?" Lone-R eyed him warily.

Icepick shook his head, his face gone completely white.

"Throw down the icepick then."

He released the pressure of the table, allowing Icepick a small space in which to lift his hand. Icepick fumbled at his wrist, produced the weapon, and let it drop to the floor. Glancing at Calypso, Lone-R jerked his head at it.

"Go pick it up."

Calypso did as commanded and only then did Lone-R drag the table away from Icepick, who slumped against the wall, groaning.

"Let's get him on the bed," Calypso said, moving to support Icepick. Lone-R joined her and they lifted him carefully. "Do you have a doctor here?" Her tone was urgent but Lone-R was slow to respond in kind.

"Yeah. Bones."

"Go get him."

"I don't wanna leave you alone with him."

"Just go, Lone-R. The poor man can scarcely breathe. I hope a rib hasn't punctured his lung."

Lone-R picked up the icepick and handed it to Calypso.

"If he makes a move, you stick him with this, you hear?" Then he spun toward the door and took off running.

§

It was several minutes before Lone-R came racing back with Bones. In the meantime, she made Icepick as comfortable as possible, stoked the fire against the chill of the coming dawn, and then pulled the chair beside the bed and bent over the patient solicitously.

"How are you feeling?"

Icepick nodded, looking grim. "Alive," he wheezed.

Calypso smiled at him. "Where there's life, there's hope," she said reassuringly.

She gazed into the fire, debating with herself, and finally asked, "Why did you do it? You had a chance. Lone-R, I mean. I saw how open he was. I saw the icepick in your hand. Why did you put it away?"

She looked at Icepick with something close to affection.

"And of course, don't answer. Talking will only make things worse. I just want you to know that I know. You sacrificed yourself willingly—again."

She wanted to touch him, to soothe him, but refrained. Instead, she began to hum a tune from her childhood, hoping that Icepick might be touched by Dvorak's sad and lilting song.

"*Songs my mother taught me/in the days long vanished/Seldom from her eyelids were the teardrops banished...*" she sang in a soft, almost whispered soprano, accompanied by the reedy wail of wind beyond the sill.

When tears began to slide down Icepick's face, she bent close to him.

"Do you want me to stop?" she whispered.

He rocked his head on the pillow, *no.*

Calypso kept singing and humming until she heard footsteps pounding down the hall.

"They're here," she whispered, and wiped away his tears with the hem of her skirt.

§

Calypso stood before the assembled Ghosts. Even Icepick, his ribs bound, was propped in a chair among the others, his place guarding the door next to Lone-R taken by El Lobo.

"This room," Father Keat began abruptly, "was the court of the Inquisition. The Jesuits believed in the power of the Inquisition and that was one of the beefs the king had with them. But the ones who built this place weren't about to quit. They would kidnap notorious people from town or local Indians and torture them. Most often, they ended by putting them to death. It's all in the journals they kept. So we all feel right at home here, right brothers?"

The men nodded their agreement. Father Keat shot a crafty look at Calypso.

"How's that make you feel?"

"Queasy."

"Too much blood and guts for you?"

"Yes."

"Well, it's time, then, to tell the rest of the story. Haven't you been wondering why we're wearing these monk clothes?"

"I have been."

"Okay. Here's the deal. I bought this place for a reason. I bought it with money I got running a secret CIA operation in Africa. They pay well for somebody to do their dirty work. All that was involved was to fly over certain villages in this plane they set me up with and drop incendiary bombs.

"No problem, right? So I fly over, drop the bombs, the villages go up in flames, and I just circle around, and watch as people run out of their houses with their clothes on fire. Or their hair. Or they're dragging the bodies of old people who can't walk. Or their children who are injured or maybe dead.

"I've got Willy Nelson singing on a tape deck and I'm thinking about how I'm going to go on a big drunk when I get back home. And all of a sudden, it hits me.

"I look down and I see—really *see*—the damage I've done to innocent human beings. I get this rush of sickness and I up-chuck all over myself. I feel like I can't breathe. Like I'm wearing a shirt of fire myself. Only it's not going to kill me—it's just going to eat away at me for the rest of my life.

"When I got back, I knew I'd never be able to do that work again. So what the hell was I going to do? That was when I met El Lobo in Dallas and he told me about this place in Mexico where he'd been hiding. And it came to me: I was going to buy it and make a home for retired killers. I knew other guys who were getting too old for it anymore. They were tired. They wanted out.

"So that's what I did. We fixed the place up and we established our perimeters. The only people we had to worry about were the local Indians, and they won't come near the place because they think it's haunted.

"There's the occasional hiker. We used to just kill them and bury them out back to fertilize the fruit trees. But as time went on, we started not feeling good about that.

"So we switched to Scopolamine. If we can catch them on the boundaries of the property and give them the drug, like we did you, we just lead them away and when the drug wears off, they don't remember a thing."

"Why didn't you do that with Hill and me?"

"Because El Lobo couldn't track you past the cave. And you told him when the drug took over that you'd come *through* the cave from the Urique Canyon. He knew that was impossible and he couldn't figure out how you could still be lying, with the Devil's Breath in your system. So he brought you here."

"And Hill, too?"

Father Keat didn't respond.

"So you present a challenge to us," he continued. "Frankly, we don't know what to do with you."

"I'd rather not fertilize any fruit trees."

"That's understandable."

"May I ask a question?

"Of course."

"You're a group of killers. Don't you have internecine conflicts? I mean, what keeps killers from killing one another? I had a roommate once and before we were through, I wanted to kill *her!*"

She smiled for the first time since her capture, and she thought she caught the wraith of a guffaw rising from the Ghosts.

Father Keat nodded.

"We've had our problems, especially at the beginning. We came down here, a bunch of freewheeling guys, and we worked hard but we partied hard, too. We drank. Did some coke. Brought in some women.

"Pretty soon, all sense of discipline broke down. A couple of the guys started a feud and ended up killing each other, one with a knife, the other with a gun at point-blank range."

"Did you bury them under the fruit trees?"

"We did. The orchard was just getting started. Birdman went under an apple tree and Saw made the orange tree take off like crazy."

Calypso couldn't stifle her smile.

"I see. So what happened to change things?"

"We knew it would never work unless we got some control over things. So we started having assemblies. We talked until we thought talking might be a new form of torture. We made some rules. Things started to settle down."

"There must have been people who didn't like the new rules."

"In the end, there were only a couple of hardcore guys who couldn't adjust."

"Apple trees?"

"A mango and a date palm, if my memory serves me."

"Killing seems to answer most of your needs."

"It used to. Over the years, we've changed, most of us. *Transformed* is maybe a better word. We've recognized our guilt. We've experienced our shame. We've taken vows not to do harm anymore. We practice martial arts. We meditate. We eat clean food and don't do drugs or drink—much anyway.

"Finally, we realized we're nothing but a bunch of monks. A brotherhood of ghosts. So we bought ourselves some monk robes and here we are."

Calypso nodded.

"Very admirable," she said drily.

ട

Father Keat called Lone-R to witness again.

"Tell her what happened to you," he commanded.

Lone-R folded his hands in front of him and dropped his head to stare at them.

"I was in LA after San Quentin," he began, his baritone softened by remembrance, "and I gots a job. It was just shovelin' dirt. Day labor. But I was tryin' to go straight.

"I was workin' with a bunch of Mexicans and they thought I didn't know Spanish. So they started makin' cracks about black men, callin' me names. All under their breath and then everyone'd laugh. It went on all day, and I was gettin' madder and madder. Then one of 'em who's workin' next to me throws a shovelful of dirt right in my face and I just exploded.

"I swung my shovel back and I caught that guy right in the arm, and I heard the bone break. I hit him again—brought the edge of the shovel down on top of his shoulder and just about cut his arm off. Blood started to squirt everywhere.

"The other guys were paralyzed. Just starin'. The guy was on the ground but I hit him again in the head. And then I just kept beatin' and beatin' on him, until he was a bloody mush.

"Finally, the other guys came for me. I hit a couple of 'em and they dropped. Before the others could get to me, I just threw my shovel and ran. They chased me for a couple of blocks but I was too fast.

"Finally, they gave up, but I kept runnin' until I came to the beach. I ran across it straight into the surf and I stayed in there, scrubbin' off the blood 'til I thought it was safe to come out. Then I went down to the rail yard, hopped a freight goin' east and ended up in Dallas.

"I probably wouldn't of cared about killin' that guy except that when I was cleanin' myself off there was this gob of stuff plastered to my cheek, and when I peeled it off, it was some of his brains, all white and slimy.

"It made me puke. And I thought about how just a few minutes ago that guy had been thinkin' with that white slime. Thinkin' bad thoughts but still he was able to think. And now he was just a bunch of jelly, layin' in a pile of dirt.

"Somethin' clicked in me. Like I was in the dark and I flipped the light on. I don't want to kill no one ever again.

"I came here and I grow vegetables. I gots tomatoes nine feet tall in the summer. Right now it's fall, so I only gots greens—chard and kale and some lettuce and cilantro. Maybe I can show you later."

Lone-R concluded with such a note of boyish pride that Calypso felt a stab of compassion toward her jailor.

Father Keat nodded. Lone-R went back to his post at the door and The Knife took his place up front. He looked at Father

Keat with the forlorn eyes of a dog left out in the rain and Father Keat gave him a nod.

"Well, like I said before," The Knife began, "I was a hired killer for twenty years and proud of it. I bought a shop for my dad and my mom had a car. I helped my brothers and sisters go to college. They all got good professions because of me. It never occurred to me that what I was doing was wrong because it was always making everything right.

"But one day I was doing a job. All I had to do was shoot this guy from a distance with a sniper rifle. So here he comes down the street and I aim and pull the trigger, and just at that very instant, this little girl darts out in front of him and I'm watching through the scope as the top of her head explodes.

"Jesus Christ! I'm ready to throw myself off the rooftop! I couldn't live with myself. I found out who her parents were and I sent them all the money I had, a hundred thousand dollars, anonymously. I tried to buy my conscience quiet but it didn't work.

"I was ready to shoot myself when Keat, here, calls me up and says he wants to talk to me. So you can guess the rest. I never married. It was easy to fold up shop and plant my ID on a bum I found dead down by the river.

"Well, okay. No. I didn't find him dead. I killed him. But it was a mercy killing, believe me. Then I had to cut off his head and hands so they couldn't ID him. It was my last job. I don't want to kill anyone again, ever. I swear to you. I'm done. So I came here and I do the cooking, and I try to make my peace. You know. With the guy upstairs."

The Knife looked close to tears, his bald head bent, his shoulders sagging. "And the worst part is," he said in a voice that choked back a sob, "I had to leave my old dad without saying goodbye and him with cancer, too. I swear to God, I'd die every death I ever meted out, if I could just have seen my father before he passed. Christ! What a mess I made of my life!"

The last words were squeezed out in a rasping whisper. Then The Knife dropped his head to his chest and wept.

§

Lone-R came from the door, put his arm around The Knife's shoulders, and lead him back to his chair.

The room was more than silent. It was as if the torrent of The Knife's shame had swept them all into a whirlpool that was sucking them down into the darkest moments of their lives, moments filled with blood and violence and the irredeemable selling of their souls.

As if on cue, the sun ducked suddenly behind a cloud and the room went dark. With a rising shriek, wind slammed the wall of windows and rain fell in a racketing deluge. An icy draft swept through the room and the fire guttered on the hearth.

Father Keat sat behind his judge's desk with his head bowed, staring at his folded hands.

"It's hard," he said at last, "when you realize you've become horrible through your own diligence at homicide. People think criminals are crude and have low intelligence, but we Ghosts see it as a spiritual problem of intelligence gone awry."

Calypso found herself on her feet, gazing at the collected men, who stared back through sad eyes. She had no idea what to say, but knew she needed to say something, to lay some kind of balm on their collective psyche.

They looked at her expectantly, and Calypso realized it was time for her to give her own defense. What could she say to move the hearts of a roomful of assassins? It seemed that her case could only come out right if it included sending light into the darkness of these men's hearts. Maybe she even had been guided here for that very purpose.

"A wise person once told me," she began, thinking of Father Roberto in Chiapas, "that all things are sacred to those who are led by spirit—who are subordinated to mercy, ennobled by love, dominated by truth, and restrained by justice."

She let her eyes glide from one grim, watchful face to the next.

"I have come among you quite by accident. When I learned who and what you are, I thought I would never find mercy, love, truth or justice here."

She stepped forward, her long skirt swaying, her dark, silvered hair drawn over one shoulder and her green eyes somber.

"Yet, what I expected and what I found were quite different. I discovered men who had committed terrible crimes, yes. But more importantly, I found men who have experienced genuine remorse. Who have known deep anguish of spirit. Who have repented of their dark deeds.

"I am not a simple woman. I have lived in the world and I know how wicked and violent and greedy and cruel it can be. I know that, this very moment, there are men and women in places of power whose crimes rival yours and probably exceed them. And I know that remorse and repentance are the furthest thing from their minds. Which makes your transcendence of your actions all the more amazing and admirable.

"I can't absolve you. I don't have that power. But I can tell you what I know about human behavior. We all make mistakes. And we keep making them until we realize they're mistakes. And then, we don't do that anymore.

"You've all made a huge leap in consciousness, from killing to not killing. You killed when you didn't know any better than to kill. Now, you don't kill because you know better."

She knew she was babbling. She looked at the faces of the men, turned up to her with a kind of expectation, possibly with hope. She wondered how long it had been since any of them had even seen a woman, as she lifted her hands and opened her arms to them in a gesture of inclusion and forgiveness.

"All I ask of you," she concluded, "is that you allow me and my friend Hill to go free. Your secret is safe with us. We are honorable people—just as I now believe you to be."

A shuffle of feet, a murmur of assent and nodding of heads erupted from the audience. Calypso felt a surge of hope until a harsh voice called out. It was El Lobo, frowning at her from his post by the door.

"You're a liar! You swore, even under the Devil's Breath, that you came through the cave from the Urique Canyon but that's impossible. So why should we believe anything you say? Maybe you're here to spy on us."

Another voice shouted from within the audience, "Yeah! I think you're lying, too!" Several more voices joined in the chorus of suspicion, until Father Keat's gavel came down in a single, sharp rap.

Shaken, Calypso gathered herself and answered, "It *is* true that I came through the cave from the Urique to the Batopilas canyon. I can show you how it's done, if you like."

"I've spent years exploring that cave, and I know that it's impossible." El Lobo's tone was surly.

"Then it's imperative that I show you. And I would like to request that others come, too, so that I have fair witnesses."

She addressed this last to Father Keat, who nodded impassively.

"And I also request that my friend Hill be present."

"Why?" Father Keat asked.

"Because I need to know he's alive and unharmed."

"Or what?" El Lobo sneered. "Are you threatening us?"

"Not at all. Hill is my friend and I'm worried about him."

She turned with an expansive gesture to the men seated before her.

"You may be a company of Ghosts, but I can see that you're also a company of friends. Wouldn't you be concerned for your friend if he were captured and held against his will?"

"One thing at a time," Father Keat demanded. "In the meantime, I'll go with you to the cave myself. Who else will to go?"

A few hands were raised and Father Keat picked eight men, Lone-R among them.

"It takes at least twenty-four hours for the entire passage," Calypso said, needing them to understand the magnitude of the undertaking. "It won't be just an afternoon jaunt."

"We've got nothing but time here," Father Keat said, with a strange, twisted smile. "And you need to understand something: if you can't prove this to us, there will be consequences."

He paused to let the threat sink in.

"We'll go after lunch," and he motioned for Lone-R and El Lobo to take Calypso back to her room.

S

The afternoon was cold but the rain had ceased as Calypso and eight Ghosts set off for the cave. The men had changed from cassocks to camouflage and were carrying weapons.

Calypso, wearing the same dirty clothing from the last cave crossing, relished the fresh air and cool sunshine, surprised at how just two days of confinement had dampened her natural optimism. A small wind played along the edge of the canyon, and the cliffs rose coppery against a very blue sky swept clean of clouds. She concentrated on these things so that she didn't have to think about what lay ahead.

As far as she could imagine, the only way to prove that there was a passage to the Urique Canyon was to take one of the men through. That meant going back into the tube not once but twice. If she allowed herself to think about that, it would sicken her and she would bolt. So she kept her eyes roaming, taking in the way nooks in the stone held small caches of rainwater, tinted turquoise by reflected sky.

The men moved at a vigorous pace, making her aware that, although not young, these men were extremely fit. El Lobo led the way, bounding up onto stones and leaping down again with his namesake, Lobo, close behind. Father Keat brought up the rear. No one spoke a word.

When they reached the grotto, she was surprised when everyone stopped, turned to the Virgin of Guadalupe on the back wall, and said silent prayers. Calypso joined them, praying fervently that she would have the courage to carry out the terrible passage through the tube. Then, without a word, the men fell into formation again, with Calypso in the middle, and they dog-trotted down the steep, narrow game trail, then worked their way uphill through the boulder field to the mouth of the cave.

They shed their daypacks and pulled out headlamps. Then, with solemn eyes, they turned to look at Calypso. She fitted her headlamp over her forehead, wrapped her long hair in a chignon at the base of her neck, and took a deep breath. "Okay," she said, "let's go."

§

They clambered into the cave, El Lobo and Lobo leading, Calypso going second. It was clear that not everyone had been into the cave before. There were brief exclamations of discovery and surprise.

El Lobo stepped back and with mocking gallantry, waved Calypso forward. "After you, milady."

Calypso got her bearings and found the tunnel leading toward the tube. Without a word, she ducked into it, knowing that the men would follow—all except one left at the entrance as guard. She felt the rush of adrenaline that always accompanied the first minutes of a dive into the depths of stone. Her body screamed to be released back into sunlight and fresh air, but she subdued her impulses and willed herself forward.

An hour later, scraping and swearing, the men arrived one by one out of the tunnel into the chamber holding the entrance to the tube. When they were all assembled she said, "This is it. Who's going to go in with me?"

"Go in where?" It was El Lobo and his tone was scornful.

Calypso turned and pointed to the base of the far wall with its narrow aperture. "There," she said.

A moment's silence elapsed as all eyes followed her pointing finger, and their collective headlamp beams converged. Then a murmur arose.

"You've gotta be kidding," someone said.

"No way," came another voice.

"That's impossible," El Lobo said.

"No," she said adamantly. "It's not impossible. And I'm going to prove it to you. Who's going to come with me?"

For the first time, El Lobo looked uncertain.

"This is some kind of trick," he said. "She's gonna get one of us in there and pull some kind of fast one."

He laid his hand on the head of the wolf. The animal stood stock still, staring at Calypso.

Calypso was growing impatient. She knew her resolve would fade if she didn't go into the tube soon. The very thought of it was making her heart race and her breathing accelerate.

"Fine. So we've come this far but now no one will go with me to prove that this can be done?"

"I'll go." It was Lone-R.

Calypso hesitated, her face stricken.

"What's the matter? You afraid to go in there with him?" El Lobo jeered.

Calypso shook her head slowly.

"No. It's just that the passage is very tight. My husband is a big man and so is Hill, and they could barely squeeze through. I'm afraid for Lone-R that he might not be able to get past the smallest part."

She scanned Lone-R appraisingly. He had shoulders like a pro football player, his head was large, his arms and legs massive.

"Truthfully," she said finally, "I don't think you'd fit. And it's a terrible thing to get wedged in there. The first time I went through, I got stuck and I thought I was going to die. I wouldn't wish that on anybody."

Father Keat looked from one man to the next, and no one would meet his eye, except Lone-R.

"El Lobo," he said at last, "you're the one who thinks this can't be done. You're the one calling Miss Searcy a liar. I nominate you to go and I call for a vote of those assembled."

He raised his own hand and looked expectantly at the others. One by one, some quickly, others reluctantly, their hands went up. Only El Lobo's did not. "Looks like this is your gig,

El Lobo," Father Keat said grimly. "Better get a move on. We'll expect you back in two days, give or take a few hours."

To hide her apprehension, Calypso bent to check her pack. She fastened the drag line, checked her extra batteries, and the small store of rations from the monastery larder.

Finally, she straightened and said, "Okay. Let's go then," and dragging the weight of Hill's fate behind her along with her pack, she lowered herself to the floor and squirmed into the mouth of the tube.

§

No matter how many times she had passed through it, the living entombment of the tube taxed Calypso's courage almost beyond bearing. Now, there was the added stress of El Lobo's presence behind her, driving her on. Of one thing she was certain: he could do her no harm during the passage. His arms and hands would be pinioned.

With that small comfort she wriggled forward, already feeling the lowering of the ceiling, the squeezing in of the walls. Behind her, she could hear the exertions of El Lobo, his muttering and his exclamations of fury, as he barked his elbows or cracked his head.

It took some time before her ears picked up another sound. It was muffled and faint, but distinct from El Lobo's exertions. The realization came as a shock: the wolf had followed his master into the tube! It, too, was worming itself along behind him, emitting small groans and yips of protest. Calypso's heart was moved by this show of loyalty and it occupied her mind as she slithered deeper and deeper into the tube.

As she approached the lowest spot, she fought back the feeling that the stone was slowly, ineluctably pressing down—that it would not stop until it had flattened her. To distract herself, she began calling instructions back to El Lobo. "We're coming to the lowest part. I know it seems impossible, but the tunnel will narrow even more. Keep your arms at your sides and wiggle yourself forward using your hips and feet. In the smallest place, you'll have to turn your head to the side to fit your skull under the rock. After that, flatten your shoulders and push with your toes. Once your shoulders are through, the worst is over."

She listened for a response, but all she could hear was a kind of low keening coming down the tube, like the sound of distant wind. She assumed that the terror of the stone had struck and knowing that nothing could save El Lobo now but his own courage, she wriggled onward.

She arrived at the lowest place. Turning her head to the side, she felt the cool stone beneath her cheek as she slipped her head through. It was like being birthed, she always thought, each time she came through that terrible constriction.

Was a baby conscious and terrified by its passage down the birth canal? Had she been, at her birth? And what would ever invoke lifetimes of reincarnation, knowing that this terror awaited, every single time? Surely, the pleasure and privilege of life must be great to overcome such memories!

She pushed with the toes of her boots and inched her head and shoulders through, then her hips, and finally the pack. It caught crosswise for a few moments, during which her breath came in the gulps anticipating panic, but she managed to hook her toe under the line and give it a sharp upward jerk and the pack slid through.

She was several feet beyond the narrowest part when she realized that she was no longer hearing any sounds behind her.

"El Lobo?" she called, but there was no response.

"El Lobo!" she yelled. Still nothing. "Christ!"

The thought of the man behind her, paralyzed with terror, unable to proceed or retreat, moved her to pity. Even the most macho of men met unknown parts of themselves in the narrows of the tube. She would never forget Javier's response the first time they traversed it.

He was leading and when he came to the narrows, he froze for several minutes. He said later he was trying to find a way to fit his head under the stone, but that he was afraid they had come to a dead end and would have to backtrack. The thought of that, he had said, was more terrible than going forward and the panic of it drove him through the aperture like a hammer driving a nail.

And while all that was happening, Calypso had been lying face down, her arms pressed to her sides, with the weight of the living stone descending like a huge mechanical press that she once had seen crushing wrecked cars. When finally they both had squirmed out of the tube into the cavern, they had lain in a heap, entwined in one another, and wept.

As she strained to hear him, El Lobo was transmogrified from a menace to a suffering being, face to face in the terrifying embrace of his own mortality. She wished that she knew his real name, the one given him by his mother and father, the name that called him to supper and tucked him into bed each night. If she knew that small secret, she might be able to coax him forward.

"What is your real name, El Lobo?" she asked.

Silence.

"Your name is the magic word."

Nothing rational she could say would make the smallest difference now. Intuition was guiding her.

"Say your name, turn your head to the side, and push with your toes."

She strained to hear a response and heard instead his labored breathing. Then it came to her.

"Turn your head, *mijo*, and push with your toes."

The Spanish endearment passed her lips softly: mijo, my son.

The narrows confronted each person with his or her deepest horror and released them through their sweetest hope. For her, it had been her mother's voice, singing at the piano, as distinctly as when she was a child curled in a chair in the music room. For Javier, it was a blinding jolt from the fingertips of the Virgin of Guadalupe, who appeared and disappeared like lightning. And for Hill, it had been the sudden opening of a crack in the stone, revealing an ethereal guide and filling his lungs with pure, cool air. Perhaps for El Lobo, it would be his mother's voice, crooning.

A muffled sob reached her, stifled by stone, but poignantly alive.

"Push, mijo," she called. "Push with your toes. Wiggle your hips. You're almost through, mijo, trust me."

She listened with all her being and heard faint scraping sounds.

"That's right. Keep moving. Keep pushing, mijo."

The sobs were more distinct now. She moved forward, so that the pack would not impede his progress. And thus, slithering and calling encouraging endearments, Calypso forgot her own terror, and saved the sanity of her bitterest foe.

§

When she reached the cavern, Calypso, still moved by compassion, reached to pull El Lobo out of the tube and help him stand. Behind him, shivering and whining, came the wolf. She kept a steadying hand on El Lobo's arm as she reached down to comfort the frightened animal. El Lobo tottered forward and leaned against a boulder, his headlamp sending arcs of yellowed light across the chaos of the cavern floor, in time to his wrenching sobs.

Calypso knelt and put her arms around the wolf, pulling its thin, shivering shoulders into her breast and soothing over and over, "It's okay. It's okay now. What a fine creature you are. It's okay. It's okay."

The animal leaned into her, almost toppling her, because her own legs were rubbery from exertion.

She rose and went to El Lobo, saying gently, "You did well. You were very brave."

"My mother," he said brokenly. "She came. Why would she come?"

"Because she loves you."

He shook his head and doubled over in a renewed fit of weeping. Hands braced on knees, he sobbed in bitter, wrenching groans, his face glazed in tears and runnels of mucus. He tried to speak, but his words were twisted and tormented by explosive sobs and hiccups.

Calypso bent close to his face. "I'm sorry," she said, "I didn't understand that."

"I did it," he managed to gasp. "I killed her. I killed my mother."

Calypso's eyes shut in horror, and it took all her resolve to say calmly and with assurance, "Then obviously she forgives you."

§

They proceeded through the cave, ascending the cliff at the back of the cavern and twisting through labyrinthian tunnels, but the mood of their expedition was not healthy. Calypso was grim and focused, harboring her energy to make the technical aspects work, including hoisting the wolf in a makeshift harness.

El Lobo was ominously quiet and haggard, refusing to talk even when Calypso addressed him directly. She began to suspect that the passage through the tube had unhinged him. For a man like him, being reduced to groveling terror was a humiliation that would demand extirpation.

Fearing that his homicidal instincts had been resurrected, she kept a wary eye on all his movements. She wondered how she would ever get him to go back through the tube, once he had proof that the cave was a complete passage between river canyons.

"You know"—she said, as they stopped for a rest, leaning against the walls of a small chamber—"we don't have to go all the way through. It should be obvious to you by now that this cave extends between canyons, just like I said."

El Lobo glared at her through narrowed eyes.

"What do you mean?"

"I mean we could just turn back now and save our strength."

"And go back through the tube again?" His voice teetered on a knife-edge of hysteria.

"Yes. We'd have to go back through the tube. There's no other way."

"Then we go forward. There's no way in hell I'm going back through that tube."

Calypso stared at him, perplexed.

"But once we get to the other side, we won't be able to get off the cliff. It comes out on a ledge almost four thousand feet above the river. We'll have to turn back eventually anyway."

"How did you get down to the ledge?"

"I rappelled. But there's a big bulge of rock between the ledge and the top of the cliff. You can't get back up that way."

"You said under Scopolamine that you and your husband had done it."

"My partner."

"You called him your husband under the drugs. They don't lie."

"If that were the case," she retorted acidly, "you should have believed me about the cave in the first place."

He lowered his eyes and nodded.

"Yes, I should have."

They sat for several moments in detente, each lost in private ruminations.

Finally, El Lobo burst out, "No. I'm not going back through that tube. We have to find a way off the ledge. How did you and your husband—partner—do it?"

"There's a climbing route set up with pitons. But I've never climbed lead before. I always followed Javier. There's no way I can do it. I'm not strong enough or a good enough climber."

"Well, you're about to become better at it," he growled. "You're going to lead us off that ledge."

Calypso shook her head despairingly. "You have no idea what you're saying. It's suicide."

"I'd rather commit suicide than go back through that tube." It was a flat statement of his truth. She could tell he was immovable.

El Lobo scrambled to his feet. "Come on. Let's go. I want out of this place. It creeps me out."

The wolf stood, too, shaking its thin shoulders and staring at Calypso with its expressionless hunter's eyes.

"What about Lobo," she objected. "We won't be able to drag him up."

El Lobo looked at the animal with a down-curling of his lips.

"Then let him stay behind."

"But he'll starve to death!"

El Lobo shrugged. "Let him starve."

ȿ

Calypso led the way forward, her mind frantically gauging the chances of surviving either the devil behind her or the deep blue sea of air in the Urique Canyon. Images of trying to climb the cliff, of slipping, falling and hurtling into the abyss filled her mind.

Thoughts of turning back brought equally disastrous images of confronting an enraged and unbalanced man. For good measure, her legs were starting to shake from exhaustion. She knew she didn't have much reserve left.

Dimly now she could hear the rush of water as they approached the great siphon and its whirlpool. The wolf stopped and pricked his ears. El Lobo gave him a vicious prod with his knee.

"Get going!"

Calypso missed seeing the blow but heard the yelp of pain and saw the wolf cringe. El Lobo was rearing his foot back to give the animal a kick when Calypso yelled, "No! Stop!"

El Lobo lowered his foot and glared at her without a word.

"He hears the water rushing," she explained. "Don't you hear it? It means we're getting close to the end."

El Lobo threw his chin toward the sound.

"Well, let's do it."

"I need to warn you—there's a dangerous spot up ahead. The rock is very slick, so move carefully. Secure every step before you transfer your weight."

El Lobo tossed his head with impatience and snarled, "Just get the fuck on with it."

Calypso shrugged and continued on. The roar became louder, so that their voices could no longer be heard above the clamor of water, as it rushed around its stone basin in a sucking vortex. Calypso turned again and signaled El Lobo to be cautious, then began her move onto rock slick with spray from the raging water.

The water was higher than when she and Hill had passed this way. The heavy rains on the surface must have fed the deluge. She was forced to climb higher on the sloping rock, where the roof slanted down onto walls only three or four feet high.

Bent almost double, she put her hand out to steady herself as she ducked under the lowest part. Immediately, she felt the rock become less dangerous, where the surface was shielded from spray by a small protrusion of the wall. She braced herself to catch her breath and turned to watch El Lobo's progress.

He was moving too fast, not stopping to place his feet firmly. His method was to skim across the slippery stone as fast as possible. Behind him, the wolf padded carefully, its yellow eyes flashing metallically in the light of the headlamps.

Suddenly, with a shout, El Lobo's feet went out from under him and he hit the rock on his hip, hard. In a flash, he was sliding toward the water, clawing helplessly at the impervious stone. Before Calypso could think to react, he slid into the water and was whipped halfway around the pool on the outer fringes of the terrible vortex.

He swept past her, floundering, trying to swim, his face a rictus of terror. As he continued on toward the spot where he had fallen, the wolf crouched, as if offering itself as a handhold.

El Lobo threw himself toward the animal, grabbed a fistful of its silky ruff, and hung on. The wolf dug all four paws into the stone, its body straining.

For a moment, it looked as if it could stabilize the situation, but then, with terrible slowness, it skidded across the wet surface, its toes splayed, its claws extended, until it too lost its grip and was pulled into the maelstrom.

El Lobo threw his arms around the wolf's neck, trying to keep his face above water as the whirlpool's energy pulled them both in. Around and around they whirled, in ever smaller circles as they fought to escape.

Finally, with a terrible scream, they plunged into the heart of the spinning water. The wolf was sucked down first. El Lobo's horrified eyes stared at a ceiling illuminated by the mad gyrations of his headlamp's beam.

Then he was gone.

S

Calypso leaned panting against the cave wall, overwhelmed with horror. Digging her fingers into tiny holds, she leaned her forehead against the damp stone and wailed.

It took many minutes to recover self-control. Then, not daring to look at the water again, she inched forward until her feet met dry rock. She sank to her knees, fell forward onto the stone, and then lay gasping for many minutes more.

At last, she was able to collect herself. She sat up, took a deep breath and reviewed her options.

If she went back, even should she summon the strength to do so, she would have to pass again through the tube, and then explain to The Ghosts why El Lobo was no longer with her. Surely they would accuse her of murdering him.

If she went forward, she would come to the ledge and the technical climb to the top of the cliff. Either way, the options were impossible.

"Give me a third option," she muttered but received no answer.

In the end, the same motivation impelled her that had moved El Lobo: the cave was beginning to creep her out. She longed for the light of the entrance that she knew was just beyond the waterfall.

She pushed herself from the rock and trudged onward, remembering how, almost gaily, she and Hill had passed this way so recently. How quickly their lives had changed! Was Hill still alive? Was Javier? She touched the cool orb of the locket beneath her sweater.

"You're useless," she muttered. "How about some answers?"

She came to the supply room. She and Hill had devoured all the stores, but she had food in her pack and stopped to eat. Her legs were trembling with fatigue, and her hands fumbled with the wrapping of the emergency food bar that The Ghosts had provided. She sat, her back against the wall, chewing mechanically, too exhausted even to cry.

As she ate, she allowed herself a few sips of hope. She was just a couple of hours away from the cave entrance. What if, freed from El Lobo's menace, she could find the courage to climb the cliff? The ledge was only a hundred feet below the top. If she allowed herself to rest, surely she could do it. She had done it before.

She blotted out the image of Javier hauling her the final ten feet like a sack of potatoes. She felt sure she could do it, and as she lay down to nap she clung to that slender red thread of hope, the way she had clung to his climbing rope.

She awoke to the roar of the waterfall, too tired and sore to move. She had to talk herself through every move: sitting up, opening her pack, replacing the batteries of her headlamp. Standing was the hardest. Her legs didn't want to accept responsibility for the rest of her. Then the straps of her pack became twisted as she slung it on her back and she fumbled with the buckle. Finally, she was ready to proceed.

She took one last look around the little room, at all the comforts she and Javier had provided for their enjoyment and sustenance in days when all this was just a rumor in their minds, like clouds far away on the horizon. Then, with a sigh, she hitched her pack on her hips and began the last leg of the cave transit.

§

The entrance to the cave glowed at the end of the long tunnel. Calypso toiled up the last grade toward the square of light as if it were the radiance of the Holy Grail. She had barked her knuckles in the narrow part of the final passage and was sucking on them, wondering if the light was dawn, daylight, or the last rays of evening.

She had lost all track of time but knew it was not possible to traverse the cave in fewer than a full twenty-four hours. She couldn't imagine that she had gone so fast. Because it was afternoon when she had parted company with The Ghosts, she reasoned that the glow ahead must be morning.

She stepped from the cave entrance and from behind its sheltering slab of stone, with a sense of profound gratitude for the simple facts of light and fresh, moving air. As the gulf of the Urique Canyon spread before her, she was gratified to see that the sun was barely above the eastern horizon. It cast long, indigo shadows among the spires and blocks of the far canyon walls. A chill morning wind played along the stone ramparts and swallows dipped and shrilled in boundless air.

Dropping her pack, she flicked off her headlamp, pulled it from her head and threw it in the top compartment of the pack. Leaving the pack behind, she walked to the far end of the ledge, and with scraped and weary fingers fitted and buckled the climbing harness, uncoiled the climbing rope under the iron ring, and clipped it to her harness.

From her vantage point at the farthest end of the ledge, the bulge of stone above her flattened where it joined the cliff face. All along the edge of the swell, she could pick out the pitons Javier had hammered into the stone, by the long, blue shadows they threw.

Like blue spikes bent by enormous force, the shadows were driven by dawn light across the rock face and then curved along the swelling belly of stone. They reminded her of nothing so much as the Crown of Thorns.

Sighing, she clipped her rope to the iron ring where she had not so long ago secured herself to catch Hill. This time, it would catch her, if she were to fall. Facing the cliff, she scanned for handholds. Then, saying a prayer, she reached her foot out from the edge of the ledge, placed in on a small knob of rock, and launched herself onto the cliff face.

§

Calypso was climbing well, despite the morning chill and the weariness of her limbs. Javier's pitons were closely placed, no more than five or six feet apart, because of the complete verticality of the pitch and the minimum of hand and foot holds. She stopped at each to install a carabiner from the climbing harness, securing her rope at successively higher levels.

She was probably fifty feet above the ledge, and twenty feet to the right of it, when she heard a slight grating sound. Before she could think, the piton on which her weight depended ripped from the stone with a *spoing.*

Suddenly, she was plummeting through space. Her weight hit the end of the rope, which tightened on the next piton down. The force of her fall was tremendous and after a moment's hesitation, that piton, too, ripped from the wall. She tore through still another piton, before one held.

She dangled, stunned, bruised, and scraped, over the canyon's emptiness, on her nylon thread. Half-conscious, swinging over the gulf of air, she experienced the liberating sensation of flight. The river, a faint thread of deep green at the bottom of the gorge, flashed in and out of view as her pendulum swung.

She hung, slack and addled, long after the swinging ceased, hearing the faint creak of the rope, and sensing the air's play across her scalp, as if her hair were wind-ruffled feathers. A seductive temptation urged her to let go, to fly down into the chasm, like a swallow dipping toward the river.

It was her own shadow against the red stone of the cliff face, like an indigo silhouette of the condemned on a gallows, that shocked her back to consciousness. Groggily she realized that she had hit her head.

Her brains felt scrambled. When she shook her head to clear it, blood flew past her eyes. Dazed, she moved her limbs one at a time, making sure no bones were broken. Wiping blood from her eyes with the sleeve of her sweater, she forced her mind to concentrate.

She was several feet below the piton that was holding her and had lost almost a third of her upward progress. As her mind cleared, she began scanning the rock to find a purchase on the stone. To her right, the cliff bellied outward and she thought she could climb back up to the piton along this less than vertical slope, if she could just find a hand- and toehold.

She spotted a small knob of rock, but it was just beyond her reach. Kicking her legs, she swung toward the slant of stone. On the backward swing, she pumped with her legs, gaining momentum, praying that the piton above her would hold.

Her feet connected with the cliff, and she pushed off again with real force, increasing the arc of her swing. This time, her feet hit the slanted part of the rock and her hands caught and held the knob. Her hips swung into the rock face and then backward, the momentum almost pulling her off as she clawed the rock with all her strength.

She was perched on tiptoes, her hands around the knob, when the giddy swaying ceased. She took a moment to orient herself and then began to clamber upward.

A strange phenomenon took command. She was highly energized, her limbs were strong and sure, and her eyes were keen to find the smallest hold. Adrenaline taking hold she surmised and then dismissed it, as her entire concentration was exerted on the climb.

She came to the piton that had sustained her and then passed it. She kept on climbing, past the sites of the failed pitons, moving up the vertical rock like a fly.

She remembered Javier's story, years ago, of having fallen from this very cliff as a child and of the Rarámuri shaman who had pulled him up again on an imaginary rope. She held that image as she climbed. Somewhere up there was a man with long black hair blowing in the morning wind, his loincloth flapping as he hauled her up, hand over hand.

She came to the still intact pitons, snapped the rope on with carabiners and kept climbing, stopping periodically to wipe blood from her forehead with the sleeve of her sweater.

At last she came to the final ten feet, the portion Javier had always hauled her over because it was so difficult. She knew, however, that Javier had been able to navigate this almost smooth stretch of rock. A determination grew in her. If he could do it then, by God, so could she.

Moving cautiously out onto the last pitch, she called up the picture of Javier climbing it—how he had stretched, where he had directed his reach, and his feet. The holds were there if she could bring them to mind. Her concentration was total, and she experienced the cliff not as vertical but as a horizontal plane over which she was crawling, free from the downward tug of gravity.

Finally, with a final grunt of exertion, Calypso pulled herself over the edge of the cliff. She wriggled on her belly until all of her was lying, exhausted and shaking, behind the wall that demarcated the cliff edge from the courtyard of Rancho Cielo. With a final effort she snapped the rope into the iron ring for safety and then lay with breath singing in and out of her lungs, too spent to move or even to rejoice in her accomplishment.

At last, a queer, smoky smell jarred her consciousness. What could it be? It was too strong for the fire pit. She got onto her knees and crawled the few feet to the wall, put her hands on top and pulled herself up.

She looked into the courtyard, blinked, and then looked again.

There was nothing there.

The house was gone. In its place was a pile of still-smoking timbers.

She gave a cry of anguish and horror and was about to throw herself over the wall, when two men came through the shattered courtyard gate on the side nearest the road. They were dressed all in black, with protective vests and helmets, and carried assault rifles. One raised his head and pointed, then came sauntering toward her.

§

The man jumped over the wall and looked along its length but there was no one there. He gave a cursory glance over the edge at the cliff face and then feeling the magnetic pull of empty space, turned dizzily away from the edge.

"What is it?" his companion called.

The first man clambered back over the wall.

"It was nothing. I thought I saw a woman but it must have been a bird or a ground squirrel."

His friend laughed.

"You're always seeing women, amigo. In the clouds, in the trees, in the whorehouse. Now you're seeing them in squirrels!"

He laughed uproariously at his own joke and his friend joined in.

"Still," he said, shaking his head, "I swear I saw a woman. But there was nothing there."

§

Flattened against the cliff face, hanging from the iron ring, Calypso listened as the men's voices moved away. There was just enough length left in the rope for her to continue her rappel on the single strand. Feeling hopeless, she began the perilous descent back to the ledge.

Once down, she huddled against the wall, convulsed in sobs. She threw herself down with her back to the cliff, the climbing rope still attached to the harness around her hips, her entire body wracked with terrible grief.

Complete desolation encompassed her. It was not the first time in her life that terror and loss had overcome her. She remembered the night she had spent in the forest in Chiapas with the old shaman woman Atl, while their village was burned and its people murdered, and the paralyzing fear that Javier was dead that had overwhelmed her then.

Today was far worse. Her home was burned to the ground and she could only imagine that Javier had died defending it. She was alone, stranded on a ledge almost a mile in the air, and the only way out was through the exhausting traverse of the cave and the horror of the tube, only to face a band of executioners. For the first time in her life, she was tempted to simply give up, to take the few steps to the edge and jump.

The utter aloneness of her situation was the most terrible part. Even El Lobo's company was preferable to this desolate solitude.

"If only I had someone," she whispered. "Anyone, God."

She wiped her face on her sleeve and with shaking fingers undid the buckle of the climbing harness. She pulled it from her body and then slumped against the stone again, staring out into the void of the canyon.

The far walls fell away in massive blocks of standing stone, shadowed blue beneath a fleet of clouds. Swallows dipped and dove only a few feet from the edge, and a pair of peregrine falcons flirted through the air and then came together in instantaneous mating. The day held all the elements she loved about living in Copper Canyon—except her home and the man without whom life was meaningless.

§

She knew how easy it would be to die here—of exposure first or of injury or starvation. That she had survived the climb to the top seemed superhuman and the frantic rappel back down miraculous. She needed to make a decision about her fate but grief clouded all judgment. Finally, it was pure animal hunger that awakened her to her immediate plight. She dug in her pack for another emergency food bar and sat chewing it as slow, heavy tears coursed soundlessly down her face.

Repugnant as it was, she knew that her only hope for survival lay in yet another transit of the cave. In her mind, she traced the way through, but when she came to the entrance to the tube, her imagination balked. Did she have enough energy left, to make the day long trek through darkness and danger? Did she have the courage to face the tube again?

She had no answers but knew that if she didn't try, she would sit here on the ledge until she sickened and died. With a ragged sigh, she delved again into her pack, pulled out her headlamp, and fitted the band on her head. Then, struggling to her feet on wavering legs, she shouldered her pack and turned with a leaden heart to the entrance of the cave.

ᘏ

Chapter 10

ʕ

The Cave

Calypso was too exhausted and too distracted to be fully in control of her body. She cracked her head in low places, scraped her arms where it was narrow. The blackness of the cave surrounded her as intentionally as a succubus. And with every step, her grief for Javier pressed on her heart like a gravestone. She felt mythic, like some unhappy soul who would wander forever beneath the earth, lost and grieving like the Piper of Keil.

She came to the waterfall and stopped to fill her water bottle from its chilly waters, then staggered into the little chamber that housed supplies, too spent to go further. Dropping her pack, she rummaged in one of canisters for an old, moth-eaten alpaca serape she remembered stuffing into the bottom and found it along with a wool shirt of Javier's.

Burying her face in the shirt, she caught the faintest whiff of his scent, and it nearly devastated her. Throwing the serape on the ground she collapsed onto it, rolled herself into fetal posture, and clutching the shirt under her cheek, fell instantly into exhausted sleep.

ʕ

Hours later, she awoke with a start, sure that some anomalous sound had awakened her. Heart hammering, she lay perfectly still, ears straining.

Was it possible that the men from the courtyard had followed her? It seemed impossible—unless of course they had forced either Pedro or Javier to give up the secret of the cave and how to access it. She scarcely breathed as she allowed her ears to hunt the darkness for clues.

There it was again! Definitely a sound she had never before heard in the cave. Not a human noise, however, but an animal one—a small moan, followed by a high, sharp yip. Calypso sat up, scrabbling for the switch on her headlamp. Rising unsteadily, she ventured into the main cavern and cast the light over the water of the pool.

Nothing.

She listened acutely but heard nothing more. She was about to go back to her bed when she heard it again, above the roar of the waterfall, coming from further down the cavern toward the whirlpool. She went back to her pack and retrieved her flashlight, glad of its extra light, and its possibilities as a defensive weapon.

Inching down the cavern, she heard the noise again, louder this time. She shone the flashlight around, searching for the source, but saw only damp stone dancing with grotesque shadows.

"Hello?" she called out. "Who's there?"

She was answered by another sharp yip. Flashing her light toward the sound, she saw the fearsome vortex of the siphon's pool and shuddered, remembering. Then, at the edge of the light, she glimpsed something silvery. She shone the beam onto it and gasped in dismay.

Lying on the very edge of the whirlpool, its hindquarters still immersed in the black water, was the wolf! And what was more, it had its head raised and was looking at her, its eyes flashing yellow in the light.

"Lobo!" she shrieked. "Oh, my God!"

She ran forward and only stopped when she felt the slippery give of wet rock beneath her feet. The wolf lay only a few feet away, but the rock sloped perilously into the water and she didn't dare approach any closer.

The wolf regarded her steadily, then lifted his head higher and gave another yip. Lifting his sodden tail from the water, he waved it momentarily, and then it subsided, as if it were too heavy to bear. Lobo's head dropped, too, lying on the wet stone in obvious exhaustion.

Calypso set down her flashlight and lay on her stomach. Reaching out her arms as far as she could she called, "I'm right here, Lobo. Can you reach for me?"

The animal whined and stretched a paw toward her, but a yard of slick stone still separated them. Calypso did not want the animal to strain, for fear that he would dislodge himself and slip again into the horrible sucking maelstrom. She stared at him in perplexity and the animal stared back.

On sudden inspiration, she pushed to her feet saying, "Wait! Don't move! I'll be right back."

Picking up her flashlight, she turned and wove her way as quickly as possible back to the supply room. She dug in one of the canisters for the spare climbing rope stored there and dashed back to the whirlpool, terrified that the wolf would no longer be there but would have been swept away in the intervening minutes.

With relief she saw the bedraggled silvery mound at the water's edge. Kneeling, she fashioned a small loop in the end of the rope using a slipknot, lay again on her stomach, and tossed the loop toward the wolf. Jiggling and snaking, she inched the rope closer and closer to the wolf's paw.

"Help me, Lobo," she urged. "Raise your paw."

The wolf's eyes, that had been focused steadily on hers, shifted to watch the wriggling approach of the rope loop. When the rope was almost touching, the animal lifted its paw a few inches.

Calypso flicked the rope and the loop struck the wolf's foot but fell back, empty. Undeterred, Calypso tried again and then again, until finally, on the fourth attempt, the loop flopped onto the wolf's foot, and with a slight forward shove of Calypso's hand, settled around its leg, six inches beyond the ankle.

Calypso rolled to her left to get a sideways pull on the knot, to avoid pulling it off the wolf's leg. Gently at first, and then more vigorously as she felt the knot tighten, she tugged on the rope.

When the knot was tightly set, she and the wolf locked eyes, both apparently aware that this was an all or nothing endeavor. Calypso knew all too well that if the loop were to slide off while she was in the act of hauling the wolf to safety, he would slip irretrievably back into the water.

"Don't struggle, Lobo," she said softly. "Just let me pull you now."

She wrapped two coils of rope around her wrist, aware that it was a dangerous thing to do given the dead weight of the half-drowned creature but not caring. She would rather be pulled into the water and die with the wolf than endure another heartbreaking loss.

She gave a tentative tug, watching the knot, praying it would hold. Feeling the tension on the rope, she began to haul on it, one hand over the other. The wolf's leg stretched out and still the loop held tight. Calypso put her full strength into the rope now and felt a slight give as Lobo's body inched forward on the rock. She scrambled to her feet and stepped back to take up the slack, lest the animal slip backwards.

With agonizing slowness, the sodden body of the wolf slid away from the seething water. The steep incline of the rock, however, exerted tremendous oppositional force. Calypso braced her feet, steeled her arms, and kept pulling.

Just when the wolf was almost within reach, the loop suddenly slipped upward toward the paw. Calypso groaned in despair and gathered in the slack before the animal could backslide. She held the tension but was afraid to pull again, for fear of losing him altogether.

Then the wolf, exhibiting the intelligence for which his kind was known, bent his paw back, forming a hook to catch the loop. Calypso jerked the rope to set the loop in the crook, and began slowly and carefully to pull again.

Finally, she felt the wolf was within reach. Reeling in the rope, she lay on her stomach and reached her free hand toward the animal. Her hand met the damp fur of his paw and she set her fingers like a steel trap, into the sinew of his leg. She reached to take hold with her other hand too.

"Don't move!" she cautioned.

The animal lay perfectly still as she shimmied her hips backward, raising him imperceptibly up the slope. A few inches more and she was able to grab the animal's other front leg.

With this increased leverage, she dragged him almost to the limit of the slick rock. She scooted back again and with one final heave, pulled the wolf's shoulders free of the slope and onto dry stone.

Now, she could embrace him around his torso and pull his hindquarters up, too. Finally, the entire beast rested on dry rock. They both lay panting and exhausted. The wolf lifted his tail and brought it down with a slosh, in one sodden gesture of gratitude. Then it closed its eyes and appeared to sleep.

Judging that it was safe to leave him for a few minutes, Calypso hurried back to the supply room to retrieve an emergency space blanket. Returning to the wolf, she rolled the sodden creature onto the blanket and then dragged him back to the supply room.

Using Javier's shirt, she dried the animal as best she could. His limbs were ice cold. She wrapped the space blanket around his body and pulling her own makeshift bed next to him, she pulled the wolf to her to give him her warmth.

How had the animal survived? She tried to imagine how the waters might have swallowed El Lobo but not his companion. She recalled in vivid detail those last moments, when El Lobo had clutched the wolf in terror.

Somehow, in the throat of the vortex, El Lobo must have released his grip, and the wolf had caught an upward swirl of water, to be spat out. And it had lain there, half-dead, too exhausted to pull itself to safety, or perhaps aware that the stone was too slick to traverse, all the while she was climbing the cliff, grieving on the ledge, and finally, sleeping.

She feared that the creature, although rescued, might still die from hypothermia. Curling herself around him, pulling him closer, she nestled the back of his head under her chin. Spooned about him like a lover, with a final, fleeting thought that her prayer for companionship was answered, she fell into exhausted and oblivious sleep.

§

She awoke to pitch blackness and the squirming animal heat of the wolf. Groping for her flashlight, she illuminated the creature, trussed in its silvery mylar blanket like a Christmas turkey.

Lobo reared his head and whined as he kicked his legs to free himself. Calypso freed the trapped end of his blanket and he unwound himself, scrambled to his feet, and shook himself mightily.

"Well, good morning!" Calypso laughed at his gyrations and sat up. "How about some breakfast?"

She dug in her pack and came up with a food bar, the last but one.

"I'll split this with you."

She opened the wrapper, broke off a piece, and offered it on the palm of her hand. The wolf sat and with gentle lips bent to receive the tidbit. Calypso broke off a piece for herself. In this fashion, they shared out the bar, which was gone far too soon.

As she was stowing the wrapper, Calypso reflected that it would be no contest,if the wolf had decided to eat *her*, and that his failure to do so might constitute a tacit kind of bonding. She reached a tentative hand to the animal's head.

"Good boy, Lobo. *Bon appétit.*"

§

The traversing of the cave now took on a dreamlike quality. The fantastic shapes of the rocks and their dancing shadows, the boulder-littered passages, the hoisting of the wolf down cliff faces, all passed in a sort of fugue state.

The blunt force mental trauma of her burned home and of Javier's death was in abeyance, as was her sense of fatigue. She and Lobo swam through the depths of darkness in slow motion, as mindless as archaic fishes suspended in the black deeps of the sea.

When they came at last to the low hole that was the entrance to the tube, Calypso sat and shared the final energy bar with the wolf.

"Will you follow me?" she asked, resting a weary arm on the creature's silky neck. "Goose me, if I stop?"

She fumbled the batteries from her headlamp, inserted the last fresh ones, and tossed her pack aside.

"No need for this," she said vaguely. How good it felt to have the wolf's intelligent eyes watching her lips, as if he understood every word!

"Are you ready?" She gave the wolf's face a last caress and sank to her knees. Crawling, she ducked into the opening to the tube.

"I can't help you once we're in here," she called back to him, "but I know you can do it."

She turned her head and saw the wolf sitting at the opening, his ears pricked, watching her. He whined but did not move.

"Come on, boy," she called. "Let's go!"

She shuffled forward on hands and knees and was relieved to hear the wolf scrabbling along behind her.

§

The narrows of the tube were no less terrible for having passed successfully through them a number of times. As the stone pressed inward, constricting her movements and forcing her to wriggle along like a worm, Calypso kept her thoughts on the wolf and how dreadful this place must be for a free-running creature.

Only when she got to the tightest part, as she was inserting her turned head through the oppressive stone, did thoughts of Javier finally break through.

Oh God! Not now, she thought frantically, as she pushed with her toes and wiggled her hips. But it was too late.

Javier's absence broke in on her in a mighty wave of desolation. Caught with her head through the narrows but her shoulders still on the other side, she was guillotined by grief. She collapsed, unable to summon the strength or volition to proceed. Sobs wracked her and with each heave of her chest, the terrible stone compressed it again like a cruel trap.

She saw again the smoking rubble of her home. Smelled its terrible stench. Saw the armed attackers, vigilant, predatory, and triumphant. She imagined the people of the ranch, trapped inside and burned in the inferno, Javier among them. Saw a burning beam fall, trapping him. His fruitless struggles to lift it off, as his clothing caught fire, and his lungs singed from smoke and heat. Witnessed her sweet life vaporizing—her paintings, her collection of Rarámuri basketry, the ancient Egyptian locket box. Her clothing. His.

At each small holocaust, she wept anew. Her rosebushes took flame. Her beds of herbs. The benches tucked into shady nooks near the house. The birdhouses Javier had built for her.

All, all.

It was the darkest moment of her life. If she died there in the stone's embrace, she would not care. She thought bitterly of some spelunker of the future, worming his way to this spot, only to be met with her grinning skull, and the thought pleased her.

Just let me die, she thought. *Just let me die.*

How long it continued she did not know. All time had ceased and she existed in an eternal torment, a living hell. At last, however, she was brought to her senses by a shrill whine. A cold nose touched the exposed skin of her ankle. She might wish for death, but the creature behind her wanted to live.

She pushed with her toes, digging in. She squirmed her hips, inching forward. Life returned through these peristaltic movements. The tube widened. A breath of clean air wafted through its confining length. Recalled to life, Calypso bored her way, head first, into the future, as lowly a creature as ever was born.

§

She knew she was near the end of the terrible passage when she smelled cigarette smoke. The first thing the beam of her headlamp picked up as she exited the tube was Lone-R, sitting in a pool of lantern light, smoking.

"Lone-R!" she exclaimed, rejoiced to see another human.

"Oh, shit!"

He erupted upward, his arms coming defensively before his face, his legs crouching. He peered into the shadows where Calypso sat, blinded by her headlamp.

"Shit, you scared me!"

Calypso moved to the side, as Lobo's snout emerged from the hole. Soon, all of the wolf was standing by her, shaking himself.

"You're smoking," she said inanely.

"Oh, yeah." He stubbed the cigarette out guiltily. "Don't tell nobody. We're not supposed to."

Calypso nodded, too spent to respond.

"Where's El Lobo?"

"He's not coming."

"What do you mean, not coming? Where the fuck is he?"

"He's dead."

"Oh, man. Don't tell me this."

"It was an accident. He fell."

"You know what they'll do, right?"

"Kill me?"

"No. Put you under the Devil's Breath, again."

She nodded wearily. "Beats being killed."

She looked hopefully at the pack by his feet. "Do you have food?"

Lone-R eyed her appraisingly. "Yeah. Sure."

He dug in his pack, came up with a sandwich in a Ziplock bag, and handed it to her. "Here. Peanut butter and honey."

He watched as Calypso ripped the bag open, tore the sandwich in half and gave one portion to the wolf. Both of them, he observed, ate like wolves. Calypso's rumpled jeans hung on her. Overnight she had gone from slender to thin. Her face was crumpled with a degree of defeat he could only guess at.

"Was it bad?"

She looked at him with heavy, red-rimmed eyes, and nodded. "The worst." The sandwich was gone and she looked hopefully again at his pack.

Lone-R shook his head. "I ain't got no more food."

He nodded toward the passage leading outside. "Let's blow this place. It gives me the creeps."

§

The late afternoon sun was sitting just above the rim of the canyon when they emerged from the cave. Calypso considered trying to escape but knew she was too physically and emotionally depleted. It was all she could do to navigate down through the boulder field toward the trail. As she trudged in front of Lone-R up the narrow game trail toward the grotto, she kept her head down, willing each step, while Lobo padded docilely behind her.

Just below the grotto, they were accosted by a sentinel named Buddy, a tall, raw-boned man in camouflage, carrying a shotgun. He stood on the edge of the little plateau and watched them toil up the steep trail.

"Where's El Lobo?" he called.

Lone-R looked up at him and shook his head.

"It's bad."

Buddy said no more, and took up the end of the line as they gained the flat. Lone-R went to the grotto, filled his canteen and offered it to Calypso, who drank greedily, while Lobo went to the pool and lapped as if he could never be filled. Buddy watched it all impassively, his shotgun cocked in the crook of his arm.

When their thirst was satisfied, they began the ascent of the even steeper and narrower trail to the monastery. Calypso immediately began to have trouble with the climb. Her feet slipped on the loose gravel and twice she stumbled badly.

On a particularly rough section, where the trail wove through a boulder field, she fell. She tried to get up, but her legs would not hold her. Lone-R, who was several feet above her on the steep slope, gestured for Buddy to stop as he was about to prod her with the barrel of the shotgun.

"No, man," Lone-R shouted, leaping back down the trail to Calypso—but not before Lobo had turned on Buddy with his teeth bared and a deep growl rumbling in his chest. The wolf couched beside Calypso, his yellow eyes trained on Buddy like scopes, clearly prepared to rip the throat out of anyone who touched her unkindly.

Lone-R assessed the situation and said, "She can't do it. It's too steep." Calypso had rolled herself into a sitting position, leaning against a boulder, and was nursing her elbow.

"Listen," Lone-R said, squatting beside her, "you're too tired to do this. I'm gonna carry you, okay?"

She shook her head. "You can't."

"Yeah. I can," he said flatly, and sliding his arms under her knees, he lifted her. "Shit, I carry more than this on my dinner tray in the refectory every night."

He turned, and setting his foot firmly on the trail, took a step upward, and then another. Lobo fell in behind, turning often to watch Buddy, who brought up the rear at a respectful distance.

Lone-R was, Calypso thought, like a tractor. The man's massive muscles rolled over the terrain, indifferent to impediment. She leaned her head against his steely shoulder and closed her eyes, feeling safe for the first time in days.

§

It was evening, before they reached the monastery. The sun had set behind the cliffs. The sky darkened from blue to violet, and then red flamed up in the west, as if the cliff tops were afire, setting Calypso's grief ablaze again.

Her legs were numb by the time they entered the courtyard of the great stone building, where Lone-R set her down on a wooden bench. He stretched his arms over his head, and Calypso imagined that they must be numb too.

"I'll go get Father Keat," he said, just as the massive door opened and their leader stepped out, forbidding in his black cassock.

"What's this?" he asked acerbically.

Calypso, Lone-R, and Buddy began to speak all at once, and Father Keat held his hand up for silence.

"You," he said, pointing to Calypso. "You go."

She began to explain, but was overcome with a fit of weeping, as she got to the part where El Lobo was swept away.

"She's tired," Lone-R said, "and she's starving."

"Put her in the guest room and bring her some supper," Father Keat commanded. He turned on his heel, his skirts flying, and ascended the stone stairs, pulled open the door, and was gone.

Buddy followed him, leaving Lone-R, with almost courtly grace, to escort Calypso and Lobo, who would not leave her side, to a new room. This one was on the ground floor, had no bars on the windows, and was comfortably furnished with antique furniture.

Lone-R bent to start a fire on the hearth, saying, "The stuff in here is original—the bed, the table, that trunk. All of it. It was just sittin' here when Father Keat took over the place."

Calypso turned to take in her surroundings.

"It's beautiful," she said. "Even the paintings are original?" She stepped closer to look at a large, rather primitive oil painting of the canyon and the mission, framed in a gilt-laden Baroque frame.

Lone-R rose from the fire and shrugged. "Yeah. I guess. You'd have to ask Father Keat." He stepped toward the door. "I'll go get you some food."

He went out and then stuck his head back through the door. "Oh—there's a bathroom through that door," he said, pointing to a heavy paneled door on the right wall. "If you want a bath." Then he was gone.

It was nearly an hour before Lone-R returned with a tray laden with steaming food. In the interim, Calypso had bathed and washed her hair. When his knock came, she was sitting by the fire, wrapped in a bathrobe she'd found hanging on the bathroom door.

Lone-R set the tray on a small table near the warmth of the fire, with a flourish. Lobo lay stretched on his side, near the flames.

"You look better."

"I feel better."

She bent her face over the steaming food while Lone-R removed two bowls from the tray. One, full of sliced meat, he set beside the wolf. The other, Lobo's water bowl, he took into the bathroom and filled with water, then put it on the hearth.

Calypso attacked the food. Instead of the usual rice and beans, there were roast chicken, fresh squash, and roasted potatoes with plenty of butter.

"This is delicious," she said in surprise. "I thought you all lived on rice and beans."

"Naw. That's just Father Keat's way of gettin' your attention."

"It seems so odd to me," Calypso said, "to have a guest room in a place where you normally execute your visitors."

"It's for the FNGs."

"FNGs?"

"Yeah, the Fuckin' New Guys. When they come to sign on, they get the royal treatment. I got to stay here myself."

"What if they decide they don't want to stay?"

Lone-R looked at her meaningfully. "Father Keat can be very persuasive."

"So do you recruit? I mean, how does anyone ever learn about this place so they can join?"

"Yeah. We gots a recruiter. Someone will know someone else who's on the lam, or dead broke, or hurt, or ready to retire. Our guy goes lookin' for him. But we're at maximum capacity now. Someone'll have to die before we recruit again."

"Someone just did."

"Yeah. Well, I guess you're gettin' the royal treatment 'cuz you kind of helped get rid of a problem."

"El Lobo?"

"Uh-huh. Nobody trusted him. I mean, we're all spooks here but he was spookier than most. A nut job."

"Sociopathic?"

Lone-R shrugged. "I guess. Whatever that means."

"It means he didn't care about anybody but himself," she said between bites. "That he was a pathological liar, a really skilled manipulator. That he was charismatic and people wanted to follow him..."

"Yeah! That's the problem. He convinced a few of the guys he should be the leader, not Father Keat. He was always underminin' Father Keat's authority. It was startin' to be a problem, you know what I mean?"

Calypso nodded. "Yes, I do. A sociopath causes trouble wherever he goes. They rile things up, start people fighting among themselves."

"Yep. That was El Lobo."

"Did he abuse Lobo?" she asked, laying a hand on the wolf's head.

"He was startin' to. Guys would see him kick Lobo or hit him. But if they confronted him, he'd deny it. He'd accuse them of workin' for Father Keat, to make him look bad."

Calypso nodded. "Yes. That's how a sociopath works. They do no wrong—it's everybody else who's doing wrong to them."

She took a sip of water, gazing into the fire.

"So you think Father Keat is actually relieved that El Lobo's gone?"

"That's my take on it."

Calypso was starting to nod. The hot food and warm fire were calming the anxiety that had driven her in the last days. Lone-R reached for her tray.

"You better go to bed. You're gonna have a big day, tomorrow."

When he was gone, she staggered to the bed, pulled back the covers and fell in. She was asleep, almost as her head touched the pillow.

§

After breakfast in the morning, Father Keat came for her. He stood by the fire, refusing her offer of a chair, his face grim.

"You realize that there are men here who think you killed El Lobo?"

"Yes, I expected that."

"You'll have to undergo interrogation again. Under scopolamine."

"I expected that, too."

"It's a complicated situation here," he said. "Every one of us has blood on his hands. Lots of it. In a sense, I guess you could say that every one of us is a sociopath."

He hesitated.

"But most of us have found a way to live with what we've done. Maybe we can't always feel remorse like most people do, but we want to stop killing. Maybe it's for selfish reasons. Most of us are tired and just want to live quietly now." He looked at Calypso, to see if she was following him.

"I understand," she said.

"Some of us got into killing from having a bad start in life, like Lone-R or Icepick. I guess me, too. I was just a poor, barefooted kid on the Mexican border. I had to be tough or die.

"It's like that with most of the men here. But there are a few—just a handful, really—who get off on killing. Who are using this place as a hideout until they can figure out how to get on with their kicks. And El Lobo was at their center. Now do you see how complicated this has gotten?"

"Do they want me dead?"

"Oh, yeah! And they want to be the ones to do it."

Calypso shuddered. "What will you do?"

Father Keat walked to the window and stood looking out, his hands behind his back.

"First, I'm going to hear you interrogated by one of our specialists in interrogation." He held up a hand, without turning from the window. "You won't be harmed, I promise you."

He hesitated again.

"And then...?"

"And then, if you're telling the truth about El Lobo dying by accident, then..." He sighed. "I haven't got a fucking clue what I'm going to do."

"I assure you, I'm innocent."

Father Keat turned from the window with a sardonic smile.

"No one in the twenty-first century is innocent, Miss Searcy. People just have varying degrees of awareness of their guilt."

§

They took her to a room without windows, one she was sure from its grim and comfortless look must have been a torture chamber during the Inquisition. Father Keat was there with Icepick and a few other of the older men. They allowed Lobo to follow her and he came to lie at her feet. Lone-R stood guard by the door.

One man came forward, wielding a syringe. He was tall and broad-shouldered, with the look of an aging bull. His eyes were hard in a handsome face, beneath a fully shaven head, and they seemed to penetrate into the depths of her own.

"Do you remember me, Miss Searcy?"

She shook her head. "No."

"That's because the last time we met, you were already under the influence of the drug I'm about to administer. My name is Cat, and I am a former interrogator for the CIA. I am about to inject scopolamine, also known as Tree Datura, Brugmansia, Toé, and Devil's Breath.

"This time, the dosage will not cause you to overdose or hallucinate, but it will cause you to speak the truth. When you come out from under its influence, you won't remember anything that has passed here. Do you understand?"

"Yes."

"There are sociopaths who can lie and still pass a lie detector test, but no one can outwit scopolamine. Are you ready?"

She was too paralyzed with fear to speak. She squared her shoulders and nodded her head. The man came forward, took her icy hand in his, and plunged the needle into her arm.

ʕ

When she first became aware of herself again, she was sitting in the armchair by the guest room fire. Lone-R stood by the door holding a shotgun. She glanced dizzily around the room and saw that the shutters were closed and locked from the inside. She was slightly nauseated and she had a cracking headache.

Lone-R caught her eye. "You back?"

She nodded, frowning. "How long?"

"About six hours."

"My vision is blurred."

"Your pupils are still dilated."

"What did they think?"

Lone-R shrugged. "Who knows? They don't share that stuff with me."

Lobo got up and came to stand by her chair, poking her in the arm with his nose. She wafted an insubstantial hand toward him and laid it on top of his head.

"What happens now?"

"We wait. You hungry?"

Calypso thought about it. "Maybe. I feel kind of sick to my stomach."

"Food might help. There're some sandwiches there, on the tray."

Calypso bent to take one and then turned to Lobo. "You hungry?"

Lobo's feathery tail gave an answering swish.

"Okay. We'll share." She tore the sandwich of bologna and cheese in half and dropped the wolf's half into the bowl on the hearth.

"Did I say anything that surprised you?" she asked Lone-R, around a bite of sandwich.

"Ha, yeah!" he said with an ironic laugh. "We. . .none of us had any idea what you went through. Everyone was shocked."

"Really?"

"Well, hell yeah. El Lobo drowning. Falling down the cliff. Your house burned down. Your husband probably dead. Finding Lobo." He waved his arm expressively. "Shit! You're one tough cookie, lady."

"You think he believed me? Father Keat?"

Lone-R shrugged. "If he didn't, he missed a good chance."

"Why are you guarding me then? Did I say I'm going to try to escape?"

"Nah. It's not that. It's El Lobo's crew. This one cat, Jimmy the Butcher. He heard your testimony but he still thinks you're lyin'. He's threatenin' to kill you."

"So you're here to protect me?"

"Yes, m'am."

Calypso reached dreamily for the second sandwich, split it with Lobo and took a bite, her eyes still gazing, slightly unfocused, at Lone-R.

"Nothing like this has ever happened here before?"

"Not that I'm aware of."

"It's hard, you know? Not remembering. And humiliating. Like I could have made a fool of myself and I'd never know."

"You didn't."

"Tell me, will you? Tell me every single thing so I can remember it now. Give me back my memory. Please?"

Lone-R considered Calypso, with her long hair in a wild aura around her haggard face, then looked at his feet and nodded.

"Okay."

He recounted the entire six hours—the questions Cat had asked; her responses; Father Keat's question, whether she simply might be hallucinating everything; and Cat's reply that she would not have been able to give an account consistent with her first interrogation if she were.

"And you cried a lot."

"I did?"

"Buckets."

"But I didn't cry in the cave. At least, not that much. Only in the tube."

"You said that, but Cat said it was because the scopolamine touches down into the subconscious, so you get a person's true responses to a situation."

"So I was really just a big baby."

"No. So you kept goin' in spite of overwhelmin' odds. You gots to remember—these guys have been there and done that. Shit! They'll probably make you an honorary Ghost!"

There was a knock at the door and Lone-R called, "Who's there?"

"Me." It was the unmistakable voice of Father Keat.

"You alone?"

"Yes."

"Give the password."

"Holy shit!"

Lone-R lifted the bar on the door. Father Keat bustled in and gestured with his head for Lone-R to close the door fast. He had replaced his cassock with camouflage and he carried an assault rifle with a handgun holstered at his side. "We've got to get you out of here," he began without preamble. "All hell's breaking loose." This observation was punctuated by a distance volley of shots. "El Lobo's crew is holed up on the third floor. They think you killed him and they want revenge."

"They didn't believe my testimony?"

"Lady, you don't understand. In the bad guy world, if you even *imagine* that someone has done you wrong, you do them. Otherwise, you lose respect."

"There's a problem. I still can't see very well. And I don't think I can walk down the trail. I'm kind of shaky."

"That's not a problem." He turned to Lone-R. "Get her out to the back courtyard, pronto."

"Yes, sir."

Lone-R lifted the bar on the door and Father Keat was halfway through, when he stopped and turned back to Calypso.

"Listen," he said earnestly. "You did a helluva thing these last couple of days. And I don't just mean El Lobo."

"All I've done is stir up trouble for you."

"No. You've flushed out the rats. Every organization's got 'em. Now, we do a little rat hunt is all. This place needed a good cleaning up."

He hesitated, then shoved the door closed and strode across the room. Taking Calypso's hand in his, he bent at the waist and laid a courtly kiss on its back. "You're a helluva broad. I've had four wives in all and all of 'em put together couldn't make half of you."

He dropped her hand, ran to the door, peered out as he drew his weapon, and was gone, leaving Calypso with her mouth agape.

Lone-R grinned. "What'd I tell you?"

He came across the room to her. "Madame," he said, bowing at the waist, and offering her his arm. She hung onto it and he pulled her to her feet. "Can you walk?"

"Yes, I think so."

"Then let's get you out of here. Pronto."

§

Chapter 11

LONE-R LED CALYPSO THROUGH A LABYRINTH OF CORRIDORS, PAST WHAT WERE, BY OBVIOUS SMELLS, THE KITCHEN AND REFECTORY. They hurried by a large room where a small cadre of men was practicing tai chi, and out a tall set of double doors at the back of the building.

They were in a courtyard paved in river cobble set on edge for drainage. Across the way, a hundred feet distant, stood another stone building with large, sliding wooden doors.

As Calypso and Lone-R crossed the yard, two men were engaged in wrestling the doors open. Then they ducked inside, and Calypso got a glimpse of some kind of machine, glimmering back in the shadows. In seconds, the men emerged, pushing a small, sleek helicopter with someone already at the controls.

As Lone-R pulled Calypso toward the chopper, the turbine kicked on with a scream and the rotors began to turn.

"This is it," Lone-R yelled. "Where you and me say goodbye." He yanked open the passenger-side door.

Stunned by the sudden change of events, Calypso threw her arms around his neck in a brief, fierce hug.

"You're a good man, Lone-R. Don't you ever let anyone tell you otherwise," she shouted over the increasing whine of the turbine.

She stepped up into the chopper and reached down to Lobo, who was cowering in the wind of the rotors, his silver and black fur thrashing.

"Come on, boy. Let's go!"

The terrified animal slunk on its belly to the door, and Lone-R boosted him in and slammed the door. He stepped back and raised his hand in farewell as the chopper immediately began to rise.

The craft took a dip to the right and as it did, the windshield suddenly crackled into a spider web pattern.

"Shit!" the pilot exclaimed.

They were thirty feet off the ground now and as they banked hard right, she saw Lone-R rolling for cover into the stone outbuilding. As they spun up and away, she caught a brief glimpse of faces at the third floor windows of the monastery, saw the muzzle flash of their guns, and heard the ping of bullets hitting the fuselage.

Then they were screaming over the terra cotta-tiled roof and the abyss of the canyon fell away underneath them. Red cliffs embraced the small craft parenthetically, the river uncoiled its aqua length, and the entirety looked as peaceful as if none of the foregoing mayhem had happened at all.

§

"You okay?" It was the pilot, and Calypso, who was still straining to see the last of the monastery, turned to him and was amazed to see Cat at the controls.

"Yes. I think so. Are you?"

"Oh, hell yeah. Takes more than that to even get my blood pressure up."

"I didn't know you had a helicopter. It's a nice one—or was."

"It's a Sikorsky S-434 turbine. State-of-the-art. But it needed a few bullet holes to add character. We were kind of embarrassed by how pristine it was."

"Why do you need one?"

"You can ask that, when it just saved your skin? Besides, when we're not rescuing fair maidens, we've got business to transact. And we fly into El Paso now and again to shop, too. Where do you think that bologna in your sandwich came from? This is our glorified shopping cart."

Calypso busied herself, arranging her feet so that Lobo could curl more comfortably on the floor. In doing so, she spotted a machine gun, mounted on the firewall.

"Shopping. I see," she said drily. "Are you taking me to El Paso then?"

"Oh, hell no. Jimmy the Butcher's got friends there."

Calypso waited for him to say more, but he flew calmly on in silence.

"Where then?" she asked finally.

"Someplace no one's going to look for you. To a friend of mine, who'll take you to another friend."

"And then what?"

Calypso's heart was sinking with the sudden realization she had no place to go, no one to return to. She had no money, no credit card, no ID, and deeply regretted leaving her pack behind in the cave. All she had was the clothing on her back and a guardian wolf with the generic name of Lobo. How far could she get with that?

As if reading her mind, Cat said, "My friend will fix you up. That's his specialty—getting people established across the border."

He threw a stern glance at Calypso. "You do realize your time on this side of the border is over, right?"

Calypso's eyes filled with tears. "I hadn't really thought about it."

"Well, start thinking."

Calypso bent to bury her fingers into Lobo's ruff, her head turned to the window. She didn't want Cat to see the tears that insisted themselves on her, despite her effort to suppress them.

"Go ahead and cry," he said gruffly. "You've got a right."

Tears brimmed over and streamed down her cheeks.

"Where's my friend, Hill?" she asked suddenly. "Did you kill him?"

"Oh, hell no. Why would we do that?"

"Then where is he?"

"I put him on Toé and gave him some strong suggestions about just having had a nice parting from you and Javier at your ranch. Then we took him to Chihuahua and put him on a plane. He's probably just getting over jet lag in Paris, about now."

Calypso's shoulders sagged with relief. "Thank God," she breathed.

Cat snorted and said sardonically, "No, actually you can thank me."

§

The chopper flew low through twisting canyons, always northwestward. They crossed the summit of the Sierra and skimmed along its steep western slope. At last, Calypso felt the craft beginning to descend. Looking down, she saw a little shack nestled in a fold of hills amid scrawny oaks, black rocks, and brush.

"End of the line," Cat said as he brought the bird down in a dirt yard.

Vortices of dust rose around them as the rotors slowed and finally came to a stop. When the dust had cleared a bit, Calypso could see a grizzled man standing in the door of the cabin. Cat shoved his chin toward him.

"There's your next connection."

He opened his door, slid out and went to talk to the man, while Calypso got herself and Lobo out on the other side. The two men approached her.

"This is Rat," Cat said. "As in Desert."

Calypso reached to shake a grimed, leathery hand. Rat stood about four foot ten, by her reckoning. He was wearing rough white cotton pants of a Mexican peasant, although he was clearly Anglo, a grungy singlet stained coffee brown, and scuffed and sloping huaraches. She could just see eyes of piercing blue above a bulbous nose, within a cloud of wildly curling, desert tan hair and beard. He could be, she thought, anywhere from twenty-five to seventy.

"He'll take you on the next leg," Cat said. "I gotta get back. I'm missing all the fun."

"I can pay you all for your trouble," Calypso stammered. "Once I get my bank account straightened out..."

Cat held up a restraining hand.

"It's on the house," he said. "We haven't had this much excitement since the last time. We were getting stale. We owe you."

He reached a large and powerful hand to her shoulder, pulled Calypso to him and kissed her soundly on the lips. Then he turned and trotted back to the chopper.

Just as he was pulling the door shut, Calypso called, "Cat!" With his eyes trained on her, she smiled broadly, threw him a kiss, and mouthed "Thank you!"

His head jerked with a chuckle, he flashed a salute, the turbine whined and in a suffocating cloud of dust, he was airborne. In seconds, he and the helicopter were gone, with only the hammering echo of its rotors rebounding from the dry hillsides.

§

"So" Rat said when the dust had settled enough to speak. He looked her up and down. "You ready to roll?"

Calypso looked around her. Besides the decrepit shack, there was a lean-to filled with firewood and hanging strings of drying chilies, another sway-backed shed, and endless miles of scrub.

"Where?" she asked, bewildered. "How?"

"Aha!" Rat exclaimed.

He held up his forefinger, cautioning her to wait. Like an unwashed leprechaun, he bounded to the shed and dragged the door open. Back in the shadows, Calypso could just make out a large grill grinning at her, with chrome teeth secured by a fat lower lip of chrome bumper.

Rat disappeared into the shed. There was a moment's silence, then the *thunk* of a heavy car door closing and the deep, throaty roar of a big engine kicking over and revving.

Suddenly, out the door of the shed flew a huge powder blue boat—a 1960 Cadillac Eldorado Biarritz, almost twenty feet long. The ragtop was back, revealing plump white leather tuck-and-roll seats. The two-door convertible throbbed and shimmied from the power of its engine and from the blasting of its tape deck, already scorching the air with the Rolling Stones' "Paint It Black."

"Hop in," said Rat, deadpan. "Three hundred forty-five horses at your service," and he tipped a nonexistent hat. His head barely showed above the dash.

Calypso's eyes swept the car from its massive hood, over six feet in width, along its bullet-shaped sides to its pointed tail fins. The only anomaly was that its sleek body was jacked up on a massive undercarriage and oversized, knobby tires that still sported elegant, crest-embossed Cadillac wheel covers.

She opened the passenger side door, pulled the white leather seat forward, got Lobo safely installed on the back seat, and then slipped into the front. She groped for seat belts but Rat just shook his head.

"Not in this model," he said.

Gripping the wheel and ramming the four-speed transmission into gear, Rat slammed his foot to the accelerator. The car dug in like a racehorse in the starting gate and then with a tremendous lurch, fountains of dirt from the rear wheels and a graceful S-shaped fishtail, it leapt forward, and charged out of the yard.

Calypso shrieked as they appeared about to crash straight into an outcropping of black rocks, but Rat hauled on the steering wheel and wrenched them onto a narrow track that was more rock and rut than drivable surface. Down this he tore, apparently with no sense that modulation of the accelerator was possible.

Rat reached a small, grimy hand to the knob and cranked the tape deck to maximum volume. "*I see a line of cars and they're all painted black...*" wailed two built-in speakers on the back deck.

Wind whipped Calypso's hair and she hauled it in, twisted it into a rough rope and coiled it into a knot at the nape of her neck. The locket hammered against her chest in response to the jolts of the road, like a metronome metering the rhythm of fate.

"I could not foresee this thing happening to you..." the Stones sang, and Lobo threw his head back and howled in agreement.

Rat drove by looking through the spokes of the steering wheel but this did not diminish his exuberance. Wind flattened his bushy tan hair against his skull and streamed it behind him like a snarl of fishing line. His beard pressed against grinning teeth and his short fingers, sun-creased and lined black with dirt, drummed time on the perforated leather of the wheel.

On and on, down the endless desert track they roared, trailing a tall rooster tail of dust. The autumn sun spread flat, white light over rough tracts of blue-gray shrub and jagged, misshapen stone. The Stones sang, Lobo howled, and Calypso hung on, fearing for both body and sanity.

Bushes growing on the verge of the almost impassable track scraped along the sides of the car, shrieking. A blast of fall wind sent a cloud of dead oak leaves into the air as they whizzed through a small copse. Leaves pelted them and so did "Gimme Shelter."

"Oh, a storm is threat'ning/My very life today/If I don't get some shelter/Oh yeah, I'm gonna fade away," Mick Jagger wailed.

"War, children, it's just a shot away/It's just a shot away." The relentless, driving rhythm underpinned the contrapuntal madness of the car's lurching frame, its pounding shock absorbers and hammering leaf springs.

They raced across a desert slope, the Cadillac tipping almost forty-five degrees. Calypso, on the downhill side, looked into a nest of black, jagged boulders, like a mouthful of rotten teeth waiting to crush and mangle.

"Ooh, see the fire is sweepin'/Our very street today/Burns like a red coal carpet/Mad bull lost your way..."

Her mind was a blur of images, backing wildly through recent chronology, as if to create a drag that would slow forward momentum—the chopper's windshield suddenly bursting into a shattered web; the smoking timbers of Rancho Cielo; the face of El Lobo as he was sucked down...

"The flood is threat'ning/My very life today/Gimme, gimme shelter/Or I'm gonna fade away..."

They plunged from the slope down into a dry arroyo of sand and boulders. With a tremendous jolt, the convertible high-centered on a rock but Rat pressed even harder on the accelerator. The vehicle kicked up a fountain of sand, dragged its scraping undercarriage off the rock, and shot up the other side like a charging bull. Calypso saw one of its elegant wire- and crest-decked hubcaps roll off down the wash.

"War, children, it's just a shot away/It's just a shot away/It's just a shot away/It's just a shot away/It's just a shot away..."

S

Rat drove until the Cadillac ran out of gas. It was late afternoon and they had descended from the hills into flat desert flecked with low, widely spaced bushes of dusty gray-green, and small cacti with very long black thorns. The track, while still rutted and rough and only one car wide, now had two distinct wheel tracks, signs of increased usage.

Rat coasted to a stop and immediately hopped out to open the trunk. Calypso unfolded her legs, which felt drunkenly unsteady on the sandy soil. Lobo hopped over the side of the car and trotted off into the desert.

The capacious trunk, Calypso saw at a glance, was filled with sloshing red plastic gas cans, several large caliber carbines using high velocity magnum cartridges, a Barrett .50 caliber sniper rifle, and a case of dynamite. An open metal pail of blasting caps listed beside it, along with two detached *huevos del toro*, drum magazines for the AK-47 and AR-15 assault rifles she glimpsed, shoved into the rear of the trunk. She closed her eyes and looked away.

She walked out into the desert to get away from Rat's endless, off-key humming, as he slurped gas into the tank. *"It's just a shot away/It's just a shot away/It's just a shot away..."*

After the racket, the near silence of the desert was almost hallucinogenic. A cold wind rattled the dry limbs of the scrub.

A small bird cheeped repeatedly somewhere close at hand. A hawk cried, up near the sun. The thrumming of branches in the wind seemed to repeat the urgent rhythm of the song's chorus.

She searched the horizon with dry, reddened eyes looking for any sign of civilization and saw none. She scanned the ground, hoping to find something—an interesting stone, a shard of glass, a bit of rusted metal—to act as talisman, but there was only yellow sand.

All too soon, Rat tooted the horn. Calypso turned back and was relieved to see Lobo bounding toward the car from the opposite direction. In a graceful leap, he cleared the side of the car and took up his station in the center of the back seat. Calypso climbed in, Rat punched the car into a wheel-spinning start, and in an instant they were flying through the desert again.

S

It was just turning dusk when they spotted an obstacle in their path. It appeared that hunters in a big four-wheel drive truck were changing a flat tire, taking up the entire track. Two men in camouflage stood with shotguns broken over their forearms while a third squatted, laboring at the rear wheel. All three heads came up in alarm as the Cadillac hove into view.

Rather than slowing, Rat sped up and with a sudden heave, wrenched the wheel to the right and charged off the road into the desert, mowing down a bush, and dodging a small outcrop of stones. Calypso gave a whoop of surprise and the tape, that had been silent between songs, suddenly yielded up "Sympathy for the Devil" at top volume, conga drums throbbing.

"Please allow me to introduce myself/I'm a man of wealth and taste/I've been around for a long, long year/Stole many a man's soul and faith..."

"Trap," Rat shouted.

Calypso doubted it. She had an unobstructed view of the hunters as she and Rat crashed past them through the sagebrush. All three were open-mouthed with astonishment by this apotheosis of a powder blue Cadillac convertible, charging along as if powered by Satan himself. Clearly, this was straining their credulity as well as their masculinity.

Their complete befuddlement struck her as so comical that she began to laugh and then to howl, until tears streamed down her cheeks. Lobo, possibly experiencing a pack moment, threw back his head and howled, too. Calypso's final view was of the three, open-mouthed and moving zombie-like to the front of their crippled truck for a last view, as the Caddy roared back onto the road with the Stones blasting.

"Pleased to meet you/Hope you guess my name..."

Calypso had lost count of how many times the Stones tape had replayed. "Don't you have any Credence Clearwater?" she shouted over the din.

Rat's head was pumping in time to the beat. "Who?"

Evening fell as a flaming western sky gradually cooled to ash. One of the car's dual headlights had been knocked askew so that its beam penetrated the roadside desert, giving evidence of approaching civilization. Beer cans, many laced with bullet holes, lay among the cactuses in increasing numbers. Enclaves of dead refrigerators, sagging couches, and spine-broken recliners sprawled amid the sagebrush.

At last, in the distance Calypso saw a flash of light, then another and another, until the phenomenon proved to be the rhythmic pulsing of a red and yellow neon sign alternately reading, FOOD/ BEER. She realized she was famished and not just for food, but for human companionship other than that of the crazed and uncommunicative Rat.

Still at high speed, Rat cranked the wheel and slid sideways into the dirt parking lot of the roadhouse. Slamming on the brakes just short of a line of parked cars and trucks, he brought the Cadillac to a halt with a final fishtail flourish. The persistent wind carried the dust of their arrival over them in a rain of fine particles, as the Stones finally fell silent, with a final yowl.

"Love is just a kiss away, love is just a kiss aw..."

"We're here," Rat announced with evident pride in his accomplishment.

Calypso looked around her. Other than the tar papered bar building there was nothing else around. The shadowed desert stretched off in all directions.

"Where?" she asked.

Rat didn't answer. He was already out of the car heading for the saloon doors, from which the sound of a honky-tonk piano and the smell of cooking were wafting. Calypso pushed the hair from her eyes and allowed herself to admit her hunger.

Pushing the door open and standing to straighten the same dirt-crusted jeans and sweater she'd worn in the cave, she said, "Come on, Lobo, let's go. This doesn't appear to be a place where we're expected to dress for dinner."

The wolf stood on the back seat, his nose to the wind. Then, apparently approving the smell of cooking meat, he leapt over the side of the car and came to stand by her knee. Calypso dropped her hand to his broad head.

"Stick with me, kid," she said. "I have no idea what to expect."

§

As Calypso shoved open the bar door, the interior air hit her, warm and humid, bearing the unmistakable smells of beer, cooking meat, and sawdust. The room was foggy with cigarette smoke, backlit by neon beer signs, and a single mirrored ball over a tiny dance floor, where two couples shuffled in clenches that looked more like wrestling holds.

In a back corner, she could just make out a figure bent over the keyboard of an antique upright piano. From the sound of it, several keys were missing and the rest were untuned, but the pianist was nevertheless eliciting from them an energetic and playful boogie-woogie.

A long bar underscored the entire right hand wall, with a handful of men slouched on barstools or standing next to it. A bartender moved through the murky air, his faceless black shadow twinned in a cloudy back-bar mirror.

Calypso stood swaying indecisively in the dusk midway between the door and the bar, taking it all in, her entire being alert for trouble. Rat was nowhere in sight.

A brief image of her abandoned backpack flashed through her mind, where it sat inside the entrance to the tube, and where it might remain for all eternity until it became petrified. It was a mark of the trauma she had been through that she had abandoned her identification, credit cards, money, and even her cherished pocketknife and lipstick. Now, she was so hungry she felt faint, but how would she buy food?

"No dogs allowed, lady." The shout shocked her into the present. The bartender was coming from behind the bar, wiping his hands on a limp towel. He pointed to the door. "Get that mutt out of here."

Calypso stood frozen to the spot, shaking her head.

"I..." Her knees felt weak and her brain too tired to function. "I..." she tried again.

"Just get it out of here," the bartender insisted.

He reached to grab Lobo by the scruff of the neck. Instantly the wolf crouched, his teeth bared, and a menacing growl rumbled from his chest, audible even over the jaunty clanking of the piano. The bartender jerked his hand back. Sudden silence fell over the bar and all eyes turned to take in the action.

Calypso mustered her strength and said with dignity, "He's not a dog. He's a wolf."

"In that case," a voice behind her said, "I say the animal stays."

Calypso felt her strength give way and her knees begin to buckle. She turned toward her defender, already toppling. When she collapsed, she fell straight into the arms of Javier Carteña.

§

He carried her to a table back in the shadows near the piano, where he sat with her on his lap. Her hands were dug into his sides like grappling hooks, and her tears had already soaked his shirt front. The longer he held her, the sobs, instead of diminishing, became more torrential.

Like a dam bursting, the accumulated sorrows, terrors and grief of the past days poured forth incoherently. Her mind was blank as a wiped slate, but her animal body was acutely aware of his animal body—the specific warmth and steeliness of his chest, his feral scent, the cherishing lock of his arms around her.

Her entire life and world were collapsed into their united being like that compacted matter said to exist in space, so dense that one cubic centimeter, if dropped on Earth, would pass right through it and out the other side.

Javier rested his chin on top of her head and let the magnitude of her emotions flow into his scorched and blackened interior. Nothing else mattered now. It was all inconsequential. The house could be rebuilt. The land and its people defended. In time, all could be even better and stronger than before.

Calypso's miraculous appearance was his wellspring and her tears were priming the pump. Where she had been, what she had experienced he did not yet know, but he would find a way to heal it. With her by his side, everything again was possible.

ʕ

They lay in the narrow, lumpy bed of a nameless motel planted in the desert beside a section of highway long bypassed by a freeway. In the room next door, a drunken couple were arguing, their inchoate mutterings and shouts penetrating the thin walls like the rumbling of beasts. The bedclothes stank of mildew and cigarette smoke and the carpet gave off the sickly sweet odor of cheap cleaner. On it, Lobo stretched beside Calypso's side of the bed sound asleep.

To them, it might have been the antechamber to heaven—or to hell. They were heedless of all things future, knowing only the present, with its endless possibilities for mutual intermingling. They lay wrapped into one another, their bodies annealed by sweat and tears.

"What's this?" Calypso asked, frowning as she ran her hand over a large welt on Javier's arm.

"Just a burn. It got pretty hot up on the wall while the house was burning."

Calypso shuddered. "My God, Javier!"

"And what about this?" He ran a tentative finger over a bruise that ran from her left cheek up into her hairline. It was the brooding purple of an eggplant and stippled with small scabs.

"I fell climbing the cliff. The pitons ripped out."

"Pitons? Plural?"

"Three, I think."

"My God, Caleepso!" He wrapped her closer to him. "You could have died."

"I considered it. But then, so could you."

They lay tangled in one another, contemplating how close they had come to losing one another, until mere proximity soothed them. Between long periods of pure, silent rapture, they told bits of their stories, attempting to piece together the puzzle of the last few days.

"So it was that little guy—how you call him? Rat?—he brought you to the bar?"

"Did you see that beat-up Cadillac in the parking lot when we came in? He brought me in that. That's probably him next door, wooing his lady."

"I can't believe that car could make it through the desert."

"Neither can I." She explained about the contents of the trunk. "Besides being a rolling bomb, it was the *Ride of the Valkyries* and *The Charge of the Light Brigade* meet Mr. Toad's Wild Ride and a drug-addled Rolling Stones concert."

Javier chuckled and kissed her forehead. They were silent for a moment, fitting that piece into the developing picture.

"Was anyone hurt, Javier? In the battle? Our people, I mean?" She tensed, awaiting the worst.

"Yes. Juan was shot in the arm, and Martín has a head wound. It's not too bad. They'll recover." He could feel Calypso's body relax. Then her hand stole over his chest and down his length.

"I can feel that everything is in good working order here," she murmured.

"Woe-man!" he growled, fending her off. But it was too late. Despite their exhaustion, their bodies demanded a deeper reunion and with squealing and listing bed springs, they obliged.

§

In the morning, ravaged by hunger, they went to the slovenly diner attached to the motel. The waitress, wearing a greasy apron over an unwashed uniform, dramatic false eyelashes, and metallic gold flats covered in food spots, frowned at them as they pushed through the door.

"May we let Lobo come in?" Calypso asked, holding the door ajar, with the wolf's long nose inserted in the crack.

The waitress shrugged. "Whatever."

Calypso glanced into a steam- and grease-clouded mirror behind the counter as they took a booth. She was still in the mud-crusted clothes she'd worn in the cave. With wet hair, no makeup, a glowering bruise, and her face gleaming with the rancid hand cream supplied by the motel, she looked spectral. Javier had been wearing the same shirt and jeans for days, smeared with soot and blood, and his face, above a field of stubble, was haggard.

"Now there's a pair to draw to!" Calypso laughed.

Javier, gazing at her across the table, took her hands in his. "You are the most beautiful sight the world," he said earnestly.

They ordered outrageous quantities of food—steak, fried eggs, bacon, waffles, pancakes and biscuits and gravy, and a plate of *machaca* for Lobo. Even the watery coffee tasted ambrosial to them.

"So I still don't understand," Javier said to her as their breakfast was cooking. "Where were you before you were with Rat?"

"I was in the cave."

"Yes, but how did you get from the cave to Rat's place?"

"I..." A frown creased her forehead. She set her coffee cup down with a puzzled look. "I..." she began again.

"I know you weren't in the safe house in Batopilas," Javier prompted. "That was the first place I looked."

Calypso shook her head slowly. "It's very strange but I don't remember. I was just suddenly there in Rat's car and we were racing through the desert."

"I called Hill in Paris. He remembers saying goodbye to us at the house before he left for the airport."

"But he was in the cave with me."

"I know. Pedro told me."

The waitress approached with the first round of food. She set the plates down, slammed a bottle of catsup in the middle of the table and departed. Calypso slipped the plate of machaca under the table and was gratified to hear Lobo's greedy lapping. She and Javier attacked their breakfasts as if they were wolves themselves.

"It makes no sense," Calypso said, gesturing with her fork. "If Hill was with me in the cave, then he couldn't have said goodbye at the house, because while we were in the cave, the house was burning."

"Exactly," Javier agreed as he sliced into his steak. "I told him that but he insisted. I started to suspect he was hiding you in Paris. I wanted to go there but my passport burned up."

"So how did you end up in the bar last night?"

"That's another strange thing. The owner, Bill Hartman—the guy who was playing the piano last night?—he called my cell phone. He said he had important information for me—too important to say over an open line. He said to come to the bar, so I did."

"Did you know him? Before this, I mean?"

"No."

"Weren't you afraid it was a trap?"

"It was a possibility."

"But you came anyway."

"Yes."

"And then I arrived."

"Yes."

They stared into one another's eyes, mystified.

"Maybe we could ask Rat," Calypso suggested.

"I thought of that but his car's already gone."

The second round of food arrived, and Calypso spread the entire paper cup's-worth of whipped margarine over her waffle while she thought.

"None of this makes sense," she said flatly.

"No. It doesn't."

"Where are we, by the way? I mean, is this the US or Mexico?"

"We're right on the border. I think we might be a couple of miles inside the US."

"But that's over two hundred miles from the ranch! And there was no border crossing."

Javier laughed. "How do you think all the drugs get across? My guess is your friend Rat is one of the guys who ferries them. And it's closer to three hundred miles."

Calypso poured a flood of syrup onto her waffle. "I don't understand any of this."

"Try to remember. Where did you find Lobo?"

"He was in the cave."

"Where in the cave?"

"All the way. He was with me all the way. I had to haul him up the cliff, after the tube."

"Think, Caleepso. When did you first see him?"

Calypso put her fork down and gazed out the steamy window into the bleak dirt parking area, backtracking in her mind's eye. It was like trying to remember a dream, teasing out its details.

"He came through the tube after El Lobo," she said finally.

"After who?"

"El Lobo. He was a very bad man, and he was in the cave with me."

"Why?"

Calypso sat and thought, then shook her head. "I don't know. I can't remember."

"Maybe you have a concussion. Did he hit you?"

Calypso ran her hand over her head. "It doesn't hurt anywhere, except from the fall."

"What happened to him? Why is Lobo with you instead of with his master?"

"Because..."

Calypso frowned with the effort of remembering.

"Because..."

Then it hit her. The image of El Lobo's agonized face as he was sucked down the siphon filled her mind. She put her hand across her mouth, feeling she might vomit.

"Oh God!"

"What, Caleepso? What?"

Several puzzle pieces came together at once.

"I went through the cave with Hill. Then we camped at the grotto. In the morning, El Lobo came. He came up really close to me and he blew something in my face. And then I was in the cave again and instead of Hill, El Lobo was with me and he fell in the whirlpool. Then I climbed the cliff and saw that the house was gone and I thought you were dead, and then I went back into the cave and Lobo was lying on the edge of the whirlpool, even though I was sure he was sucked down, because El Lobo was hanging onto him..."

She stopped to take a breath, her startled eyes glazed with tears.

"My God, Javier!" she finished. She put her hand to her forehead and stared into her plate of half-eaten waffle, deeply shaken.

"Scopolamine," Javier responded succinctly.

"What?" Her eyes were suddenly alert.

"Scopolamine. They blow it in your face and you forget what you do next. You lose your own will and do whatever they ask you to do."

She was nodding, her face filled with remembering.

"Yes. Yes, I think you're right. There are images...people. They're swimming around in my mind. Insubstantial, like... like ghosts."

"That's why Hill can't remember either. They must have given him a hypnotic suggestion while he was under the drug. He really believes he said goodbye to us at the ranch, but I thought he was lying to protect you."

He put his hand on hers and said gently, "You'll have memory loss from it. Some will come and go. Some will be gone forever."

The waitress approached, wiping her hands on her apron and casting a wary glance under the table.

"You all through here or you want more food?" She threw an ironic eye across the laden table, with its litter of half-eaten food, dirty plates, cutlery, coffee cups, water glasses, syrup pitchers, and wadded napkins.

"That should hold us until lunch," Javier said with smooth courtesy, as he laid several bills on the table.

Calypso suppressed a smile and reached under the table to scratch Lobo's broad, furry head. Then they exited the booth and pushed through the finger-grimed glass front door into a gloriously clear and cold desert morning.

§

The three of them climbed into the cab of Javier's truck with Javier at the wheel, Calypso nestled next to him and Lobo by the window.

"Where do we go now?" she asked, suddenly realizing with a pang that they had no home to go home to.

"I've been thinking. There's a new house in the workers' village that's almost finished. We can move in there."

"But the cartel is there. I saw them when I climbed the cliff."

Javier scanned her face, frowning, then shook his head.

"No, Caleepso."

"Yes! They were wearing protective vests and carrying assault rifles. I saw them!"

Understanding flooded his face.

"Ooooh! You must have seen the soldiers."

"Soldiers?"

"The governor sent in soldiers to protect the ranch. I called him after the attack."

"So it's safe to go back?"

Javier nodded. "Yes. So we'll go through Chihuahua City and buy some furniture. I have to talk to the insurance agent anyway."

"And we have to apply for our passports again."

He nodded. "That, too."

Calypso's smile was impish. "Because I have a proposal."

Javier, reaching to put the key in the ignition, straightened at her tone and looked at her warily.

"Yes?"

"I know you'll want to rebuild the house."

"Yes?"

"So I'm thinking you could ask Pedro to supervise that. He was there the first time you built. He knows the whole process and we have good builders among the workers."

"Yes? And?"

"And then, you and I could take a little vacation. We haven't gone away together for years."

"A vacation where?" But he was already smiling, knowing.

"A vacation to...well, you know...to France."

And then in a rush, "We could stay with Walter in Paris for a few days. And then maybe go to the South and rent a cottage in some little village somewhere. Maybe near Avignon. I love Avignon. And I could write. Because my manuscript is gone, you know, because of the fire. My computer, too. I'm going to have to write the whole thing again. And you could write, too. Write about the cartels, and the killing, and the corruption in the government because of all the drug money..."

Her face was suffused with enthusiasm and Javier could not help but smile. "What?"

"Caleepso, Caleepso," he said shaking his head, bemused, and ruffling her hair.

"Well—what do you think? Would you?"

He reached to start the truck, backed and turned it, and headed out of the parking lot. He glanced both ways and then turned onto the old highway, headed east. Calypso regarded his profile fixedly, knowing that much was going on behind that impervious facade.

He threw a glance at her.

"What?"

She laughed. "What indeed? Could you stop being a rancher for a while? It's been a long time since you wrote *The Speaking Sword*. Maybe your country is calling you to write another book. Nothing really happens by accident, you know. Maybe the universe is booting us out of Rancho Cielo for awhile so you can write."

Javier rose up, bracing himself on the wheel, and settled again into the seat, taking a firmer grip at the helm.

"We talk about it," he said and then put an arm around her shoulders and pulled her closer. "Later."

They drove into morning sun still low on the horizon. The angle of light cast long, blue shadows from the base of yucca trees and cactus, striping the yellow desert sand.

Lobo thrust his nose out the crack in the window, his nostrils flaring, taking in the rich, sagey scent of the desert air and other smells that only his clan could register. The old highway was pitted with potholes, the white line was worn away in spots, and the truck rattled and jounced as the three drove on into their future.

ട

Chapter 12

Paris

THE THREE OLD FRIENDS SAT IN FRONT OF A SMALL FIRE IN THE SALON OF HILL'S APARTMENT ON PLACE DES VOSGES. The remains of their supper had been cleared away and their little digestif glasses of cognac were half-empty. A stillness had fallen, such as only old and dear friends find comfortable.

"Scopolamine, eh?" said Hill, breaking the silence. "You know, I never did drugs in the sixties and seventies when everyone was experimenting with them. I was too busy reporting in Vietnam. But then one night, a bunch of marines up on the DMZ pulled me into their hootch and insisted I smoke pot with them."

He laughed, his eyes lost in the past.

"I got so damn stoned. We laughed all night. Christ, we had a party!"

He bent to pick up the poker, rearranged the burning logs to his satisfaction, and settled back into his chair.

"The next day, those guys went out on recon and only three came back." He shook his head and sighed. "Fucking war."

A small pause ensued, as each thought about the scarification that war and drugs had wrought in each of their lives. Calypso broke the silence.

"It's a wicked drug, Walter. I've been researching it on my new laptop. They say people are robbed while they're under the influence, and they're so open to suggestion that they actually help the robbers rip off their own homes. Then, when they come out from under it, they can't remember a thing. Other people have to tell them what they did. It's scary! You ought to write an exposé, now that you've had personal experience."

"Maybe I will. Or maybe I'll leave it to the young bucks. I'm pretty happy, just poking around Paris for little scandals. You'd be amazed how many of those there are."

"Drugs are destroying the culture of Mexico," Javier cut in. "The cartels are making so much money that drugs are the main export in my country now. How crazy is that?" He took a sip of cognac.

"Think of the infrastructure that's required to produce that kind of profit: the importation of cocaine from South America; the farming of opium and marijuana in Mexico; the processing, packaging, warehousing, shipping, and smuggling into the US; the distribution and sales. And then the arms trafficking, money laundering, bribery, and surveillance, the placing of connected people in high political and military places. But if you ask anybody in the government, they just shake their heads and say they know nothing about it."

Calypso smiled to herself as she rolled her glass between her fingers. She knew she was hearing the opening salvos of Javier's next book.

"They say that between one and ten million dollars of illegal drugs pass over the border from Juarez to El Paso every single day!" she added. "And that's just one single port of entry. Somebody's getting really stoned in the US."

"What we need to do is find that guy and stop him!" Hill said, deadpan.

Calypso laughed. Even Javier shook his head and grinned.

"Seriously though," Hill continued, "an associate of mine in London did a piece on how drug money saved global banks from collapsing in 2008, when the speculative capital markets imploded. He quoted the head of the UN Office on Drugs and Crime as saying that the only liquid investment capital available to some banks in 2008 was the actual cash they were taking in, literally by truckloads, from the cartels. He said over three hundred and fifty billion dollars of drug profits were absorbed into the economy that way."

"No one wants to say the real truth," Javier added, "that the federal police and the Mexican Army have administered drug trafficking for decades and are recruitment centers for paramilitary assassins. Or that the big banks in the US—Bank of America, Wells Fargo, the big names—are laundering billions of dollars for the cartels, as we speak."

Hill nodded. "Yes, and don't forget who else profits from the so-called War on Drugs. In the US arms sales are huge, private prisons are bulging with drug mules and small time dealers, and the prison guard unions count on that for their pay raises. Even the racists get their kicks, because criminalization of drugs mostly locks up people of color. The US government knows all that and turns a blind eye."

"El Chapo Guzmán was Mexico's most-wanted capo—and he's also been featured in *Forbes* on their list of billionaires, as if he were just another businessman!" Calypso added.

"And even now that he's been captured, he'll just run his business from prison." Javier's face was dark with disgust. "Nothing will change."

"Who ever would have thought that we'd have personal experience of the power of the cartels?" Calypso said thoughtfully. "I mean, we knew what was going on around us and we prepared for an attack, but I don't think I ever really believed they'd bother us when they have so much else going on. But here we sit. All three of us have been touched. Javier's had to fight them physically and you and I have been under the spell of their drugs, Walter. Parts of our memories are expunged forever, along with our home and my manuscript. Did you ever expect that such a thing would happen to you?"

Hill suddenly sat up straight.

"Manuscript?"

"Yes, the one I'd almost finished about the locket. It burned up in the fire."

Hill pushed himself from his chair.

"Excuse me for a moment."

Javier and Calypso sat waiting for his return. She shot him a glance and he nodded imperceptibly. It was late. Time to make their excuses and head to bed.

Hill returned holding a box, which he handed to Calypso with a flourish. "Yours, I believe, madame."

It was a manuscript box, dinged on the corners, smeared with mud, but still recognizable. Calypso ripped open the flap and peered inside.

"Oh my God!" was all she could say.

"What?" Javier asked.

"It's my manuscript! Walter—how in the world...?"

Hill grinned triumphantly.

"It was that morning of the attack. We were running for the cliff but then I went back, remember?"

"Yes. For scones."

"And for your manuscript. I stuffed it in my pack. I was determined that you were going to finish telling me the story of the locket, come hell or high water."

Calypso sat dazed, staring at the stack of printed pages in her lap.

"I can't believe it!"

"Believe! And another thing you'd better believe is that while you're here you're going to read the rest to me. I'm not going to let you depart until you do."

"But it's not finished."

"Then finish it."

"That's what I intend to do once we get to the South. I thought I was going to have to rewrite the whole thing. Now it's only a few pages. But I need to settle in somewhere before I can write them."

"Then read what you have and I'll come to the South to hear the end."

Javier smiled and nodded. "That would be good."

Calypso reached out a hand to Hill. "It's a deal. That's the least I could do. How can I ever thank you?"

"By starting tonight. Read a few pages for me. We left off where..."

"I know, I know. Where Blanche de Muret jumped down the well."

"Yes," Hill said eagerly.

"Not tonight, Walter. Javier and I are still jet-lagged. But tomorrow night, I promise I'll read everything I've got. Then you'll have to wait for a couple of months until I can finish it."

Hill's lower lip shot out in a pout.

"If we wait until tomorrow night, something terrible will happen. Maybe war will be declared with aliens from deep space. *Something* will keep me from ever hearing the end of this damned story."

"No, Walter. Everything will be fine. Go to bed, now, and tomorrow I'll read you the rest. I'm amazed you haven't read it yourself."

"Oh, no!" He looked shocked. "I would never do that. This book is your intellectual property."

"Well, your patience and ethics will be rewarded. Tomorrow."

Calypso rose and held her hand out to Javier.

"Come along, my love, before this persuasive man has his way with me."

Hill stayed seated, staring sullenly into the fire.

"Tomorrow then," he said glumly.

"Goodnight, Walter." She bent and kissed him on top of the head.

Javier patted him on the shoulder as he passed and murmured, "I never win either. Just imagine trying to live with her!"

"I do," Hill whispered, after they had disappeared down the hallway to the guest room. "I do. All the time."

§

Javier lay with Calypso's head on his shoulder. Freshly pressed sheets of old, embroidered linen rustled as she burrowed her body toward him until her entire length was nestled against his.

"It's so nice to be here," she sighed.

"Do you miss it?"

"What? Paris? This place?"

"All of it."

Calypso raised up on her elbow, her face hovering over his, so that her hair made a tent containing them both.

"Javier, my love, there is only one thing, *ever*, that I have truly missed—*you*. I don't even know how many days we were apart because of the attack, but to me they were an eternity. All the rest of this," she waved her hand at the guest room walls in a gesture meant to include Paris and the entire rest of the planet, "is superfluous. I can live without everything else. I don't even want anything else. All I want, or have ever wanted, is you."

"So you won't mind, when our vacation is over, going back to Rancho Cielo?"

"Will you be there?"

He laughed. "Yes."

"Then I'll be happy. Or maybe you'd like to move to Jupiter. I hear the ambient temperature there is about minus two hundred and thirty-four degrees. I'd go there, too, if you were there."

She settled back and nuzzled her cheek into the swale of his shoulder.

"Of course," she murmured, "you'd have to buy me a new wardrobe."

He laughed, bent to kiss her, and found her already asleep.

§

The next night, the three friends again sat by the fire after supper. Calypso opened the manuscript box and pulled the sheaf from it. "Ready?" she flicked a teasing glance at Hill.

"For about a decade," he said. "Read on." He reached to pour each of them a refill for their glasses.

"You remember, we ended when..."

"Yes, yes," Hill said impatiently, "I remember!"

"Okay then," Calypso said, "here we go." Then, adjusting her reading glasses and taking a sip of cognac, she began. She read until midnight, recounting Blanche's jump down the well, her rescue, the meeting with Caspar and then with Allia. She read until her voice was hoarse, then begged off until the following night.

The next evening, they went out for an early supper at a little bistro close to Place des Vosges and then walked home in the dusk. Traffic roared in the distance on the Champs-Élysées and small bright pink, oblong clouds floated in a sky of unearthly electric blue. Calypso strolled between the two men, an arm linked in each of theirs.

"I haven't been this happy in years," she sighed.

"Because you're in Paris?" Hill asked.

"No. Because we're all together again. Because we're all alive and well. It's a miracle, don't you think? Given what we've been through?"

Both men nodded. Her question threw them both into a wordless place of gratitude.

"Expansion and contraction," Calypso went on, "that's what we've endured. First, we're on the edge of the abyss—endless void and light. Then suddenly, we're in the cave, with its constriction and darkness. Or in Javier's case, in a conflagration of blood and fire. We've all led big, expansive lives—and then, we've been reduced, compacted. Just to have survived it makes me happy."

"I guess it proves we're flexible," Hill said.

"And invincible," Javier added.

Calypso pulled them both in close to her as they strolled, their footsteps synchronized. In the center of Place des Vosges, a beautiful young model in an ankle-length mink coat was posing near the fountain while the photographer, all in black, ducked and wove, snapping his shutter. The girl preened and pouted and strutted, and the three passersby smiled to themselves as they passed.

Nothing of this world meant a hoot to them anymore, Hill reflected. He, Calypso, and Javier had passed through a veil into an alternate reality in which the rewards of this world, no matter how provocatively displayed, paled in comparison.

In comparison to what? he asked himself, then smiled, knowing he was loved.

§

They were settled again by the fire.

"Tonight we'll finish all that I've written," Calypso said as prelude.

"I'm sad to hear it," Hill said, "but at least I'll finally know the end."

"You remember that we left off last night, with Blanche being prepared to meet Sa Tahuti?"

"Yes, after Allia told her the story of Isis and Osiris and of the underground community," Hill nodded. He turned to Javier.

"When Calypso and I first met here in Paris, I told her we had known one another in a life in ancient Egypt. I thought I was kidding at the time, but this story makes me wonder..."

Javier nodded. "Yes. Somehow, it all sounds familiar to me, too. Even the part about Sa Tahuti trading bodies. The shamans talk about things like that, too."

The men looked at Calypso expectantly. She adjusted her reading glasses on her nose.

"Ready?"

Without waiting for a response, she began.

§

The Story of Blanche de Muret Continues

Let the readers of my affidavit be sure, this long story told by Allia taxed my credulity, as it must certainly tax that of those who read it. I was in fear that I had fallen in with the most hardened devil worshippers and witches, who traded souls as some people trade lemons for bread.

Yet, the community of the Ammonites—for that is what they call themselves—was as gentle, mannerly, and generous with Christian charity as any one might encounter. Also, I had the assurance of Caspar, King of Nubia, with his Christian cross blazoned upon his forehead, that I was quite safe from demonic forces. Indeed, he soothed my fears by saying that the Egyptians' spiritual development was of such a level that even Christians might envy it.

Still, as the reader may well imagine, I was dubious especially of the one called Sa Tahuti, for such magic as she practiced was completely beyond my understanding. I am ashamed to say that my own ignorance became a sort of prejudice against this person, well in advance of actually meeting her. I prepared myself as best I could to confront one who seemed to me at best a bald-faced liar and charlatan, or possibly one demented and delusional, and at worst, demonical.

None of these objections did I raise with Allia, for she clearly was bent on seeing this introduction into being. The next day, she and several attendants—new women whose faces I had never before seen, just as Allia had predicted—bathed and clothed me and arranged my hair according to the simple and fastidious ways of their community. Dressed in a long white linen gown rather than a tunic, I was led by Allia by a way I had never before been, far into the recesses of the cave.

At last, we came to an anteroom where Allia, with one last flounce of my skirt as her eyes swept me head to toe, departed, leaving me alone. Again, I was in a room that had been plastered and painted with the lively, elongated figures of everyday Egyptians at work. These were harvesting grain beside the river, where hunters in boats were aiming their arrows at a flock of geese.

Charming as these scenes were, however, I could not subdue my nervousness. How was I to deport myself with this ancient woman I was about to meet? About what could we possibly converse? And what would I do, should I mistrust or even hate her on sight? Nothing in my upbringing as a highborn lady, careful as it was, had prepared me for such an encounter.

S

Therefore, it was a great relief to me when a girl about my own age came to fetch me into the inner chamber. Like the others, she was clad in a simple white linen gown, with the exception that her hair hung loose in a black cascade, clear to her waist. She greeted me with an engaging smile and motioned me to follow her, saying, "There is no need to be afraid, Blanche de Muret. Sa Tahuti has only love for you."

The apartment to which she delivered me was much like Allia's, appointed with fine ebony and gold furniture, while the walls were covered in hieroglyphics and figures of gods and goddesses. It was, withal, a cozy room, for many candles were burning, bouquets of fresh flowers, and plates of luscious fruits were set about, and the divans were covered in beautifully embroidered coverlets.

"Please sit," the girl said, indicating a divan covered in a field of stitched flowers. "I understand from our good Caspar," she began immediately that I was seated, "that you have certain apprehensions about this meeting?"

I was torn between twin desires to be truthful about my misgivings and to give no offense. "I have nothing in my experience to prepare me for an encounter with a being such as Sa Tahuti," I managed to stammer.

The girl smiled sweetly and said, "I understand," and then sat gazing at me expectantly. I grew restless under her gaze and said, rather crossly I regret to report, "When shall my audience begin?"

The girl smiled again, this time with a real twinkle in her eye and said, "Why, it already has!"

I stared at her dully, not in the least comprehending. Was it possible the old crone was spying on us to see what manner of person I was? Finally, I shook my head and with knitted brows said, "I don't understand. I'm sorry."

She regarded me cheerfully and responded, "But here we are! We are talking. The audience has begun."

A bolt of shock ran through me. I stared at her, aghast.

"But surely..." I faltered. "No. It cannot be..."

I stared at her some more and she, as composed as she could possibly be, gazed back. At last I managed to gasp, "*You* are Sa Tahuti?"

A delightful, impish grin flashed across her face. She didn't say a word, but only nodded, her eyes never leaving mine.

"But... I thought..." I stammered. I could not finish but collapsed in confusion and mortification, my head hanging low.

In a flash, she had crossed the space between us and with her hand beneath my chin, raised my head up, so that our eyes met and held. I had a strange sensation of a tremor, hot and intense, running from her hand to my head and this feeling soon expanded, coursing down my arms and legs and prickling along my entire torso, front and back. At this close range, the eyes I stared into were infinite as the night sky and older than time itself, and so filled with wisdom and compassion that I dropped my own eyes in humility.

"Do not resist me, Blanche de Muret," she whispered. "You have come far and suffered many hardships and terrible losses to be by my side again."

"*Again?!*" I shrieked. I felt oddly light-headed and terribly confused and unsure whether I would burst into tears or run screaming from this uncanny child-who-was-not-a-child. The very walls around me seemed to warp and waver, as insubstantial as heat waves.

Finally, the accumulated griefs of these many months of pilgrimage, captivity and death were a bursting dam. Tears and wailing consumed me and I collapsed into the arms of Sa Tahuti!

ℌ

How long she held me, rocking and whispering comforts in a strange tongue, I do not know. It seemed my tears would go on forever and just when I thought I might regain my composure, a fresh bout would overtake me.

Images of my homeland in Languedoc, green with spring and white with blossoming fruit trees, were followed by intensely real imaginings of my beloved parents. I saw their faces, looked into their eyes, felt their love. And my darling brother Godfrey cavorted across my sight, running happily in fields of new green wheat, dotted with red poppies. With each of these visions, a fresh stab of grief and pain reduced me once again to helpless sobs.

When at last I came to myself, I lay upon the divan with a flowered coverlet over me. Sa Tahuti sat beside me, hand upon my brow, softly singing a sweet, soothing, monotonous chant, over and over. I lay beneath her touch like a piece of boiled laundry—limp and unresisting.

"You have been long away, Blanche," she said quietly. Regarding me tenderly, she continued, "It is necessary to have this great cleansing upheaval, Blanche, so that these difficult events and beloved persons do not come to live in your bones as disease. Those things that are not brought to consciousness can turn to poison. I see that now your aura is cleared of much dark and brooding energy."

I looked at her in incomprehension, without the smallest notion of what she meant by her words. I began to ask for clarification but Sa Tahuti laid her finger across my lips.

"Shhhhhh, now. You must sleep. You have worked very, very hard today. Tomorrow we will talk and I will answer all your questions—even the ones to which there is no answer." She smiled mysteriously, laid her hand across my eyes, and in an instant, I slept.

In the night, I had a strange, disturbing dream. I seemed to be in the body of a boy child and I was wandering in the dark, frightened and weary. All around me, voices echoed but I could make out only the barest shadows of moving beings, and the language these shadow people spoke was unknown to me. Lights flared and flashed randomly and nowhere in this dream could I find comfort.

I awoke in tears to find Sa Tahuti sitting beside my bed. I told her the dream, sobbing, "I have a terrible feeling that I am witnessing my poor Godfrey in Hell!"

Sa Tahuti soothed me with gentle words and kindly strokes along my brow, saying, "No, no, dear Blanche. It is nothing of the kind. You are beginning to remember, that is all. Quiet yourself, now, and as soon as you have broken your fast, I will explain to you what you have seen in the night."

§

Then began a part of my adventure that to this day astonishes me, although I doubt not that it is true, so vivid were my memories and so cogent were the explanations of Sa Tahuti regarding them. For she explained to me that, in her presence and guided by her great power, I was beginning to recall a life in which I had known her before—in the person of the older son of the very Pharaoh who had fled from Philae, so many centuries before!

That day, Sa Tahuti invoked in me a trance and, with her voice as guide, I wandered again in the darkness of the cave. I felt the loving presence of my parents and their servants and experienced again the terrible grief of losing my baby brother—only to have him live again as an uncanny child, the infant Sau Tahuti.

"Your brother is one of those valiant souls who incarnates again and again, with the sole purpose of bringing the souls of those he loves to fuller spiritual awareness. When he dives back into the Other World, he is as confident as you are when passing through a simple doorway," Sa Tahuti told me. "Although you grieve for him, there is really no need to do so. He has agreed, before he ever entered life, to come to your aid and then depart."

"Which brother, in which life?" I asked, confused.

"In both."

"Are you telling me," I asked in astonishment, "that Godfrey is the same soul as the Pharaoh's baby?"

Sa Tahuti smiled. "Yes, Blanche. That is what I am telling you."

But why would his death, and the grief with which it had harrowed me, serve me? I could not understand how such suffering would be beneficial, nor why my beloved brother would choose to put me through such anguish. Sa Tahuti was patient with my protestations and answered them calmly.

"Such grief as you have known is like the blow to an egg against the side of a bowl. Until the hard shell of total identification with the ego is broken, one can never truly love, any more than one can cook with an unbroken egg.

"And sometimes it happens that the most effective way to accomplish this access to love is to lose it. Fierce as was your devotion to Godfrey on the pilgrimage and sea voyage, you did not truly love him until you saw him naked upon the slave block. Then your heart broke and with that breaking, love flooded in."

As much as I desired to resist this line of reasoning, I knew in my heart that Sa Tahuti spoke the truth. I had been bound to Godfrey by bonds of duty and honor, until the instant of his ultimate helplessness in the slave market. The rush of grief and loss which swept over me then was a great wave of love, against the power of which I was completely helpless.

Sa Tahuti continued gently, "Was it not the same with the one you call your Savior? When he was most helpless upon the cross, was he not most powerful? In breaking the hearts of his followers, did he not open the floodgates of their deepest love and longing?"

I had to yield, then, to Sa Tahuti's superior understanding. All that day and for many to follow, she spoke to me of the laws of life by which the whole universe is governed. Much that she imparted was lost to my child's understanding, but much remains with me to this day, and indeed, will do so until my dying breath. Most vividly do I remember her closing remarks.

"Always remember and never forget, dear Blanche, that the universe turns upon the axle of love. Love is the horse that draws it and love is the wheel. And love is the road upon which the great wheel of the universe travels. All is love. Nothing exists but by the power of love. To attain the ability to love is worth any hardship, any suffering, any grief. Every tear you shed lubricates the great, cycling wheel of being that is love and love only. Never, ever forget this."

With these words our long and rich audience drew to a close. By this time, Sa Tahuti, despite her physical appearance, was transformed in my eyes. I knew her with my heart to be a being of infinite age, wisdom, and power. I was in awe of her and yet also felt her to be my dearest and most intimate friend. How this can be cannot be explained by human discourse. Sa Tahuti was and is a miracle for which there are no words. It seemed there could be no further gift that she could give me, and yet, that is what now transpired.

"I have something that I will pass into your keeping, Blanche de Muret," she said solemnly. "It is an object of great antiquity. Two thousand years before the birth of the one you call the Christ, it was made by hands that knew the magic from the beginning of the world."

She rose from her divan and went to a table where sat a small chest inlaid with ivory and precious stones. Raising the lid, she withdrew something, which she clasped in her palm and then raised to her lips in a reverential kiss. Then, turning to me, she spoke in a voice that shocked me with the power of its command.

"Rise, Blanche de Muret! Receive your due. I place this jewel upon you as a token of the esteem and holy love of the Great Mother."

So saying, she slipped over my head and around my neck a chain of gold, upon which depended a locket of wondrous beauty. I began to stammer my thanks but Sa Tahuti silenced me.

"Be still! You have no idea what has been entrusted to you. No thanks of yours can encompass the magnitude of this gift."

I was taken aback, for the sweetness of Sa Tahuti's demeanor had transformed, in those instants, to something terrible and stern. I felt a huge presence fill the room, pulsing against the walls, invisible but entirely palpable. Whatever it was, it seemed to be using Sa Tahuti as its voice. Her entire body shuddered with the force of the words that spoke through her.

"I lay upon you today both a gift and a burden, Blanche de Muret. This locket, small and cunningly made as it is, contains the seed power of the universe; a tear of the Great Mother; the Egg of Fate. You will keep it with you always. You will wear it daily. You will learn from it as you have learned at the knee of Sa Tahuti. And when your time comes to cross over to the next world, you will pass it on to your descendants and they to theirs, through an unbroken lineage."

My entire body began to stream with sweat, and I shook like a dry leaf in the first wind of autumn. I felt both deepest, most humble gratitude and a crushing weight that descended upon my heart like a millstone. The locket burned against the skin of my breast like a coal.

"There will be times when the gift must pass to a male heir. He is never to wear the locket, only to keep it safe until it can be passed to one who is worthy. The locket itself will choose. Never fret. The locket knows its own course. It was set at the beginning of the world and nothing can alter its trajectory through time and space. You are one blessed by the Great Mother, Blanche de Muret. Go in peace."

With that, the voice ceased. The immense pressure of living energy diminished and then faded from the room, leaving me weak and shaken. Even Sa Tahuti seemed momentarily overcome.

We stood for many minutes in silence, each, I am sure, collecting herself again after so shattering a visitation. I thought, then, of Moses and the burning bush; of Mary at the Annunciation; and of Mary Magdalene meeting the risen Savior in the garden. It seemed not possible that one such as I, a mere girl and a lost one at that, might receive direct commune with God and yet, so it seemed to have happened.

§

At last Sa Tahuti spoke, her voice returned to its usual sweetness, but not without a tremor trembling through it.

"You have received an incalculable blessing today, Blanche de Muret. And an incalculable burden. From this day forward you are an emissary of the Great Mother. She has spoken."

I do not know what moved me to argue philosophy with Sa Tahuti at that moment. It was as if the locket itself demanded that I speak my truth, difficult as it was.

"But Sa Tahuti," I exclaimed, "in Christian thought, all are beings of free will! If this task is imposed on me, how then can it be other than that my free will is violated?"

Sa Tahuti nodded with complete understanding.

"You have spoken well, Blanche. What you must understand is that time is much greater than you imagine, as are the dimensions of reality. You have agreed to take on this task in this life, but you have forgotten because you made this contract in the world between worlds, where souls go between earthly incarnations."

Then I understood that she spoke the truth. I felt in the depths of my being that this locket and its fate were inextricably intertwined with my life, and that this was a situation in which my heart and soul were completely complicit.

I gazed at Sa Tahuti with this dawning understanding. Our eyes met and held, and I knew that our time together had come to an end.

Gently, Sa Tahuti embraced me and I her, and it shocked me to feel how slender and small was her body. Why, I was taller than she! I felt I held a younger child than I in my arms, and it was not until I stepped back and again met her gaze that I felt the renewal of awe at her very being. She smiled then, graciously and with perfect understanding.

"I am as is the Great Mother, Blanche—ever ancient, ever young."

So saying, she took me by my elbow and steered me toward the door. I went unresistingly, but with great sadness pouring into my heart, like water into a vessel. Beyond the linen curtain of the doorway, Allia stood in the antechamber, waiting patiently.

"Here is our sister, fresh from her initiation," Sa Tahuti said to her.

Sa Tahuti took both my hands in hers, looked deep into my eyes and said, "Do not be sad, child. We are never far parted and when we are, we must hold the hope ever green in our hearts of our coming together once more. We shall meet again. Over and over again, we consecrate ourselves to the work."

"What work is that?" I gasped, for I was close to tears

"Why, the work of bringing love into a loveless world, of course!" With that, she kissed me most sweetly, full on the mouth, then turned and with a flick of the curtain, disappeared.

I stood with my hand to my lips, for her kiss had imparted such powerful energy there that it left me stunned. I understood in those instants what the Scriptures mean by *an holy kiss*.

I barely felt Allia's hand as she took me by the elbow and guided me back the way we had come. I moved as one in a daze, but a pleasant one, misted in the scent of orange blossoms and dazzled by sunlight.

§

Gradually, I became aware that we were in a part of the cave where I had never been. This awareness came through my feet, for they suddenly informed me that we were ascending.

Coming out of my trance, I looked around in confusion. The cave was just giving way to a manmade tunnel, neither broad nor high, yet not terribly confining either. It was apparent that we were climbing, as if up a steep ramp.

Allia was in the lead, pulling me along by my hand. I sensed both an urgency and a lightheartedness in her.

"Where are you taking me at such a great rate?" I teased.

"Great rate?" Allia shot back. "You are as balky as an old donkey! You may as well be sleepwalking."

We laughed together and I felt a sudden influx of such joyous energy that I could scarcely contain myself.

"Where are you dragging this old donkey *to* then, Allia?"

"Well you should ask. We are almost there. Just around this corner and..." She smiled mysteriously and tugged me onward so that we were almost trotting. We rounded a corner and a short length down the tunnel, were confronted by a massive wooden door.

"Here we are, then, Blanche de Muret. The threshold to your new life. Are you ready?"

Not having the slightest idea what I should be ready *for*, I yet assented. "Yes," I said boldly, for my heart was leaping with joy for no reason that I could ascertain, "I am ready!"

With that, Allia swung the portal open and a great, burning, dazzling ray of sunshine shot into the tunnel! I was on the surface!

I stepped forth into the courtyard of the safe house, greeted by the scent of flowers, the songs of birds, and the laughter of children. And who should my sun-dazed eyes see, rushing toward me with arms open wide to greet me, but my beloved Caspar, King of Nubia!

I sank into his arms like a bird returning to its nest. There are no words for the joy I felt. All I can say is that the Great Mother had prepared for me a day that healed the last of my woes, for no sorrow can dwell where such joy lives.

§

Paris

Calypso stopped for a sip of water. "Still with me?" she asked, glancing at her companions. The two men nodded and she took up the manuscript once again. " Here we go then. We're almost done."

§

The Story of Comte Henri Charlemagne de MontMaran Continues

"And that, my dear Maria-Elena, is enough of that for one night—which I fear is actually now morning. Are you still alive?"

The Count's voice, although gravelly with use, was lighthearted, even gay, as he slapped the cover down on his bound edition of Blanche de Muret's testimony.

"Yes, Monsieur le Comte, I am indeed!" Maria-Elena sat forward in her chair so that he might see her face by the firelight. "That is the most entirely compelling story I ever have heard!"

"Yes, it is extraordinary. So much so that, when Blanche de Muret was returned to France by her Egyptian friends, she was scarcely believed—which of course is why she wrote this testament in the first place. The Inquisition had not quite yet begun in earnest, you understand, but it was not too soon for the church to level charges of heresy against her."

"Oh, dear! That poor girl. What a life of upheaval she led! What became of her?"

"She stood trial. It has come down through family legend that she defended herself quite ably, but was bound for prison, despite that. It was her Cathar heritage, of course, that worked against her. But then a quite astonishing thing happened: charges were suddenly dropped. Not another word of accusation was leveled at her."

"How could that be?"

"It seems that a certain young man had listened carefully to her testimony and was convinced of her innocence. The young man was impressed, we are told, by her brilliance and her skill at argumentation. Day after day of the trial, she beat back the arguments of the prosecution with splendidly reasoned defenses. Of course, it also did not hurt that she had grown to become a very beautiful young woman!"

"Did the young man rescue her?"

"Yes, in a sense. He did not scale fortress walls and carry her away by night on horseback, if that is what you mean. But he was the first and favorite son of a family of immense influence in the realm. There was nothing his father would not have done to grant his son's every wish.

"The life of a poor simple girl was nothing to him, but as it meant a great deal to his son, the father used his power and authority to intercede on behalf of Blanche de Muret. Even the Archbishop dared not intervene, as the father gave generously to the church. And so, Blanche was saved from certain torture and imprisonment and a slow and terrible death."

"But what happened then? Did they fall in love?"

"Sadly, no. The boy was already betrothed to the daughter of another powerful lord. It was a match that was to unite two feuding fiefdoms and so must be consummated. The two did, however, correspond throughout their lives and were, as far as I can tell, the best of friends. And Blanche did find a mate, obviously, or I would not be here to tell this tale.

"She was wooed by a young man from a good, solid family and she accepted his advances. They had five children. It is all written in the family records. Four were boys and one, a girl. As you can imagine, it was the girl who inherited the locket upon her mother's death. She and Blanche were my ever-so-many-great-grandmothers."

Maria-Elena sat on the edge of her chair and faced him fully.

"This locket, Monsieur le Comte—Blanche makes record of having received it but she never describes it. What did it look like? Was it a thing of great beauty?"

The old man drew in a breath and let it out very slowly, as if he were summoning his courage. He nodded his head, as if listening to an internal prompt or argument. When his eyes met Maria-Elena's, they had lost their merriment and were dark pools of sadness.

"Well, you may ask, Maria-Elena," he said.

Hefting himself to his feet without another word, he crossed the room on bowed and spindly legs to a small table. On it sat a box inlaid with ivory and precious stones.

"This casket traveled with Blanche from Egypt," he said, lifting the box. "Who knows how old it may be? Certainly, it dates back to the pharaohs but how far back is anyone's conjecture. Family rumor has it that it was a small-scale model of the one created by Set to entrap Osiris."

He brought the box back to the fireside and laid it on Maria-Elena's knees. "This is the dubious gift I wish to give you, Maria-Elena, this box—and what it contains."

He hovered over her with a heavy sigh.

Maria-Elena sat for some minutes, her hands stroking the marvelous box, her fingers wandering over its jeweled protrusions.

Finally, the Count ordered her sharply, "Open it! Open it now or I shall never have the nerve to give it to you!"

With cautious fingers, Maria-Elena turned the latch, carefully lifted the lid and allowed her eyes to fall upon what was cached within. Her brow knit with confusion and astonishment as her hand withdrew from the depths, where it had been pillowed on a frayed linen cushion, a gold chain and at its end, a round locket the size of a large coin.

Maria-Elena brought the locket close to her face and examined it carefully. "Oh," she breathed. "It's *beautiful!*"

Lying on her palm, a jewel of extraordinary workmanship, was an enameled disk, surrounded by cunningly wrought gold. In itself a precious object, it was the image worked in enamel that was truly wondrous—an exquisitely rendered portrait of a bare-breasted mother with a boy child upon her lap and extending a golden orb, as if offering it to someone.

"It is an image of Isis suckling Horus," the Count said. "But you have seen the same image in Christian churches, I know, of Mary with the infant Jesus. You see, one secret that this object encodes is that the Great Mother is present in all religions. Her names may change but her presence is ever One and the same. That was one of Sa Tahuti's lessons to Blanche de Muret.

"And there was another: whomever would take ownership of this necklace did so because it was foreordained that she should do so. No man is allowed to wear this chain about his neck. He is not even to consider himself the owner of this jewel but only its conservator, until such time as its rightful owner should appear." With a sigh and a cracking of his knees, the count sat down heavily into his chair.

"I am an old man now, Maria-Elena. I have waited a lifetime for that one to come. And I believe life has reserved the best for last: it is to you, Maria-Elena Villanova y Mansart, that I now bequeath the locket of Sa Tahuti."

§

The Story of Maria-Elena Villanova y Mansart Continues

"And so you see, my dear Roberto, that what I have here is a very precious thing. And because I will not be able to guard it any longer, I am passing it on to you." She ran a loving hand over the top of his head.

"But, Maman! Why don't you use the locket to heal yourself? You said it is magic!"

"Yes, my darling, that it is. But it is not that kind of magic. It is the magic of foreseeing the future. That is how I knew I was ill. Long before the tumor was visible on the doctor's X-rays, I knew it was there. I was *told* it was there! There is a voice that speaks, sometimes in dreams, sometimes during the most mundane tasks of the day. Never has it been proven wrong."

"What use is it, then, if it can't heal you? What good does it do to know you're sick before you're even sick? I think it's a terrible old thing and I don't want to have it. Give it to Tia Isobella or to Grandmother!" Roberto's smooth brow furrowed beneath his thick black fringe of bangs.

"No, Roberto. This locket cannot be given to Isobella or to my mother. They are women of the world. They have no interest in such matters. They care about banquets and ball gowns and how much money is tucked away in the bank. They would not understand the importance of this locket. In fact, if they had it they would probably sell it and use the money to buy a jewel of modern design. You are the only one to whom I can entrust it, Roberto."

She scooted Roberto away from her and sat on the edge of the bed.

"See this?" She picked up the inlaid box from her bedside table. "You must always keep it in this box. Keep it by your bedside. It will bring you vivid dreams."

"But I'm a boy! The locket doesn't like me."

Maria-Elena laughed.

"Oh, Berto! The locket *loves* you! Don't you see, the heart of the Great Mother is attached to this locket. She will never fail you. Her love is even greater than my own."

"No! I don't believe it! Give it back to the Count then."

"Berto, that isn't possible. You see, I hadn't been gone from the Count's chateau for more than a week when I received word that he had passed away quietly in his sleep. And do you know what, son? His old saluki, Saladin, died the exact same night! Isn't that remarkable?"

"If you own the locket and you are sick and about to die, then the locket is bad luck. I don't want it."

"Roberto, you don't understand. You are fighting fate, my child. This is the life I agreed to live before I ever came to this world. And you, my son, have agreed as well. You knew before your soul entered my womb that you would one day be the conservator of the locket. It is more important than you know. The locket must go on. It must move toward its next owner."

"Why?"

"Because the power of the locket can intervene in events, Roberto. It helped Sa Tahuti lead the Count's grandmother to the well that saved her from the harem and helped her escape persecution by the church. It has transformed the lives of all who own it, even my own.

"I was a careless young woman, Berto, when I went to the Count's chateau. When I came away, I was changed. I knew in my heart that what he had told me was true. I knew it was my duty to protect the locket throughout my life and to send it onward to its next owner at my life's end.

"All these things come from the power of the locket, Roberto. I ask you again: please safeguard it for me until its next owner appears."

§

The Story of Father Roberto Villanova y Mansart Continues

"At last, the boy that I was capitulated, Señor Hill. Who can say if it was the power of the locket that overcame his resistance or the power of his love for his mother? Either way, the locket passed that day from Maria-Elena Villanova y Mansart to me, her son. And within a week she, like the Count before her, was gone.

"Throughout my life I have protected the locket in its box. It has sat by my bedside and given me strange dreams and caused me to awaken with unusual knowings. Who can say why, Señor Hill? It is not for us to know these things but only to honor what we know to be true.

"So that, my friend, is the very long and involved answer to your question about what I am doing here in the forests of Chiapas. I was urged by these inner messages to be here. That is all I know and all I need to know.

"In the meanwhile, there is plenty for me to do. It's not as if I were stranded on a desert island. Everywhere I turn in this place, there are those who need my counsel and encouragement.

"Thank you for listening so patiently to this long story. You are a good listener, my friend."

§

Calypso stopped reading and let the sheaf of pages fall into her lap. The three friends sat for quite a long time in silence, until Hill finally blurted, "You ended your book with *me?*"

Calypso turned to him with a smile.

"Not really," she said. "The book's not done yet. There's something more, but I don't know what it is."

"Something you forgot? Maybe you could write to Berto and ask."

She shook her head.

"No. I've spoken with Berto and he feels the story's complete." She gazed pensively into the flames. "I think whatever it is will come to me, while I'm editing the manuscript in the South." She shrugged and flicked a smile toward him. "That's all I know."

Javier was sitting lost in thought. Finally, he said slowly, "Do you think we are in that story? That we have lived those events?"

Calypso shrugged. "Who can say? Does it sound familiar to you?"

Javier frowned. "It's the repetition of the pattern that makes it familiar. The cave, the destruction of an old life, and the terrifying passage toward a new one. The friendships that save lives. The old, wise women like Allia—and Atl, in Chiapas. Doesn't it all sound familiar?"

Hill nodded. "I got a twinge when Blanche was saved by the young nobleman. I felt very sure that he loved her deeply but was forced by circumstances to be with someone else."

His eyes shifted from Calypso's to Javier's and back again to Calypso's.

"It's no secret among us that you're the love of my life, Calypso. The only difference is, I never married anyone else, this time around."

Calypso reached for his hand, brought it to her lips and kissed it.

"Then, thank you for rescuing me from the power of the church. I really have no desire to be tortured, in this or any other life."

The golden Empire clock on the mantel chimed the half-hour. Slowly, the conversation turned to other matters.

"We've got to be up early," Calypso said at last. "The train to the South leaves at eight."

They stood. Each recognized a certain awkwardness among them, and each realized it came from the profound deepening of their bonds with one another. "I'm going to miss you," Hill said and raised his arms to embrace them both.

The three stood entwined by the fire for several moments. No one could speak because tears constricted their throats. At last, with a final squeeze, they broke apart.

"You'll come to the South then, Walter?" Calypso asked softly.

"Of course. How could I stay away?"

"Good. We shall meet again. Over and over again we consecrate ourselves to the work."

Her smile held a hint of mischief as Javier pulled her away toward bed.

§

Brignac, Languedoc, France

Spring was just beginning to touch the garden of the rental property on the edge of the old stone village. Rosebuds opened their thick, silky petals like the sensuous eyelids of the goddess. Deep in blue shade, acanthus lifted its softly purple spires amid ruffs of black-green leaves. In *vigne vierge* scrawled across the stone facade of the converted orangerie, an energetic pair of wrens labored over a nest. Swallows swooped and chittered in a pale, misty sky.

They had been on the property less than a week and Calypso was still discovering its secrets. Where she sat, a thick canopy of plane trees sheltered the sun's scant warmth, despite the seething of their upper branches in chill tramontana.

Like water cascading, the roar of wind drowned other sounds, so that she was startled by her visitor. Lumbering down a pathway of pale golden gravel, its head stretched forth in earnest effort and its tiny black toenails pushing aside stones like a bulldozer, came a tortoise big as a salad plate.

"Well, *bonjour!*" Calypso crowed with delight. "Would you like to share my strawberries?"

Her hand darted into the old Chinese blue-and-white bowl in her lap and she flourished a succulent red fruit. The movement attracted the tortoise. He turned his leathery neck and gazed at her with sad black eyes that seemed to speak of a strawberry-less life and multitudinous other sorrows.

Calypso knelt beside him and offered the strawberry in front of his hooked and armored nose. In one snap, the tortoise bit the fruit in half, closed his eyes in apparent bliss, and savored.

Having swallowed, his eyes flew open. They had lost their dolorousness and looked at her with dawning wonder and expectation. Calypso kept supplying strawberries until her bowl was empty.

"That's all," she said, shaking her head. "I'll bring you more tomorrow."

As if understanding perfectly, the tortoise blinked at her and then turned away, resuming his ponderous promenade.

"For a French tortoise," Calypso called after him, "you understand English very well."

She set the empty bowl on the rusted and listing café table and pulled the metal chair at an angle so she could gaze at a different part of the garden.

Down an allée of plane trees shading a path lined in overgrown boxwoods, she could glimpse the facade of another building. This, the rental agent had told her, was the former great house of the owners of the *mas*. Far from her notion of a farmhouse, it was three stories of the same pale golden stone as their rental, which was a remodel of the estate's former orangerie.

The rental agent had said that the mas was owned by the same family that had built it in the eighteenth century.

"But now the children don't care about it," the slender, chic French woman had said in charmingly accented English. "They want the city life now. Someday, they will sell this place to a developer and there will be little houses here, instead of a garden."

She sighed, as if this conjecture were already an inevitability.

Almost without realizing it, Calypso left the table and drifted down the allée toward the old house, drawn by the melody of wind and birdsong as by a Siren's song. Her feet crunched on gravel. A nightingale sang from the depths of a pomegranate tree starred with vermillion blossoms. The scents of mint, of myriad blossoms, of water, and, of sun-warmed soil rose to greet her. Walking almost on tiptoe, she was mindful of rupturing a deep, dreaming peace.

The great house stood silent and shuttered behind its apron of pale gravel. Faded blue wooden shutters showed signs of rot along the bottom edges, and the lintel was softly crumbling above tall double front doors. Under the verge of rosy terra cotta roof tiles, swallows swooped around a small village of mud nests.

All around the house, in sharp contrast to its stolid bulk, the overgrown garden danced and flounced in rushing air. A rich warmth, the fecundity of earth, hung like perfume beneath the thick canopy of old trees. A small grove of old olive trees off its western flank hummed with wind, flashing the silvery undersides of leaves like the tongues of mechanical birds.

It was a scene of enchantment. To Calypso, the great house was as potent a container of mysteries as had been the now-incinerated locket box. She felt the magnetic languor of it in her bones and it held her captive.

The house stood with its massive weight rooted in the fertile, vine-bearing earth of Languedoc, austere in its gravitas, yet somehow welcoming. There was a buttery softness to its hewn blocks of stone, a giving quality. Were she to accidentally brush against its walls, she felt her sweater would come away marked with pigment, a calligram communicating the soul of the old building. The house held the same sad, dreaming quality as the eyes of the tortoise, as if human company and events had bypassed them for too long and left them lonely.

Slowly, she made a circuit of the house. Its facade, facing south, presented the dignified central entrance portal, capped by a simple Greek pediment, with long windows on either side, balanced in number down its length. She imagined how the long, narrow fenestration would let in light in a special way, illuminating rooms with nobly high ceilings, rooms zinging with the force and energy of perfect proportion, with the cosmic intelligence of the Golden Mean.

On the east side, the house dreamed under the shade of a huge plane tree, perhaps eight feet in circumference. Calypso imagined lying in bed at night in a second-story bedroom, the windows thrown open to incessant shifting and rustling of leaves.

The north side of the house had smaller windows and clearly turned its back on the icy blasts of the north wind. A door on its eastern corner led, she imagined, to a mud room where work shoes would be shed and hands washed after a day in the fields or garden.

On the west side, to her delight, a central double French door opened onto a pergola covered in vines. She stepped into the shaded space. Simple Ionic columns upheld an iron basket-like superstructure, over which grape, wisteria and *vigne vierge* clambered enthusiastically. A rustic table, sloping and chapped from weather, sat outside the shuttered doors. In her mind's eye, Calypso saw the lady of the house coming through the open doors of a morning, tray in hand, bringing coffee and croissants for *petit dejeuner.*

Beside this kitchen door, a Roman fountain with an austere triangular pediment still spilled spring water from its lion's-mouth aperture into a basin shaped like a scallop shell. The water rippled across the mossy green bowl and spilled over the edges to fall into a still larger seashell, four feet below. From between the hewn blocks of the fountain's body, maidenhair ferns hung down the facade, dripping water from their delicately incised leaves. The soft splashing of the water sang a contrapuntal melodic line against the basso of the wind.

Surely ghosts lodged in this enchanted place, trailing veiled memories of vanished ages—perhaps even astonishment at the passage of Hannibal's elephants that had lumbered through Languedoc two hundred years before the birth of the Christ. The house stimulated her imagination: the clatter of hooves and crunch of gravel as a coach arrived; the heavy drone of cicadas in summer heat; workers coming in from autumnal fields, sheened with sweat, carrying scythes or baskets of grapes; snow edging the cornices like frosting, during the long, silent winter. History, culture, and memory would flow from the opened doors and windows as surely as spring water flowed from the Roman fountain.

§

She was so deep in reverie that his voice startled her.

"Here you are."

She jumped guiltily. "Oh! I didn't hear you come." She stood uncertainly, as if caught in a questionable act.

"What are you doing?" Javier approached her curiously.

"I was just..." She swept her hand toward the house. "You know..."

"You have that look," Javier said, half accusingly, half teasing.

"What look?"

"Like you're either starting a new book in your head or planning something big." He put an arm around her shoulders and squeezed her to his side. "I think I caught you just in time."

"Maybe not. I think it's too late."

"I have to watch you or you'll fly away." He massaged her shoulders. "Are those tight muscles I feel—or wing buds?"

She threw him a glance filled with a plea that rose from her heart. "Javier..." Her eyes searched his face, begging for understanding.

"What, Caleepso? What?"

"I've been thinking."

"Yes." The old, dipping, and rising intonation, denoting *obviously*.

"And I think we've been out of balance."

"What do you mean?"

"I mean that...Let me think how to say this...You know I love Rancho Cielo."

"Yes."

"And of course, you do, too." She frowned, searching for words to express her morning's revelations. "But it's only part of who we are, Javier. Northern Mexico's wild and it's exhilarating. It challenges us with hard work and with harsh weather and difficult politics." She wouldn't meet his eye.

"Yes. And?"

"And this morning I'm realizing that there's another part of me. And of you, I think. One that wants rest from the difficulties. Safety even. And roots in a culture that's more than just five hundred years old." Her eyes flew to his.

"I feel safe here, Javier. And I feel the history that's saturated into this soil. Think of it! The Celts, the Egyptians, Phoenicians, Greeks, Romans, Moors, the Franks, and the Gauls. Charlemagne, the Count of Toulouse, the Cathars and the troubadours, chivalry, and courtly love. Romanesque and Gothic cathedrals, pilgrim trails, the Black Virgins..."

She stopped for breath, her arms outstretched, as if they could embrace thousands of years of French culture.

Javier looked at her there, so earnest and graceful, dappled with golden coins of light beneath the dancing plane trees, and his heart filled with both love and sorrow.

"You don't want to live at Rancho Cielo anymore, Caleepso?"

She came to him and took his hand, raising it to her lips, then resting it on her heart.

"Javier, of course I want to live at Rancho Cielo again. I'm as eager as you are to see the new house. But I also know that *this*"—she gestured toward the house and garden—"has been missing in our lives.

"Imagine going to the opera in Montpellier! Or having neighbors who want to talk about Lamartine or Proust, instead of cattle insemination or the local cartel death toll.

"You and I are unique, Javier. We can live in both worlds—and we *need* to live in both."

Javier fought with the bitter disappointment that was rising in his throat like acid. It felt as if Calypso were in revolt, disparaging everything they had built together.

"You find Mexico wanting, Caleepso?"

Her look was exasperated as she pulled away from him. She stood with her back to him, her fists clenched. Her shoulders heaved as she took deep breaths to calm herself. How could she communicate to him the longing that was rising in her, the deep and persistent need? Difficult as it was, she had to speak her truth.

"No, Javier. I don't find Mexico wanting. But I find it *Mexico.* Think of it as cooking. I love Mexican cuisine—but does that mean I'm a traitor if I also like French food?

"Something in me is going unanswered, Javier. Some part of me that longs for *this!*"

She flung her arm toward the desolate pile before them.

"You're just having house envy, Caleepso. Once you have a home of your own again, this won't seem so urgent."

"No! I am *not* having house envy! I have a genuine need—a need right in my soul—for France. Mexico is raw and difficult, Javier. It's the wildness and the mystery that I love about it. Here in France, the centuries have tamed the land but in a kind way. A way that honors the soil and brings up this kind of richness and beauty from it."

She spun, holding her arms out as if presenting him with the full beauty and mystery of the old garden.

"You won't find this in Mexico," she said stubbornly. "It's too far south and the water's too scarce and the plants that grow here won't grow there. I can't replicate it in Chihuahua. And this is the very thing that my soul craves."

"I didn't realize how much you hate Mexico."

She stamped her foot in frustration.

"No! I do *not* hate Mexico. That's so unfair! I've given the better part of my life to Mexico. And after what we've just been through, it's a wonder one or both of us didn't give our lives, period. You could have been killed, Javier! I thought you were. And I could have been, too. Climbing that cliff was the hardest thing I've ever done. When I fell, I thought I was going to die. And let's not even *think* about going through the tube—*three times!*"

Flames were scorching his heart again. How could Calypso do this, when the new house was half built and a new start was almost theirs? He tried to collect his thoughts.

"What is it you *want*, Caleepso?"

"I want to buy this place and renovate this house," she said. It was straightforward and simple—how could he object?

"And what about Rancho Cielo? You taking up bilocation now, Caleepso? You becoming a shaman?"

"We could live part of the year at Rancho Cielo and part of the year here. Pedro can run the ranch for us while we're away."

Javier frowned. "You think Pedro can run it as well as I can?"

"It's not a matter of who runs it best. Don't you see, Javier—it's time for us to retire. Oh! Don't get me wrong," she added hastily, "I know we'll never really do that. We both have too much we want to accomplish. But we've been working hard for years, Javier. It's time for a change. Life is more interesting that way. And it's part of being in late midlife, to keep growing in new directions.

"Besides, I know you have a new book in your head. And I know you can influence your country more by writing it than by doing hand to hand combat with the cartels."

"I can write it at Rancho Cielo," he growled.

Calypso knew this stubborn mood and how obstinate it could be, but she persisted.

"But you won't and you know it. There are a thousand distractions to keep you from it. If the sheep aren't lambing, then it's the cattle needing branding or the haying or shoeing the horses or..." She raised her hands in a helpless gesture. "You know it's true, Javier."

And he did. He knew in his heart that everything she was saying was true. He felt the urgency of the book pressing inside him. He felt a weariness that was the need for a long physical rest. He knew the pressure of the endless rounds of work on the ranch. And he understood Calypso's need for safety and some time out from the perilous political realities of the northern

Sierra and the cartels. Why, then, was his heart so set against her and her proposed project?

"I don't want you to do this, Caleepso. I want us to go home to the ranch like we planned. I feel like you lured me here to France, knowing that you didn't want to go home again."

Calypso shrieked in rage. "That is *so* not true! This place ambushed me! I'm astonished by its hold over me! It's like the locket—its irresistible. I'm as surprised by this as you are."

The wind was picking up. The canopy of branches lifted and seethed in agitation. Their shadows pooled about them in the late morning sun like cast-off clothing, his as upright and rigid as a post, hers dancing with frustration, and streaming with windblown hair as if emitting coils of energy.

They stared at one another, her eyes pleading, his adamant.

"We're out of balance, Javier," she said again. "We need a change of pace." Even to her it felt feeble in the face of his resistance.

"I'm going to do this thing," she said with more conviction. "I'm going to take the money from the last two books and I'm going to buy this place and renovate it. Please stay and help me. Please, Javier."

He stood his ground, still staring at her, his face hard and closed. Then he spun on his boot heel and strode down the garden path toward the rental without a word.

"Javier!" she called after him. But he did not answer and he did not stop. When she got back to the orangerie, he was gone.

ଌ

Calypso stood her ground but being separated from him proved to be a living hell. She was surprised, at first mildly and then with increasing alarm, to find her heart so lacerated by simple absence. That such passion existed, unguessed, caused her to question her entire being: If this could loiter in the recesses, what else might be there, lurking? What was possible for her? Of what acts of self-betrayal or self-sacrifice might she be capable?

As weeks went by, the feeling grew in force until it was a hurricane of grief and loss that flung her about the bed at night and bowed her shoulders by day. The quiet, orderly life she was accustomed to inhabit was ripped apart by the force of these winds. Her mind was like a corrugated tin roof—everything around and within her seemed to flap, squeal, groan, or shudder from the unseen gale. Food lost its savor. Her skin grew pale, all blood having sunk, she surmised, by some psychological deep-diving effect, into the core for self-preservation.

She stopped seeing friends, the slow rituals of the cafés seeming tedious now and meaningless. Not given to drink or drugs, she could find no anesthesia for the howling pain. She went sleepless, walked ceaselessly, sat and stared.

Without warning and in the most inappropriate places, tears would start, brim over and roll. All she could do was turn away from the curious or sympathetic, whose lame ministrations revolted her, knowing there was no way to stop the flow until some secret source went dry or shut its weirs for a period of replenishment.

She was utterly helpless in the throes of it all and too absent-spirited even to be angry about it. She must have arrived, finally, at the iron gates of love. Hammering there was bloodying, exhausting.

The word *Please!* can be flung into the empty maw of the universe only so many times without losing its apotropaic powers. A sense of fatedness began to settle upon her like smothering smoke. She could taste its bitterness. It burned her nostrils and left her throat parched and scratchy. Her heart, always so glad and eager, hunkered down in the quivering, terror-stricken passivity of mortified flesh. The world was absolutely void of solace.

Then, in her cowardice, she would consider packing her bags and returning to Rancho Cielo. She would hover in this meek, servile place for a day or two, and then come out fighting.

A thousand times she vowed simply to throw him off. Willed herself to forget. To move on. But like a mother bird whose nest has been robbed by the dark probings of a raven, her mind flew in endless circles, shrieking and grieving around the emptiness that had so lately been full of life and promise.

There seemed to be no remedy. No cure for the endless hemorrhagic flood of sorrow and longing that was bleeding her to pallor. She listened for his step on the gravel path. Sat by the phone, knowing he would not call. She read and reread a careless note he had written and stuck on the orangerie refrigerator, seeking to draw some faint scent from it, some tincture of love that surely must have motivated its posting.

Her eyes, blurry from weeping, looked blankly into the future without seeing a single flicker projected on that white screen. Would she creep back to Mexico, leaving her heart's longing unfulfilled? Without him there, there was no plan. No meaning. No point in continuing.

She feared her health would collapse. She thought of walking into the depths of the garden, where the shrubbery was overgrown and almost impenetrable, and putting a pistol in her mouth.

In the hurricane's eye was the stillness of death.

§

Two factors saved her. The first was the somewhat sly realization that Javier must be suffering just as badly as she was. They had been together far too long for her to ignore either his emotional pain or the intellectual rigor he would be bringing to the issue of their separation.

He would count up the years she had spent by his side in Chiapas, nursing him back to health after his imprisonment and torture, helping him build Rancho Cielo, and acting as a full partner in both the ranch and in their political activities. He would not forget to add in the sale of her Paris flat to Hill, even though she had made that decision on her own.

Against that summation, in the other pan of the scale, he would throw his own devotion to her. And what else? He had resisted every suggestion of hers that they take vacations, travel a little, relax more. In her more rational moments, she knew he would be deeply troubled by the emptiness of that side of the balance. Not that she wanted him to suffer, of course, but some obstinate place in her at least demanded the fair hearing that she had not gotten.

The second factor was the property—and if she was rigorously honest with herself, it was the fascination with the old house that really saved her. To distract herself, she threw herself into negotiations with the owner of the mas. To her surprise, it was just as the rental agent had suggested. The owner was not only willing but eager to make a deal with her for the sale of the entire property.

She would never forget the first time she entered the old house. The heiress to the estate, an attractive, businesslike young woman who drove over in her BMW from Narbonnes to show Calypso around, was an executive in an international chemical conglomerate. She breezed through the shuttered rooms, throwing out dismissive gestures at all the collected treasures of generations of her family.

"All this old stuff!" she exclaimed, pulling a two-hundred-year-old faience plate from the depths of a kitchen cupboard. "I can have a dealer come in and get it out of your way, if you want."

Calypso's heart leapt and it was all she could do to reply calmly, "No, I'd like to include the furnishings and all in whatever price we finally arrive at, if that works for you."

The young woman wrinkled her nose and shrugged. "That's fine with me. I'm a minimalist myself. I can't bear all this fusty old stuff."

Calypso downplayed her interest slightly, saying, "I'm sure there will be a couple of pieces that I'll want to keep and I can dispose of the rest."

She cast her eye over the treasures for whose continued existence in the house she was now responsible. She peeked at Provençal armoires and Louis Quinze and Seize fauteuils. The contents of the house ranged from early to late Baroque with lovely Rococo pieces, to second phase of Neoclassical with its elegant ebony and gilt evocations of Egypt of the Napoleonic era known as Empire. All stood patient and forlorn under dust covers. She felt as if she were negotiating the release of prisoners of war, of entire families that would otherwise be separated at best and demolished at worst.

Finally, over cups of coffee, they settled at the orangerie dining table to talk business. Calypso was not unmindful that, for all her disparaging of the contents of the house, the young woman was more than aware of their value. After an afternoon of haggling, the two women settled on a price.

ꞩ

Despite the eagerness of the owner to make the sale, the negotiations for the purchase of the property were more convoluted than Calypso had imagined. She was obliged to engage a notary who could deal with the legal complications. Bureaucratic delays were lengthy and frustrating. Nevertheless, she was able to make a contractual agreement with the seller so that she could begin renovations on the house, even before taking legal ownership.

Luck was with her. She heard about a retired builder in the village, Monsieur Signac, and set about to convince him to take the job. He wandered through the rooms of the house, smacking walls with his fist to demonstrate the plaster falling away in dust, bouncing on the upstairs floors to test the integrity of the wood, humming dejectedly over antiquated wiring, and snorting in disgust at the unorthodox web of lead plumbing pipes.

He spent two days in isolation, making calculations, during which time Calypso paced the property and took to biting her nails. Finally, on the morning of the third day, the builder appeared, papers in hand.

They sat at the garden table, their coffee growing cold, and hammered out an agreement and a price. They shook hands and Monsieur Signac announced that work would begin the following day.

He arrived at seven the next morning with two stout-looking assistants, who immediately began erecting two portable metal sheds on the gravel apron in front of the house, one for a tool shed and one for storage of the furniture. By afternoon, the two young men, Luc and Jean-Pierre, were engaged in moving massive armoires, beds and sideboards into the shed. By evening, both sheds sat filled and locked, their silvery sheen looking strangely alien through the garden growth, against the backdrop of golden stone.

§

The work went on for months. Summer passed in heat and clouds of dust, as walls were rid of rot and replastered. Electricians came in their square vans and rooted in the depths of the house, as did plumbers. A sheet metal specialist raised an ungodly din for weeks, installing ductwork for central heating and air conditioning. A roofing contractor began pitching broken roof tiles into the yard, and barely finished securing the house before the coming of the autumn storms.

A blustery autumn turned into a dismal winter of cold wind and torrential rain. Working under portable lights, the men began the finish work. The parquet of the upstairs floors was stripped in preparation for refinishing. Plaster was smoothed in preparation for painting. Original wallpaper was restored. New faucets were installed over old basins.

A seamstress in the village, Madame Simard, labored over yards of hand-blocked Souleiado fabric making draperies and cushions. Calypso made excursions into the neighboring towns and villages, always returning with some treasure to feather her nest. The pile of boxes and bags grew in the second bedroom of the orangerie.

§

Everything, in fact, was going well except her relationship with Javier. He had, of course, headed straight home to Rancho

Cielo after their tiff. At first, he refused to speak with her on the phone, to the consternation of their maid, Maria. "I tell him, Señora, but he no come," she wailed. "When you come home? We miss you!"

As the weeks went by, he deigned to hold brief conversations, during which they discussed the weather and the present state of the cattle herds and not much more. Calypso was grateful even for that. Both carefully avoided the subject of the new house each was tending into existence on separate continents.

She ended each conversation by saying, "I love you."

"I love you, too," he would say, but it sounded stiff and not very convincing.

§

One day in early spring, just after the signing of the final papers, Monsieur Signac came to the door of the orangerie with an odd look on his face.

"Excuse me for bothering you, Madame Searcy, but I think you should come see this," he said without preamble. "I don't know what to make of it."

Calypso slipped on a sweater and followed him down the gravel path toward the house. The rains had stopped for a few days and the gardens were just beginning to shake off the winter's hammering.

"I had Luc working on the floor back in the mud room this morning," Monsieur Signac said as they hurried along. "I saved that for last because it gets so much traffic from the workmen."

Calypso nodded. "Yes, I remember discussing that."

"The tiles were uneven in the back corner, as you may remember. It didn't matter as long as that big armoire was there. But now it's very obvious. The tiles there aren't eighteenth century and don't match the rest. So I had Luc chisel them out so we can replace them with antique tiles."

"Good," Calypso said.

She pulled the sweater tighter about her as the wind kicked up and showered them with pendant droplets from the garden's canopy.

"But something strange happened."

Monsieur Signac stopped and looked her in the eye. Calypso stopped, too, and gave him a puzzled look.

"Strange?"

"Yes. The floor under the newer tiles was wood, very badly put in place. So I told Luc to tear it out so we could do the job right."

"Yes?"

"And he broke through into...well, you should come and see for yourself." He turned without another word and led them around to the north side of the house with its single, austere back entrance near the west corner. Calypso followed, mystified.

The back door gave into a room about fifteen feet square, with one long window on the west wall. Directly across from the entry was the door leading into the kitchen. The corner to the left of the kitchen door that once had been occupied by a large Provençal armoire was now a gaping hole.

"What on earth?" Calypso exclaimed.

Monsieur Signac handed her a large flashlight.

"We haven't gone down yet," he said. "It is your right as owner to descend first."

"Down?"

Calypso's voice was dubious. She approached the hole, which breathed a cool and faintly musty draft into the room, and angled the flashlight's beam into its dusky depths. Starting just beneath what would have been floor level were steep stone steps leading down into darkness.

"Oh my!" She glanced at Monsieur Signac with a wry smile. "It's a dubious honor you're offering me."

"If you like, I will go down first," the builder offered gallantly.

"No, I think I want to do this myself. Just be listening for screams, please."

He gave a stiff, ironic bow.

"At your service, Madame."

§

Monsieur Signac held out his arm for support, as Calypso stepped into the hole and planted her foot on the first step. The flashlight's beam revealed that the stairs were wedge-shaped and wound downward in a tight spiral. They were also very high, so that after descending three steps Calypso was forced to relinquish Monsieur Signac's arm, as she was already almost a yard below floor level.

"I'll just lean against the wall as I go down," she reassured him.

In three more steps, she had curved from his view and was fully under the existing floor. She was in a narrow shaft not more than nine feet wide, entirely filled by the staircase.

In three more steps, she had completed one whole revolution of the spiral and the sense of depth was beginning to close in on her. Light from above had dimmed nearly to blackness at this level, as she discovered when she accidentally hit the flashlight's switch against the wall. Instantly she was plunged into darkness and she let out a small shriek of surprise.

"Everything going well?" she heard Monsieur Signac's voice from above, blunted by the thick stone.

"I'm fine," she called back, aware that there was a slight edge of hysteria in her voice. "Still descending."

She groped the switch on and lowered herself a few more steps, feeling like she'd shrunk down to ant size and was lost inside a seashell. Two more steps and the light picked out a landing only three more steps below her. She lowered herself cautiously, her feet scraping on the grit of ages. She was grateful that the stairwell was unusually dry, with no slippery mold or moss to make the descent even more treacherous.

Finally, she reached the bottom and a small landing, barely big enough to contain her. Straight in front of her nose was a heavy wooden door, arched at the top, with a handsome, hand-forged iron latch. She reached eagerly for it and then hesitated.

What if there were a chamber of horrors inside? An old prison cell, where people were left manacled to the wall until they went mad from darkness and isolation and then died? She laid her hand against the cold metal and asked herself if she had the courage to face the worst—knowing full well that her curiosity would not let her wait much longer.

At last, she depressed the latch and pushed against the door with her shoulder, realizing that the opening was so low she would have to duck. With surprising ease, the door swung inward and Calypso crouched through into a low room.

She swung the flashlight's beam. She was in a round space perhaps twenty feet in diameter, with a vaulted stone ceiling that barely cleared her head and then sloped down to half that height near the walls. She recognized the construction as very old—possibly Romanesque, making it roughly a thousand years old, or even Roman, which would mean it was around two thousand years old. She had expected the space to be dank and slimy and was impressed that it was watertight and dry.

The room was empty except for a central mass slightly taller than she was and covered with a linen sheet grown yellow with age and dust. Teepee-shaped, it sagged into the crevices of what lay beneath with finality, as if it had been dipped in plaster, and had ripped in several places from its own weight. Clearly, it had been undisturbed for a very long time.

She tried to lift the sheet from the object it covered, which sat, apparently, on a table or dais. The covering was stiff and resistant, however. It was more the texture of canvas, she realized as she tugged at it. Wrestling with it only covered her in a landslide of cascading dust and grit. Coughing, she backed off, thinking she would have to return with a stout pair of shears to cut the covering away.

Running her light over the mound, her eye caught the corner of a table with an elegant Louis Quinze leg and a glint of metal, where she had dislodged the right-hand edge of the tarp. Her flashlight illuminated a whirling cloud of dust motes as she stepped forward again and slid her hand beneath the edge of the fabric, across what felt cold and smooth like a marble tabletop. It met with a solid rectangle, which she dragged out and lifted, then quickly lowered to the floor as it was very heavy.

She squatted and ran her light over the object. It was a box about a foot long and five or six inches wide, with a metal framework covered in gold work and antique cut gems. The sides and top of the box were of thick, beveled rock crystal. It must be a reliquary, she reasoned, one of those precious containers in which the bones of a saint lay in honor.

She was stunned by its beauty and richness but even more by something else. It took her a moment to realize it. The reliquary was the same size and shape and of a sumptuousness equal to the now-lost locket box.

ʖ

Calypso laid the flashlight on the stone floor and slipped out of her sweater. Wrapping the box in it so that nothing showed, she tucked it under her arm, took up the light again and stood. With one last look around to make sure she hadn't missed anything, she ducked back out of the vaulted room and closed the door.

Going up the spiral stairs was harder than coming down. Her knees protested against the high steps and she had a hard time keeping her balance with the flashlight in one hand and the box tucked under the other elbow, the way a running back would snug a football. Tottering and scraping, she made her way to the top where Monsieur Signac waited, staring worriedly into the darkness.

"Ah, Madame! I was just about to come down looking for you!"

"Thank you, Monsieur Signac. It's not so far down, really, but it's very steep."

She handed the flashlight to him and took his proffered hand so that he could pull her up the final three steps.

In answer to his questioning look she said, "There's a door at the bottom, leading into a Roman or Romanesque vault. There's nothing of interest there except this box." She waved the sweater-wrapped parcel. "I'll clean it up and let you see it later."

"What is your pleasure regarding this stairwell, Madame? Shall we put the new floor over it?"

"No. What I would like you to do is to create a door that is flush with the floor and covered with the same tiles. And I'd like a flush-mounted lock on it."

"Very well, Madame. I can do that."

"Thank you, Monsieur Signac. And thank you for calling me. It was quite a surprise to know that this exists under the house." She turned to go.

"Oh! And" she turned back as if it were an afterthought, "please don't go down there or let Luc or Jean-Pierre go down. It's very steep and I don't want the insurance liability."

"As you wish, Madame Searcy," and he bowed stiffly with a slightly ironic smile.

§

Calypso surprised herself with her protectiveness of the newly found space. As she hurried through the windy garden toward the orangerie, she wondered at her response. Whoever originally had floored-over the stairs must have done so for a reason. Like a detective, she didn't want the scene contaminated until she could understand more about what had occurred there.

The orangerie was still warm, although the fire had died down. As she stepped into the salon and laid her parcel on the table, she shivered, pulling a shawl from the back of her armchair and throwing it over her shoulders.

Then, like a surgeon unwrapping bandages, she began the careful extrication of the box from its knitted wrappings. Prongs holding the jewels caught in the yarn and the little metal legs with their lion's paw feet were poking rudely into the knit. It took several minutes before the crystal container stood in the light of day on the marble tabletop.

She went for a damp cloth to wipe the crystal clean. As she did, the beauty of the box became more and more remarkable. Now she could see that the interior was lined with crimson silk, although to her relief, no saint's bones appeared to be present.

Finally, she put her thumb to the delicate clasp and released it. Raising the lid with great care, fearful of breaking a hinge, she surveyed the interior. The red silk lining was striated with minute tears, all down its length. Only one thing was contained within—a small piece of paper, rolled like a scroll. Gingerly, she picked it up between thumb and finger and then lowered the lid.

Going to her desk, she placed the scroll on the desktop and began with careful fingers to unroll it. Although its edges were dog-eared and it was plainly of some antiquity, the paper was surprisingly supple. Soon writing in an elegant hand, in sepia ink, began to appear. Unrolled, the entirety was about eight inches long. She weighted it with books, top and bottom and along the side edges to keep it from curling up again and went for her magnifying glass.

The ink was faded and in some places almost invisible, and the handwriting was more showy than legible. It took her the better part of an hour to decipher its message. As she did, she wrote an English translation on a yellow legal tablet.

> *I write in haste. News has reached me of terrible events in Paris, Lyons and Nantes. As a nonjuring priest, I am now condemned as refractory clergy, and fear for my life. It is said that three of our holy bishops and hundreds of priests have been massacred by angry mobs, as the Legislative Assembly has dissolved into chaos. The noyades for treason under the direction of Jean-Baptiste Carrier have killed many hundreds of both nuns and priests, along with many simple folk who were stalwarts of their parishes.*
>
> *Until now, revolutionary fervor has been mild here, involving only the removal of the bell from the church*

> *tower, and the sealing of the church doors. Tonight, however, a mob is gathering in front of the Mairie, and I fear for my life. With the aid of good Monsieur M., I have removed the sacred figures from the church, hiding them for who can say how long, until such time as it is once again safe, through the agency of Our Lord, to worship as a Catholic again.*
>
> *I write this in full faith that such shall be the final outcome, as an apostate priest of the constitutional clergy, and a faithful servant of our Holy Church, and its head, Pope Pius VI.*
>
> *So be it. May God have mercy on those who make such desperate measures necessary, and upon his humble servant,*
>
> *Father Xavier S.*
> *This 6th day of September, 1792*

Calypso put down her magnifying glass with a troubled heart and wrote the final words of her translation on the tablet. She went to her laptop and looked up the word *noyades*, discovering that, as she had thought, it meant *drowning.* Her mind was agitated by the drama of the priest's terror. What became of him, she wondered? And was that tarp-covered mound in the vault, then, the holy figures from the local church?

Her memory of French history from the time of the Revolution was sketchy and she decided to do a little research to settle herself. She spent the remainder of the day at her computer, tracking down bits and pieces of information that fleshed out the priest's letter.

She discovered that in August, 1789, the state cancelled the power of the church to levy taxes. The new revolutionary government made the issue central to its policies, declaring that all church property in France now belonged to the nation. Confiscation began and church properties were sold at public auction.

Then, in July 1790, the National Constituent Assembly published the Civil Constitution of the Clergy, stripping the clergy of their special rights and making them employees of the state. All priests and bishops were required to swear an oath of fidelity to the new government on pain of dismissal, deportation or death.

The pope at that time, Pius VI, spent almost eight months deliberating on the issue of whether to grant French priests Papal approval to sign such an oath. On April 13, 1791, the pope instead denounced the new French Constitution, effectively splitting the French Catholic church. Abjuring priests, called *jurors*, became known as *constitutional clergy*, while nonjuring priests were called *refractory clergy*, the term with which Father Xavier had been labeled.

During those disordered months as the Legislative Assembly, the successor to the National Constituent Assembly, also dissolved into chaos, the church was increasingly viewed as counterrevolutionary. Social and economic grievances among the people boiled over and violence directed toward the church and her clergy erupted all across France.

In Paris, during a single two-day period beginning September 2, 1792, three church bishops and more than two hundred priests were massacred by angry mobs—the beginning of what would become known as the September Massacres. Calypso found that the *noyades*, or drownings, were mass executions for treason under the direction of Jean-Baptiste Carrier and involved thousands of people, including nuns and priests. The executions took place in the Loire river, which Carrier himself called *the national bathtub*—all of this a precursor to the Reign of Terror the following year, with its use of the guillotine called *the national razor*.

Obviously, Father Xavier had good reason to fear for his life and it was only reasonable for him to assume that his church would be desecrated. Who, she wondered, was *the good Monsieur M.* and what was his fate for helping the priest? Perhaps the *Mairie*, the city hall of Brignac, would still have records from that period. She made a note to do some research there when time permitted.

Toward the end of the afternoon, she went again to the house, where Monsieur Signac was just finishing up for the day. She found him sweeping up in the corner where she had left him earlier.

"Ah, Madame!" he exclaimed. "Come and see if you approve. I have fashioned a door here, you see, and affixed the tiles."

He demonstrated to Calypso that he had created a door from thick exterior plywood and attached it to a floor joist with a piano hinge. Already the tiles were mortared in place and a single tile, its center bored through, held a flush-mounted lock surrounded by a metal ring for lifting the door. The level of the tile aligned perfectly with the surrounding floor.

"You've done a fine job, Monsieur Signac," she said warmly. "The door simply disappears."

"Yes, and I've made a metal loop on the under side. When you want to open the door, you can put the loop over this hook I've installed in the wall, so the door won't fall shut while you're inside."

He demonstrated by opening the door, swiveling the metal loop outward, and then hooking it over a stout steel hook set into the plaster of the wall.

"This is excellent," Calypso said. "I'm very pleased with what you've done."

Mr. Signac beamed and handed her the key to the lock.

"This should keep your insurance liability safe," he said with a knowing smile.

Calypso wondered if he had already been down the stairs, even before he had come to fetch her that morning. Something in his smile told her that he knew she was protecting something more than just her insurance premiums.

§

She hadn't been back at the orangerie for more than five minutes when the telephone rang. To her amazement, it was Javier.

It was the first time he had called her in all the months of their separation. She braced for bad news.

"What is it?" she asked. "What's happened?"

"Nothing, nothing, Caleepso. Not to worry. I just called you to let you know the house is finished."

"Finished! That's wonderful! Congratulations!"

"I thought you might like to see it." His voice held a ghost of his old teasing tone.

Calypso hesitated only for a moment but already she knew it was a moment too long.

"I'm just finishing up here, Javier. In a couple of weeks I'll be able..."

"Never mind," he snapped. "Is not important."

"Javier..."

"I have to go. Bye." And he hung up.

Calypso replaced the receiver slowly, not sure if she wanted to cry or scream in rage. In the next couple of days, Monsieur Signac had promised, the house would be ready for the gang of cleaners he had assembled from the village.

Floors would be scrubbed and waxed, windows washed, fixtures polished. Draperies would be hung and carpets unfurled, all in preparation for moving in the furniture and the dismantling of the annoyingly moderne metal sheds in the front yard.

It was almost more than she could bear to think of leaving now. It would be a psychological *coitus interruptus* that would only make her resentful of Rancho Cielo. She had pages of diagrams for the placement of furniture and hanging of paintings. She even knew which of the heavy old handwoven linen sheets, with their looping hand-embroidered monograms and tatted edgings, went on which bed in which room. It was unthinkable, unbearable, unfair to have to leave now.

She sat staring out the window of the orangerie, gnawing on her thumbnail. This was like a return to the earliest days of their relationship, when Javier had turned abruptly cranky and impossible, and she had expended every wile in her arsenal to break through, without success.

The garden was darkening toward evening. Down the dusky, shadowed path came the tortoise, lumbering along in innocent expectation of his evening slices of fruit. Something in his blameless and irreproachable assumption of friendly plenitude mirrored her own.

She had made a bond with the creature, almost a pact. They were partners in the rediscovery of this mysterious and neglected place. At that moment, her loyalty to the reptile felt greater than the one to Javier and her heart swelled with affection for the simple old creature, even while her eyes stung with tears.

She went to the kitchen, washed a handful of cherries and pitted them, and then went out into the cool, windy evening, where the tortoise was just arriving at the kitchen stoop. She sat on the bottom stair and offered the creature his first piece of fruit. He waved his nose in front of it like a perfumer appreciating a new fragrance and then took the cherry from her fingers in one gulp.

"It's just you and me, kid," Calypso said mournfully. "I'm not going back, you know. Not yet, at least. So stick with me, okay?"

The tortoise raised his creased, leathery head and gazed at her with his bottomless black eyes. Was it her imagination or did she feel in that moment a jolt of love and understanding that almost rocked her off the step? She reached into the bowl for another cherry and she continued to supply her friend's supper as the sun sank and the penumbra of evening descended upon the garden.

§

She slept poorly that night. Sometime in the blackest hours of the early morning, she awoke with the stirring conviction that she needed to see the figures in the vault. She lay under the soft, cozy duvet and tried to talk herself out of so rash an adventure.

It was dark. There was no one to help her lift the door, which was heavy with tiles. The stairs were steep and treacherous—if she fell, no one would find her for hours. And lastly, why didn't she just go back to sleep and gratify this urge in the morning?

She stayed in bed, following the conviction that rationality would win in the end. She turned on her side, organized her pillow just so and composed herself for slumber.

Within minutes she was thrashing about, seeking a new position, as if to ward off the attack of the idea, which insisted itself upon her relentlessly. Finally, feeling disgruntled with herself, she turned on the bedside lamp and lay staring at her clothes, where they lay flung over the back of a chair.

She imagined getting up, putting them on, finding the flashlight and shears, opening the door to the chill and windy darkness, and setting out for the house. Even this dismal scenario, however, would not quiet the inner promptings.

At last, with a sigh she threw back the covers and lunged through chilly air toward her clothing. In minutes, she was crunching down the garden path toward the house behind the round disk of the flashlight's beam.

The big building stood against the night sky, a blacker blackness. She rounded its western flank, hearing the sostenuto of rustling olive leaves beneath the fountain's treble. She inserted her key into the lock, threw one glance into the surrounding darkness, as if looking for someone to stop her in this madness, and entered the house.

Monsieur Signac had, of course, closed and locked the door to the stairwell. Calypso knelt and inserted the brand new key into the lock, aware of the sharp, limey smell of fresh mortar. She hoisted the heavy door by its inset ring, hoping that the mortar was fully set and the tiles wouldn't all slide off when the door went vertical. Holding the flashlight between her knees, she wrestled the door upright, and managed to secure its metal loop over the hook in the wall.

Below her, the stairs spiraled down into darkness like the grinding screw in a meat grinder. She felt the hair on her arms rise at the thought of descending, all alone, into their depths. She set the flashlight on the floor with its beam angled over the opening, sat down on the floor, and swung her feet onto the first stair. Picking up her light, she aimed it into the darkness below her and began a slow, very cautious descent.

§

Her heart was jarring in her ribcage as she stood, finally, before the low wooden door to the vaulted room. The space between the foot of the stairs and the door was so narrow that she felt as if she were in her own coffin. Reflexively, she reached for the locket and fingered it beneath her sweater. Then, drawing in her breath, she depressed the latch, shoved the door open with her shoulder and ducked into the secret room.

She had shoved a couple of votive candles and a book of matches into her pants pocket before leaving the orangerie. Setting the flashlight on the floor, she knelt and lit the candles. The two small flames threw weak illumination over the room, but their warm light was comforting after the harsh glare of the flashlight. She set them to either side, where they would not throw her own shadow over the work to come.

Then, pulling the shears from their holster on her belt, she rose and turned toward the mysterious tarp-covered teepee in the center of the room.

Old and rotten as it was, the tarp resisted the blades of her shears. She bore down until her fingers felt raw, cutting stroke by stroke into the covering, realizing that the shears would be sprung and have to be replaced after this night's work. She managed to cut three long slits up the side of the mound before she developed a blister on her finger.

After that, she set the shears aside and began inserting her fingers into the rotted rips in the tarp. With sufficient strength and a few sharp jerks, she managed to open the rips into long vertical tears.

After about an hour she was covered in dust and grit, and the tarp hung in tatters but what lay captive underneath was still obscure. Taking up the shears again, she began to cut horizontally across the thin strips with a kind of desperate determination. As each strip fell away, a lengthening incision appeared across the face of the mound.

When the horizontal cut was a couple of feet long, the tarp suddenly shifted backward from its own weight, startling Calypso. She jumped back with a yip. It was almost as if human hands had tugged the covering sheet from behind. Then, her eyes fell on the incision again and she gasped.

"Oh my God!" she exclaimed.

Picking up the flashlight from the floor, she aimed it into the cut and then stared. Looking back, from where he was cradled on a sturdy arm, was an infant, smiling at her with sweet serenity.

She was frantic, then, to see the rest of the statue. Cutting, ripping and tugging, she managed finally to dislodge the tarp. With a final yank on its backside hem, she felt its inertia give way and in one sliding movement, it released its hold and crumpled to her feet. She raced around to the front and taking up her flashlight again, spotlighted the entirety of the statue.

What she saw took her breath away. Her legs buckled and she sank to her knees.

"It can't be!" she breathed in wonder that bordered on terror.

Centered in the cone of the flashlight's beam, a statue almost four feet high of a mother and child stood resplendent upon an elegant Louis Quinze table. Carved in wood, colored in polychrome, and shining with gold gilt, the Queen of Heaven and her Son gazed with divine, untroubled calm into Calypso's astonished eyes.

Calypso shook her head dazedly and exclaimed, "*You!*"

She switched off her flashlight and let it fall to the floor. In the light of the two candles, the figures above her seemed to move and breathe in the soft, flickering light.

Calypso felt a hot wave of emotion erupt from the very pit of her being. Sobs spewed from her like molten lava. Cradling her forehead in her hands, she bent at the waist and with her elbows braced on her thighs, fell into an attitude of obeisance. Cries arose from her that even she could not interpret with what was left of her rationality. They ripped from her throat unreservedly, a mixture of grief and ecstasy.

She howled her stark amazement and disequilibrium. Her body seemed to fly through undifferentiated space at warp speed, with fragments releasing and falling away, until she was only a soul, hurtling through endless void like a comet. With one imperious glance, Our Lady had released her from earthly bounds and set her on a timeless and infinite journey.

When she returned from it, she found herself still kneeling before the Mother of God. Her knees ached, her thighs screamed for release, and her shaking hands were saturated with tears.

How she was able to climb from the depths and to lower and lock the door, she was never able to remember. The only image that remained of the time between her return to consciousness and her arrival back at the orangerie was of her own hands, moving as if disembodied, taking the two candles from the floor, and placing them reverently before the throne of the Queen of Heaven.

§

"This is truly remarkable." Calypso read the e-mail from her friend Eleanore with weary, strained eyes, the day following her discovery. "If this is real—and of course we would have to do many tests to prove it—then you have discovered a kind of missing link."

Calypso could imagine Eleanore in her office in the depths of the Louvre, that was crowded with files and diminished by three looming walls of shelved reference books, bending in disbelief over the photos Calypso had e-mailed her. Her friend, an art historian of the Middle Ages, was almost as amazed as was Calypso.

"This image clearly draws its iconographic references from Egyptian prototypes of Isis suckling Horus," Eleanore's email continued. "If testing shows that it predates other Black Madonnas—and I suspect it will—then this image is a perfect example of the transition between the worship of Isis as Queen of Heaven and the veneration of Mary by the same title." She ended the message with a question, "When can I see Her?"

Since her discovery, Calypso had been busy. Although Monsieur Signac had arrived with his crew of cleaners that morning, Calypso had declared the back entrance and its room off limits. Then, borrowing extension cords and moveable work lights from the builder's shed and refusing all help from him or his assistants, she had made numerous trips up and down the stairs to the vault, setting up lights. Finally, she brought her camera and tripod from the orangerie and disappeared into the back of the house, locking herself into the back room, much to the mystification of the others.

Having taken shots of the statue from numerous angles, she downloaded the photos and sent them to Eleanore, who had an international reputation as an art historian and an impregnable position at the Louvre, because of her expertise. On a day when she had expected to be overjoyed with the progress on her new home, Calypso was largely oblivious to the work being accomplished in other rooms. As she dismantled the lighting and lugged it up the stairs, her thoughts were solely on Eleanore's response.

Now, as she bent over the screen of her laptop, gnawing on a hastily made sandwich, she felt a wave of emotion at her friend's evaluation. Living beneath her new home was an ancient and heretofore unknown aspect of the Divine Feminine, Her fire and compassion hidden deep in earth and darkness and forgotten, diminished or derided on the surface.

Calypso was certain that it was She who had called her to buy and restore the property; She who brought Calypso to defy even Javier and to risk their love in order to secure Her future.

How unthinkable that the property might have been sold for a housing development! What if She and Her vault had been mindlessly desecrated by a bulldozer and then simply covered over, never again to know human reverence? Calypso shuddered at the thought.

Accustomed to the power of the locket and to the sometimes shatteringly prophetic dreams is brought, still Calypso was amazed by the power of the call of the Black Madonna, as she had come to think of the statue. In Her, nature had become conscious matter—mere wood had become a living channel of the divine through the agency of human attention, love, and devotion.

In recognizing what drove her to buy and renovate the place, even at the expense of her relationship with Javier, Calypso had endured the eruption of an inner volcano of passion—her love for the soil of France, for its aesthetic, and for the history saturated into its soil—all now embodied in the statue of Isis/Mary. Furthermore, the uncanny realization that the image of the Black Virgin was identical to the one on the locket!

She brought up ancient images of Isis and Horus on her screen, side by side with one of her frontal photos of the statue. They were almost identical. Each held her Infant on her lap with her left hand and each had both breasts bared. The only difference lay in that the traditional Isis figure used her right had to guide her left breast to her child, while in the transitional figure, the breast in the right hand had been translated into a globe, which She extended to all.

Calypso stared at the orb in Her right hand, feeling she understood the iconographic shift. Divine consciousness, the milk of the Mother, would eventually expand to encompass the globe. Moreover, the globe was a mandala whose center *is* humankind, a center which is the consciousness humans bring to it. Spheric wholeness and completion are the milk the Goddess offers.

She flipped down the lid of her laptop and went to sit on the kitchen stoop to finish her sandwich. Her thoughts shifted to Javier and his patriarchal world of business, politics, warfare, and violence. She longed for a world at peace, where the inclusive values of the Feminine could be expressed—and she knew, in all fairness, that this was ultimately what Javier had expended his life trying to establish in Mexico.

She knew, too, that for all her love of France, it too had had long periods of violence, ignorance and warfare, as Father Xavier's letter had shown. It was not Mexico that was the crucible of human disorder but throughout the ages, the human heart.

Suddenly, her longing for Javier was almost unbearable. Each of them, in their desire for that elusive peace, was creating a sliver of it in their chosen corner of the world and each hoped that the other would share in it unreservedly. In their desire to give one another this anointing in the Divine Feminine, they had almost torn their love apart. She didn't know whether to cry or laugh.

On impulse, she went into the house and made a call to Rancho Cielo, even though she knew it was already late at night there. The phone rang and rang and rang. With a sad heart, she replaced the receiver and went to see how the house was coming along under the ministrations of the cleaners.

As she walked down the garden path, her hand went automatically to the locket beneath her sweater and she fingered its cool orb to calm her agitation. How could it be that the image on the locket was the same as the image in the vault? Although made perhaps three thousand years before the statue, still the Isis of the locket held an orb in her extended hand.

Overcome by this strange synchronicity, Calypso sank onto a stone bench, her mind singed by an echo of the delirious flight of consciousness of the previous night. What was time, really, or consciousness or matter that was shaped intentionally to expand it? It was all an unfathomable mystery.

She sat for many minutes until the feeling of dizziness passed. Then she pulled herself together, rose to her feet and went toward the house, vowing to focus for this afternoon on cobwebs and sawdust only.

ʂ

The house was nearly clean. The crew had started at the top, on the *troisième étage* and worked downward. When she arrived, they were on the ground floor. The smell of lavender soap hung in air damp from still-drying floors and windows. She found Monsieur Signac tinkering with a window latch to assure its perfect functioning.

"Is there anything left for me to do?" she asked.

"No, Madame. I think all is well in hand. We can even begin moving in furniture upstairs if you would like. Luc and Jean-Pierre can be spared from cleaning now, I think."

As if a switch had been thrown, Calypso found herself suddenly as eager to have her house in order as she had been driven, that morning, to photograph the statue.

"Are the drapes hung up there?"

Monsieur Signac nodded.

"Yes. All the draperies are hung on the second and third floors. We are waiting for the windows all to be cleaned before we hang them here on the ground floor."

Calypso gave him a radiant smile.

"Then let's get going!"

ʖ

It took four full days to move into the house. Luc and Jean-Pierre worked like Trojan slaves, heaving and wrestling into place the massive armoires, chests of drawers, tables, and desks. The rest of the crew, liberated from cleaning, brought the boxes and bags of treasures she had purchased during the months of renovation, in a long procession from the orangerie through the garden to the house.

In the kitchen, ivory-handled knives and silver flatware were washed, polished, and carefully laid down in newly painted drawers. In the salon, study and bedrooms, paintings were hung, chairs and couches posed in groupings, and beds assembled and made up. Calypso ran herself ragged, going up and down the stairs to the calls of the crew, asking if the placement of a table was correct or if she liked the positioning of a painting before it was hung.

Each night she collapsed into bed with a growing feeling of joy, made inexplicable in the face of her longing to see Javier.

It was as if the two were growing in direct proportion to one another: the more finished and delightful her new abode, the more, too, her heart pined to see and touch the man of her heart.

§

It was late Friday afternoon when Monsieur Signac finally released his crew. He and Calypso did a quick tour through the rooms beforehand, to make sure that last minute cleanups were finished and all was in perfect order.

"Well, Madame, do you approve?" Monsieur Signac asked when they reached the salon.

The rays of late sun slanted in almost horizontally, touching glowing parquet, polished furniture, and gleaming accessories with a nostalgic golden glow.

"It's perfectly beautiful!" she exclaimed. "You've created something special, Monsieur Signac. I can't imagine that anyone else could have done what you've done. I can't thank you enough."

The builder smiled in genuine pleasure.

"It was nothing, Madame Searcy. A house like this, it is so well made even an old broken-down carpenter like me couldn't spoil it."

Rather than reply, Calypso reached for his hand and held it in both of hers. Their eyes met, and the deal they had sealed with a handshake so many months before was completed without a word said.

As Calypso walked back to the orangerie, she realized that the house was ready for habitation. The cleaning crew had even brought over her clothing, had moved her food from one kitchen to the other, and then had cleaned the orangerie, as well.

She fished in her pocket for the keys as she did a quick walk through, looking for things that would need to be transferred in the future. Her laptop still sat on the desk and she coiled its wires into her pocket before hoisting it under her arm. With a last look around, she stepped through the front door and locked it, making final one phase of her life, even as she was about to begin a new one.

Walking back to the house, she encountered the tortoise, toiling along in the same direction.

"You must have gotten the word," she said companionably. "Treats at the kitchen door over here from now on. Understand?"

The tortoise didn't stop to look at her, but continued his earnest shuffle toward the house.

"You are the most understanding of creatures," Calypso marveled. "If only my husband understood things so clearly."

She bade the tortoise good evening and went toward the welcoming salon lights of her new home.

She was standing in her new bathroom, arranging the items of her daily toilette on an étagère by the lavatory, when it hit her. She stared at herself in the mirror in dismay.

A woman of late middle age stared back at her. Her long hair was pulled up in a knot on top of her head and her newly washed face had smooth, unlined skin. What struck her were the eyes. They spoke of humor and intelligence and a depth of experience that, as a younger woman, she had only hoped to gain. She looked like someone who would understand the full implication of what she was about to say.

"You called him your husband again," she said to the woman in the mirror. The woman looked back at her silently, apparently as quietly bemused by this revelation as was Calypso.

S

In the night, wind seethed in the plane tree outside her new bedroom window. As she had anticipated, it was a delicious sound, like the very soul of the huge old tree singing the secrets of earth's day. In it she heard birdsong and rain, the glad shouts of flowers as they opened their petals to the sun, the slither of lizards and the slow scratch of the tortoise along the garden's gravel.

With this recitation of the day just past came bruits of the one to come, as if the duende of the *genius loci*, cornucopia in his left hand and libation bowl in his right, were sitting in the branches, humming the new day into existence. Calypso lay long, listening to the singing of her new life into being.

Her mind was filled with ecstatic images of the rooms that were now hers to inhabit, with plans for the renovation of the wildly overgrown garden, and with imaginings of the dishes she would prepare in her new kitchen. She had yet to even turn on a burner of the new La Cornue stove that sat, solid and massive as a bank vault, in blue and gold splendor against the east kitchen wall. In her new study, a Louis Quinze desk already held her laptop on its inlaid leather top, just waiting for her fingers to allow inspiration to flow.

So many future delights danced and fluttered through her tired brain that at first she could not even approach slumber. Her entire body relished the cool, smooth finish of antique linen sheets. The high-ceilinged space around her seemed to zing with energy, as if rejoicing in its own beauty of proportion and its softly tinted new plaster. Occasionally, her eyes drifted open and wandered toward the dark bulk of the marble mantlepiece and her imagination lit a winter fire there, relishing the coming of long nights of rain, its rush and splatter syncopated with the rising and falling of the flames.

Only in the bass undernote of the wind did her mind pick up the thread of another narrative. Her hand stole from her side toward the empty half of the bed. She fell asleep with Javier's face rising before her, his lips drawn in that perfect arc that precedes a kiss.

§

In the morning, Calypso dressed in old jeans and an indigo sweater, slid her feet into a pair of slouching blue and white striped espadrilles, wrapped a bright scarf around her neck, and hurried downstairs to her kitchen. It was the first day of her new life and she was determined to stay aware in order to soak in every delicious detail of it, moment by moment.

Everything was new to her. The kettle she filled with water was a copper one she had found moldering greenly in the cupboard on her first inspection of the house, now polished and gleaming in morning light. She managed to light the burner of the new stove and put the kettle on to boil, ground coffee in an antique wooden hand grinder, and slide the grounds from the little drawer into her French press. Each act was a tessera in the mosaic of her new life and world, invested with the sacred importance of ritual.

While the water was heating, she opened the west side doors and shutters and went out under the pergola. Its vines filtered golden morning light onto the restored wooden table. She threw a fresh white linen tea towel down on the tabletop and brought out a basket of bread, a plate of butter, a pot of local strawberry jam that one of the ladies of the cleaning crew had brought her, and laid out flatware and an antique faience plate.

Back inside, she stood before the Provençal hutch and its shelf of cups and saucers, choosing carefully which would become her morning favorite. Finally, from among Limoges cups covered in hand-painted roses, Lunéville with innocent bouquets of flowers and Minton with elaborate oriental designs, she chose a large hexagonal cup of white Paris porcelain, decorated only with a gold ring around its lip. Even though it had a chip along the edge and its saucer was mismatched, Calypso responded to the dignity and resilience of the two hundred-year-old vessel.

"When I'm your age, I'll have a few chips and dings, too," she said.

Setting the cup on the counter, she filled it with hot water from the kettle and then filled the French press. From the drawer of the hutch she produced an antique tea cozy stitched like a Provençal *boutis* in a charming cicada pattern and, from a cupboard, a worn Empire tole tray in chapped red enamel and spotty gold.

She depressed the French press and the smell of hot coffee welled up blissfully. Putting the press on the tray, she popped the tea cozy over it, added a bowl of brown sugar cubes, a little pitcher of cream and the warming cup, and carried the tray outside.

Settling in behind the table, faced so that she could look down the sun-dappled length of the pergola, she poured her coffee, and slathered bread with butter and jam. A small breeze shivering through the leaves of the plane trees and the Roman fountain's languorous plash, were rustic music spiked with birdsong. Calypso thought, then, of the figure in the vault. Down in darkness, like an anchor for a ship bobbing in a pleasant harbor, the Goddess radiated her joy up and outward, filling the world with song.

Sharp concussions of footfall on gravel interrupted her musings. Before she could rise to investigate, a voice behind her said, "There you are! I've been hammering on the front door."

Her body convulsed in shock and joy.

"Is it *you?*"

She pushed back her chair, twirled to face him, and collided with his onrushing chest. His arms went around her, pressing her to him, and she smelled the scent that, since their first embrace almost fifty years before, had annihilated all reason in her. She buried her face in his shirt and clung to him, her arms wrapped around him.

"Oh, my God, Javier!" was all she could say, and was not surprised when he was too overwhelmed to respond.

§

They sat half the morning under the pergola, catching up. She plied him with food and coffee, which he accepted but did not eat in the intensity of their chatter. Their coffee grew cold. Wasps trekked through the jam on their plates, unheeded. They bent toward one another, holding hands across the table, lost in the amazement of being together again.

"You've been traveling a long time," Calypso said.

"Yes. Two full days. But you won't believe it, Caleepso. I was in such a hurry to get here, I forgot my passport back at the ranch. It took four days to get a temporary one issued. Can you believe something so stupid as that?"

He rubbed his head, amazed at his own mistake.

In her mind's eye, she traced his long journey down from the Sierra into Chihuahua City. The unbearably convoluted and frustrating bureaucratic hassle over the passport and then the airport, the flight into El Paso, then onward to New York, the change of planes, the hop across the Atlantic, then customs and the rush across Charles de Gaulle Airport from the international terminal to the domestic one and finally, the short flight to Montpellier. It made her tired just to think about it.

"You rented a car in Montpellier?"

"Yes. I spent the night there last night, at the Palais Hotel. I wanted to come last night, but I was too tired."

"I've missed you." Her chest was compressed with emotion and it came out in a whisper.

"I have missed you too, Caleepso. I need to tell you something."

She was suddenly wary. What if he had come to insist that she come back to Rancho Cielo? Or worse, unbearable to think of, that he was so tired of missing her that he wanted out—wanted a fresh start, so that the wound of her absence could heal?

Tears glossed her eyes and she could barely wheeze, "What?" It came out more sharply than she had anticipated.

He pulled his hand away, stood, and brought his chair around to her side of the table. She turned her chair to face his and he reached for her hands with both of his.

"Caleepso," he began, in a voice so serious that it terrified her, "I need you to know that..." He stopped and gazed down the length of the pergola, collecting his thoughts. "That I have been thinking."

He stopped to look her straight in the eye.

"There has never been a time when you did not support every single step of my life, starting that very first day in Berkeley. You have never denied me anything my heart really wanted. You've followed me into warfare and into a kind of exile in the mountains. You've helped me build the ranch and to rebuild my life."

Calypso smiled slightly, hearing the listing that she had anticipated. The only real issue, she knew, was what he had included in the other pan of the balance.

"When you decided to buy this property, I was angry. I thought you wanted to leave Mexico for good. I thought maybe you even wanted to leave me. I went a little crazy with that thought. I couldn't really believe it but I couldn't let it rest either."

He let go of her hands and rose from his chair. She looked up his tall frame to his beloved face, now furled in thought, and knew the verdict was about to be pronounced. She braced herself for it, with her fingers curled around the frame of her chair's seat.

"And then I thought about what I've done for you. I took care of you after the rape. That was the start. And I killed a man for you—but my guess is you don't consider that a plus. I built Rancho Cielo with you in mind. I wanted it to be beautiful and big and strong, so you would feel safe and happy there. And you know, Caleepso," his eyes sought hers with a kind of desperation, "I have always loved you. I would give my life for you."

She nodded and swallowed the lump in her throat.

"Then maybe six days ago, I felt something. Just a knowing. And I knew I had to get to you fast. Were you in danger, Caleepso? I was certain I needed to come to you."

"Only in danger of dying of loneliness," she whispered.

"But nothing happened about a week ago? I had a big hit of your energy, Caleepso. So strong, I dropped what I was doing—I was building new gates for the courtyard—and I just ran to my truck and came."

"About a week ago?"

So much had happened so fast. She rummaged her memory for something that could have jolted him, almost six thousand miles distant. When it came to her, she covered her mouth with her hands in astonishment.

"Oh! Of course!"

"What?"

There was no way to explain it to him. She realized he would have to experience it for himself. She took him by the hand, saying, "Come," and led him into the kitchen. Taking up her ring of keys, she unlocked the door leading to the north entry room, now set up as a mud room and laundry. The same huge Provençal armoire that had guarded the secret stairs was now centered on the wall, leaving the door in the tiled floor unencumbered.

She knelt and unlocked the concealed door and struggled to raise it. Javier shot out his arm and with one heave, pushed it back against the wall and held it, as Calypso maneuvered the metal loop over the hook in the wall.

"If this thing ever fell on you," he said severely, "it would kill you."

"Swatted down like a fly! That would be an ignominious death, for sure," she smiled.

She reached into the armoire and produced flashlights for each of them. "You'll need this. Be careful going down. It's even more treacherous than it looks."

They spiraled carefully down into darkness. When she reached the landing at the bottom she said, "I'm very sure that you're about to see what—or who—brought you here with such speed."

She turned and smiled at him, where he balanced on the bottom step, one hand braced against the stone wall of the stairwell.

"Watch your head. This door is very low."

As they ducked into the vaulted room, the beams of their flashlights immediately spotlighted the statue. Calypso heard Javier gasp and turned to see that he was struck speechless, his eyes fixed on the figure before him. They stood for a long time with their lights playing over the polychrome and gold surface of the Queen of Heaven.

"Caleepso!" Javier breathed at last. "It's the same figure that's on the locket!"

"Yes."

He approached the image and reached out to stroke it but drew his hand back before his fingers touched the surface.

"This is more than a statue," he said, stepping back. "This has power!"

Calypso nodded.

"Yes, you're right. It does."

She went to him and took his hand.

"A few days ago, I was completely overwhelmed by Her energy. Stunned by it. Almost knocked senseless. It seemed to me that time and space were liquid, like a big wave that was washing me into a sea of—of I don't know what. Pure consciousness, maybe."

Javier was nodding, even before she finished.

"Yes. I felt it. It felt like you were dissolving."

He put his arms around her and pulled her close.

"I was scared, Caleepso. So scared that something had happened to you."

They stood embracing one another for long minutes. At last, Javier whispered, "She did it, didn't She? She brought us back together."

Calypso nodded, her cheek rubbing against his shirt.

"Yes," she said softy, "I think so. I believe She has both the power and the intention to do that."

At last, they turned away from the serene and infinite gaze of the Goddess and ducked back through the arched door.

S

Calypso spent the remainder of the day touring Javier through her new domain.

"I think She held you off with the passport problem," she said, nodding her head toward the floor, "so we could finish the decorating. It would have been anticlimactic if you'd come in the middle of scrub buckets and sweating movers."

Javier made polite murmurs over every room. Only when she opened a door and said, "And this is *your* study," did he show genuine surprise.

"Mine? You made a study for me? How did you know I would come?"

"I didn't. I hoped."

He nodded, his lips pursed.

"Caleepso," he said, drawing her to him, "I told you this morning I need to tell you something."

Again, Calypso's heart sank. "What?" she whispered.

He cleared his throat, looked down at his boots, and then back at her, his lips still pursed.

"What I want to tell you is this. . .I have been a colossal jerk. I came here to ask your forgiveness. And now I see that you've already forgiven me."

He waved his hand around the study, with its deep leather chair, broad desk and walls of bookcases awaiting books.

"How can I ever thank you?" His voice broke and his dark eyes were limpid with unshed tears.

Calypso raised her face to his and kissed him then. It was a kiss holding all her pent-up doubt, sorrow and longing, all her creative passion, all her joy at his closeness. All her love.

Javier received the kiss in the same spirit. His soul encompassed her in an embrace that knew no time, no place, and no end. What did it matter, if they were in Mexico or France? On Earth or on the Moon? In the twenty-first century or any other, past or future? As long as they were together, everything was possible.

S

Mist that had crept inland from the Mediterranean was just lifting its veil to the clear light of dawn, as Calypso slipped behind the leather-topped desk in her study and began to write. The dream was still heavy upon her and with eyes closed, her fingers flew across the keyboard.

After an hour or so, she heard Javier get up and go down to the kitchen. In the quiet house, the ground floor rustle of water flowing into the kettle and the fierce grinding of coffee beans were audible, but her inner vision persisted.

Javier was just entering the study to put a cup of coffee beside her as she wrote *FINI* and straightened from the computer.

"I'm done!" she crowed. "Free, at last!"

Javier grinned. "Good morning."

She stood and put her arms around him. "I'm a free woman! I just wrote the final scene of the book. What do you say we go to the coast today? Let's eat a huge breakfast and then drive down to the shore. What do you think?"

He pulled her close and kissed her. "How can I refuse you on the day when you're liberated from that thing." He nodded toward her laptop. "It's as if you've taken a lover, when you're writing. I'd better take you away before you start a new book."

They prepared omelets fat with avocado, onions, and cheese, and ate them ravenously out under the pergola, watching wrens coming and going to some secret nest where babies screamed mercilessly for *more*. After cleaning up the breakfast dishes, they packed more food for a picnic—bread, cheese, olives, and a bottle of local wine. Calypso gathered sweaters and hats while Javier loaded the basket in his rental car.

"Ready?" he asked, keys in hand.

"Ready." She pulled the front door shut behind her and almost skipped across the gravel to the car. "I don't know why I feel so unaccountably gay this morning," she said, as she folded herself into the passenger seat.

"Because you've just finished another book?" He went around to the driver's side and lowered his length into the tiny interior. "Or maybe because you get to ride with me in this little clown car?"

Calypso smiled, pulled down the visor to check her lipstick, and nestled her purse beside her on the seat.

"No," she said as they pulled away from the house. "It's that, but also something more. Maybe it's simply being with you, my love!" She gave him a radiant smile. "Or because it's spring. Or because we're in the south of France. Or maybe all of the above."

They drove through the awakening village and turned onto the auto route leading south to the sea. The roadsides were thick with red poppies that had yet to open their dewy heads to the sun, and the vineyards were just beginning to show a few tendrils and leaves, like topknots on the black zigzags of the old vines. A little veil of sea mist floated seaward and even the somber olive groves seemed to sparkle with silvery inner fire as the morning breeze flounced their leaves.

They drove in silence, so deeply absorbed in communion that no words were necessary. Coming to the coast road, Javier turned left with the aqua ripple of the Mediterranean to their right.

They hadn't gone far when Calypso exclaimed, "Look at that little point of rocks! Let's go out there and explore."

Without a word, Javier pulled the car onto the shoulder, got out and then went around to help Calypso extricate herself.

"We both have legs too long for French cars," she said, laughing as he pulled her to her feet.

Hand in hand, they crossed the road and went down an embankment, heading for a small promontory crowned with sea- and wind-worn rocks. Shore birds swooped and cried in the chilly air and the tang of salt was sharp and clean on the wind.

After a few minutes of clambering, they found themselves on top of the point, looking out over the restless blue skin of the sea. In both directions, the coast swept away in a gentle curve as if Earth were embracing her glittering waters.

"How beautiful!" Calypso exclaimed.

She ventured out to the edge of the rock and peered over. Below her, slow waves rolled up to the outcrop, splashed lazily and retreated.

"Be careful!" Javier said, slipping his fingers into the back of the waistband of her jeans. "It's still too cold for a swim."

Calypso laughed and spread her arms, leaning outward, moored by Javier's firm grip. "I'm flying!" she cried joyfully.

They sat down with their backs to a sun-warmed rock.

"I almost forgot to tell you!" Javier said suddenly. "A very strange thing."

Calypso felt a jolt of foreboding.

"What?"

Javier raised a calming hand.

"No, nothing bad. Just strange. I was out with the cattle early one morning, just before I came here, and Lobo was with me. But I got busy with the cattle and next thing I know, Lobo is way over at the edge of the pasture near the woods.

"At first I thought my eyes were playing tricks, because Lobo was leaping and running and spinning around. But then I saw that there was another wolf there, too. They were playing. And then Lobo looked at me—a very long, hard look, Caleepso—and then he just turned and trotted away with the other wolf into the woods."

"Just like that."

"Yes."

Calypso's eyes glazed with tears. "He saved my life, you know."

"You saved *his* life."

"Well, yes. But if he hadn't been with me that last time through the tube, I think I'd still be there. I would have given up. I wanted to die. It was Lobo's nose on my ankle, so cold and wet—so *alive*— that spurred me on. Without him, honestly Javier, I think I would be dead now."

Javier took her hand and held it lightly.

"Lots of liberation this year," he said gently. "From the past, from work in the present, from dreams of the future. Don't they call a year like this *fateful?*"

She sighed and looked again out to sea. "He's not coming back, is he?"

"I don't think so."

"But he's not lost either—is he?"

"No. I don't think he is. I think he's gone back to his people, the Wolf Clan."

She nodded and clambered to her feet.

"Then it's just you and me, my love. And the sky's the limit."

He pushed to his feet and took her hand.

"Maybe there are no limits," he said. "Just the illusion of them."

He jumped from the shelf of rock and then turned to lift her down. She was almost insubstantial in his hands.

"My God, Caleepso!" he exclaimed. "You need fattening. Let's forget the picnic and go to that restaurant we passed down the road."

"Okay. Let's."

Hand in hand, they scrambled through the rocks toward the car.

"You know, I just remembered something, too," Calypso said, swinging their clasped hands.

"What's that?"

"That under scopolamine, I called you my husband."

Javier stopped on the shoulder of the road and turned to look at her.

"Is that so?" he said, studying her face appraisingly.

Calypso only smiled in response.

"In that case, we'd better eat a big lunch. It's going to be a bigger day than we planned!"

She smiled at him. "You think?"

He nodded, his eyes filled with a new light. "Yes. I think."

"Where?"

He shrugged. "Anywhere. How about in the next town we come to?"

He opened the car door and settled her into her seat, then went around and folded himself behind the wheel.

"I have a better idea."

"What?"

"How about in the vault with the Goddess for a witness? I'm sure we could find a notary crazy enough to do it—for a price."

He nodded. "Yes. I like that idea. Let's go have lunch and then we can start making calls."

"What about rings?"

"What about them?"

"We'll need some."

"What about an antiques store? Would they have any?"

"Maybe."

"Then we'll stop at every one we come to between here and home."

They glanced at one another in surprise. Calypso smiled.

"Did I hear you say what I thought you said?"

"Yes. Home. But don't forget, we've got two homes now. Like His and Hers bath towels," he grinned his impossibly enchanting grin, "only bigger." He started the car and pulled from the shoulder.

Calypso smiled radiantly at him. "No, not His and Hers—Ours and Ours."

§

"Will you have to give the statue back to the church, Caleepso?"

They were lying in bed. The window was thrown open and night wind brought the sigh of the plane tree and the clear treble of falling water into the room. It was really too cool for open windows but it made snuggling more expedient.

Calypso, cradled against Javier's chest in deep relaxation, answered dreamily, "No, I don't think so. It's odd, Javier. I asked Monsieur Signac about the desecration of the church here in Brignac. His family's been here since before the Revolution. He told me that a family named Moreau returned the holy figures to the church sometime in the nineteen-fifties. They'd been hidden in an old granary on their mas all that time."

"So that was the Monsieur M. who helped Father Xavier?"

"That's what I'm assuming."

"Then how did the statue get here?"

"That's a good question—and I have no answer. It's sitting on a Louis Quinze table so it had to have been placed there sometime shortly before or after the start of the French Revolution in 1789. The making of Louis Quinze-style furniture pretty much died along with the monarch."

"But it could have been put on that table last week," Javier said reasonably.

"True, but then there's the reliquary and the letter. It seems safe to assume that they were put there at the same time, since the box was under the same tarp as the statue."

Javier kissed the top of her head. "You should have been a detective, Caleepso."

"Ummmm hummm." She sighed luxuriously.

"Maybe there was an official set of statuary for the church and then a secret one, that the parishioners didn't know about."

Calypso erupted into activity, squirming until she could look him in the eye by the light of the candelabra on the bedside table.

"You know, that's a really good theory. What if our statue was kept hidden, like something apostate? Many churches were built on the ruins of earlier holy sites. Maybe when they built the church here in Brignac, they dug into an older site—Roman or maybe even an Egyptian one. The Egyptians had a major port on the Mediterranean just a few miles from here, you know, called Ratis. There are all kinds of stories about them bringing images of Isis into the area."

"What was the name of the woman who sold you this place?"

"Landrieu, why?"

"I thought maybe her name might have started with an 'M', too."

"No...but she's married. That's not her maiden name." Calypso's voice was rising with excitement. "The family that started this mas lived here until Madame Landrieu's grandparents died in the mid-sixties Their name was Martel!

"That's got to be it, Javier! Father Xavier must have had a much deeper friendship with the Martel family. Otherwise, he wouldn't have entrusted the statue to them and they wouldn't have made the effort to hide the stairs like they did."

"Or maybe She's always lived here. Maybe they put the table under Her and the tarp over Her and then closed the stairs to protect Her during the Revolution."

"That's a possibility, too."

Calypso lay thinking about what little was known of the Black Virgins of southern France. Local myths told that many of the Black Virgin statues were discovered in natural settings like caves or grottoes, or hidden in trees, or buried in the ground near springs. Farmers plowing their fields sometimes turned one up or were alerted to its presence by the strange behavior of their animals that refused to cross the spot where a Black Virgin was buried or were unusually attracted it.

As she explained this to Javier, Calypso remembered that it also was said that a Black Virgin brought from the spot in which She was discovered and placed in a Christian chapel would disappear. Then somehow, She would make Her way back to the place of Her discovery, as if She could not bear to leave Her association with the earth and its life-giving waters and vegetation.

"So if you move Her from here, She might just return anyway?" Javier felt deeply, unaccountably moved by these stories.

"It's possible. One thing I know for sure—if I'm supposed to do anything besides leave Her where She is, I'll know about it." Calypso dangled the locket in the candlelight. "This thing won't let me rest until I do what's right. In fact, I feel like this locket's a homing device and it brought me here in the first place."

"It's very strange, Caleepso. Strange and wonderful." He pulled her close to him and they lay in candlelight, listening to the sounds of the night that flowed through the open windows.

"What will we call this place, Caleepso?"

"Ummm...how about *Notre Dame des Bénédictions Terrestres*?"

"*Our Lady of Earthly Blessings?* It's kind of long—and besides, it sounds like we're living in a church."

"Are you sure we're not? Anyway, it will have to do until morning."

They lay quietly for a space. Then, "There's an excavation of a Roman villa just a few miles from here, did you know?" she murmured, snuggling closer under his arm and pressing her cheek against his chest. "Right now, this moment, is so timeless, I feel like we could be Romans in a villa two thousand years ago."

He pulled her closer. "Maybe we are," he said pensively. "Maybe we are."

"One thing I know: we are blessed, my love." She sighed and flung a sleepy arm across him.

"Yes, *mi corazón*, we are."

A gust blew through the window, flouncing the drapes and snuffing the candles. In the darkness, wind spiraled through the room, dispersing the fragrance of flowers and wet earth. Out in the branches of the plane tree, an owl gave a short, whistling hoot. Somewhere in the garden, the old tortoise was dreaming his earthen dreams, while the water of the spring trickled endlessly from its fountain like muted laughter rising from the depths of the earth.

S

Epilogue

THE VOICES OF THE WINDS WERE COMMANDING. A solitary figure gazed across the valley, beyond which the bluffs with their rock-cut tombs glowed white and merciless on the horizon. The heat of midday was stifling and the figure turned briefly to take in the distant ribbon of green that demarcated the river.

Between the healing waters and the valley of death were the winds. They rose up in black, whirling columns, as tall as those on the portico of the temple. She counted thirteen in all, each with its separate voice that whispered or screamed, chuckled or wailed. In her memory, there had never been so many—and her memory was long.

When humankind became riled, nature did, too. This she knew. Political intrigue, social injustice, bigotry, religious intolerance, astounding greed—these were just a few of the ills that stirred within her culture like an evil potion brewing and bubbling on the back of a mighty magician's stove. The spirits of the natural world were rising up in complaint against the human miasma.

She faced the whirlwinds and bowed deeply. The voices of the wind bade her and she knew what she must do.

"I will do what I can," she spoke into the turbid air. Turning, she walked back toward the river, her white linen skirts billowing about her in the hot wind.

Once in her priestess's chambers, she refreshed herself with water, bathed and put on a fresh linen tunic and skirt. Wending her way into the heart of the temple, she came to the holy of holies, with its tall diorite image of the goddess and her son. Prostrating herself on the stone floor, she prayed for wisdom and for the power to manifest it.

She had not lain long, prostrate at the feet of Isis, before her mind was flooded with an image. A golden locket dangled in her mind's eye and a voice said, "Make this and I will do the rest." She studied the image until she knew every detail and then it slowly faded.

Rising, she bowed deeply to Holy Mother, backed from the chamber and then hurried away in search of her friend. She found him in the royal goldsmith's shop, where coals glowed red on the forge and bits of gold work in various phases of completion littered the workbenches.

She explained her mission to him and sketched in great detail the image she had been shown. When she withdrew from the studio, it was with assurances that her project would take priority, but also with the warning that it would take many months to accomplish what she requested.

Months passed. *Peret*, the season of growth and *Shemu*, that of harvest, finally faded into *Akhet*, the months of the annual inundation by the waters of the Nile. As the waters receded and the green sprouts of barley began to show across the fields, she kept her vigil still, praying and performing ceremonies of power. A holder of the wisdom of the true lineage, she abjured all that did not pertain to her project. She ate no meat, drank no beer, abstained from sex.

Peret was again passing when her friend summoned her to his shop. With pride, he handed her a box of sumptuous beauty, inlaid with ivory and precious stones. A look passed between them. Bowing, she left the goldsmith's studio, wrapping the box in her veil as she went.

For the following week, she performed the ceremonies that she had prepared, scrupulously following the old methods. She let her heart open and felt the flow of love pass through her from above, into the object in the box. When she slept, which was infrequently and for short periods, she wore the object around her neck.

At last, she made ritual ablution once again and with the locket around her neck, went down the long stone corridors of the temple to the inner sanctum. Prostrating herself before Isis, she began to pray.

When the power took her, it was as if she had been struck by lightning. Her body was galvanized by a pure current that flowed through the top of her head and up from the soles of her feet, to blend their currents in her heart. From her heart, the combined flood erupted, turning the locket burning hot against her chest, as she lay in a rictus of wonder and terror.

At last, like the Nile at the end of *Akhet*, the energy ebbed, leaving her panting at the feet of the goddess. A voice, motherly yet regal, said, "It is done. Beauty can never be destroyed, only lost or hidden for a time. My wisdom is eternal. In every generation, there now will be one who partakes of it. You have done well."

The priestess rose to her knees, kissed the locket, and bowed to Holy Mother. Then she backed from the room and went her way beneath the gaze of the Sphinx and within the shadow of the pyramids.

The dust of centuries blew over those proud monuments. Dynasties rose and fell. Egyptian pharaohs were succeeded by Greek rulers and they in turn fell to Christians, who in time ceded powered to Muslims. Cultures crumbled, bitter wars were waged, fortunes were made and lost, emperors rose and died.

Through the centuries, the locket traveled on, worn about the necks of both high and humble, noble and peasant, but always seeking its own—that woman in whom love ran pure, and in whom the love of the Goddess manifested a life of service to Her greater goal.

Each dipped into some small portion of the living river of Her bounty and Her love, as it flowed through the ages. Imbued with magic from the beginning of time, the locket moved through cultures and across oceans and continents. It is moving still. Therefore, be without fear. All is well.

§

[illegible] sanction to [illegible]

[illegible] then.

Then the [illegible] It was as if [illegible] lightning. Her body was [illegible] down the [illegible] head and [illegible] her face [illegible] in her [illegible] The [illegible] burning [illegible] as she [illegible]

At last [illegible] the Sphinx [illegible] at the feet of the [illegible] yet [illegible] My mission is [illegible] there now will be one [illegible] you have done well."

The goddess rose to her knees, [illegible] and bowed to [illegible] Then she [illegible] the gaze of the Sphinx and walked into the shadow of the pyramid.

The [illegible] century blew over those [illegible] Ptolemies [illegible] and fell, [illegible] Greek [illegible] to Christians [illegible] power [illegible] died.

Through the [illegible] high and [illegible] noble and [illegible] seeking [illegible]

[illegible] small portion of the [illegible] magic [illegible] through [illegible] and [illegible] well."

Acknowledgements

First, many thanks to publisher Lou Aronica, who has brought *Well In Time* to life through his new and exciting brain child, The Story Plant.

Thank you to all who helped in the creation of this book: John Van Dam for technical support; Write On Women Ellen Stewart, Patricia Harrelson, Shelley Muniz, Ann St. James, Cynthia Restivo, Blanche Abrams, and Carol Biederman, for their comments on the manuscript; Steve Weldon for technical climbing expertise; Linda Nielsen for her excellent interview; Mark LaPorte for his expertise in wine; Melanie Stewart for webpage design and Mic Harper and Kath Christensen for the author's photograph.

Thank you to Jeffrey Kennedy and Jean-François Martin of magical La Missare, in Brignac, France, for their graciousness as hosts, their depth of knowledge of things French and their generosity of spirit in sharing their lively friendships, the beauty of their region, and their many refined and eclectic interests.

Thank you to Cécile Pradalié and family for their hospitality at their home and ateliers and for the mesmerizing hours in their marvelous eighteenth-century garden at Fouscaïs.

Thank you to Alain Maulat, Jerôme Prevost, and Tom Garnier for a lovely afternoon of tea and conversation in their magical apartment in Saint André de Sangonis.

Thank you to John Gibler, whose *To Die in Mexico* and *Mexico Unconquered* were invaluable resources; to Richard Grant and his *God's Middle Finger*, who comes as close as anyone has to explicating the madness that is the Mexican Sierra Madre; to Dr. Tom Soloway Pinkson, author of *The Shamanic Wisdom of the Huichol*; and Jay Courtney Fikes, author of *Unknown Huichol: Shamans and Immortals, Allies Against Chaos*, both of which deepened my understanding of that mystical people.

Thank you to the Dream Girls: Gael Amend, Debbie Dodge, Marianne Jacobsen, Pam Marino, and Sandy Alarcon for the many years of friendship, laughter, struggle, and honesty that have buoyed me through long months of writing.

Thank you to Renaissance women Reggie Hein-Dossi for her intimate understanding of the creative process and her wonder at the workings of the psyche; and Gwynne Popovac, whose sensitivity to the natural world enlarges my own. Your support is life giving.

Thank you to the students of my former prison writing classes, and especially to Madniz, whose great spirit electrified those gatherings and gave us all hope. Gentlemen, your stories are altered here but the spirit of contrition and the harrowing wisdom that you demonstrated are, I hope, unchanged.

Thank you to those men who appear herein as Father Keat, Cat, Icepick, and The Knife, unknown and unsung warriors and heroes of the Cold War: I do not share your politics, but I have tremendous admiration for your courage and expertise. Living shadow of American might, the Ghosts exist because of you—and I hope you find as happy a finale to your own complex lives.

And thank you to your polar opposite, Father Roy Bourgeois, campaigner for social justice and fierce adversary of the School of the Americas.

Thank you to Javier Aguirre for traveling with me through Mexico, and into the heart of Chihuahua's Copper Canyon, and for the years of adventure for which *no hay palabras,* and to his family, for welcoming me so graciously into their homes throughout the region.

Thank you to the many friends who sent encouragement during the writing process, among whom are Roxanne Williams, Hope Werness, Louise Jolly, Greg Ford, Julie Loar, Carol and Hubert Culpepper, Vonna Breeze Martin, Alexander Chow-Stuart, Susanne Nishino, Glenn Taylor, Barbara Briner, Marsha Van Winkle, Cindy Surendorf, Wang Kai, Sylvie Carnot, Lloyd Battista, Tammy Horn, Anthony Dossi, Ted Denmark, Marjorie Thoman-Lomas, Erik Nielsen, Christel Zaluga, Sarah Cohelo Webster, Cristie Holliday, Pam Horner, Karen Kress, Rick Shears, Susie Carrington, and my beloved sister, Carolyn Takhar. The world would be a bleak place without you.

Thank you to my adorable fur children, Sophia Rosemaria whose glorious sunning of her belly is the acme of sensuality; Maclovio, who brings the fearlessness of Chihuahua to his daily battles with marauding Mr. Sniffles; and our dear, departed Panda, whose mischief is sorely missed, for all the love and comfort their pure hearts provide.

Finally, to my husband David Roberson, without whom this book would never have been finished, and who has given with such generosity of spirit and loving kindness more than he will ever receive in return, the eternal thanks of my grateful and loving heart.

A Conversation With Suzan Still

with Linda Nielsen, author of Lasso the Stars

§

Talk a bit about the title, Well In Time.

When I first conceived this book, I saw it as a kind of diagram or map, with a horizontal plane representing present time. In the middle of the plane was a deep, narrow V, showing the plunge through successive generations, into the deep past. That motif was repeated physically in the deep chasms of river canyons and the descent into the cave, and culturally in Blanche de Muret's plummet down the well into a community that was still immersed in a culture thousands of years old, or in Javier's contact with the Huichol's ancient ways.

I used telescoping narratives to bore ever deeper into the well of time.Everywhere in this story the crust of present-day reality is thin, and one false step sends the protagonists and the reader plunging down into alternate realities, in the same way that El Lobo was sucked into the siphon's vortex. In a sense, I feel that we are never far parted from other times—that they are always fully present in parallel dimensions, so perhaps the well in time could be seen as what depth psychologists refer to as the collective unconscious, or metaphysicians as the akashic records.

Well In Time *is the sequel to* Fiesta of Smoke, *although it can certainly stand alone. What was the inspiration for this new book?*

Well In Time is a darker book than *Fiesta of Smoke*, influenced, I think, by the times we're living through. So many people are suffering hardships, right now—loss of jobs, foreclosures, financial and health difficulties, not to mention generalized corruption, and class, gender and religious warfare. And of course, in Mexico there is the cataclysm of drug cartel violence that is disrupting the very foundations of the country. In *Well In Time*, I wanted to address these dark matters, but also give a broader and more hopeful perspective, found in the reassurance that life is eternal, that we live again and again, and also that there are other realms or dimensions involved, from which guidance and help of all kinds emanate.

The passage back and forth through the cave, especially the so-called "tube," is very dark. What importance do you place on that?

Caves have been, since earliest times, places of initiation. By nullifying the everyday world, and blunting our chief sense of sight, a cave forces the psyche to rely on other, deeper ways of knowing to conquer primal fear. Other dimensions can intervene, in flashes of metaphysical insight. But none of this happens without terror of both the unknown and of our helplessness in the face of it.

I'm a claustrophobe, so for me the tube was the ultimate such passage—a real face-off with my deepest fear. In fact, when I was writing those passages, I would wake up in the night thinking about them, and the tube was so real for me that I'd panic, feeling like I couldn't breathe!

Why is it important to put oneself through such a terrifying experience?

In order to grow, we have to face our fears.The passage through the cave is symbolic of that confrontation. Everyone has experienced that place in life where we're face to face with the very thing that seems insurmountable. Some part of us knows that it's really not. That just like the tube, there really is a way through, albeit a very narrow, frightening and humbling one.

Sadly, some people turn back at that juncture. I think of them as people still trapped inside the mountain, because they refuse the narrow passage. They're the people with talent who never paint a picture or write a page; with intelligence, who convince themselves they're too old or too poor or not smart enough to get an education; who refuse to fight back against disability or loss. That refusal of the narrow path holds them trapped in a kind of inner darkness.

And it's also a refusal of the help that will come, if we only have faith and set out. In fairytales and myths, it's always *after* the hero has set out, faithfully pursuing his task, that help comes in the form of an animal who knows a secret, or an old woman who gives a gift, or an army of ants that helps to sort a heap of mixed grain. That kind of metaphysical help only comes *after* the act of faith, never before. For Calypso, it was the wolf Lobo and the gnome-like Rat.

So facing the terrors of the cave signifies facing the difficulties of life, for which we feel unprepared and inept and paralyzed by doubt. Some lives, like Calypso's, call for more than one such passage, and with each pass, new strength is born.

You've created a fantastic character, in Sa Tahuti.

Actually, I didn't create her, at all. The Ammonite religion still exists, with leadership claiming lineage to the ancient pharaohs. And they also claim that there really is a Sa Tahuti—or Sau Tahuti, when in the masculine form—who can transcend death, and has lived, basically, forever. I hope I haven't offended the Ammonites by using her in the book, and deeply apologize, if I have.

Her case is not isolated, either. I've read of a similar being, Baba Ji, in India, who is basically immortal, and have heard rumors of others. While this seems fantastic to us in our unenlightened state, it's probably possible for the enlightened to concentrate their energies, so as to transcend death. After all, the entire Christian religion is based on the resurrection of Jesus, and he claimed that we are all as gods, and could do everything he did, and more.

What about The Ghosts? Are they based on actual persons, too?

Yes, in fact they are. Through unusual circumstances, I know men like The Ghosts. Some I met during my time teaching in prison. Others are involved in our government's covert operations. I don't share their politics, but I have tremendous admiration for their courage and expertise. They are men of action—tough, resilient, honorable to a certain code, and lethal. Yet, I know one, for example, who literally gave the skin off his back to a complete stranger, a little boy who had been badly burned. It is impossible for the average citizen to comprehend where these guys hang out in their heads. They live, basically, in an alternate reality, which is where I placed them, in *Well In Time.*

Calypso's ride in the Cadillac is one of the wildest things I've ever read. Don't tell me you have personal experience of that, too?

(Laughing) Yes, I'm afraid that's drawn from my own experience. I've never laughed so hard, before or since. It was amazingly surreal.

The Children's Crusade is a strange tale. Is it based in fact?

Oh yes! The Children's Crusade actually happened in 1212. Modern scholars debate many of the details, but that the children, led by Stephen of Cloyes, walked the length of France in the expectation of marching to Jerusalem on the dried-up seabed, is a fact. I don't know of any modern movement to compare with it, in which young people were totally swept up with passion, unless maybe it was the Beatles phenomenon.

Fire and fireplaces play a role in Well In Time. *Can you say why your characters so often are placed before a fire?*

Fire is primal. From time immemorial humans have gathered by the fire to tell stories, recount myths and histories, and make decisions. For the Huichol Indians, Grandfather Fire is the source of insight and vision, and for European peoples, time by the fireplace is time-out, when the business of the day is left behind and more philosophical or leisurely pursuits have a chance to surface.

I use fire in *Well In Time* to demarcate those moments when the protagonists' lives are in transition, when new insights are revealed. There is, in a sense, a burning away of the old and a lighting of revelation of the new. There is safety, warmth and communion by a fire, as if the ancestors and the supernatural forces join us there, in moving forward the ongoing task of humanness.

The cave itself seems fantastic, running as it does between two river gorges.

The idea for the cave actually came from one of my prison students, who was from a place in Mexico south of Chihuahua. He told me that in his area there are cave systems running clear through the mountains, that were used to hide and move troops during the 1910 Revolution. And of course, they're used for drug smuggling, today.

The Copper Canyon area in Chihuahua is riddled with caves, many occupied by the Rarámuri, or Tarahumara as they're commonly called. Whether any cave runs completely through the cliffs, I don't know—but it's certainly not an impossibility.

There are many metaphysical events in Well In Time. *Are you using them as a literary device, as in magical realism, or more religiously or philosophically?*

I personally have experienced many metaphysical events—visions, prophetic dreams, clairvoyance, apparitions, out-of-body experiences, ESP, spontaneous healing—a kind of smorgasbord of weird stuff. So I would say that I'm simply recognizing the existence of these alternate realms or dimensions by writing them into *Well In Time*. There's nothing hypothetical or faith-based about it—it's simply experiential. I do love magical realism, however, and I think it addresses the deep mysteries, the inexplicable, in a delightful way. If the reader wants to take those events in that vein, it's fine with me!

I'm a firm believer that we've only scratched the surface of reality, and it intrigues me how these dimensions seem to flirt with us, ducking in and out of our perception in a game of metaphysical hide-and-seek. And I question: Does this flirtation have meaning for our lives, and if so, what is it? *Well In Time* is, in part, an exploration of those questions.

Talk about the violence perpetrated by the drug cartels in Mexico, and why you chose this as a theme in Well In Time.

It is clear to me that all the disruption and death caused by the drug mafias in Mexico are really to be laid at the feet of our own country. We're the ones buying all these drugs, after all, to the tune of multibillions of dollars per year. Plus, our laws prohibiting use of recreational drugs drive up the price by diminishing availability, thereby fueling the competition among cartels for the illicit monies. Drug use is bad, but the violence and death caused by making drugs illegal is far worse.

There is a direct connection between US recreational drug use, laws prohibiting it, and the assassination and terror unleashed in Mexico. You could say that drug prohibition has been an informal way to impose American cultural colonization on our neighbor to the south. That's not even to mention the allegations of CIA involvement in cocaine trafficking to the US, as a way of supporting counterinsurgency forces in Nicaragua and other places, as investigated by the US Senate Subcommittee on Narcotics and Terrorism.

The violence perpetrated by the cartels is so horrible as to be almost unspeakable. People are decapitated and dismembered, burned in barrels, disappeared. Their family members are murdered. No one is safe, and the fear becomes another type of murder. When I first started traveling in Mexico, years ago, it was safe to go out at all hours of the night on city streets, and people were open and friendly. Now, the streets are empty at night in some cities, and the happy din of culture is silenced. That kind of suppression through terror is murder of an entire culture.

Just days after one trip to Copper Canyon, a cartel attack took place just blocks away from the home where I was staying. You can see it on YouTube. (http://www.youtube.com/watch?v=tltWQKNLWYg) I had passed through that intersection numerous times, during the days before the attack. It brought home how personal the problem can be.

In *Well In Time*, Javier trains his workers as a vigilante army, which is actually happening in Mexico, as people fight to retain their lands, homes and lives against encroaching cartels. It's a deeply distressing situation, and at this point there's no real answer, although legalizing recreational drugs in this country would certainly be a start.

What's next for Suzan Still as a writer? What can your readers look forward to?

Well, I'm not making any promises, but I *think* I'm going to finish a book I've started, set in Malta. It's very different from the adventures told in *Well In Time* and *Fiesta of Smoke*, or even in *Commune of Women*. I want to slow the pace of the narrative way down, and enjoy the deliciousness of each small increment of the male protagonist's movement toward a new consciousness of women and the feminine. I have some delicious pitfalls prepared for him!

There are, however, five other partial manuscripts awaiting my attention, and one of them might tempt me away from the Malta book. And then, heaven forfend, there's that moment when an entirely new idea insists itself on my awareness! I get about an idea a week for books, and I'd have to lead ten more lives to finish them all.

Is there anything more you'd like to add about Well In Time, *before we close?*

I wanted to present the terrible reality of drug violence in Mexico, and the suffering of the people because of it. There is much that we can do in this country to mitigate that, starting by simply educating ourselves to its reality, and to the causes underlying it. To this end, I would highly recommend John Gibler's book, *To Die in Mexico: Dispatches from Inside the Drug War*. It's tough to read, but it gives the real deal, that we don't often get to hear.

I also want to say that it's my hope that *Well In Time* will give readers hope, despite its dark passages. The world itself is going through a dark passage, right now, and it's easy to become discouraged. I want this book to encourage people to look at the bigger picture, the one spanning not decades but millennia. In that context, humanity really is moving forward, becoming more just, better educated, more aware of itself as a force for good or evil.

And also in that context, there are eternal verities that span cultures and centuries, that root humankind to earth in wholesome and loving ways. I think it's safe to say that almost every person wants to be loved, to raise a family in safety and abundance, to practice their beliefs in freedom and without prejudicial treatment, to experience good health and sound education, and to eat and sleep in peace and plenty. We're linked to one another and to past and successive generations by these simple and natural things. They're things that we can seek for ourselves and our loved ones, and can help to provide for those lacking them. In that way, culture is stabilized, and with it, the lives of each one of us.

Javier and Calypso represent two people who love life and one another. They're willing to struggle to improve not only their own lot in life, but that of others, as well. That's a simple credo we can all take to heart. If *Well In Time* influences even one person to think and behave more positively and optimistically and generously, I will feel the book is a tremendous success!

Reading Group Questions

What would you consider to be the main theme or themes of *Well In Time?* If you were to recommend this book to someone else, how would you summarize it?

Which character do you prefer, and why? If you could go to lunch with one of these characters, which one would it be? What questions would you ask him or her, while dining? What topic would you most want to discuss with this person?

What did you know about the drug cartels in Mexico, before reading *Well In Time?* What did this book teach you, or how did it change your opinion or impression of that situation?

The narrative moves through both space and time, from present-day Paris to Chihuahua, from Europe to North Africa; from 2014 to prehistory. Which place or time did you find most interesting? Why?

The character of the Huichol shaman, and of Sa Tahuti, introduce an element of the unknown and metaphysical. Do you consider their world to be purely fictional? Have you ever known of or been influenced by unseen powers, or had contact with a shamanic culture?

What does the title, *Well In Time*, mean to you? What is its relation to themes of reality and illusion?

The characters of the Ghosts are based in real lives and activities. What do you think about international events being influenced by such people? Are their activities a brutal necessity, or an abhorrent evil? Are these men redeemable in your opinion? Is their shadow world necessary to our own peace and prosperity?

How do you imagine the lives of the characters, after the novel ends? What decisions will they make, and how have they been altered or transformed by their experiences?

Is there a moral to *Well In Time*? What have you learned about the world and about yourself, from experiencing this plunge into other times and other realities?

§

To understand more about drug violence in Mexico, watch these YouTube videos:

http://www.youtube.com/watch?v=LpIyaIHsJbc

http://www.youtube.com/watch?v=8XiSnCt9fDc

http://www.youtube.com/watch?v=Amn4JqM4JEo

§

To reach Suzan Still with questions, or to arrange a personal or telephone visit with your reading group, e-mail her at SuzanStill@gmail.com. Visit her website at http://suzanstill.com, and her blog at SuzanStillCommune.blogspot.com.